THE
VOLUNTEER

ALSO BY SALVATORE SCIBONA

The End

THE
VOLUNTEER

Salvatore Scibona

PENGUIN PRESS
New York
2019

PENGUIN PRESS
An imprint of Penguin Random House LLC
penguinrandomhouse.com

A portion of this book previously appeared, in different form, in *The New Yorker*.

LIBRARY OF CONGRESS CATALOGING-IN-PUBLICATION DATA

Names: Scibona, Salvatore, author.
Title: The volunteer : a novel / Salvatore Scibona.
Description: New York : Penguin Press, 2019.
Identifiers: LCCN 2018046079 (print) | LCCN 2018047067 (ebook) |
ISBN 9780525558538 (ebook) | ISBN 9780525558521 (hardcover)
Subjects: | BISAC: FICTION / Literary. |
FICTION / War & Military. | FICTION / Sagas.
Classification: LCC PS3619.C53 (ebook) |
LCC PS3619.C53 V65 2019 (print) |
DDC 813/.6—dc23
LC record available at https://lccn.loc.gov/2018046079

Printed in the United States of America
1   3   5   7   9   10   8   6   4   2

DESIGNED BY MEIGHAN CAVANAUGH

To Jennifer Sprague and Philip LeCuyer

I'm Nobody! Who are you?
Are you—Nobody—too?

—EMILY DICKINSON

HAMBURG

2010

The boy wore a black parka, a matching ski cap, blue jeans, and sneakers; he appeared to be five years old; and he was weeping.

He stood at Gate C3, Hamburg-Fuhlsbüttel Airport, his padded arms limp at his sides. He was talking through his sobs—not shouting or pleading, just talking to one attendant after another—but no one could figure out what language he was using. It seemed, somehow, Polish. The hodgepodge dialect of a town that ten different empires had captured on their way to someplace else.

An airBaltic flight had disgorged its passengers at a nearby gate less than an hour before. The flight having come from Riga, it may have been Latvian the boy was speaking. But by the time he materialized in front of the counter at C3 the plane from Riga had pulled away from the terminal and no airBaltic employees remained at the gate or anywhere else in the concourse. He looked up at the agents behind the counter, stating his case incomprehensibly, while two hundred travelers watched, mesmerized, waiting for Lufthansa 531 to Amsterdam.

It might have been Lithuanian.

Soon the boy was barely forming words at all; he only pointed in the direction of Gates C1 and C2. But the custodian for whom half a dozen

Lufthansa employees and passengers began to search the smoking cabins and bathrooms, and to whom the airport intercom called out in German, could be found nowhere at the lower end of the concourse.

"*Je m'appelle Laurence. Comment t'appelles-tu?*"

"*Ich heiße Elisabeth. Wie heißt du?*"

But no one could get him to divulge anything that sounded like a name. And some of the adults around him began to think that their solicitousness only aggravated his distress. Each question elicited less of a response.

A nurse from Kazakhstan knelt at the boy's side, petting his hair, but he persisted in weeping. The boy's coat fit him poorly: the cuffs fell short of his wrists. Bits of batting poked out of several tears in its shell, which somebody had tried to mend with electrical tape. A Lufthansa clerk—whose age (about sixty) and whose vast, highlighted hairdo seemed to put her in charge—tried using English, Russian, and Dutch to extract a name. Yet to the Kazakh nurse it seemed the boy *knew* they were asking for his name, and in the nightmare of his present, his withholding the name was the only thing that tied him to the lip of the chasm into which he had slipped. He aimed a curving finger toward the labyrinth of the rest of the airport, as though in search of a misstep. He let the nurse hold his snotty hand. He led her and the clerk down the teeming corridor.

A young American who said he was an EMT asked, "Would the boy like to breathe into this bag? *Quieres hablar conmigo, hermano?*"

The clerk said emphatically, "No, he is *Estländer*." But she was only guessing.

The intercom repeated in English, "Terminal 1, a child in lost-and-found," while the boy hustled along, incongruous: a body automatized with purpose, as though if you got close enough you would hear him ticking, and yet under his crooked hat his face was anarchic with spasmodic blinks and sniffles. The chest heaved in the little coat. The nurse tried to unzip it. She thought the boy must feel terribly hot. But he twisted away when she touched him. It was incredible that the head could hold so much liquid; he had been crying for so long now without a drink. The nurse and the clerk led him into the ladies' room to get him some paper towels.

After they came out, he wouldn't let either of the women hold his hand. He snatched it back when they tried to take it, and pointed this way, that way, until they began to see he was not retracing his steps after all. He was groping in a maze. For a parent. And he didn't want either of these strange women to help him. But he hoped they would stick around.

By the snack bar, a woman from Holland sat on her bag on the floor—other travelers occupied all the chairs—and watched as the boy led the other women crisscrossing through the corridor. She wore a blue polyester overcoat, a silk blouse, running shoes.

She was trapped like the others, following the boy everywhere with eyes wide, devout. But unlike the others she gripped the thing on which she sat as though willing her body not to get up. Watching. Watching.

Her hair was shaved on one side. The rest was white.

ELROY HEFLIN'S SKELETON had gained its final inch only as he was getting out of the prison in Los Lunas, when he was twenty-one. Then followed two years of raking hot asphalt in Kansas, Nebraska, Maine; stocking breakfast cereals in grocery stores; slinging heroin, crank; using; shelters or street sleeping; raw wind, the wet kind that goes through you like devil thought; dropping the junk cold, no methadone, no program; multiple antibiotic-resistant infections to contusions in the scalp; teetering through snow toward a shelter in a church, where in the dark entrance a stout figure raised its hands in seeming benediction and to Elroy's liquor-twisted mind took the shape of his father—hope even supplied the old man's face—until the figure resolved into a pink-faced rent-a-cop who snapped, "Keep out till you're sober," and shoved him backward toward the dark; then Elroy's fist swinging right for the face, a crack to the bastard's eye, a crack to the nose, blood on the ice like a taunt that made him kick the piggish body after it fell, making it screech and plead, shouting at it, "I'll come in if I want to, nobody's keeping me out"; followed by his second, longer prison bit before he joined the army, got a steady place to sleep, and his shit finally started coming together for real.

Soon thereafter, he was assigned to an Office of Defense Cooperation attached to the U.S. embassy in Riga, Latvia, as the country prepared to join NATO. Those were great days. All the men billeted in a three-star hotel—an eighteenth-century palace recently renovated with Swedish capital—that the Red Army had used for fifty years as a barracks.

His CO ate smoked trout on dense rye bread in the hotel dining room. "I want to give you some perspective," he said. "Where do you come from, Heflin?"

"Sir, New Mexico," Elroy said.

"Sit down. Where, Albuquerque?"

"Sir, Las Cruces, a place called Ramah, another place without any name west of Vado in Doña Ana County." The table was set for a meal such as people ate who never had to wash the dishes. Seven silver utensils, five pieces of china, a linen napkin, four glasses of different shapes, arrayed, gleaming, empty, with a blue tinge.

The CO poured himself coffee. "Imagine a Russian base in downtown Albuquerque. Farm boys in Soviet uniforms are eating lunch at Lotaburger. You're one of them. Your side won the Cold War without firing a shot. How do you feel?"

"Cock of the walk, sir."

"And rightly so. But you better not act like it."

The local girls were going to dress slutty, the CO explained. Elroy shouldn't let the other junior enlisted men get the wrong idea. His age meant the younger privates were likely to follow his lead. To the men, the outfits would mean, Come take me for a spin. To the girls, they meant, This is how a real European dresses, right? So hands off. The men were only stationed here for eight months. The Latvian girls wanted to get married just like anybody.

That sounded all right to Elroy. He reckoned he had become the marrying kind. And within a couple of months he had a steady girlfriend on the sly. The look, the counterlook, the approach all came so easily. Not like at home. He was drinking with some of the men in the Old City, at a café on a cobblestoned street just wide enough for a fat horse. And the waitress brought them some strawberries and dinner rolls they hadn't ordered. She wanted to practice her English.

In bed she asked him, "How come you like my ear so much?"

It tasted funny. She didn't expend much effort in washing it. He had a little bit of the USSR right here in his mouth. It tasted of sweat, sebum, and lemon-flower perfume.

"Twenty years ago," he said, "they would have sent me here to rape you and burn down your house."

"Silly," she said, turning the pages of a travel magazine. "We didn't have a house."

He awoke in her one-room apartment to find her polishing his shoes with her spit and an old sock. More than once she offered to do his laundry. No thanks, he said. He shied from a woman touching his dirty underclothes, smelling his funks and dribbles.

Dank wind, then sleet. A Sunday. He bought two umbrellas for them. They walked through the Art Nouveau district, and she pointed to the tortured stone faces in the cornice of the law school. They happened upon Mass in a Catholic church, and for a nasty joke they both took Communion, in spite of the sport of the night before. He did not know what the priest was saying, except, for the most part, he did know. Mass was Mass everywhere. He looked up at the bats hanging from the high timbers and spoke with the God of the place. He asked if he could meet her parents, but they were dead.

Her name was Evija.

He wanted to suggest she go more conservative with the makeup;

however, he respected other cultures. Before the deployment ended, he'd got her knocked up. He wanted to get married, but she didn't just yet. And through a subsequent chain of tactical decisions, each reasonable in itself but unguided by strategic vision, he found himself five years later, while stationed in northern Afghanistan, sending a third of his pay to a bank in the former Soviet Union for the upkeep of a boy he got to see about twice a year. And all the while Evija was going out on dates with a Russian theater fag, and writing Elroy emails about, Could she have his credit-card number? She wanted to take the kid on a cruise to visit Norway. He sought the advice of his new platoon leader—for once an older man, with judgment as well as training— about, Was it wise, because what if somebody intercepted the message and got his credit-card number?

His platoon leader said, "Corporal Heflin, a fucking cruise?"

He emailed her that he wouldn't pay for the cruise. Then he didn't hear from her for a few months. To force her hand, he stopped sending the money. Then, while back in New Mexico on leave, he got an email about, Due to circumstances in her personal life, Evija was moving to Spain; she would not take the child; her family wouldn't take him either; and that left Elroy; so when would he come get the boy, Janis; and apologies for such a rush, but within the month?

The army had just promoted him to sergeant. He had grown stouter, more savage. He sat before the computer in his father's retirement condo outside Los Alamos, eating a plum. The plum had detonated in Elroy's teeth and spattered his shirt with juice. He did not notice. He was leaking tears—of what? Of gratitude? He wanted them to be tears of gratitude, yes. And he laughed, free and loud. To the radiant screen he said, "I'll be damned."

TWO DAYS LATER—without a clear plan as to who would look after Janis once Elroy redeployed, and with the boy's immigration status uninvestigated, and lacking so much as an air mattress for him to sleep on—Elroy sat in his and Evija's old haunt, a café on Stabu iela, waiting. He had the blond, small-eyed looks of the local people, and the waitress threw the menus down and shot a stream of Latvian at him. He replied with a phrase Evija had taught him to enunciate without slurring: "I'll need a moment to think things through, if you please."

Evija was going to come in with the boy. Then what? Elroy didn't know.

His post in the café wings gave him both a view of the plate-glass vestibule, where patrons entered, and cover from the prying eyes in the main dining room. If his feelings had to come out now, let them. But they didn't need to do it on a stage. He sat still, hands folded under the table, waiting. He had not slept on any of the planes or in any of the airports, from New Mexico eastward. Little rashes splotched his face. His eyes were parched from airplane air. His feelings need not happen on a stage. But if they came rocketing out of his brain stem and began to ricochet across the roof of his brain, then did it make him such a child if he wanted a woman there with him to not look away?

He checked his watch. He had thought to bribe Evija with flowers, but whatever it was he wanted from her he couldn't buy. Unless she offered it freely, he wanted no part of it. Pointing at the menu, he ordered a glass of seltzer, and when it came he crouched behind a potted ficus, poured some of the water into his hand, and threw it on his eyes and the backs of his ears. He sat up, composed, hoping.

Every time he had gone to stay with Evija and the boy, Riga had grown cleaner, richer, with newer cars. The Russian stayed away when Elroy visited. Evija insisted that the Russian was a common homosexual who needed a girl to keep up the proper appearances, and that she had never kissed him on the mouth.

She cooked potato pancakes for Elroy and the kid, who abhorred sour cream, applesauce, anything presented to him as a condiment. These are the kinks of habit that evolve into our permanent selves. Elroy, as a child, had always preferred to sleep under sheets tight enough to cramp his toes. This preference had led him to take comfort in the austerities of basic training—they break you down, they build you up again, faster, tighter—and he discovered he had a talent for the breaking down, a talent for forgetting. And then a talent for acting on the impulse to kill.

The three of them used to eat on the balcony of her place. Evija called it "our place," including Elroy and Janis. She had taught the boy English and spoke it exclusively whenever his father came, so the boy could practice. He hesitated too much with his English, both parents agreed. By some private rule, he spoke it only to the two of them, and always red in the face.

In the café, Elroy was ordering a plate of chicken livers when a crone came through the vestibule, speaking in harsh tones to what seemed a trailing dog, though it was hidden from view by the low clutter of tables.

The waitress went away. The crone looked down at a photograph and cased the room. And Elroy hit the deck.

His ass remained in the chair, but his hands pressed the floor, his head bent below the table. The wood floor shone with varnish. He could not quite breathe. He seemed to have seen something without knowing it yet. The way you jerk back your hand from a hot skillet before you feel the scorch. He had shot between four and seven enemy insurgents without ever meeting the thoughtless fright of the present instant.

At last, he forced himself to stand. The woman adjusted her frayed shawl, looking around. The dog behind her was Janis, struggling to pull over the threshold a roller bag made for a child much larger than himself.

Elroy said in Latvian, "Madam?" and waved her over.

Evija hadn't come. She'd sent this emissary, this hag: in fact, he now recognized, her landlady.

If the woman and Janis had had their way, the transaction would have taken fifteen seconds. She looked at the photograph—of Janis and Elroy nearly naked at the beach in Jurmala the year before—and told the boy to go sit at the table. But he had already approached his father and was climbing into the seat next to him.

The boy told the woman in Latvian she could leave now—the phrase Evija used when excusing him from the dinner table. But Elroy wanted the woman to tell him what to do. "Don't you have anything to give me?" he asked.

The woman admonished the boy, and the boy nodded. And when Elroy asked, the boy interpreted in a whisper that she was saying Janis must not forget to take care of the papers stored in his bag.

Elroy watched the woman leave. He felt a warm thing on the top of his leg. It was the boy's left hand. With the other hand, the boy was paging through the menu as he looked at the pictures of the food. Elroy cancelled the livers, and they left without eating.

They took a bus to the airport. He strapped Janis into his seat on the flight to Hamburg.

From New Mexico Elroy had brought a coloring book and a crayon. The boy wrapped his fingers around the crayon just so, while Elroy schooled him on how to press lightly so as to conserve wax. And yet, within moments, the crayon snapped in the boy's fist. And the boy glanced up with fear in his shaking mouth, as though he was about to be whipped.

In Hamburg, fresh off the plane, Elroy took the boy to a men's room stall and stuffed his coat pocket with money.

"I didn't mean to break the crayon," Janis said. "I'm sorry."

"Where do you keep my watch?" Elroy drilled, resealing the worn tape that patched the boy's coat. Elroy needed a moment to think things through. He needed ten minutes, fifteen. He would have to buy a book about how to parent. He would have to draw up a grocery list, like cereal, health insurance, antihistamines. The boy had an allergy to dander, and the condo was covered everywhere with the fur of Elroy's father's dog. Elroy needed a moment offstage, without the boy watching, so later he could give the impression he knew what the fuck he was doing. He needed a pad of paper and a pencil.

"I keep the watch in my pants pocket," the boy replied. "I'm sorry."

Elroy said, "Say you're sorry again and I'll give you something to be sorry about."

The boy looked up, his clothed haunches suspended in the toilet seat.

"Go ahead and cry," Elroy said. "What time do I come to get you?"

Janis showed a thumb and index finger. He said, "Two."

Elroy exited the stall. He told the boy to lock it. He heard a scuffle, and the sliding of the latch. He left the men's room, mindful to keep a moderate pace amid the mad clatter of Europeans racing toward him, overtaking him on either side. The corridor reeked of burned cooking grease. He paced away, trailing his bag and the boy's toward Terminal 2. The dented wheels of the smaller bag infuriated him by persistently tipping the bag on its side. He dragged the heavy thing wrong side up. Then he hoisted it by its sissy bar, which would not retract. He blew five minutes just looking for a clock, all while getting farther from the bathroom where the boy waited.

In order to think, Elroy needed to buy a pencil. He blew another ten minutes in Terminal 2 looking for a stationery store. When he found it he realized he had, for reasons hidden from himself, left all of his money with the boy. Why had he left the boy with so much money? He didn't know. And now the cashier, who would have accepted dollars if Elroy had had any, would not let him make such a trifling purchase with a credit card. The airport intercom said something in German, like There was a kindergarten at one of the C gates. Elroy was executing a plan, evidently of his own devising, and yet he did not know its objective.

His connection to London would begin boarding in three minutes. It was already well past two o'clock. He turned back toward the bathroom in Terminal 1, planning to get a little money from the boy, buy the pencil, buy some paper, sit a moment, think, go back again, fetch the boy, and make it to the gate in time for the final boarding call. He would need to draw up an agenda, like day care, catechism classes, haircut. What could he possibly have intended by leaving the boy with all of his cash? The intercom said something in English, like In Terminal 1 there was a lost-and-found. Something in the lost-and-found. He paused, listening.

With low inexorable thumps, an escalator drew arriving passengers down beneath the floor.

He turned. Back toward the London gate, the bags dragging. Like a boat that comes about though its anchor has dropped. The wind takes it. Water all around. You need a while before you come to see you're pointed the wrong way.

JANIS SAT in a little room, an office someplace in the airport. Three kindly Germans surrounded him, their voices soft. Hot chocolate on the desk. He knew he was in Germany, so these must be Germans. And of Germans he knew exactly one thing, a saying he had heard from his mother's actor friend in Riga: *A German may appear to be a good fellow, but better to hang him.*

Do not be fooled by their chocolate.

Go ahead and cry, his father had said. And Janis had let himself cry.

Everything the Germans were telling him sounded like a question, the tone coming up sort of sweet and menacing at the end. Like, "*Flik flik, bok bok, ACK ACK ACK?*" He considered it best not to respond. Most of the grief he had met in life, such as Kit Kats withheld and isolation in the bedroom before dark while others could stay awake together as long as they chose, had come to him because he had talked.

Germany was in Europe. Latvia, his mother's country, was also in Europe. He had two homes: Riga with his mother and America with his father, though Janis had never visited there. Germany must fall somewhere in between. His mother was on vacation and so was he, but "vacation" seemed the wrong word in his case because his father's house, where he was going, also counted as his own house.

Papa will come. By suppertime. Any minute now. So Janis should save room. He wouldn't eat any solid thing they gave him. Per Papa's instructions, he had stayed in the bathroom stall until the little hand of his father's watch had reached the two. Then he had waited a little while longer. Then he had stuffed the watch into his pants and gone back to the place where they had got off the plane. And waited. Papa was not there. So Janis had missed some aspect of their scheme. However, the coming of supper was an unchangeable law that neither he nor his father could get around even if they had wanted to. Papa would have to come by suppertime. Things were very bad, but supper would make them all right again.

Janis longed for the coloring book. His father had taken it back and put it in his bag. The book had no captions and, in this respect, was excellent. He could not quite read yet and disliked feeling he was missing out on something. The book appeared to tell of a boy who feeds and tames a fox and is rewarded with the animal's friendship. The book had no title, so Janis could come up with one of his own along with names for the people in it.

He took a sip of the hot chocolate while the Germans conferred. He didn't want to cry anymore, but he was allowed. It was one of his father's instructions that he was allowed to cry.

TWO HOURS LATER, Elroy landed in London. He deplaned, walked to the perimeter of the airport, and boarded a bus that drove on the wrong side. He had met another of the world wonders—driving on the left. You kind of don't believe in it until you see it. Like the women he had watched float through the street in Kunduz, curtained in blue from cap to toes, a lace visor where the eyes should go. His platoon leader had warned them: Keep your head down. You weren't supposed to look. But Kunduz had been a *Star Wars* planet. Like, How do I process this, a kid like me?

Elroy got off the bus after a couple of stops, sneaked to the back of an apartment complex, and pitched the wicked little bag into a Dumpster. Then he figured out he could go back to the correct side of the street—see, everything went backward; maybe you do it wrong first so you can do it right later—and yes, another bus came and returned him to the airport.

Heathrow, Terminal 5. A bright, oblong construction of glass and steel between asphalt runways. Ticketing. Bag check. A placard at security expressly forbade, among other items, crossbows, machetes, pliers, firearms, lighters shaped like firearms, harpoons, and catapults.

He surrendered what he had to the conveyor belt and the screening cavern, and stepped through the metal detector, shoulders low, breathing deep. But the machine flunked him, cheeping, and a jowly attendant led him to secondary screening—asking, Did he have a pacemaker, a cobalt hip, a plate in his head?—and pointed him to the glass booth of a trace-detection portal.

Elroy breathed deep. Sometimes you went the wrong way to go the right way again. Like once, in the street of a vacant neighborhood in Kunduz, he saw a mound in the earth where the dirt lay neatly disarranged, and he got on his knees and blew on it, and he saw the pressure plate, and he stood up fast. Nobody else around. And before he knew it, he'd said, "Fuck it," and kicked the thing. Yet it didn't blow. Like God was saying, "I want you to live, you shit." And for a whole day Elroy feared nothing.

From all directions, jets in the portal walls spat air at him while the machine sniffed the chamber for cocaine, PCP, smack, methamphetamine; also for TNT, C-4, and Semtex.

A green light flashed, and the portal opened in front. A new attendant led him to a backscatter X-ray. He stood before a wall, hands raised, palms out, while a raster of radiation scanned the length of him. At the controls, a cheerless Caribbean woman with gold crowning her incisors could not determine his fault and let him go.

In the afternoon autumn light, he sat in a file of Naugahyde chairs by the bank of windows. A color had gone out of the light this week: yellow, it seemed. All over Europe, the depleted light identical. And it had transported him back to an era of leaf piles, of cottonwood leaves stuck in the waistband of his underpants. Mountains heaped and demolished.

Jumbo jets faced the terminal windows like orcas nosing at the wall of an aquarium. The haze parted. The light squarely struck Elroy's shaved face. He bathed his neck in it, raising his chin and turning. A lattice of white steel overhead.

By the gate a sign in blocky brass letters said a hamlet had stood here once, called Hitherowe, Hetherow, Hetherowfeyld. A heath with a row of houses on it. Heathrow. Scrub oak and gorse in sandy soil, where the kids played amid the vegetation and rubbish until Mother called them in for tea.

He boarded, took his seat, and the plane tore through the atmosphere.

A WHILE LATER, the Germans were trying to get Janis to do something, but he didn't know what. One of the men took off his own tie and put it on the table, asking Janis a question and pointing to him. Then the man took off his jacket too, and emptied the pockets: cigarettes, ATM receipts. Smiling, open eyes, like, See? Sort of a demonstration.

They were going to make him disrobe? He didn't know how to prevent them. A rule from his mother went, No one gets to take your clothes off you, or take anything away from you that you have. One of the Germans put her hand on Janis's hat, and he let her take it off, exposing his ragged hair, but he could not keep from crying. He was racked with hunger. They ought to feel awful about what they were trying to do to him. They made him stand up and they took off his coat. Anything might happen now. She laid his coat on the table and searched his pockets. They let him watch. They found a Kit Kat wrapper. Gum. And 263 U.S. dollars folded in half.

THE GREAT CIRCLE ROUTE WESTWARD over the Arctic.

Gravity pressed on the plane. Yet the pressure beneath the racing wings, together with the deflection against the flaps in the plane's trailing edges, lifted it up, so that its passengers hovered in the air, in a vessel weighing 830,000 pounds.

Elroy watched a glacier pour ice into the ocean. God crowded the world with wonders so you wouldn't forget what he told you to do. Elroy didn't know if he'd forgotten or remembered.

He transferred at Boston Logan and landed in Albuquerque—the fourth landing in the same day, although it had lasted thirty hours so far. The chamisa pollen caught in his nose and broke his heart. Mucus drained from his sinuses.

He had reserved a subcompact car online, but Hertz had overbooked his model, so he was given a Mustang convertible. He drove it north, with the top down, on the straightaway interstate through the valley of the Rio Grande, pointing his face straight up at the stars, which had occupied the same places over the East. He dared the car to veer out of its lane.

West of Santa Fe, he headed into the Jemez range, the thin air insufficient for his breathing, the roads black. At last he found a low adobe wall running the length of three city blocks—he was navigating by feel, almost by remembered smell, like a hound—and met a gate, at one in the morning Mountain Standard Time. He hadn't eaten since the plane from London, and his longing for food registered as a physical panic. His breath moved shallow and quick. His spine went rigid.

A guard sat at the gate in a lighted cabin doing a sudoku. He asked Elroy, in the rapid-fire English of native New Mexicans, whom he had come to see.

"But I find nothing here from Mr. Tilly that he is expecting you," the guard said to his clipboard. He required a special note from the condo owner to ring after ten o'clock.

"Come on, man," Elroy said. "I was here three days ago." He produced a packet of collection agency envelopes he had stashed in his bag earlier in the week, all addressed to him here, none yet opened. The guard scrutinized them.

The gate receded into the adobe wall, and Elroy eased the convertible into the compound. Hooded lights, rock gardens, low-slung stucco homes. He walked under the vigas of the porch and knocked.

No answer came. He tried the knob. It gave and let him in.

A DAY LATER, Janis was awakened where he slept, on a cot in the airport office, by a man wearing a pilot's uniform. He introduced himself in Latvian as Kristaps, while the Germans looked on. *Latvian to strangers. American only to the ones you know.* A system that had stood Janis in good stead before. But he had to conclude that, in Germany, a stranger speaking to him in Latvian presented a special case. The pilot was trying to trick him in some way. Papa *will* come, eventually.

Janis went to the concourse with the pilot for some milk and an egg sandwich, and the pilot asked in Latvian, "Where is your mother or father?" Angry, as though Janis had done something wrong.

And Janis said, blushing, in American, "Can I have mustard?" intending to spoil the wondrous thing on his plate, lest he succumb and eat it.

"*Where is the person who brought you here?*" the pilot demanded.

Why did it feel *good* to cry? Janis had long wondered what was the matter with him that when he cried, which was feeling bad, it felt good somehow.

Janis took the top off the sandwich, hoping the white of the egg would be runny, but it had set perfectly; hoping the yolk would be green and hard, but it gave easily when he poked it. His entire being cried out for food.

He needed to eat. But he also needed Papa to come. And all this was a test of some kind. Papa *would* come, but only if Janis kept faith and did not eat.

The pilot cursed him.

Janis gnawed at the arm of his coat. The pilot got up for coffee. Janis felt his hunger as a throb beneath his sternum and a kind of wind inside his head. He decided on the title for the coloring book. The title would be *Joe Loves Foxie, and Foxie Loves Joe Very Much.* He opened the little carton of German milk and poured it all over the food on his plate.

Around midday, they put him in a car.

They drove an enormous road. There was a big city, with ships and cranes and railroad cars. It was all so beautiful that Janis wondered whether he was in Heaven.

MR. TILLY WASN'T really Elroy's father. He wasn't even Elroy's stepfather. He had been Elroy's legal guardian until he turned eighteen. Nonetheless, if Elroy should ever get killed, the Casualty Notification Officer tasked with informing his primary next of kin would have to come out here. Whether his mother was living or dead, he didn't know.

Toward the living room he made his way in the dark, touching the walls. The cavelike dwelling swallowed every sound. A prehistoric homey smell of an old person's wool clothes drying. Under his hand on the sofa, sheets and blankets lay stacked: a bed prepared for him.

He untied his boots. A presence in this home as nowhere else seemed to see him and know, an all-embracing knowledge of what he had done and would do. Someone existed who saw it all and went on watching when each of the others had turned away.

He washed his face and dried it and came back to the living room. His eyes, seeing not in spite of the darkness but as if by means of it, became attuned to the rug—which he had shipped to the old man at foolish expense from an air base in central Asia—and to a little, second, makeshift bed that had been arranged there: a quilt folded twice to make a mattress, a pillow, an acrylic blanket. Atop the pillow, a box of apple juice with its shrink-wrapped straw affixed.

Beside him on the sofa he found a remote control, aimed it into the nothing before him, pressed its rubber button. The flickers of a gas fireplace shot up among cast ceramic logs.

Down through the chasm of the flames—the other world inside the fire—a throng of souls came falling toward him. Altogether toward his face, souls old and young, of every color and time, two by two from the flames, paired souls like two streams coursing, all of them knowing him, but none so much as turned a face to acknowledge he was there.

Firelight faintly painted the hopping room, creating a small piano with its lid ajar, printed music scattered on a table, a heap of trade magazines, jade and cactus growing amid pebbles in the bottoms of soda bottles. A money tree, a chair in the far corner, a pair of black jeans, a brown wool shirt, a gray windbreaker—the old man's perpetual outfit of a person ready to disappear in a crowd or thicket. The flickering light made the shirt move. It resolved above the shirt into a white crown like a beacon unlit. A mist condensed and hardened and embodied the clothes and hair. The grizzled head twisted and shook off sleep. The fingers swiped the corners of the eyes. "Elroy," the voice said simply.

"Fuck, I didn't see you."

Tilly—the puzzle, the elusive creature—stirred and came awake in the chair in the dark corner. "I thought you were coming with the boy," he said.

"Yeah," Elroy said listlessly.

"Did I misunderstand?"

"Yeah, it didn't work out, you know?"

Tilly's conniving dog, Mavis, appeared behind the glass door that opened onto the patio. She scratched at the pane and looked in at the old man with her ears back and her eyes gaping, like, I know I can't come in, but I'm a stupid bitch, and can I come in?

Tilly got up from his corner and hobbled to the door, holding a magazine. "What is it exactly I know?" he asked.

"Just, it didn't work out. He looks like me though, these days. A fucking miracle, right? You expect them to follow you in the face, but then you don't think they do, until they get to a certain age, and then you see it."

Tilly slid open the door, bent, rolled the magazine, and offered it to the dog, who did not really want to come in; she wanted Tilly to come out. She seized the magazine passionately in her jaws. Tilly began thereby to drag her inside, and she to draw him toward the dark. Once her forepaws touched the carpet, she knew she would lose this contest and shrieked and ran off.

Elroy went to the fridge, which contained only expired Tex-Mex condiments. "What happened to my baloney?" he said.

"I ate it," the old man said.

"No way," Elroy said, stricken. "You did, really?"

"Elroy, it's my house. I eat the food here. You ate up everything else I had, even the pears. Go to the store and get yourself something."

"Aw, man, I'd have to go all the way to White Rock." Elroy turned to address the old man's stocking feet, the left one wedged like a trowel: he had lost three toes in Vietnam. Elroy said, "You're supposed to be my dad."

AT SUNUP, as Tilly was leaving to eat his breakfast at a diner in town, Elroy awoke on the sofa and asked Tilly to get him something to eat down by the labs. He rummaged in his pants pockets—he had slept in his clothes—and discovered a crumpled mass of bills, which he handed drowsily to the old man.

Tilly picked out a piece of blue-green paper decorated with an oak tree. "What in the world is this?" he asked.

"That's a whatchamacall. A lat. Five lats—where'd all my real money go?" he asked, sitting up. He thought a moment.

"What do you want, a burrito? I'll get it for you," Tilly said, clicking the leash around the jubilant dog's neck. Wherever Tilly went, Mavis came along.

"I'll pay you back."

Tilly approached the couch, where Elroy lay cramped and crooked, and reached toward him, whereupon Elroy shrank, furtive as a wolf. Tilly folded the money that had no value here and tucked it in the breast pocket of Elroy's shirt.

Elroy's afflicted eyes itched. "I don't deserve it," he said.

"Who told you that you had to deserve it?" Tilly asked.

Part One

The Old Man

1

Tilly told people he came from Davenport, Iowa. His birth and baptism certificates both listed a family address in Davenport at 14 Greeley Street. If it were ever objected that contemporaneous maps list no such street anywhere in that city, he would have said the street was a right of way through a clump of shacks on the floodplain; mail didn't arrive there. The certificates showed he was born to one Ida Elizabeth Tilly, age twenty, father not named, on November 14, 1948. His Marine Corps separation papers listed the same date but in 1947. Otherwise all his important papers agreed.

In reality, no such person as this Ida Tilly ever lived. The person who would become Dwight Elliot Tilly was born not in 1948 or '47 but in 1950. Not in the city of Davenport but on a farm of 278 acres in the prairie north of there, nearest the town of Calamus. Not to Ida Tilly but to Annie Frade, age forty-six, and Potter Frade, age fifty-three.

The Frades had married only a year before, each for the first time. A mixed marriage of a Catholic and a Presbyterian. Each awoke the morning after the wedding certain they had done the thing wrong. Most of what they knew, they knew from livestock. Whatever far-fetched hopes either might have had at their ages that a child might result from their efforts, they were too embarrassed to say.

She bore the unlikely boy in the Frade parlor, with pages of the *Quad-County Advertiser* spread all over the rug. Potter Frade, practiced in calving, delivered him and wiped him with dish towels and painted his navel with iodine. Annie looked him over and found nothing the matter with him and gave him her breast, and he nursed, wrestling the air. He was angry and strong. If he were a calf he would already have been walking. But he was more a vegetable seed, left over in the autumn garden, that survived the snow and sprouted on its own in the spring. They called him the Volunteer. Later, they called him Vollie. His true name they never used.

Funny the documents should have given him Davenport for a home. Of Davenport his mother never spoke except to curse it. No one prospered there but financiers and chiropractors. Even the Mississippi was crooked in Davenport. She did not drink the tap water there. Frades and Marquettes, her own people, didn't come from Davenport as foals didn't come from sows.

The Frades only went to Davenport to pay their mortgages, of which they had several. Annie drove; Potter's eyes were dimming already. Vollie stood atop his father's lap inspecting the road while Potter gripped the yoke of the boy's shirt and braced him with an arm around the belly, nuzzling him and teaching him the family names of the properties they passed. All their debts his father paid in person. He enlisted Annie as a reader of contracts and bills. When a piece of paper required his signing, he drew a cypher of sturdy lines and curves, a mark that looked nothing like the words "Potter Frade" but was a phrase of some kind, the only one he ever taught himself to make. Tilly never forgot the mark and could have made a convincing copy of it in a flash: his hand remembered it like a piano melody. But he never knew its origin.

This was its origin. His father, as a boy of six, had sat in the Flat Rock Presbyterian Church tracing the letters stamped in gold foil on the back of a hymnal: *God Is Love,* it said, but the boy Potter didn't know. A half century of work having swollen and twisted the hand, the signature now no longer resembled the phrase he had begun by copying. Instead you saw the runic mark of old Potter Frade. It meant, We Will Pay.

A WINTER MORNING.

All three Frades lowered their heads over breakfast—applesauce, side pork, toast, fried eggs, marmalade, milk, sour cream coffee cake, coffee. Annie Frade gave thanks for God's grace and for the Volunteer. Vollie gave thanks for his pocket comb and, when pressed, for the cake. Potter Frade's eyes clenched with inward attention. His old neck and old head, fringed in silver hair, protruded from his old jacket, the head stony and shining like a rubbed nickel. He said, For their heifers on the meadow, for Annie, for the boy, for their disc harrow, for his knees.

Vollie ate everything on his plate and walked two miles along the icy white gravel shoulders of farm roads to the clapboard schoolhouse. Miss Travers the teacher called the roll. Four students were absent. All present students, age six to fourteen, stood with hands over hearts and pledged allegiance to the flag of the republic. At lunchtime under the jungle gym, Carleen the Quaker girl shared with Vollie a block of fudge from her lunch bucket and he the ham sandwich from his. A black car came through the noontime winter mud and slush of the road. Mr. Strieg, the superintendent, climbed out and hastily gimped into the school, swinging under him the kneeless, war-shot, famous wooden leg. When Carleen wasn't looking, Vollie turned his face to the dark clouds and gave thanks to God for all our knees—for his father's, for Carleen's, especially for the knee of Mr. Strieg's other leg, which worked.

Shortly, Miss Travers came out and blew the whistle. The children gathered into the schoolroom. The superintendent handed each a page of blue instructions still damp from a mimeograph machine. Everybody went immediately home. They were not to walk in groups or pairs.

Vollie found his silverhead father in the barn and handed him the mimeograph. His father looked toward it awhile, not quite at it, and smiled and folded it twice and stuck it in the bib pocket of his coveralls, and that was when Vollie for the first time guessed his father couldn't read. Later, at supper, rummaging in the pocket, the old man brought out the mimeograph and passed it to the boy's mother, who, lacking her glasses, held it at arm's length over the table.

Something was wrong.

His mother immediately stripped him right there in the kitchen. She ran him a bath. She told him to scrub himself well and hustled away with his clothes.

Vollie bathed, he dried himself, he climbed the stairs to his room, where the glass of the only window seemed to contain an unusual orange and blue flickering. He approached it and looked down over the snowbound nighttime fields.

What he witnessed there, the dreadful rite, penetrated the depths of his consciousness, impressed its shape upon his innermost being, and promptly vanished: by the next morning, he would never again recall what he had seen or that he had seen it. But the impression it made would harden with time, and the meaning he took from the impression, which remained with him as a feeling at once of perfect fear and perfect peace, came to seem self-evident, and probably true of everyone.

Out in the yard, he saw himself on fire.

His father stood over a steel can. Flames leapt from it. He held an iron poker at the end of which hung the burning figure, dangling by the yoke of his shirt at the very place his father would grip him when they drove. Flames shot from the sleeves, the collar. Vollie watched as his legs too were set ablaze; the ashy pants floated in the heat. His mother came out with his school shoes and threw them likewise in the fire.

Vollie stood upstairs at the window in his underwear, engulfed by a fear that was the god of all previous fears, encompassing them, compounding them into the perfect fear that was being realized right now: his father and mother were burning him alive. Black smoke, the remnant of him, rose and dispersed into the nothing of night sky. Dark— forever and absolute.

And yet.

And yet, if Vollie himself had just been turned to nothing out there, what was this limbed creature inside the house that watched it all and shivered with cold and still hungered for supper?

His self was a "who" who had burned away in the flames; but the creature was a "what" that could endure even this. The self that had seemed all of him was only a part; it could be shed and left behind.

A gust shook the house, rattling the window. Cold touched his body thrillingly everywhere.

The god of all fears had left the room. The creature had outlasted him.

As he grew older, the events of the days surrounding the fire he'd seen would come back to him in flashes: the breakfast, the walk, the unfolding of the mimeograph that he would later learn had alerted his mother to an outbreak of meningitis in the school and the precautions they must take against it.

None of these flickers would stay with him long, but one. A vision he endured within the fever that overcame him in the subsequent days. Here and there across the years, it was the memory not of the fire but of this fever vision that returned to him, shocking him with the promise of perfect freedom, but blinding him to what the freedom would cost.

He showed no symptoms of infection until two days later. He came in the house midmorning red-faced after hog feeding and was ordered to the parlor for piano practice. Minutes later his scales were no longer audible in the kitchen, and his mother found him asleep with his burning head on the keys.

He lay in bed a week. His coveralls hung from the old hook in the closet door. His mother and father were there in the room somewhere. His brain pounded. A doctor came and went away. The coveralls, hanging upright and unpersoned by him, meant he had become a ghost. He smelled boiled chicken and onions and found his father hovering over the bed with a spoon of steaming broth and his mother prizing open his jaws. The slight raising of his head from the pillow felt to him as though his neck was being broken. A priest came. By candlelight amid Latin murmuring, the priest touched with oil Vollie's eyelids, ears, lips, nostrils, the palms of his hands, and the soles of his feet. He came awake in dry sheets and slept again. He came awake in sopping sheets and slept once more, and then the vision commenced.

Moon on the orchard. Somewhere, a hog crying. The deep cold creek in the meadow. He approached the creek wild with thirst and lowered his burning head to the flowing surface that warped the face he saw in it. He saw the anguish in the face. He knew the face to be his. Then he understood the anguish not to be within the burning head itself but in the face he saw. He knew he must overcome his resistance to the cold and press the face through the surface of the water, whereby the face would be extinguished, together with its anguish, but the head would survive with the body and the rest of him. He understood the cries of the hog were in fact his own cries. Hands from somewhere pressed him toward the water. Summoning his nerve, he plunged his face through the surface.

Immediately the face and its anguish were gone. The freedom from the torture of the face was sweet relief. He gave in to the hands he felt pressing on him and fell into the creek entirely—and the body was seized with frigid alarm.

At that moment, he came to in the bright bathroom of his home, naked in the water of an ice bath. His father was dumping snow in the water from a tin pail. His mother held him down in the rusted tub.

Then he passed out again into the vision-world, the truer realm beneath the surface of the creek on the meadow. Cold and hidden and unreachable and right, submerged in what seemed his true element. Swimming in a time out of time, free of any self.

When he came to again, he was wearing flannel pajamas in his own bed amid dry sheets. He sat up a little and found a plate of soup crackers on the small table by the bed and ate one of them. The bones of his neck could turn a little now. He lay still with his eyes closed remembering his vision. Someone came in and touched his forehead and neck. From the smell on the hands of bag balm and gasoline, he recognized his father checking on the fever that had begun to subside. Vollie might have said aloud that he was better now, but he did not yet want to depart from his vision.

He loved his mother. Even as a teenager he would get up and go to whatever room of the small house she was in, and they would both stay in the room without needing to speak a word, doing whatever they were doing.

He loved his old father. He coveted what the man knew. A tacit understanding existed between them that they would have less time than other families, and his father must show him everything without delay, and Vollie must pay attention or it would be lost, what his father knew, the knowledge uniquely his, the old world in the old mind.

All the same, from early on he believed he had come too late for them, like a houseguest whose arrival wakes us from sleep. The arms that lifted him couldn't sustain his weight for long. He had come unnaturally late and represented an unnatural burden. Nature would eventually free them from it, but how? He would be cast off. Nature would find a time, an instrument.

SALVATORE SCIBONA

.   .   .

WHEN THEY HAD MONEY after expenses, they went to Davenport and
Potter Frade made his mark and signed the money over to the bank
that owned their mortgages. He could have bought the Dressler property when Dressler retired, but he paid down debt instead. He could
have demolished the derelict barn from which tin roof sheets flew off in
windstorms and he could have bought the timbers and siding to build
a new barn, but instead he sent Vollie up to the roof of the existing barn
with a pop-rivet gun and a bucket of tar. Casey Reese up the road fell
from his hayloft and broke his back. The swampy parcel of his large
pasture came up separately for sale. Vollie would have quit his job
chicken catching for a season and would have laid new drain tile
through the pasture by himself—he understood his father's old knees
were too feeble to lay tile anymore—and they could have fed twenty
more head of cattle, but his father said no.

Vollie said, "You'll cancel that debt if it kills you."

"That's right," his father said.

"What if it kills me?"

"Nobody ever got killed waiting to build a barn."

"I never see our money," Vollie said and spat on the meadow they
were manuring.

"Look around you," his father said. "Right here's where the money is."

A meadow, a heap of a barn, a pasture, a ditch covered with asparagus ferns, two hundred acres of shorn stalks awaiting the snow.

AT AGE SEVENTEEN, Vollie Frade propped his bicycle on a phone pole
and approached the casement glass door of the Clinton County Savings & Loan with his conscience in knots and his wicked money in his
jacket. The money was not wicked in itself, it became so as he brought

it to the teller's window and stood filling out the application for an account in his own name. Money, unlike underclothes, belonged to one's family and not to oneself, yet here he stood printing both the family name and the true first name no one ever used, which befit the occasion since who was this bastard preparing to do this closefisted thing?

The money in his jacket came from when he had worked as a chicken catcher and, since his aunt had died and left him her bicycle, as the mechanic's gofer in Lost Nation. He had not turned over all his earnings to his mother and father; a portion, a residual, had accrued to him by mutual agreement, and he had saved it in a paint can with a slot punched in the lid. Nevertheless, from time to time his mother would come and need some of it, popping the lid off with a screwdriver, taking only what the bill required, pounding the lid back down with a hammer as Vollie watched.

A bird of prey spanned the top of the application form and bore on its breast the shield of the CCS&L while its wild eye hunted something beyond the paper's edge. He printed the name, the address, the date of birth, the amount of the initial deposit. A line of dots invited his signature. He did not sign. The moment distended as in a spell of nausea. To sign was to horde and betray. It was to bring a curse upon himself. He didn't recognize the force compelling him to do it. He didn't understand why he wanted it so badly. He could not bear to do something so cruel and irrevocable to his own people, to take what was his away from what was theirs, when all they had they had offered him and would leave him when they died.

With a shock, he signed.

The curse began to work its evil at supper that same day.

"I got my eye on this Grand Prix," he said.

"And what might that be, my lamb?" Annie asked.

"Mamma, that's a—" Vollie took the plate of scalloped apples from his father but did not look at him, and Vollie's neck and shoulders squared and he spooned the fruit and dribbled its browned sugar syrup on his rib chops. His face went hot. He said, "That's a car."

There wasn't any question what his father would say about this.

Annie said, "And will you tell us about it?"

Potter said, "We got a car."

"It's a green car that needs a transmission rebuild."

"And you can do that, can't you?"

His father repeated, "We got a car."

"Pretty sure I can rebuild it on this model, yes."

"And then you could sell it back and turn a profit, you mean."

"Yes, or I could—"

"Doesn't smell like a profit," Potter said.

"I could maybe."

"People always want cars so there would be a demand," Annie said.

"Smells like an expense."

"You could put an ad in the church bulletin and turn it right around."

"I could do that, yes, if I wanted," Vollie said, "or use it for other things."

"He doesn't have any such intention of selling," Potter said.

"Or you could park it on sixty-six by Marion Kierkoff. He'd let you. Where people could see it with a sign on the window."

"He has an intention of one thing."

"If I wanted, later, yeah," Vollie said. "I could sell it up there or anywheres."

"With a sign that says for sale and the asking price, the way people do, to give a sense of the sort of offer you would entertain, but you would be flexible depending on how much time and money you had already sunk into it."

"One thing and one thing only," Potter said.

"Or I could use it awhile first."

"Intention of *driving fast*."

"Oh, not too fast," Annie said. "He wouldn't drive it very fast. Would you, lamb?"

"Then he'll smash up and break his back. I say no."

"I feel sure you would obey the posted speed limits, wouldn't you?"

"Mother, we got to say no at this time," Potter said.

"I guessed you would say that," Vollie said.

Annie got up and straightened the serving dish for the pork, the dish for the apples, the dish for the bread. She sat back down.

"I ain't going to fight you," Vollie said.

"Nobody appreciates how a boy wishes to go in charging, screaming his head off, and get things done," Annie said. "This really is too bad."

"We have to say no at this time. We got no spare. We got no cash on the margin at all."

Vollie said, "You figure you win now."

Annie and Potter looked at each other dumbfounded and mutually inquiring. "What?" they both said. "Win what?"

Potter's old face was rumpled and blotched as a pie. In perplexity he said, "What is there—"

Annie said, "What is there to win?"

THE NEXT DAY Vollie fed and watered the hogs, cut school, biked into town, took the bus to Davenport, forged his father's inscrutable signature on the document that demonstrated parental permission for recruits under eighteen, passed his physical, and was enlisted in the United States Marine Corps. He made it back to Calamus in time to withdraw all but a dollar from his account at the S&L.

He told Potter and Annie, "I don't have to explain anything. Here's my money."

"Jesus Christ, what have you done?" Potter said.

When Annie quit shouting she said, "I'm surprised they let a person just take himself away like that."

"We could stop this if we went down there and I said that ain't my hand that made the mark," Potter said. "Except I figure you'd only find some other way."

It hadn't until that moment occurred to Vollie his swindle of forging the mark might succeed. He had supposed, without quite knowing it, that Annie would drive them to the recruiter in Davenport and Potter would say, That ain't my hand. I'll show you my hand. And come morning Vollie would be back feeding the hogs, school in daytime, and the Lost Nation garage until supper. He hadn't thought so far ahead as finding any other work to consume his day, least of all soldiering, of which he knew not a thing; he didn't even hunt, they had no time for hunting and no spare for shells. But his father foresaw his actions before he himself saw them. His father's mind was a coat wrapping Vollie's will, confining it but also comprehending it. Knowing it for him because he was too young yet to know it himself. He could act on his will and follow it, but he didn't *know* it. He needed his father to tell him where his own will was taking him. Elsewise the crazy idiot thing, his will, racing avidly like it did, would have him shooting off the edge of the earth before he thought to pack a bag.

"That's right, I'd find some other way," Vollie said and went upstairs to the small room with the window that overlooked the yard. His coveralls hung from the hook in the closet door. It was only then he understood that nature had found its time and way of casting him out of the home he had never hoped to leave, and that a force more powerful than his will had employed him as its instrument.

2

Okinawa was a fever dream of mosquitos and Falstaff beer.

A Marine Corps rule said they couldn't put Vollie on the plane to deploy if he was too drunk to walk unassisted across the tarmac and up the stairs into the bird. Why did command make a rule like that if they were going to give you liberty to see the town the night before you flew out?

A buddy he'd met stateside in survival training, a ranch hand from New Mexico, was teaching Vollie to drink himself sick. "The belly got to get swole up," his companion said. "Loose that belt. Let the bubbles in down deep. You're a beer camel now. They'll put me on that plane in ten pieces is the only way. Tie me together in the cargo hold. We used to keep camels on the ranch. Two of them. Brother, could they drink up the whole irrigation ditch. See now, the way you doing, either breathing or drinking, that there is a mistake. You got to keep up breathing while the beer goes down. There, you got it. They'll have to ship me in a crate because I ain't walking." He had a head full of cuspate teeth, and when he snored in the bunk the eyes drew open, showing only the grisly whites while the irises pointed elsewhere within the skull. His name was Bobby Heflin.

They headed to a different bar. Everywhere in the street people were trying to sell them laundry detergent, beer and cigarettes by the case, shaving products, all the brands of home in bright familiar packaging with the power to transport him back to what already seemed a previous life: long afternoons under the lift in the dank garage, where a transistor sang catchy odes to gum and window cleaners and he timed the turns of a ratchet to the rhythm of the jingle beat.

They got to the new bar. Vollie took a seat at a long plank table where some squids were playing bridge, he could see it was bridge, concentrated and insular and leaning back to hide their cards amid the narrow quarters of the table like a crowded raft. Heflin went away for more beers. Vollie removed from his shirt pocket a letter several months old, soiled and worn in its folds from his opening and closing it.

The letter had been delivered to him on base in California and came from the preacher at home, writing for his father, saying his mother was in the hospital with hives, probably out of worry for Vollie's well-being, but he shouldn't think about it, or about them; he should keep his mind on what he was doing, keep his head down, and keep away from automatic weapons if possible. Which was funny; Vollie had already been trained to maintain and fire a .50-caliber machine gun.

Then back on the Okinawan street and everybody trying to sell him more detergent. Tide, the washday miracle, cleanest washes you can get. Winston, the filter blend that makes the big taste difference. Falstaff beer that satisfies your taste for living. A C-141 came in low enough you could see the light crenellating behind its engines and a red cross painted on its tail fin, so its cargo would be what? Casualties, he figured. Get the package with the spear and you'll know enjoyment's here, because it's Wrigley's here, the biggest little treat in all the land. All this while he stumbled in streets lit beautiful as Christmas yards, and every moment more beautiful as the tropical dusk settled in, the neon red lights everywhere invited him into establishments with silhouettes of what he had learned was a martini glass. You could also buy a squatting ape carved out of a hollowed coconut with a slot in its mouth for your spare change. You saved your money like that instead of blowing it on beer and trinkets to send to your folks who had no need of conch shells that carried home the sound of the soughing sea.

Vollie led Heflin toward a cocktail lounge. Or maybe it was the other way around, Heflin led Vollie. Or the other, other way: both of them led by the red neon figure of a martini glass suspended over the establishment's door. The place inside swarmed with marines, you'd think an invasion was on, skinny pimpled white black, laughing idiots eager to get mown down to the ankles, reaped like corn, addle-eyed in the bar noise. Heflin had gone away again, because here he was coming back with two fresh cans. "Give me your life," he shouted. Except it was *knife* he'd said, and turned the beers upside down and stabbed them on the bottom and showed how to cover the hole then flip it right side up, crack the top, slip the tab into the can, and shoot the beer. All this Vollie did, but the beer tasted wrong. His can had halfway drained, the black and yellow crest and the logo lion's head leering, before it became clear the discombobulating foreignness of the beer consisted in its being hot beer, hot as blood. Then the beer was empty, Falstaff the choicest product of the brewer's art, and Heflin howling like a spanked dog, and Vollie felt a baseball bat smack him in the eyes: felt that way, hold on, it was only the hot beer like a blow to the head. A girl—a perfect Japanese girl with shiny clothes—came by with a tray of Singapore slings and said, "Your job is to die," except inflected like a question. "The hell it is," he said. She repeated, "You want to buy?" Yes. And how. Another for his buddy? Yes, for the cowboy too. Look at his shark teeth. Don't kiss him, your mouth'll get stuck in there. And the girl went away. If you were under the influence they weren't supposed to put you on the plane. It bewildered him the motleyness of what you could buy from a single market stall—only he was pretty sure he was still inside the cocktail place and only thinking about the market stalls flanking the street outside—all the products of home though he was in Japan, and also face paint, magazines, hi-fis, porno, decals extolling the honor of the Third Marine Division, the Fighting Third; all for sale from the same codgers in the street, no distinctions whatever to clarify what you were supposed to buy from the one stall rather than the other, which was too confusing, and that was why he wanted to go back under the neon silhouette of the cocktail glass into the lounge because the silhouette of the cocktail glass clarified things, made it plain what you were supposed to do in there. Except if he was looking at the sign he was outside, and how was he outside? He actually *was* outside after all. Because his drink was inside, so he went back in there. He sat on a high chair, and another shiny girl, a penumbra of light around her like a saint in a picture, wearing a brilliant, lithe, vertically striped dress like pulled taffy with a fluorescent light rod stuck in it she glowed so, approached him carrying a tray of plastic tumblers, red and frothy with straws and a quarter round of pineapple clipping the lip of the drinks and asked, Would he like a long beverage?

Later, he would remember the chair. A spindle-back chair that turned on ball bearings. He would remember he was sitting in this chair taking the plastic drink from the shiny girl, then not being greedy with the pineapple slice, taking only the one bite to avoid the sneaky shards of pine that hid in the flesh. And he would remember he had yet to pay the girl and turned in the chair with a dollar in his fist lest she vanish before she could be paid, a sudden swinging turn that swept the chair from under him, and the very next thing—no time elapsed at all, a perfect glue or weave between the days—the very next thing, there's a voice, a staticky voice over an intercom saying, "Gentlemen, fasten your seat belts, you are landing in the Republic of Vietnam."

. . .

YOU'D SEE A GUY was scared. They were all of them scared out of their minds even while stoned, but you'd see, what was it, the eyes too open, too reactive to movement and sun glints on passing scooter windshields; eyes too certain they could see it coming, the moment, the fell turn; a crouchy way of moving around even when the guy had no gear to hump; and it all amounted to a greed to go on living, laced with the knowledge it was not to be. Like, I know I ain't getting out of here. And then a few weeks later, you'd hear that guy was dead.

There wasn't any sense to make of this phenomenon. Unless God didn't like you expecting too much and he punished you for it by giving you what you expected to get. And you might think, all right, then I'll go ahead and expect to make it home. But that was just vanity. No available facts supported such a foolish assurance. Within a week of his arrival in the country, Vollie was picking shards of the head of a lance corporal off his shirt, a boy nearly his same age, and hair attached to the shards that smelled of smoke and Brylcreem.

You'd see a guy stop short three times while tying the same shoe, stop to look up at moonlight flicking off a rock while the river moved on it, stop and look, stop and look. And a month later that guy would be dead.

He knew a marine in Da Nang, a chancre mechanic who only ever saw combat when John Wayne got bayoneted at the Alamo on the TV in the hospital rec room—but scared as a crippled rat. What harm was going to come to him in a hospital ward in the big city where all he ever shot was penicillin? A shy marine, and he had that look of not just scared but, I see it coming. And then he was dead.

He had managed to get shot in the stomach on a park bench by a twelve-year-old boy with a homemade pistol, not even a VC, though you could never know for sure. And the boy said, once they caught him, tears gooing the face, a long breathless convulsive fugue of repeated something that turned out to mean, "I didn't know it was loaded. It was a game. I didn't know it was loaded. He gave me Percodan for my mother's back sometimes. I wanted to show him my pistol. I didn't know it was loaded. He gave me potato chips from his lunch outside in the parking lot. He was my friend. I didn't know."

The lesson was, anything you love so bad that everywhere you look you see how you're going to lose it, that thing will be taken from you. Even your life.

So Vollie had a mantra—he had learned to meditate from Bobby Heflin, of all unquiet people, who'd read some magazine articles about Buddhism and a Buddhist's all-eclipsing indifference to property, to life, to limb. Vollie had a mantra and he sat still in the dark on his bunk with his back against the plywood hooch wall at Dong Ha with his eyes half closed and his folded feet aflame from fungal itching, and he breathed deep and said within the mind, It don't mean nothing. Into his consciousness came a vision how he would lose his hand, the right hand that played the melody on the Baldwin upright back home, and he said without speaking but enunciated as it were crisply in the mind, It don't mean nothing. Not that the fear didn't mean anything, or the vision or the pain, but the *hand* didn't mean anything. Then the vision of reaching into a hole in the ground, a hidden tunnel entrance, with the left hand, the harmony hand, reaching into the ground in the jungle knowing the VC had a whole world of interconnected tunnels, whole supply channels underground. A whole division might be waiting down there to bite off the hand so why was he doing this? But he was doing it in the vision and saw with lightning clarity, the way amid the shadows of rain coming through thickening air at night the lightning makes a cut across the sky and everything comes alight as stark as noon, he saw the hole explode and the fire leaping out of it, and his own blood spitting on his face, and these two stumps at the ends of his arms like when a kid walks on the road in winter without gloves and bunches up the fists within the cuffs, except the hands were not hidden, melody and harmony, they were gone. And of the hands he said crisply in the mind, They don't mean nothing. And he saw his silverhead father sneezing in the hog barn, ailing in his bed, and said, It don't mean nothing. Meaning *he* didn't mean anything, the aging man at home, the red and here-and-there peeling face awaiting his return. And he saw the farm with only his mother to work it, it didn't mean nothing. Cracked drain tile clogged with earth and flooding the meadow, it didn't mean nothing. The apple trees unsprayed and the fruit eaten to pulp by curculios, it didn't mean nothing. And he got up and went into a tent where a couple of other dirt-caked convoy drivers lay on cots asleep before a TV hooked to a generator showing a police movie, all sirens and shadows and waxy hair, the unsteady horizontal hold on the black-and-white screen catching the moment, the scene, and losing it and the scene running away like a loose blind, then catching it again, shadows and then glowing white human faces close to the camera, and Lauren Bacall looked out of the convex box into the night that reeked of monsoon funk, with lust and reproach in her face as if to say, I dare you to forget me too.

THE COUNTRY had been on fire from the moment he had first landed. He'd only ever seen a big civilian city from the insides of planes or airports, and now he was outside on the tarmac—in his undress blues and carrying a seabag, and the uncountable Falstaffs and Singapore slings were exacting their revenge on his head and guts—in a city, Da Nang, that was home to hundreds of thousands and was taking artillery fire, smoke rising like giant ghost trees from the rooftops.

Within a couple of hours he was assigned to the 26th Marines at a supply depot in the rear at Dong Ha, from which he was to run convoys up the dirt roads to the forward combat bases near the DMZ at Camp Carroll, Lang Vei, Quang Tri, something called the Rockpile, and another spot that was just an airstrip really as it turned out—a road, a cliff, and an airstrip on a low plateau outside a village called Khe Sanh, although whatever human life in the village had been raptured lately, right before he passed through it the first time, so lately the cats were still delicately eating scraps in the hot trash heaps, the cats the souls of the sinners left behind.

Convoy orders were nice and simple: keep going. A long line of trucks in single file, twenty, fifty, sometimes a hundred trucks. You get a flat tire, you keep going. He drove an M54, a five-ton truck with ten wheels, and you could afford to lose a tire so long as it wasn't in front and keep on up the slick road to the combat base. A truck disabled by whatever mechanical failure or land mine, you ditch that truck and keep going. If it obstructs the road you push it off the cliff, don't matter if your mother's inside. Do not stop. They were running candy canes and powder charges and everything between, building supplies, shovels, canned milk, but the cargo and any disabled truck could be replaced. Two minutes stopped on a mountain road was plenty long enough for a convoy to get sighted and blown to hell from incoming.

Squads of grunts were guarding the road, on patrol or some of them dug in, or some of them hiding in rock formations because up near the DMZ the place could have been Mars for all the cover any vegetation provided. But you hardly saw these dug-in or hiding squads and fire teams until you were right on top of them. And while the convoy headed back to Dong Ha the afternoon after a drop, the grunts guarding the road would throw a bag into your truck as you drove by, a burlap or polypropylene woven bag usually used for sandbagging but with a rock in it to make it sail like a projectile and you'd snatch it coming in your window. Inside was a passel of rumpled lists of the supplies they needed: razor blades, rations, bullets, cigarettes, soap. Somebody wrote, *Chicken soup or orange juice—we all got colds.* It was Christmas every day, and Vollie was Santa Claus taking requests. Every list pled for beer, but he couldn't find any for the longest time.

Do not stop the convoy. He heard it in his dreams, dreams of incoming artillery and RPGs, and when you woke up that was no dream, that was the explosion in the deep distance. One-hundred-twenty-two-millimeter rocket fire and 100-millimeter artillery fire coming from some goddamn place. A little *thump, thump, thump.* You counted the seconds until you heard the bangs commence and thereby figured out how many miles away the guns were. From up by Khe Sanh came rumors of a new gun. A big NVA gun, never before used in the field. One hundred thirty millimeters, accurate to crazy distances, hitting cargo planes the minute they landed and making Swiss cheese of the airfield. What with the Phantom fighter-bombers crisscrossing the sky at will you'd think they could find those 130 millimeters and knock them out. The 130 was better artillery even than the Americans had, or anyhow than the Marines did. This piddly-size country, in fact half a country, with these piddly-size people, where did they get such a gun? Rumor said the guns were hidden across the Laotian border, in tunnels dug into the eastern flanks of the mountains under dense foliage, and the guns rolled out and fired and rolled back in their tunnels untraceably. Every rumor had a tunnel in it. Scuttlebutt about a wayward shipment of candy bars—where did they go? Some tunnel rat found them later, a whole pallet of Snickers in a room in the earth with a dog guarding it, tied to the pallet and dead.

Laos being neutral, he might have asked somebody how come the enemy got to run supply lines through it and bury their monster guns there and fire them, and how come we were building our camps here and waiting to get shelled instead of driving over the border and killing them first? But such questions arose and blew off like mist, because boot camp had trained the mind to sneer at questions and forget them. To live in the body and let it reason in its thoughtless way, to jump and dart precisely, respond machinelike. The machine of the body is at peace with itself and knows only peace. That other structure, the command structure, the mind, the nerves, that part suffers and fears and knows conflict. And what for? When you could be just four limbs, a pelvis, a head, a torso? It seemed silly in boot camp the way the drill sergeant would curse you out if ever you said "I" or "me." But there was some truth in this practice it took training to reveal. You stop calling yourself your name, that ain't your name anymore. You stop calling him "I" and call him instead "this recruit," then that's all you are. Maybe that's all you ever were, a bag of flesh and bones at peace. They cursed and beat and humiliated out of you any notion of what was called thinking for yourself. Nobody ever got out of boot camp able to say, Sergeant, I think there might be a better way to get this job done. You'd learn something and think you'd forgotten it until a high-pitched whisper came through your tent. And then you had jumped out of the tent and into the trench with your lid on and your M16 in hand before the laggard mind told you what you'd heard was, rather had been, a sniper bullet. The boy's dumb body knew faster and better than his mind did.

Sometimes the roadside grunts put mail in the sandbags along with the rock and the rumpled list, and if they were dug in far enough from the road you had to square up, high on the mount atop the cab, to snag the thing from the air like a long fly to the outfield, and inside was a letter to Mr. and Mrs. Stanley Routenberg of Livonia, Michigan, and a rumpled note to the convoy demanding, if not beer, at least a couple of hundred pounds of grass. All Vollie had for them to drink was Coca-Cola. It turned out some guys made a casserole out of rations cooked in Coke. A Puerto Rican from the 2/9 Marines told him that was how you were *supposed* to cook pork, which was comical, trying to tell a Clinton County boy he didn't know how to cook a pig.

There were whole villages made of Coke cases, and the ingenious Vietnamese had pleated together roofs for their huts out of the dissected Coke cans. The convoy had to slow up through one such village, and they should have known better because as they rolled into the village no kids were flinging themselves at the sides of the trucks, begging for candy and rations. Everybody was in a hut someplace.

Then a bomb detonated in the road. A Marine artillery shell, most likely, that had failed to explode and been rejiggered into a land mine. The mine blew off the front end of the truck right ahead of his. Three men flew up and away from the explosion, but they still had their legs and scrambled, flesh hanging in strips through smoldering fatigues—the automatic marine body that scrambles before it needs to understand—and climbed into the back of Vollie's truck. The convoy plowed teetering right over the cardboard village, right over the Coke huts, running who knew what, rice bags or people, under the listing axles, and the convoy did not stop. It got to Camp Carroll ahead of schedule carrying mail, tents, diesel fuel, kerosene, Winston the one filter cigarette that delivers flavor twenty times a pack, two wounded, one dead. He was Santa Claus and the mailman and a teenager driving tons of munitions through a monsoon-slick road in early February with *rat-a-tat* sniper fire in the distant hills as normal as birdsong. Winston's got that filter flavor.

Then back in Dong Ha he found the Quonset hut where the squids were hiding their beer. If marines never stole from the army and the navy we could never win a war. A marine is a thief by training, tradition, and necessity caused by, Why are we always out of supplies and they're so flush? But questions blew off like fog, and another marine from his convoy group lit a smoke bomb at the far end of the depot, and the squids went running to investigate while Vollie backed up his truck to the Quonset hut, and with a dolly, a ramp, and four men pushing, they got a whole pallet of Hamm's beer into his truck and covered it, and he was out of there before the quartermaster or anybody else was any the wiser. Clean cut with smoothness aged in—Hamm's, it's the refreshingest. Then the whole way toward the Rockpile, they threw warm cases of beer down to the men popping from behind boulders, from under makeshift blinds, men joyous as retriever dogs to see the labels on the cases.

His convoy had nearly reached the Rockpile, midday, when a marine appeared like a vision hovering above the road in the distance. At first it seemed the warm beer was giving Vollie fantod hallucinations, but he'd only drunk the one, nice and slow to let the stomach take it, not even the one, a swig remained in the can he held with fingers that meantime guided the steering wheel. The hovering marine wore a painted wood sign around his neck. You could see his busted helmet and flak jacket, but the feet were too loose to be standing. He floated midair. A miracle as they approached. A marine with invisible wings. Then as they got close you could see the spike that had been introduced through his ass and into the torso, a thin spike you could spy only when you were near enough to see his face, in fact a dead Vietnamese face about fifteen years old with flies nesting in the nose, dressed in old shreds of Marine fatigues. The sign around his neck read

CAUTION:

THIS ROAD PATROLLED BY THE MAGNIFICENT BASTARDS

2ND BATTALION, 4TH MARINES

And a little drawing of a seahorse for a signature.

They slept that night at the Rockpile, or anyhow under it. There wasn't any need to drive up the crazy mountain, or any road to climb it, didn't seem. And in the morning they drove back to Dong Ha, unstopping and sometimes throwing C rations of ham and motherfuckers at the Vietnamese in their loose-fit rags who lined the roads sometimes begging for food and sometimes pretending to beg for food so you would slow down if you were stupid and they would throw a grenade in your cab.

They pulled into Dong Ha, and the grinning screeching children swarmed begging frenziedly, and the trucks pushed through with all due haste. Farther along, near the base gate, an old woman—or not so old but without any teeth, the brown smiling gums gone to leather from chewing betel nut—waved her straw cone hat sweet and friendly by the roadside. Suddenly she bent low and fished at her skirt bottom. Vollie in the cab unholstered the 1911 pistol from his shoulder, or his hand unholstered it, jutted it out the window, and aimed it, the peaceful fleet hand that did its work while the laggard mind raced to understand what was happening.

Then the old woman, unfazed by an automatic pistol aimed at her face by a dumb white teenager in a truck, pulled her skirt up over her belly and pulled down her shapeless drawers calling, "Fucky-fucky five dollars."

His hand drew his pistol back within the cab. The trucks rumbled on inside the gate, inside the compound, and the men refueled and parked at the tire shop and went to the mess and then to their bunks.

He had never seen a woman's privates before, he had seen pictures and he had dreamt dreams, but the mind so unswerving in its misguided notions and expectations could not shake all night the weirdness that the fucking part was in the front of her, whereas in the female of all the other animals he could think of, you found the fucking parts behind. The frontwardness, the face-to-face aspect of human fucking was itself backward. But no, that was another lie of the discordant mind. The body didn't know we were made to do things the wrong way—it didn't know this thing that wasn't true. It got a hard-on all the same to see a woman without her clothes, even decrepit; though perhaps the hard-on came from the pistol he had aimed at her face and had not fired.

Ham and motherfuckers was ham and lima beans and even the starvelings up at Khe Sanh didn't want them.

Do not stop the convoy.

But then one day while they were taking apart their pallets at Khe Sanh—uncommon to stop at Khe Sanh, rumors of a hell of a ruckus up there what with the RPGs and the 130-millimeter guns, so the Marine Corps was supplying mostly from the air—he heard a noise. He was unloading into a hooch and he heard a noise. He looked around him. The four other guys in the hooch unloading with him were already gone. The smoke from their cigarettes hung where they had stood, but the men had vanished, and he ran out of the tent aware he was a step behind something important, and the body knowing more as always threw itself in the trench outside the hooch and landed on a dead grunt who, wait, was not dead but crouching, ducked and covered, in a stream that, wait, was not a stream but a trench filled two feet deep with water. The grunt threw Vollie off him. Vollie landed in the water of the trench. Six men crouched there half submerged. The sun was setting through the drizzle. I have heard incoming real close and so I am in a trench, reported the idiot laggard mind, and I am afraid. Then the artillery was everywhere, the surface of the airstrip around him bubbling like the surface of boiling stew, and they stayed in the trench until the sun had set two more times. Somewhere in there he heard a whistle and saw his truck blow up and he figured he would be here at Khe Sanh a while longer.

LUCKY HE HAD DISMOUNTED his .50 caliber from the truck an hour before that first barrage, intending to take her apart and clean and oil her that night and remount her the next morning when they would have headed home to Dong Ha, sort of making nightly love to her, or to be honest not making love, about which he knew only the basic engineering strategy, more like grooming her, getting her ready like a sow before the fair, brushing, greasing. That the .50 caliber had not been destroyed with the rest of the truck was to prove useful in the two months he was stuck at Khe Sanh and made his home on the ground between the airstrip there and the trenches at the base perimeter.

Everybody in the convoy who manned a .50 caliber had a name for it, usually stenciled with spray paint in the mounting plate above the cab. Guns named Winter Night, Mafia Inc. I, Mafia Inc. II, Voss, Shirley. His he named Hog Butcher, and his intimacy with her was such that, some weeks later, when the grunts mounted her atop the sandbags on the morning the NVA finally came at them in person, a crush of figures like ants, innumerable, he almost snatched her down from the trench lip, fearful lest some harm should come to her and resentful these thieving bastards should touch her. Despite her name and job, he knew the Hog Butcher to be female.

He wasn't the only truck driver stuck at Khe Sanh. Once that big assault started, they couldn't get anybody through to sweep the road for mines and his whole convoy was stranded. Later, no road remained to sweep. Nothing fitting the term appeared to lead from the place. The base was an island in a lake of clay that bubbled with incoming and aerial bombardment. Mortar attacks killed several of the other drivers in the convoy, and he inherited one of their trucks, another M54, thankfully a diesel.

One guy stuck there had come in driving a gasser so old it might have seen action in the Second World War, and almost certainly in Korea. Unluckily for the driver this model had a stopcock in its gasoline tank, and as supplies ran short, the tank became the only source of cooking fuel for anybody in that part of the base. Theoretically you could cook with diesel fuel, if you liked the taste in your food of licking the Devil's sulfur ass. The thing to do was to get yourself an empty tuna can and fill it with dirt, soak it in gasoline purloined from that old truck, and set it afire under the grate of your pot. Good eating could be prepared this way, but rations ran tight. And it seemed the Marine Corps had no plans to attempt another convoy anytime soon. For weeks, the perimeter of the airfield was bombed and rocketed and napalmed to an extent that he was kind of getting used to the noise. He lived on a plateau with fire surrounding it everywhere. The question-asking apparatus having been extracted, it didn't occur to him to ask anybody what was out there to bomb so. He couldn't really see what they were trying to hit. It was another driver who asked one of the infantry sergeants what were they bombing. "The enemy, knucklehead," the sergeant said. "Don't you know when you're under siege?" Vollie could not see any enemy. He saw earth afire.

The enemy was underground.

Then there were transport planes, C-130s mostly, the Hercules, supplying them now because evidently no more convoys, but it pleased him the pilots followed the old convoy rule. Do not stop. A Hercules sitting still on a landing strip made a plum target, juicier probably than a stopped convoy since the flames would rise higher in the sky if it was hit. If you are too far away to count the number of your enemy dead, how else to measure success but by the height of the flames? So the pilots did this number where the plane flew low over the strip, sometimes low enough to knock off a man's head if he were standing there. Its hatch dropped open in back, and a grappling hook in the airstrip snagged a loop of cord dangling from the hatch, and the plane kept going, the plane did not stop, but the cord inside was attached to a long succession of supplies on pallets that shot out of the cargo bay and somersaulted as the Hercules cleared the strip, never having touched down.

The base was getting shelled incessantly, the airstrip was a mess, and men ran out there to fill the holes with dirt and cover them with steel land matting while new shells made new holes farther up the strip. Meantime, everywhere around him except a few hills was under equally endless but much higher-flaming aerial bombardment from his own government. Yet he saw no NVA, he did not see massed troops. It was a siege in theory only. And there he was outside playing basketball with the grunts sometimes—the NVA couldn't mortar every inch of the compound at every minute so why not get some exercise?—and when he couldn't sleep playing George Gershwin or Schumann songs on a mute piano he had made from a sawbuck tabletop and a Magic Marker, and it got so he could hear the music in his mind, even his mistakes, and steadily improved with this perverse way of playing piano, music minus sound leaving only the boy's body at peace in articulate motion, alive and in time to the moving numbers that measure and govern everything from Schumann to jet propulsion to the pressure of the blood in your arteries. And he boiled rations over the tuna-can gas stoves. And he was probably going to die, they would be overrun, and it didn't mean nothing.

Sometimes in the distance earth and sky would explode in light at no notice. It was nighttime, then for a long moment it was daytime in front of you. Not a rending of the sky and a flash as from lightning, but a world that opened and opened from below, a world with a sun inside it that burst forth from the ground. Then the skeptical mind caught up and said the source must in fact have come from above. And that was when you looked up wondering where in the hell did that come from? The whole world made new with light out of the darkness.

Only then the roar reached you.

This was an Arc Light. Bombs, many bombs, ton after ton after ton, flown from Guam in B-52s and dropped all at once in the lower stratosphere and falling for miles through the uninterrupted dark, or else if it was daytime through the dome of uninterrupted sunlight that cups the planet like the lid of an eye, through rain and tropospheric disturbances and thickening air into the radiant warmth of the lower atmosphere, falling too fast from too far to be seen or heard or suspected, toward the brown and green smoldering terrain west of a river north of a road, toward a plateau between a mountain and piedmont hills, encampments and trenches, long supply channels underground, people down there armed and waiting in the dark. And it was beautiful when the bombs struck, all at once in one place, and made a roar like nothing on earth. The B-52s flew so high you could neither see nor hear the planes themselves, usually three of them, thirty-five tons of bombs in every payload. You didn't know they were anywhere in the country until they had long since flown away.

The split second of wild peace before the sound.

Arc Light. And the roar.

And if you were an NVA, that might be a nice way to die, since we all have to die some way. Just there and then not there. A century from now a crater would remain where you had been taking your last piss in a tunnel in the dark, a bowl big as a house in the ground where one night you got Arc Lighted to Paradise.

Then it was dark, late February. The Puerto Rican, Espinoza, had got hold of a pint of bourbon and shared it with Vollie, who had never drunk bourbon or whiskey. It tasted like Coke boiled to a gravy and cut with lighter fluid. He feared to smoke as he drank it lest he catch fire. Espinoza sometimes appeared to be itching his privates through his pocket while working a sunflower seed in his lips; in fact, he kept a rosary in the pocket and was mumbling prayers. He carried on this way even while they drank bourbon and played cards late at night in Vollie's tent. It was about two in the morning when they had emptied the bottle and Espinoza got up to head back to his tent by the ammunition depot, but a minute later he came back saying he couldn't see his hand in front of his face out there in the dark and fog. So Vollie made sleeping room for him in the tent he'd made, his makeshift Khe Sanh home on the dirt off the airstrip which was really, the tent was, nothing more than a half tent made from a parachute pegged to the dirt on one side and tied up to the door of his new truck on the other. And Vollie fell into dreamless inebriate sleep.

Then he woke up yelling, "It hit me. It hit me."

Espinoza could be heard wrestling with the parachute tent walls, tearing the top edge of the thing away from the truck, unable in the total dark of foggy moonless night to see the open flap of the enclosure, the side Vollie kept open to let the breeze in and through which shrapnel had just evidently flown and drilled Vollie's face, his arms, his throat.

"It hit me," he said. The splatter somehow soft it was so warm. He couldn't move or see. Unaccountably he had been hit only in the parts of him his fatigues didn't cover. If he couldn't get out of here it was probably because his legs didn't work. "It hit me," he said to nothing and no one and looked down to where his feet ought to be but saw nothing. However, it was dark.

Mind and body at last rendezvoused, and he sent his foot a message, speaking it aloud to put all his parts on notice to attend. "I'll stomp my foot, and if I hear it then it's still there." The muscles of the upper leg then contracted, and a low quiet peaceful stamp sounded amid the nylon of the tent enveloping him like a shroud. He convened likewise with the other foot.

Outside, Espinoza said, "Who the fuck you talking to? Get under the fucking truck, man."

He wasn't hit, Vollie wasn't, not exactly. Mud had splattered his face, neck, arms. A shell or a rocket had exploded nearby and blasted the mud through the opening of his tent. He discovered this under the truck, itself not the soundest of places to hide from a barrage. A couple of artillery flashes gave them a visual notion how to make it to the trench. They bolted for the perimeter. This entire interval—waking up believing he was hit, the experiment with his feet, the communing of mind with lower extremities, sliding under the truck, and hustling out to the perimeter and down into the trench with grunts already awake in there and firing—had taken about as long as it takes to butter a piece of toast.

The grunts in the trench had mounted the Hog Butcher on their sandbags and they were firing her. They had already used all but one box of the ammunition at hand. But Vollie had stolen and hidden about twenty boxes of it from a Hercules drop he had helped unload, stolen because that is what a marine does, and secreted them in a hooch about fifty yards away under a case of toilet paper, and he saw the ammunition they had streaming out of their boxes and jumped out of the trench and darted top speed at the hooch, which under the circumstances seemed far away as bumfuck Egypt.

He ran fast. Every step a stroke of wild luck. He turned a corner. In another artillery flash the hooch appeared low and dark through smoke. He had never run faster. But somebody had cut down a dead tree for firewood, leaving the stump three feet off the ground, and he struck it at a sprint right in his privates. He convulsed and screamed as though hit again, but wasn't hit this time either, not for real. He'd rammed his nuts into a tree. A parting of the smoke and something like dawn light coming over the mountain. And he made it to the hooch and over-turned the toilet paper, they called them sweet rolls, gathered three ammunition boxes, and hobbled in his nut-crumpled state expecting to be hit and then to explode with all the rounds in his arms and the in-coming; and he was going as fast as he could, the eyes on the destina-tion, the trench, to get behind the sandbags; but higher up, going on solid ground and running back toward the perimeter with the little parting of dawnish light, he had another vantage than before; and the light better; one of the boxes threatening to fall; and he tried to keep the eyes on the trench, to get back there; but he had this other vantage now, and the eyes looking upward squinted against the smoke—and that was when he saw them.

He had seen VC before, guerrillas, and he had seen shells coming and the 122-millimeter rockets. But now he saw the enemy themselves, the true enemy out of their burrows, the NVA massed and swarming on human legs.

They were like ants, the way ants swarmed over a dead animal in the meadow, except they all were running this way. A few had made it near enough already you could see their shirts crisscrossed with bandoliers. And the laggard mind said, Hold on, those people over there want to kill me. All this in the two seconds before he got his head and his boxes down below the line of sandbags. He crouched. His privates screamed in pain. The grunt who had commandeered the Hog Butcher switched with him and got low to feed the machine her bullets from the new boxes while Vollie manned the machine, the Hog Butcher, who was in actual fact an antiaircraft weapon that to fire directly on human beings violated some article of the Geneva Conventions, so said the scuttle-butt. Five rounds, pause, five rounds, pause; microscopic bits of the lands in her barrel flying out of her muzzle; and the red tracers stream-ing like bits of glowing rope afire, fast at first then slow and peaceful in the deeper distance, then careening off at sharp angles when they hit a rock or for all he knew some kid's brain bucket, his helmet, whose trac-ers were coming right back at Vollie reciprocally, but the NVA tracers were green across the low almost-night sky, a field of arcing and sud-denly careening red and green tracers, four invisible rounds between every tracer, the colors like Christmas lights, and the Hog Butcher jammed.

She jammed. He opened her from the top. It was like a vivisection. He had to use his asbestos gloves. She was so hot she could take off his skin if he touched her. And he dumped a bottle of 30-weight motor oil all over her innards and her exposed chamber and closed her up, and the grunt refed the chain of long cartridges and remounted her, and Vollie went back to firing.

Like ants or a tide. And the tracers came rocketing out of the barrel hot and red like wishes that seemed to slow as they sailed farther away, tracers that sometimes took a sharp upward or outward turn like wishes gone wrong when the tracer hit a rock or helmet or another bullet amid the profusion of rounds five times as numerous as were visible, and ricocheted. And he saw some of the people convulse, falling backward through the tracer fire. They were coming fast, and Vollie was near enough the command post to hear a radioman cranking the phone and calling out coordinates.

Do not stop the convoy.

Other scuttlebutt said command had started the rumor about the Geneva Conventions to save money on the big expensive .50-caliber cartridges.

He aimed his weapon at the tide, the tracers like wishes or seed corn you scattered away from yourself and that disappeared into someplace you couldn't see. It was a wish because you sent it out of you but you couldn't know what would come of it. The machine sent a shock wave of recoil through all his bones, one-two-three-four-five pause one-two-three-four-five pause. He ducked down to help unload another box of ammunition and asked the grunt, "Who's he calling?" meaning the radioman.

"New Jersey, I guess."

That was a joke, the radioman calling the prestigious state back east where Annie Frade had once gone for a cousin's wedding and come back with a picture book about skyscrapers for her boy.

However, it was neither a joke nor a state. The grunt said, "Naw, man. The *ship.*"

The battleship. A recommissioned dreadnought, the *New Jersey*, with 16-inch guns revamped and rumored to be out of dry dock in Philadelphia and headed this way. Vollie fired and fired continuously and yet resignedly; what with the numbers, the ants, they were about to be overrun. Do not stop the convoy. And he kept firing.

Then it was as if somebody far away as Davenport had fired a cannon at the barn in Calamus and hit it square in the roof. And hit it again. And hit it again. Right where the ants were swarming there was a shock wave and a wall of fire and clouds that rose in columns and bloomed flowers of ash, dirt, smoke. Espinoza ran out to the hooch and came back with more ammunition for the Hog Butcher. Vollie kept firing. Turning to his left and right like a radio dial. Those must have been the shells coming from the *New Jersey*. You heard them shearing the air overhead, then a shock wave and a cloud, impossible magic as if an object could have knowledge—the shells coming from afar in the sea and landing right where the radioman had directed them.

It took less than ten minutes for the Phantoms to fly the hundred miles from Da Nang. All down the long NVA lines the enemy were swarming and firing, and the shells blew them up, and Phantoms flew low dropping napalm on the people. And more 16-inch shells came from the *New Jersey,* or wherever, shearing the air.

His orders were not to stop the convoy. He looked behind him. His second truck wasn't there. Motherfuckers had driven off with his truck. No, they hadn't, the truck was that pile of twisted smoking steel, rubber, and canvas. He had lost a second truck. Each truck cost about what their farm cost, and he had lost two of them.

Nobody had told him what any of this—the airstrip, the siege, the bombardment—was for.

When he got back to Dong Ha after it was over, an Easter card waited for him with his mother's signature in it alongside his father's mark, and a two-dollar bill, an old bill dated 1953 but crisp. She had ironed it.

He kept on unaccountably not getting killed. He caught a fragment of an RPG in his foot, the hot flash went right through the toe cap of the boot and the foot and the sole of the boot somehow without striking a bone. That was all right, he found new boots, size 11 wide, in the depot at Dong Ha and he went back to the convoy.

The trucks were running as before along Route 9, such as it was a route. Anyway it was passable now, and they were resupplying the forward combat bases again as though the months at Khe Sanh had never happened. He wondered what his father would say to learn Vollie was on his third truck. He missed his father and mother too much to write to them. Espinoza didn't write home either, on the clever theory you did everybody a favor letting them assume you were dead: if later you turned up living it would be a bonus, assuming they liked you.

Nobody said the siege at Khe Sanh had been broken. The place, having been an island surrounded by erupting clay and towers of fire, had simply gone quiet; and a crew from one of the rear bases had patched up the road. Vollie had ridden at last back to Dong Ha, where the dispatcher congratulated him on being alive and assigned him yet another M54. His father would have said, If every time you give this boy a truck it explodes, don't give him any more trucks.

He sweated in his bunk at the witching hour reading by flashlight a pocket manual on mines and booby traps that advised him to stay off trails, footpaths, cart tracks, other likely routes of travel. He must move where local inhabitants moved, avoid patterns, maintain intervals of fifteen meters between men and one hundred meters between men and tracked vehicles. He must move slowly. He must not attempt to outrun the explosion. He must not immediately rush to the aid of marines wounded by mines or booby traps. Frequently there was a second booby trap in the vicinity of the first. Many booby traps were themselves booby-trapped.

Sometimes on the way to resupply Quang Tri the convoy would overtake a creeping Volkswagen bus or suchlike loaded like a clown car with Vietnamese civilians—and from their perch atop the gun mounts, the men would whip empty shell casings at the roofs of the vehicles, then watch as the vehicles stopped and the doors swung open and the terrified civilians jumped out screaming and scattering.

Did he partake of this sport? Yes.

And at night he lay awake in his hooch bunk asking the dark what was this force invisible and inescapable as gravity or wind that made him *want* to do what it would have bewildered and sickened his mother and father to know he did, the force that seemed equal to, and caused by, the love he felt for them but opposite in its direction?

At present, he read, the best mine and booby trap detector in the Marine Corps was an alert and observant marine. He must be watchful for mud smears, mud balls, dung, a board on the road, apparent road repair, wires leading from the road; tripwires along road shoulders, through dense vegetation, fords, ditches, rice paddy dikes; suspicious items in trees and bushes. To support his mine warfare operations the enemy frequently exploited material discarded as trash: C rations, beer and soda cans, batteries, bandoliers. All items considered unusable by free world forces must be completely destroyed or properly disposed of.

He *must not* travel alone.

He took his out-of-country R and R in Australia with some guys from his battalion, flying Da Nang to Sydney with a layover in Singapore. They rented rooms in a Sydney boardinghouse, where his own room had a color TV in place of a window. He switched it on, curious as to the jingles in this hemisphere. The first thing the TV presented was an international news story reporting $13 million of damage caused today by a single strike on the American air base at Da Nang in South Vietnam. He asked the screen, "What the fuck?" A VC rocket strike had hit a plane on the runway evidently an hour after he had taken off from there, struck it and blew it up while he had been smoking in the cabin of a civilian airliner over Java or Borneo, where there still lived mountain people uncontacted by what was called civilization, meaning the kinds of people who made of the earth a farm, a runway, an Arc Light. What must this uncontacted fellow consider the airplane overhead in which Vollie had been flying? That it was an animal or a lesser god or cosmic litter that made its own long line of white cloud. Already the Pentagon had reported the damage of the rocket strike in U.S. dollars.

Then came ads on the TV for Tarax carbonated lemonade, because today was a family kind of day. And Caltex gasoline was butane boosted. And Desert Flower CornSilk powder gave you that natural look, no caking, no shine. Then more about the war, which according to the gentleman on TV was going poorly although there was footage of bombs stacked like cordwood, footage of the enemy running from mass bombardment, a clip of President Johnson saying, "Make no mistake about it, we are going to win," and by all accounts a wholesale routing of the enemy everyplace he had shown himself in the recent offensive.

Vollie sat on the bed with the clean cheap sheets and smoked and could not take his eyes off this program that now began to speak of "the" Tet Offensive, "the" battle of Khe Sanh. Footage followed of Khe Sanh looking rusty as Mars, accurate enough. He figured they were talking about some engagement that had happened under the French or Chinese in centuries past. But no, the man in the tweed jacket and tie on the screen looked squarely at the viewer from the authoritative noplace where they make TV and alluded to events at Khe Sanh from the present year as if everybody watching knew all about them and needed only an update. There on TV, the C-130s shat out their tumbling pallets and did not stop and took off into the smoke with antiaircraft fire scrambling up the sky after them. He looked for himself amid the footage of the dirty boys shirtless or in fatigues shoveling mud into sandbags. He smoked in the small room on the alien continent and ate black olives and spat the pits into his hand and dropped them in an ashtray. He pared his nails. He searched the screen, not finding himself in the footage. If he wasn't in the footage, had he really been there? The olives tasted like bacon cooked rare and pickled. He couldn't stop fishing them out of the jar as he watched.

NVA mortars struck an ammo dump, flames consumed it, tar-black smoke overflowed the screen. He himself had seen the dump blow, then heard it blow, then choked: it sucked all available oxygen from the blast perimeter, and he hit the pavement choking. The TV knew the dates, elevations, tonnages, kill rates. It showed the viewer what had happened and why. Yet nowhere in this comprehensive program appeared the face of Vollie Frade.

He was watching his own life without him in it.

And there was a rightness to this. A flash of recognition and hope. That he could watch without having to appear. Then something stranger but just as right. An eerie conviction returning to him from deep time. That his body wore a self like a jacket, and the jacket could be removed. Vollie Frade might look for himself in the footage; but his body looked for nothing: it only watched. It had no right name. It had no self to find.

He sat on the bed in the dark of the foreign room, elbows on knees. He got up, toes gripping the carpet. His lungs pulled in tobacco smoke; his eyes watched the screen. Hope flew like breath inside him. A rapture hope. That his self might pass away and leave his body to go on living.

The earnest gentleman on TV, grave in twisty-mouthed Australian English, told the viewer the decisive elements of the battle of Khe Sanh had been Operations Niagara and Rolling Thunder, a coordinated bombing effort of U.S. Navy, Marine Corps, and Air Force planes that had carried out the largest aerial bombardment on a single place in the history of warfare. General Westmoreland had made a great success. He had not resorted to nuclear weapons, as some had urged. A clip played from earlier in the year of a Thai colonel saying the strategic value of Khe Sanh could not be underestimated. President Johnson had had a model of the place constructed in the Situation Room at the White House.

Vollie longed for the piano in the parlor at home. The old instrument three generations in that house. When he played the piano it was his body that played, at one with its senses, its limbs, with the bodies of his mother and father and the parlor and the house. No other fictitious entities such as his self intervened. Lately only to shoot his gun felt this way. And he longed for the farm, for the taste of the water from the spigots on the farm. All the home water had long since passed out of him. If a body was mostly composed of its water, he was mostly some foreigner now.

The man in the tweed jacket described how the Americans had won the battle of Khe Sanh. The NVA had massed between twenty and forty thousand troops around this one little combat base obstructing their route into South Vietnam, a base where six thousand marines were holding an airstrip. It was a battle, had been a battle, for an airstrip. America had won at what the man referred to as unspeakable loss of blood and treasure. He said Khe Sanh was the front gate of the free world.

He said now summer had come to Vietnam—except here in Australia that meant winter. The siege was just a few months behind us all, and yet Khe Sanh was in the news this way at this time because command, having performed a review and revision of strategic priorities, had just ordered the base at Khe Sanh to be dismantled and abandoned.

VOLLIE TOOK A SHOWER, and the boys all went out for steaks. One of them asked for a kangaroo porterhouse. The waitress said they were out but she could bring them some emu kebabs.

The emu meat was lean, sinuous, and red, though an emu was a bird if Vollie had rightly understood. The waitress's mother used to render emu fat and comb it into her hair. "Welcome to Oz," she said. "Please don't kill us."

They changed into civvies and bought lambskin shoes, light as slippers, and prowled the clubs, hunting girls. White girls, in pearl earrings and skirts hemmed nearer to the waist than the knees, who expected in exchange for their attention not payment but discourse, preferably while you smiled like an innocent and not a killer who already, at eighteen, had paid for trim, a killer who both pitied and worshipped these girls for giving it away when they might have sold it dear. All you had to do was talk and smile, so it appeared from the limited success of his comrades whom he watched from the periphery of his vision as he faced the Wurlitzer, reading every word of the label of every record, often near enough a girl to smell her, wishing it were permissible to walk up to one of them and not speak but sing. He knew the lyrics to most of the Wurlitzer songs. He did not sing but listened. His lambskin toe cap, free of thought, rose and tapped the floor as it would have done were he playing this lick on the piano in Calamus and not smelling this girl, drunk from the rose and dancing-sweat odor of this laughing girl he never turned his face to see.

Then they went back to Vietnam and ran convoys again. And at the end of his thirteen months, in February 1969, Vollie Frade shipped to North Carolina, where a spit-and-polish captain who had never left North America but still outranked him by the infinite moat that separates officer from enlisted, this joker not two years out of Canoe U. and already a captain so he surely sucked cock real good, dressed Vollie down because one of the four campaign stars on his ribbon was not pointing directly upward. For this infraction the captain called him a miserable shit and an embarrassment to his uniform. He did not of course laugh at the captain, he loved him in one of the not-queer ways in which you let another man believe whatever he liked, or you let somebody lie without calling him on it, or some kid in short pants threw a rock at you and missed and turned and ran and you had the back of his head in your sights and did not fire. It was the love born of mercy.

When he had liberty, he walked around loving the captain as you can love only somebody you thought of killing, this motherfucking nun in a captain's uniform who during a junk-on-the-bunk inspection found the score of the songs by Schumann among Vollie's things and asked where he'd got it. In the mail, Vollie said, but left off the "sir" at the end. The captain burned the score right in front of him. For this and other abuses Vollie loved the captain. And to his mother and father he wrote not a word.

He walked on the sunbaked humdrum streets of Jacksonville or borrowed a car from a squid steelworker stationed there and drove as far as Myrtle Beach, South Carolina, but mostly stayed around Camp Lejeune and played piano in the Sunday-school room of a Methodist church near the base. It was all right about the score. He was working on the short pieces called *Kinderszenen,* which he had been made to play in high school and had not cared for, but which he had mostly memorized now by reading the score in Dong Ha. What he couldn't remember he put together from listening to an LP he bought of Vladimir Horowitz playing them. They had sad and beautiful names: "Pleading Child," "Great Adventure," "Perfect Happiness," "Of Foreign Lands and People," "By the Fireside," "Almost Too Serious," "Hobgoblin," "In Slumberland," "The Poet Speaks"; but the one he played most was the seventh, called "Träumerei," or "Dreaming," the one he used to play after supper while nearby his father petted the cat with his twisted hands, faintly humming in tune.

In Wilmington, Vollie went to a jazz joint and drank alone and listened to the Negro horn players. Listened and watched. Tried to let the music in. But before he could hear it all the way, the music turned to warfare in his mind. The trombonist, with only the slide and nothing to measure it by, hit note after uncannily perfect note, calculations precise as mortar fire: the powder charge, the tube, the parabolic shot that struck its distant mark.

He kept up a correspondence with the former ranch hand Bobby Heflin, who had spent a few nights in the Okinawa brig drying out but eventually was deployed to Da Nang with the rest of them and spent his thirteen months in an infantry unit around Phu Bai and had even learned to surf there and had come to Sydney with the other boys on that trip and fallen in love. He wrote it was really love for real, he was going to marry this Australian girl. Her name was Anne Marie. He compared her in his letters to horses of whom he had been especially fond in his youth: her spirit and hair and look. Vollie had been sitting on the next barstool in the Sydney night club when Heflin and the girl first started talking. Aware that Heflin was down to pocket change, Vollie waited for the girl to turn her head and order them another round before he slipped Heflin a pink, Aussie five-dollar note and pretended jet lag and said he'd better get back to the rooming house but in fact walked alone late through the night touching the cars, the trees, watching the illegible antipodean stars. Bobby would later call the money a loan, but it had been a gift. He wrote he was now on base in California teaching the cherries at the survival school how to live by foraging when trapped behind the enemy and he described with a diagram at the end of the letter how you could make a pair of moccasins out of a jackrabbit you caught in a snare.

Then Vollie opened the second piece of mail he had received that day, a telegram from Washington, and read that his father had died.

Your father has experienced a cerebral embolism, read the document.

He knew what that was. A bubble pops in the brain, smaller than a soap bubble, but it must feel like an RPG in your skull for the effect it has, a shock wave that turns a building to rubble, only it was microscopic, too small to make any sound, it would only feel like sound, a megaton burst that shattered the fortress of the mind.

He wore his dress blues that night and his high-gloss Corfam shoes, for the first time in more than a year, to a cotillion in Wilmington. The girls were like cakes in their outfits with frosting for hair, spun and spiraling high.

He danced with a girl named Shirley. The heavy makeup made her look older than she was and barely concealed her acne. He wanted to tell her she was all right, she'd outgrow it. Instead he said, "I knew a gun by your name."

She curtsied and smiled with vacant eyes. They kept on dancing awkwardly. The music was pretty loud, canned music blown from public address speakers, and when he leaned to her ear there was a reek of hair spray such that, given the dispersal of the tall hair and the oxygen separating the strands, she could have caught fire from the merest flicker. Cigarettes burned like jungle threats wherever he looked. She'd go right up.

He said, "It was a Browning fifty-caliber machine gun."

Again with the empty-eyed face smiling in plaster fixity. When the song ended she curtsied again and gave him her white-gloved hand, smiling. He took it with his own white-gloved hand and made a little bow and said, "Pleasure." She uttered in response finally a single smiling word and floated away in her confectionary dress, which hid her feet. She said the word without adjusting the smile in any way. The word was "animal."

Kinderszenen meant "Scenes from Childhood." There were *ritardandos* all over the one called "Träumerei." According to his father, Vollie never grasped what they really meant, the *ritardandos,* which was funny since Potter Frade couldn't read and couldn't play. But he had ears. And he didn't figure Vollie knew what "slowly" really meant. Real slowness. Gradually slower. A long slowing walk that ended in repose. A long easeful stride that came someplace to a finish. "You figure if you go too slow you won't get there. Vollie, that ain't so. Unless you slow down you'll get to the end and blow right past it."

The next morning, he dressed and did not eat. He left in his foot-locker the jar of change he might have used for a pay phone. He walked off base, mouthing but not yet willing to breathe the words of a telegram. He arrived at the Western Union office and tried the door, but it was locked. He walked the perimeter of the little town and went into a bar and dumped a noontime shot of whiskey in his mouth and paid for it and went outside and spat the whiskey on the street and continued to the Western Union office again and opened the door and waited in line behind other marines, behind women black and white, young and old, behind a woman bent as a tree with age, her purse dangling from the crook of her elbow—the innocent, honey-yellow, lacquered purse with a shining clasp like a target he might have shot because it was shining and moved, because it was innocent and the woman was innocent. When his turn came before the mesh-reinforced glass of the counter, he pretended he had misplaced his money clip, digging in his pockets, and let another marine go ahead of him.

His turn came again. He addressed not the clerk waiting there but the mesh inside the glass between them.

"Speak up, son," the clerk said, a freckle-spattered boy his same age.

Then Vollie dictated the telegram to his mother, saying he could not get liberty to go home for his father's funeral.

He had never lied to her before. While the clerk read the message back to him, he nearly convinced himself the lie didn't count because he had spoken it not to her but to an intermediary. Then he took from his breast pocket the little silver money clip and gave the clerk two dollars, and the clerk made change, and the thing became a lie inflicted in cold blood, and Vollie knew it.

He hitched back to base and went to the fussbudget captain's office and volunteered for a second tour of duty. Within the month he was back in Vietnam. They gave him blood stripes for his dress blues because he was a corporal now.

YOU'D SEE A GUY was scared. Oiling his pistol by the TV light in the hooch, he'd get up and peer through the mosquito netting at the door. Nobody else heard that noise? Then he'd sit back down. Get up and check the door again and sit down. Get up and sit down.

A few days later, that guy would be dead. It was the ghost of his death he had heard. But just because your wraith is hunting you doesn't mean you have to run from it.

So on his second tour Corporal Vollie Frade, now an old hand at nineteen, developed a new kind of meditation. It was still in keeping with telling the wraith, You don't mean nothing, except he did it with his body instead of his mind. Every convoy ride when he manned the .50 caliber, a position that already made him a conspicuous target, he wore a brand-new Hanes T-shirt, snug fitting, high and bright and white and plain to see for a mile around. You weren't supposed to ride atop the cab the way he did, but the design of the turret left you ribdeep in the vehicle; you weren't high enough to see properly and felt as if you were shooting up, not down; so he sat on the gun mount instead. He was shooting the new .50 caliber named Hog Butcher II. Upright and shining in the jungle, like You get one shot at me. Go ahead, fire; but if you miss, you got to know I'll take you out.

This behavior was a little crazy but kept the spirit of the first rule of a firefight as articulated in boot camp: establish fire superiority immediately. Blanket your surroundings in fire; let the enemy know the equipment you have, your eagerness to use it. In the likely event he doesn't get hit in your harum-scarum barrage, he'll run away. The aim was less to strike the enemy himself than to throw a wave of panic around your perimeter. At some point Vollie heard himself calling Hog Butcher II a "he" not a "she" and realized he had been doing that since he'd got back here and wondered why. He hated questions but still he wondered why. Then it was obvious he didn't want a girl close to him at this particular time. The body was by nature at peace with itself, but a girl touching it made the body unruly and ungovernable, and he didn't like it. None of this prevented him from going to see mama-san when he had liberty, however, because fucking was a separate thing.

The shirt when he wore it high on the gun mount made him no less fearful but did make him a wraith himself, a clean beacon of your impending end, with a tattoo on one arm of the Marine Corps insignia— the eagle, globe, and anchor—and a second on the other arm of the words ESSE QUAM VIDERI in black block type.

He had got the tattoos in Jacksonville, CATFUed drunk, aka completely and totally fucked up drunk, and awoke not remembering anything past losing a bet with some local boys in a bar. His wallet was still full in the morning so maybe he had won the bet. If he thought hard, he also remembered looking through the binder of options in the tattoo parlor, a binder like a family photo album, only it didn't appear to include any of his relations until he saw the insignia—aka the bird, ball, and chain—like the face of a progenitor whose ghost you wanted never to leave you. For a month he didn't know what the second tattoo meant. Then he ran into one of the local boys again. The boy and his Tar Heel buddies had got the same tattoo that night as they had paid to stick on Vollie. Esse quam videri. The motto of their home state. "To be rather than to seem."

At night on that second tour down south in the jungle, otherwise a thirteen-month succession of nothing happening at all, choppers flew low over the canopy. He lived in dread of having to use Hog Butcher II on an actual aircraft: if he accidentally fired on a U.S. chopper, they'd kill him for sure. But halfway into his second tour he had yet to see an NVA aircraft of any kind, so this one must be a friendly despite it was speaking Vietnamese. Yes, it was a chopper speaking in the dark. A drone and a cry. A puling noise and then Vietnamese voices real trippy, echoey and crying out, a man's voice and a reverberant woman's voice pleading and moaning from evidently a U.S. chopper over the trees.

The first time they heard the crying aircraft, all the men in his unit took cover in a ditch, the panic-struck dopeheads among them spinning out one after another cockamamie theory of what they were hearing. No theory, however, could compete for looniness with the one related as fact a month later by a pilot from the South Vietnamese air force who hitched a ride with them to the base at Pleiku.

They had heard the voices of the wandering souls, he said.

The chopper had been part of a PSYOP deployed all over the jungle to spook the superstitious VC. Somebody had recorded local actors in a studio in Saigon and got the voices mixed with psychedelic noises and horror-movie sound effects. The agonized voices pled with their relations to help them, to avoid the mistakes they had made in venturing away from their home villages to be killed, their bodies abandoned, so that their souls were caught in a no-man's-land of the dead. The female voice said, "Come home with me!" The male responded, "Who is calling? My daughter? My mother? But my body is gone. Go home, friends. Hurry! If not, you will end up like me." The project was named for the summer festival when the souls of Buddhist sinners got a day and a night's furlough from perdition to wander the country, naked, starving, homeless.

Vollie was driving the truck in which the pilot, riding shotgun and twisting to address the men in the rear, explained all this. The cab stank of the foreign delicacies, packed in a basket on the pilot's lap, that his mother had cooked for him that morning on the coast. The truck climbed into Pleiku Province. Translucent mist subsumed the road, the sort of tranquil mist Vollie had come to dread: it put the wits to sleep.

Over the racket of the diesel engine, the men in back loudly speculated as to which branch of the military was pissing away the government's money on such a project. It seemed like the navy to have a secret drama club, but the choppers they'd heard were not navy issue.

"It is not likely to be your navy," the pilot said. The project did not reflect strategic naval priorities. More likely the CIA was running it, or the Military Intelligence Corps, or some sterile outfit paid for by the Defense Intelligence Agency.

It didn't surprise Vollie that this foreign captain knew the customs of American intelligence agencies better than he did. Officers the world over shared a supernationality. They traded officer knowledge and officer lies using officerspeak, in the present case with a French accent. But he was surprised at the pilot's response when the grunt riding between them claimed the war was shrinking, a rumor Vollie had believed given their uneventful convoys of late.

"Shrinking?" the pilot sneered. Whatever was said in public, the bombing sorties on NVA supply lines in Laos and Cambodia proceeded apace, if they weren't in fact expanding. He had seen the results from his cockpit. And those sorties did no good at all. Plenty of supplies were getting to the VC anyway.

The other Americans in the truck, at ease in Marine Corps cynicism, raised invisible glasses and toasted the pointlessness of this expenditure of matériel. Only their gunny sergeant defended it sincerely. "Whatever the Air Force is dropping on whatever side of the border, it's good for one thing," he said. "Ain't no marines on the ground in Cambodia. That's all I care." Everybody liked the gunny. He had no loyalties outside the Marine Corps. His contempt for command was perfect. The more desperately command wanted to do something, the more certain he became that that thing was a boondoggle designed to kill marines.

But the pilot had grown impatient with the proud ignorance of this truckload of Americans, enlisted men all. "If marines are sleeping tonight across the border, gunnery sergeant, you would be first to know," he said with cheerless sarcasm. "Even if such operation should risk drawing Chinese or Soviets to invade these territories for their, let's say, protection. Surely command would consult you first."

The gunny was too alarmed to take offense. "Do you have scuttlebutt, sir?" he asked.

A sickened hush came from the rear—the men listening through the diesel clamor for how the pilot would answer. If command had sent two men into Cambodia, a division was sure to follow.

The pilot seemed to choose his words so as to hide his meaning. "Perhaps not every outfit in American defense complex regards public avowals vis-à-vis integrity of international boundaries with the same degree of, let's say, intimidation."

"Are we on the ground over there or not?" one of the men snapped.

Vollie aimed his eyes through the lurid mist, trusting the eyes, trying to deafen himself to the dispute, disregard all memory and expectation, willing himself to become a single eye that penetrated the mud of the road ahead and saw only what traps were hidden there.

Perhaps he had not made himself clear, the Vietnamese pilot said. It was in the interest of both sides to deploy in Laos and Cambodia but of neither to say so. Therefore, insofar as the answer to the question might be yes, it must also, at the same time and with equal urgency, be no.

LETTERS FROM HIS MOTHER reached him in the jungle—disjointed letters about the autumn weather; and marmalade; and the Lord coming to her in her sleep saying, "Be not afraid, I am with you"; and asparagus; and she didn't know what to do with the barn, it had so many holes in the roof; and he wouldn't mind, would he, if she found a tenant to farm the meadow?; and the Lord loves us every one, even in our sin; and she hoped he would understand if she had no spare to send in her card at Christmas. Each letter screwier than the last—applesauce giving way to Jesus, giving way to, Please forgive her if she sold the disc harrow since she'd already sold the tractor.

I wear this white shirt because I am the angel of your death hunting you. Or such was his understanding of his message in wearing it. In any case he was never fired on again, not once, in that attire, in that position on the gun mount. He must have looked like Caesar on triumph day. A cherry on base asked him, "What do you wear that shirt for, sir?" Vollie thought a second, cocked his head to look at the kid sidewise, and said, "Keeps the sun off. I burn easy."

HE FINISHED HIS SECOND TOUR and went back to Camp Lejeune an honorary southern boy with that tattoo and played piano alone weeknights at the same church and drove as far as Norfolk one weekend in civilian clothes to drink and look at the big ships in summertime, roaming, and after a few weeks of such drives the laggard mind told him roaming so far from base meant the body was looking for somewhere to live and not finding it. His right place was the farm, but to be from a place was to drink the water there, and now he was full of this foreign water, Vietnam and Carolina water—he had introduced discord into the body at peace, and it was lost. His three-year enlistment was almost up.

Bobby Heflin, now at home on his three years of inactive duty, wrote from New Mexico seeming a new man. He had inherited his parents' ranch, and some interesting people lived there with him now, sweet people female and male living close to the bone but trying to be gentle with each other and with their dogs and horses, and they kept no cattle except some Jersey dairy cows because the spirit of meat was death and the spirit of milk was life, and Vollie should join them when his time was up in the service. No mention of Anne Marie, the eternal bride. Heflin for the first time had typed his letter because he was trying to be deliberate with his words and concluded it with a passage from a book one of his companions was reading:

> Know the measure, know the times, study that. When you are
> left alone, pray. Love to throw yourself on the earth and kiss
> it. Kiss the earth and love it with an unceasing, consuming love.
> Love all men, love everything. Seek that rapture and ecstasy.
> Water the earth with the tears of your joy and love those tears.
> Don't be ashamed of that ecstasy, prize it, for it is a gift of God
> and a great one; it is not given to many but only to the elect.

Vollie crammed the letter into its envelope and crammed the envelope into his pocket and walked to the battalion headquarters under low strange clouds borne on ocean winds. He went to the office of the CMFWIC, aka the chief motherfucker what's in charge, a lieutenant colonel he had come to admire from the required distance for the man's talent at standing upright and looking hard and giving the impression that no part of him touched or was touched by his surroundings, even as he governed them down to their atoms by telepathy. Vollie had never seen the man speak. He sat at a steel desk with a rubberized top, writing something. Vollie asked permission to address him which was granted with a nod and then asked, if he signed up for another three years, whether he could be promised a posting not stateside but in Vietnam.

3

No, he could not, the lieutenant colonel said.

Vollie asked permission to be excused, which was granted.

The next morning, he reenlisted anyway. Soon he was indeed back in Vietnam but still farther south this time, in a place with zero signs of civilization except a trail and vast swaths of ravine and mountainside denuded by Agent Orange. In a jeep amid a convoy headed west. He had made staff sergeant by now.

The convoy went off trail and tottered over ruts other expeditionary vehicles had made. He was riding with a big lieutenant new to the country, and Vollie disliked sharing the jeep with him because if anybody ever had the look of, I see it coming, the lieutenant did: every piece of jungle rock that plinked against the chassis drew his face to the jeep floor as though land mines ever gave forewarnings or as though he had something inside him that his body wanted to wretch out the mouth.

In their line of vehicles, they carried supplies for three months; a few other NCOs; a dozen infantry, mostly cherries, for the NCOs to abuse and scare; and two civilians thick as thieves, a reporter and a botanist, both of them plainly covert intelligence.

Earlier that day at the Bien Hoa Air Base, during the send-off barbecue for the current mission, the two cagey civilians had eaten their spare ribs with knife and fork. Thus it was understood they wished the enlisted men to despise them. The lieutenant joined them at their small table, looking in this first impression the erect picture of Naval Academy confidence. He had in fact played linebacker on the Annapolis football team. As he settled into conference with the two civilians, the men he was to lead took bets on how he would attack his lunch. Nobody could hear what the three were saying. The lieutenant raised a rib to his mouth, hesitated, seemed to notice the way the other two were eating, put down the bone, and went for his silverware. Everybody at the long table saw the lieutenant waffle; nobody laughed.

Shortly, a fourth man joined the other three. He carried a plate that threatened to overflow with ribs and cornbread. He wore a freshly ironed linen suit, loose in his long limbs, the straw-colored hair neatly piled over the ears. He ate with his hands. Immediately, the others at that table began to do likewise. Snatches of an aristocratic southern accent were heard, but what he had to say, on which the other three were hanging, did not reach the long table.

Scuttlebutt said this fourth man was supposed to be a civilian importer of cleaning supplies who happened to find himself on base today at chow time. The pretense that such a figure—the dubious man of commerce, of whom there seemed to be several afoot on every base at any time—had come all the way out to Bien Hoa in the service of private industry was a charade no one needed to believe. Its audience was theoretical. It allowed such a man to follow rules of engagement other than those he would have had to follow if he were wearing the uniform of the government he obviously served. Under whatever pretextual blankets and jackets of security clearance and subtleties and misdirection and outright lies, he was free. The enlisted men did not resent this freedom, they envied it. Before the convoy left the base, the fourth man had disappeared.

Once in the sweltering jeep, the lieutenant's confidence evaporated. He did not speak. He wore no shirt. As he braced against the irregular tottering of the vehicle, his shoulder blades threatened to slice through the sweating flesh of his pale back.

The convoy continued across the wilds, sunward through the afternoon and evening. Vollie hadn't realized Vietnam stretched so wide across down here. The men were going to defend an ammunition dump. He knew nothing more of the mission except, now, that the dump was located suspiciously distant from base.

When they arrived after nightfall, another NCO in the unit they were relieving asked him, "Are we still nowhere?"

This man had misjudged Vollie's security clearance in the operation.

"Guess so," Vollie said. "It doesn't look like much."

"But all this is still not happening, right? And we were never here? Or can I tell the boys they've been abroad the last two months? They know it anyway."

That was how Vollie figured out for sure he was in Cambodia, where, officially speaking, for geopolitical reasons above his pay grade, he was not, and neither were his men.

They slept that first night in their trucks. At sunup, the trucks and the jeep were refueled from tanks within the camp, which had no vehicles of its own. The men of the two units all shook hands. The old unit drove off, taking all the vehicles with it, leaving Vollie's unit immobilized and exposed in unfamiliar territory.

The men went inside the rude enclosures, roofed with fiberglass sheeting, and picked their bunks. The lieutenant then called them back outside. He ordered them to strip and burn their uniforms. He pried open a crate among the supplies they had brought and gave them black pajamas to wear such as the locals used. They were to be a sterile unit now.

None of the men knew quite what a sterile unit was supposed to be, but it was clear from that first morning that the status of the camp had been revised. The previous unit had not been relieved but, at least on paper, withdrawn. Someone had found out about the camp and ordered it dismantled. Someone else was claiming to comply with the order while in reality flouting it. And to have it both ways, their own unit had been removed from the chain of command. This last conclusion was unmistakable. Anybody could see the lieutenant was taking his orders from the two civilians.

They had radios but did not use them. They had food and water purification tablets and plenty of cigarettes. They had oceanic depths of such quiet as a living jungle permits and they had long sleep and the tedium of a mission easy and peaceful as holding your tongue. No one came to draw from their stores of matériel. They had Bayer aspirin, mouthwash, shampoo. And they had what seemed a cloak of perfect invisibility until the morning the two civilians took half the men on a survey eastward down the trail.

In their absence, a single shot was heard.

Then, an enfilade.

The ill-defended camp was attacked by NVA regulars from the east and west at once. Vollie saw their uniforms and AK-47s. Here and there he saw their eyes, and later he would remember impossibly having seen the very bullet that tagged him in the back and lodged there, on the left side, between his spine and kidney. A lance corporal requested the lieutenant's permission to radio for air support. The lieutenant said yes. Then, doubting his authority to disclose their location over the air, said no. Within minutes, the lance corporal and four more men had been shot dead.

The camp that was not there was overrun. Vollie, the lieutenant, and a surviving cherry were tied up in ropes that were not there. And they were transported over many hours in vehicles that were not there, blindfolded and bleeding from the injuries they had not sustained, and they only knew the vehicles had entered some kind of cavern when the motors cut off and there were no jungle sounds that did not exist around them, of wild boars not running through the pine and mangrove trees, of ducks not flapping, of the classified drizzle that did not become static in the mind.

He was dragged, still blindfolded, from the vehicle and put on his feet. The invisible world in which he was impelled to walk narrowed immediately to a dirt tunnel through which his shoulders scarcely fit. For miles he shuffled in a crouch while a jailer he never saw prodded his back. At last they reached a vestibule within the tunnel where he and the cherry were tied up again and left. A space like an earthen pot, wet and cold. The two men listened for jungle noises, city noises, anything from the surface.

Only nothing sounds reached them. The double-nothing sounds of a tunnel that did not exist and men who were not there for an expanse of time that never took place and could not be measured anyway since they saw neither sunlight nor starlight, and what is time without its measure? *Know the measure, know the times, study that. When you are left alone, pray.*

Here, his long work began. The work toward which he had been groping since the moment in childhood he was plunged through the surface of the ice bath. The work of becoming no one. In the total dark, he closed his eyes. He studied the difference: the one dark with him, the other without.

"STAFF SERGEANT FRADE?" rasped the cherry, Wakefield, chained in the dark to what they had decided was the junked remnant of a Soviet-manufactured field artillery carriage lacking its barrel, "what was the name of your high school football team?"

"We didn't have enough boys for football." Vollie sat upright, exposing the suppurating hole in his back to the air—better dank air than wet dirt.

"Basketball then," said the failing voice. Wakefield came from Arkansas. He had three brothers and five sisters. He had not once in his life slept in a room alone.

"The Comets."

"Tell about a Comets game. Beginning to end, how it all went down. I'm trying to do like you told me and not think about my throat, sir."

"You aren't dying yet, Wakefield. You'll be all right."

"My throat's tighter than a widow's twat, sir."

In addition to a broken leg and collarbone, Wakefield had been running a fever from which he got not even the relief of sweating, he was so dehydrated. They both were.

Vollie did diamond push-ups until the wound in his back stung too badly to continue. Wakefield, who hardly stirred anymore except to squeeze a little piss in a hole they had dug, counted for him. "Now tell about a game, sir, please. I know you don't like to talk about yourself."

Vollie sat up in the dirt, panting, his head and shoulders against the dirt wall, his back arched, air to the wound, grasping at memories that quickly escaped him. He couldn't remember a single game in which he'd played. He told instead of one he had watched—must have watched, though he could not recall the stands or bench where he would have sat, what he had eaten or drunk while watching. An away game at Maquoketa in which the Comets had won in the final seconds. He remembered watching, not playing. However, it was a fact that he had played guard in every minute of every Comets game of that season. These competing realities he could not square.

. . .

"Do you hear him?" Wakefield asked.

The lieutenant was praying again in a vestibule farther down the tunnel. Vollie heard but said he didn't.

"Yes, you do," Wakefield said.

"His prayers are his business."

"Why is he praying out loud if he doesn't want us to hear?"

"To hear himself."

"How many sisters and brothers do you have?"

"I told you," Vollie said.

"Not any? Did they die?" The voice of a sick child, trusting. "I got eight." Pride smoothed the croak in his throat.

"You told me. I won't forget."

"I guess that's a lot. I mean that's enough. Mom will manage."

"Don't talk like that."

The lieutenant's low emphatic murmured prayers continued like weather.

"Staff Sergeant Frade?"

"What is it, Wakefield?"

"I want to live, sir."

"Attaboy."

Time.

Space.

He lay unmoving on the tunnel floor, inwardly at work. He was remembering the life he had led while unremembering his own place in it. Life continued here in the dark, ungoverned by the normal sequences, the diurnal patterns, the tidal routines of body and consciousness. The girl brought water in an aluminum bowl, or she didn't. He pissed and shat, or he didn't. The thing he had formerly understood as himself was only a cluster of phenomena, predictable and repeated. In their absence, this illusory entity, his self, was withering away like a weed under a tarp.

The lack of patterns. The three captive men were kept in separate vestibules, or the two enlisted men were kept together and the lieutenant sequestered, or all three were confined in one space. Chains or lengths of manila rope bound them to the artillery carriage. Teenage boys came behind carbide lamps dragging equipment through the tunnel and moved the captive men to out-of-the-way vestibules where they were kept separately for unknowable durations, possibly endless durations, so that they each separately might be occupying their timeless separate graves. Cold rice came in folded newspaper bundles, or it didn't. Leafy broth in a cup. Wakefield stank of rot, humming Christmas carols. They dragged him away on his blanket, making room for a crate to pass. They dragged him back.

They confined Vollie in a larger vestibule, lighted. A kind of workshop where children and grandmothers in pajamas filled empty tomato-juice cans with explosive and road gravel, and enveloped them, with great solicitude, in empty cans of beer: grenades homemade like dumplings.

Wakefield, unable to stand or crawl, was dragged away and dragged back.

Their captors bore their own convoys on foot underground, shadowed crates on creaking wagons, and they dragged Wakefield back into the vestibule with Vollie, or they didn't. The lieutenant through an air shaft apologized to space, the dirt. Vollie did not listen to the private words of dark confession.

His bones and blood, his fingers—all his parts participated in hunger. If rice came, he devoured every grain before he had a moment to taste it. Then he woke Wakefield and fed him his equal portion, reminding the boy to chew.

It was difficult work, the reconfiguration of world in absence of self, and he approached it with commitment. The rerecording of innumerable bike trips down Route 61, Clinton County, the waterhemp being weeded—all of it having happened now without him. All qualities refined out of being. All attachment. Needful, invisible work, like the distillation, within the lungs, of oxygen from crude air. What was left: a being, alive.

The lieutenant and Wakefield were dying, he could smell them dying. But he was not.

"STAFF SERGEANT FRADE," Wakefield said. "They know we're down here, don't they?"

Vollie twisted his back, stretching the cramped and spasming lumbar muscles until they emitted a new hurt, and keeping the hurt there in the muscle, dwelling in the hurt. "Probably," he said.

"But I'm afraid if it's them spooks who got us into this, then nobody else knows."

"It's all right if nobody knows."

They rarely saw or heard their captors, who came and checked the ropes or chains and brought water, or didn't. No efforts were made to extract names or serial numbers from them, which Wakefield took to mean they were not being held as prisoners of war but as chits to trade. "If the mission was classified, then us disappearing is classified. And we'll just be MIA forever. But why are they keeping us alive unless they think the spooks will pay something for us? What do you think we're worth?"

Vollie didn't answer, and Wakefield said, "I feel really awful today."

"Your throat's better."

"That's right. Thank you for reminding me, sir."

"You'll make it, Wakefield."

"Okay, thank you, sir."

But Vollie feared for the boy that his throat had opened only because the body was giving up.

THE BODY WAS GIVING UP. The thin rank body that often fell asleep even as it ate, while Vollie hungered, feeding it. The body surrendering to its wounds as Vollie's own body did not. The body preparing to die that could not have hungered the way his own body did. The boy's body that did not deserve to eat because it refused to struggle.

THE LIEUTENANT COULD BE HEARD from afar through a communication tunnel talking a blue streak. A three- or four-person confab in which he played all the voices. Later, when he was tied up with Vollie and Wakefield, he mostly shivered unspeaking. His shivers rustled the pebbles under him. Wakefield asked how many brothers and sisters he had.

Once, the girl put fish or some other sweet-smelling mash atop the rice, and Wakefield, rousing a little, wanted them all three to say grace. The lieutenant by then spoke only when alone, and Wakefield gave thanks to God for his loving-kindness and their good fortune and said amen. Vollie listened for the prayer to end and did not partake of it. Then he ate.

He put the mash in Wakefield's mouth and Wakefield chewed. He fell asleep while he was chewing, and Vollie woke him up and told him to swallow.

The lieutenant was taken away.

THE BODY THAT REFUSED to struggle still could eat. Wakefield's body. It breathed and stirred.

After perhaps two days without food, a Vietnamese boy behind a lamp came with rice, two packages wet and cold in paper, one for Vollie, one for Wakefield. The boy went away. Vollie unwrapped the first bundle and ate, licking the paper afterward, listening to his companion breathe. His hand then grabbed the second bundle—not his own hand, but the hand of the no one he was becoming—and unwrapped it and brought the rice to this no one's mouth, and the mouth ate again.

The next time food came, he again took what was his from what was theirs and ate it, and took the rest and ate it too, while the other body slept.

STRANGE WORK, only possible in the absence of time. The arrangement of impressions in memory came loose and came together again without him. Twilight slogging through the muddy pasture. Music and spring rain. The people he had known and loved. All of it falling away from him in the dark.

The other body began to die more quickly now.

Vollie was cold, or he wasn't. He lusted for more rice, or he had descended beneath any want. No time governed the intake or outflow of this breath. Whether his feet remained his feet, he could neither confirm nor deny. The hair on his body was mostly dirt.

Maximum possible forgetting.

The wound in his back had closed on itself.

KNOW THE MEASURE, know the times, study that. When you are left alone, pray. But he was never really alone until the lieutenant and Wakefield died at last. That happened four months after they were taken into the tunnel. It could have been half or twice as many months. There had been less to eat, then almost nothing. Wakefield died. Then the lieutenant died real fast, and Vollie was alone. He never figured out what the lieutenant was sick with, a new illness he got at the end. He coughed a lot, but Vollie didn't catch it. By and by, their bodies were taken away. He was led elsewhere within the tunnel into another equipment cavern, where most of the time his hands and feet were tied to the wheel of a buffalo cart so that he sat or curled himself on the rubble floor but could not lie flat or stand. Lucky he had Heflin's letter to read and sometimes a kid would come by with a lamp. *Love to throw yourself on the earth and kiss it.* He memorized the letter. *Love all men, love everything.*

It was now in the nowhere no-time realm of tunnel dark—after the bodies of the lieutenant and Wakefield had been taken away, after his bones had seemed to bend to fit the shape in which they were constrained, after time had lost its nature as a duration leaving only its nature as a medium in which the things endured that had never come into being and could never pass out of it—that his vision came back to him:

The farm. Moon on the orchard. Night frost in the high grass that cracked underfoot. The cry of a hog. Thirst. He approached the creek in the meadow. No one else about. His head burning. The warped reflection in the creek of the anguished face he knew to be his own. The fear of the water's cold. The recognition that he had come from this water and must go back into it now.

When his eyes penetrated the water, the face disappeared as though it had never been. The person lost his nature as mind, a venue of conflict, as bearer of a name, leaving only the nature of a body swimming in the body's medium of water. Vision time merged with tunnel time. He had fallen once before from the vision into the frigid bath, his mother holding his feet, his father dumping snow in the water from a pail. He understood that night in the bath to be only one of many births he had known. And all the births had already taken place. Each was the repetition of a previous birth. None had happened first. His soul lived only temporarily inside the medium of time and subject to duration. It endured otherwise, nameless and faceless, outside of time in peace.

THEN A GIRL CAME.

Weeks or years had passed.

She put a coarsely woven bag over his head. There were men's voices.

The ropes at his feet were untied. He was prodded in his back to stand. The back did not straighten for several minutes; the bullet was still lodged in it from the long-past day the camp had been overrun. By and by he was prodded to walk. He counted his steps and figured they walked about five miles always in the dark and he always crouching and continually hitting his head on the dirt or rock tunnel walls made for smaller people.

They stopped in the tunnel and pulled the bag up a little and tied it over his eyes and gave him a cup of rice to eat. They pulled the bag back down and tied it and they kept going. He figured about three more miles. Slowly, gradually more slowly, as his strength was giving out. Then an unmistakable sewage smell, and he was walking on a harder surface through cold stagnant water to his ankles. Then there was a ladder. His hands were placed on the rung of a ladder. He heard curt commands, and there was a jab to the legs, and he climbed. After the ladder they walked perhaps another fifty yards, he always crouching.

Then he smelled leaves. Then through the bag light seeped. Green, yellow, and orange light stabbing his eyes. *Kiss the earth and love it with an unceasing, consuming love.* He rode in a vehicle. He was given water to drink under the bag, then they retied the bag snugly under his jaw. When the vehicle stopped he was prodded to step out of it. With slaps to his shoulders he was prodded to kneel on the ground. They retied his hands behind his back. With slaps to his head, he was prodded to lower it, which exposed the back of his neck, and the warmth of the sun penetrated the skin at the exposed juncture of head and body, and seemed to warm even his bones. His eyes constricted as if he were about to cry—to cry out his shame that the others had had to die in the dark but he was going to get to die now with the light of the sun on his neck, shame that the sun at the hour of his death had blessed him and not the others, or shame at the food he had taken—yet the no one he had become could feel no shame: he wanted only, devoutly, impossibly to go on living.

He heard city sounds. Engines and distant tangled voices. He was not prodded and so did not move. Then he heard men speaking in low-toned American English.

A sudden shuffling of feet. A smell of Brut aftershave. Hands that gripped his scrawny arms by the elbows and shoulders, and urged him to stand up.

A fumbling of fingers at his Adam's apple where the bag was tied. The bag coming off his head. A burst like an Arc Light too near to be survived. *Don't be ashamed of that ecstasy, prize it, for it is a gift of God and a great one; it is not given to many but only to the elect.*

Then he was taken to the hospital in Saigon.

4

It was there, in the hospital mess, that the civilian first approached him. The natty dresser, the last to have arrived at the Bien Hoa barbecue and the first to have left. His name was Lorch. Vollie was to learn it only there in the hospital. He really did import cleaning supplies to the Republic of Vietnam, although he could disclose to Staff Sergeant Frade that the import enterprise did not represent the totality of his dealings there. He also ran what he called a "shop" that developed intelligence products—both raw and finished products—as well as engaging, here and there, in the more modern intelligence function of covert operations. At length, he would make Vollie a proposition. It would sound at first as if the man wanted to shove him into another tunnel. With time, however, Vollie would recognize the proposition as the tracer wish that you send out of yourself red and burning when you're too young to know what you're wishing for, and that sometimes hits something hard in the dark, a rock out there, and ricochets, and starts a chain of consequences you could not have foreseen, though you willed it.

The MPs who discovered him, tied up and kneeling on the sidewalk outside a field office of the Military Assistance Command, set him on a bench in the hospital emergency room. They conferred in whispers with the intake orderly. One of them gave him a candy bar, but the strange person he had become was numb to hunger, and he didn't eat it. Nobody else was waiting there to be treated. Perhaps the war had been won in his absence. The MPs shook his hand uncertainly and went away. A nurse led him toward the showers. She gave him a bottle of Coke as they walked through the hallway afire with fluorescent light, but he didn't drink it. She gave him a towel. He stripped and washed. When he got out, she was waiting and gave him pressed fatigues, new socks, underwear, shoes. She seemed the last woman on earth. She took him to a barber elsewhere on the quiet base. While the barber cut his hair, the nurse read a magazine, standing in a corner. She led him across the hospital complex to a ward, mostly empty of patients.

Was the war over? he asked.

"Sort of," she said.

She signed some documents on a clipboard and gave him the documents to hold and told him to take a seat in the hall there and to give the documents to the orderly who would show him his bed. She asked if he would be all right waiting there by himself. He thought a moment and said yes and watched her go out the door, her legs and feet, her upward-swooping hair. The door swung closed behind her, and he never saw her again.

They gave him a private room. At night he left the room and walked the dark ward, thin as a rod beneath his clothes, barefoot, feeling the cold slick tiles.

People tried to talk to him, army intelligence, sociable marines who'd heard scuttlebutt about him. He didn't say much. He spent his exercise hours apart from the other patients, pacing the Saigon junk bazaars that teemed with people, sunlight on nameless faces. In the bazaars, unlike the hospital, no one claimed to recognize him from a previous tour or asked him whether his appetite was improving, whom they should wire with the news he'd been found, how had he kept his finger-nails pared with nothing sharp to cut them—just teeming nameless human faces young and old jostling him softly like another fish in the school, crowded under the canopies of the markets in exactly the parts of town he did not have leave to visit.

When the hospital people reiterated how far he was allowed to go from the base, he listened, elbows on knees, smoking, quiet. Then he went where he wanted. To the bazaars—or to a record store where he listened on headphones to the Beach Boys or to Schumann, to the coded language of numbers in motion in which a spirit had been try-ing since he was a small child to communicate some urgent news, some extremely important instruction that after almost twenty years he still failed to comprehend. Neck bent with the headphones on in the record store, listening, white as newsprint from the months under-ground.

During his third week at the hospital, while he was forcing himself to eat a bacon sandwich in an isolated corner of the mess, the civilian made his approach. Vollie recognized him at once from his strawlike hair but neither looked at the man directly nor otherwise acknowl-edged any compromise of his solitude. The civilian took the seat op-posite him, arranging before himself a plate of baby corn cobs, another piled with brisket, and a steaming bowl of apple fritters. "I note you like to perambulate and see the town," the civilian said.

Vollie didn't respond. He was watching a Vietnamese girl in an *ao dai* bright as waxed fruit polish the big veranda windows. Two things he could watch forever—fire and other people working. Midday city light behind her. Gleaming smog.

"Ain't it the smell mostly," the civilian was asking, "that says, 'Toto, we ain't in Kansas anymore'?"

"I've never been to Kansas."

"I mean the smell more than all these identical people under their identical hats, don't you think?"

The civilian sported loafers and shiny cuff buttons, a slim yellow tie; like an executive just off the links with that accent peculiar to the southern rich, that corporate hillbilly inflection none of them could shake even to tell a joke about Yankee talk. "What do you see when you walk?" he asked. "Khe Sanh? Calamus? Kalamazoo?"

"I've never been to Kalamazoo." Pause. "What do you know about Calamus?"

A town of four hundred people, but the civilian knew a lot, it turned out. Right down to most Union Army volunteers, on a per capita basis, of any town in the state of Iowa. Vollie himself hadn't known that, though he was descended from more than one of them.

The civilian knew a lot about a lot of things. When Vollie let slip about the 16-inch shells from the *New Jersey* that had lit up the perimeter that morning at Khe Sanh during his first tour, the civilian listened with smiling relish but then explained why it couldn't be true. The battleship had indeed been en route to the South China Sea, but by the time of Khe Sanh it had yet to cross the Pacific. The shells he'd seen had most likely come from the 175-millimeter army guns at Camp Carroll. "Anyway, the sixteen inch can't quite reach Khe Sanh, less they could've sailed the ship fifteen miles up on land." The civilian had done enough of his homework, or somebody had done it for him, that Vollie didn't see the point in trying to hide his private business. There was no knowing the limit of what this man already knew.

It was the civilian who informed him that of the men those spooks had led away from the dump the morning they were overrun, not one had made it back to base. All were presumed dead.

The civilian knew all about the tunnel, knew where some of the tunnel entrances were, knew the exact number of days Vollie had been in it. He spoke obliquely of the inside of the tunnel itself, as though he had seen and heard what Vollie alone had seen and heard. A promise seemed sewn in these allusions. That he might speak more explicitly but chose not to.

He apologized on behalf of their government—not to say he was employed in government; he did all his business on a contract basis— for how long it had taken to get Vollie out of the tunnel and for the unfortunate exigency that Vollie was never going to be allowed to tell anybody where he had been for 412 days. "Actually, you don't yourself have clearance to know where you were."

"I was in Cambodia," Vollie said.

"That ain't possible," the civilian said shortly. "Congress in its wisdom prohibited you from setting foot in Cambodia."

"Sir, I don't know exactly where that last part of the tunnel was. It only took a half day's walking before we got to the sewer under Saigon and they let me go. But when they hit us, we were in Cambodia. And they weren't guerrillas wandering around. They were NVA. They had new K-50Ms and AK-47s. Their uniforms were clean. And there were four of them for every one of us. Some hidden camp. Those NVA knew our location real good."

"I hear you, Staff Sergeant, but after the secret bombings and the incursion Congress passed a law. The law said you could not be in Cambodia. Ergo you were not. The enemy is allowed to shoot at you from behind an international boundary, but you ain't allowed anymore to walk over there and ask him to knock it off. You'd have to be real smart to understand whatever sense that makes. I ain't smart myself, so I don't get it. Neither do some of the poor folks at the Defense Department who have actual responsibility for soldiers and marines deployed in combat zones. But in other quarters of government people are more sophisticated. These people are so sophisticated they think we can save men by losing them. They can make a complex argument for why our success here is impossible. This argument is so beautiful to them that they would rather see us all fail and prove them right than see us all win and prove them wrong."

Interesting as all this was, Vollie had no intention of buying whatever the civilian was here to sell him, likely a promotion wrapped in some other secret he'd have to keep as long as he lived. Sun drenched the veranda. He wanted to go out there and take a nap. "Don't worry, sir," Vollie said. "I have no one to tell where I was."

The civilian wagged his head, bit a fritter, chewed. "Actually, you were not only not in Cambodia. Actually—and I'm sorry to tell you this—you deserted."

A laugh almost escaped him before the implications of what the civilian was saying pierced his brain. "The hell I did."

"I'm sorry, but on paper you did. And nobody looking at your files will have clearance to find out about any operations we might or might not have been conducting. I'm sorry. You ain't got a witness. There's a gap now. A gap going to get filled with desertion. Some nosey parker in the hospital already asked to refer your case to the Judge Advocate Division. Marine went off the reservation and got hungry, then he come back—that's what they think they see."

"Who the fuck are you?"

His name was Lorch. He gave it frankly. He had assumed Vollie knew it by now from scuttlebutt. "I feel we owe you a debt," he said. "I think we need to figure out how to make this go away for you. But if military justice gets interested, we can't just tell them to mind their own business. And we could hardly exculpate you by explaining you were in a place where Congress made it illegal for you to be. So we have to think creatively. I've been fixing to introduce myself so we could talk about a proposition that might tidy you up."

The lights went out. The lights were always going out. Then they came back on.

He was rotating out of country, Lorch was. His operations were winding down, sadly, along with the war. He'd had a lot of fun here, the men in the shop he'd assembled made good product, but more than that they were good friends. It would have been a terrible waste to let the bonds of trust they'd built wither away only because there was no war to fight. Once you made a bond, you ought to keep it. So they were retooling the shop in the hope their existing customers might throw them enough domestic work to stay in business. "There's always going to be a demand for intelligence, even stateside," he said. "Now. You'll be looking for a position soon, Staff Sergeant."

"I didn't know I was leaving the service."

"Unfortunately you are. You haven't been listening. You'll get to go to Kansas. To the prison at Fort Leavenworth, understand? Or you'll let me help you. They won't stick you with a month in the brig. This ain't a weekend's AWOL. This'll be desertion in wartime. You'll be locked up till about 1985."

Vollie's toes contracted within his shoes, as if he was about to jump across the table, grab the man's fork, and stab it in his devil tongue.

"I wager a position that could give you an end run around that might appeal. You don't want to hear about it?"

He believed not a word Lorch had said. Yet so much of it was plainly true that he could not even trust his unbelief, and chose to listen for some new reality he might extract that might point him where to go; because he had wanted nothing in the tunnel but to leave himself behind and feel the sun on his head, and now he stood naked at the end of a road with the sun all over his head and the rest of him, but he had nowhere to go, home least of all—it was no home of his anymore—and no one else with him.

Lorch knew how many cavities Vollie had, what were his political affiliations (none), what were his family connections in the active-duty officer corps of the four service branches (none), what were his bank holdings (nothing), how many people stateside had bothered to pester Washington as to the whereabouts of Staff Sergeant Frade while he was underground (one letter, on behalf of his mother, from a preacher who was told Vollie was temporarily stationed out of postal range), and even if he didn't get Leavenworth what did he think his employment prospects were with a dishonorable discharge? Anyway, he hadn't heard what the position was yet. It wasn't hard duty. If he had eyes and could live someplace, he could do it.

"You would embed in a stateside locality of interest and report to us what you see," Lorch said.

Having been tied up so long, he now remembered how it felt to be a threat—the rush, the appetite to cause pain, also the recognition imperfectly hidden in an adversary's eyes of what you might do and the lengths he would go to evade you. Whatever this position might entail, Vollie could see no reason Lorch should offer it to him: he could only be trying to keep a potential enemy close. Vollie said, "None of this solves the problem you say I have."

"I'm getting to that. It's standard protocol when setting up an asset like this to sheep-dip him. You ever dip a sheep? I bet you have. You dip him in pesticide, fungicide. Nothing living sticks to his fleece. That is, we strip him, temporarily, of whatever's in his files; the name, the family relations, the personnel records fall away from him for a while. This lets him move unencumbered in his new environment." At the same time, Lorch said, a rudimentary second person was created. None of this required ingenuity. A war had been waged in Laos by thousands of operatives processed in about the same way. Documents establishing the second person were inserted in files at various levels of government from which identification papers could then be obtained for the asset's use while he engaged his assignment.

Typically, nothing needed to be done with the original person's legal existence, into which the asset reintegrated at the end of his assignment. But in Vollie's case, the protocol could be exploited to scour his record. While his whereabouts remained unknown, nobody would pursue any investigation, and affiliates in the Defense Department would have time to establish a paper trail that could refute any later speculations against him. Whenever he completed his work with Lorch's shop, he would reintegrate into his old life with his good name beyond reproach, fully eligible for all the benefits of a returning veteran.

Most of the mayo-soaked bread of the sandwich remained on Vollie's plate. At least he had managed to eat the bacon and the lettuce. "Not interested," he said.

As to money, Lorch continued. The shop was not a corporation of owners and employees. It was a family, each member with his role, usually operating at significant distances from one another but all sharing in the family's fortunes. Servicemen in military units that sometimes cooperated with the shop weren't knowing participants in its operations and didn't share its revenue, but now he would be within the fold. No one involved, not even Lorch, drew a salary. Members were compensated, each according to his share, when the team as a whole made good on a contract and the customer paid the fee. "In other words, we work independently for a common reward. We take from the shared pot only what *belongs* to us," Lorch said, with the merest hint of further insinuation. "You of all people would understand that."

The food in Vollie's gullet rose to his throat. He nearly gagged. Before he knew it, he had stood to leave—

But he had stood too quickly. The blood went right out of his head.

"I respect what you've come through, Staff Sergeant. All the little decisions I'm sure you had to make. And I feel we owe you, morally if not contractually, for the way our—for the way your operation went off its rails. I don't like to owe. Why don't you set down awhile? You don't look half right."

Vollie held the back of a chair, tottering. His brain was a water balloon: as if from a distance, he watched it pop. The pressure that gave it its shape dispersed. If only someone else could share his bewilderment, his dizziness, at this moment—but of course he was alone in such experiences. And right then he understood that the person he had been before the tunnel had fooled himself to believe he knew how it had sounded within his father's silver head when the old man's artery had burst: that his father like the rest of us was alone within the cavern of his skull when he died as at every moment he had lived.

The mess was empty. "Go lie down," Lorch said with concern. "I'm sorry, I talked off your ear. Why don't you get some sleep and consider? I wouldn't take too long though, if I was you."

Vollie lay the rest of the afternoon in the unaccustomed sheets of his bunk but did not sleep. At nightfall he walked off base to the record store and stood with head bent, listening to the numbers in motion, the music scribbled in vinyl and shipped here from the other side of the world. He wore the headphones. He needed to listen close. There was something cruel about the headphones, that he should be condemned to listen to the piece called "Of Foreign Lands and People" with others present, but that they should not share it. He looked up at the Vietnamese in fine white shirts flitting their fingers through the albums in this place to which the war had brought some merchant prosperity, the elegant Vietnamese wearing headphones too but listening to other music from other times right there next to him, within the distant globes of their own brains.

The power went out. Amid near-perfect obscurity, everybody looked up. The turntables slowly losing momentum but the sound utterly snuffed as though killed. Everybody looking up. Strangers, animal in their startling, human in their namelessness. For a second, he was in the tunnel again and saw the girl putting the bag back on his head. He even felt the weave of the bag against his face. It filled him not with dread but peace. A person unseen, unknown, even unremembered—if he hoped for anything, he hoped to stay this way.

The lights flickered on in the store, and it came to him what he would do.

HE FOUND LORCH the next day, in the mess, staring with avid eyes through the cough guard at a steam tray of chicken casserole.

SALVATORE SCIBONA

The two of them sat down at a table overlooking a highway choked with cars, men and women carrying grocery bags, picking their way through the traffic. "How long can you make me go away?" Vollie asked.

Lorch, not understanding the question or ignoring it, wanted first to discuss how much Vollie could expect to earn. "The exact figure depends on the size of the gross contract and your percentage of shares in it," Lorch said. "We anticipate the typical range per operation for you will be between eight and ten thousand dollars, payable as you see fit either before or after you reintegrate."

"That's what I want to ask. The reintegration. Is it voluntary?"

Lorch's tongue discovered something disagreeable amid the casserole in his mouth, and he spat it in a paper napkin. "Either there's a pebble in here or a piece of bone," he said to the wad in his palm. "Are you listening? That was serious money I just quoted you. What do you mean, voluntary? You misunderstand."

"Nossir, I don't. It's not my behind you're covering, it's yours. I'm a mistake you made. You want me out of the way until I can't cause you any trouble. I want me out of the way too."

"You misunderstand completely. We paid a lot to get you out of where you were. We're proud of you, I mean it. We don't want you to go out. We want you to come in."

"Nossir, you want me to disappear. So do I." The roots of his hair prickled. His skin seemed an insufficient container for the pressure of the hope he could feel. His vision came back to him unbidden: the fever vision of childhood. The creek in the meadow. The twisted face and its anguish vanishing the moment he pushed the face through the surface of the water. The cold shock when he dove in fully. The body at one with all that surrounded it. The naked body swimming along the rocky creek bed. The body turning within the water to face the gleaming moon. However, in this vision it was not the moon overhead but the sun. Light all over him. And he gave himself over to crazy hope. "I'll do what you want," he said. "But only if I can go away for good."

"You're not talking about a scouring, you're talking about a hard clearing," Lorch said. "As a matter of fact, there's a protocol, but it's for people in bigger trouble than you."

"I thought I was going to Leavenworth."

"There's bigger trouble in the world than Leavenworth. There's bigger people than you. And a hard clearing takes *forever*. We can't do it in house. Half a dozen staff assistants to the deputy resource manager of bureaucratic horse shit would get to withhold approval. The transfer protocol for financial assets and liabilities alone is a nightmare. They wouldn't let you use this to run away from creditors, if that's what you're thinking. They would also set up a chain of accounts to filter any kind of trust funds, pensions, legacies that may become payable to the old entity after he's wiped out."

"I wouldn't want any kind of accounts like that."

"Maybe not; protocol says you'd get them anyway. I could look into it for you, but listen. In a sheep-dipping, the entity is rinsed and later on he goes back the way he was; after the hard clearing the entity is no longer extant. He's either killed on paper or they destroy whatever records they get access to that he ever lived. That can't really be what you want."

"Yessir, it is."

"There *is* a protocol but—you know, there's even an envelope." He described the physical attributes of the envelope and what it contained, documents making it possible for the entity and his net worth to go on living free of his past, for the duration. "You know what they call that envelope? They call it a Luke Nine: Sixty-two: 'No man, having put his hand to the plough, and looking back, is fit for the kingdom.'"

It was the rapture hope, taking shape.

"You don't really want that," Lorch said. "Your head ain't straight.

You haven't done anything wrong. Think what you owe the people who made you."

BUT IT WAS of those same people and what he owed them that he must not think, that he would refuse to think, and that in the end the man he became would never learn to stop thinking. Long after Vollie Frade had mostly disappeared from his mind, his mother and father—on whom he had turned his back in order to face the void that seemed his true home—would abide in his inner world, with terrible sweetness. The smells of their hair, their snores. What good did it do them to be thought of? His heart shared its substance with them and could not be made to love them less. However he tried to excuse, his heart would not allow him to forget what he owed them. His debt never diminished. The interest compounded. Someday, to someone, it would be paid.

Lorch was eager to get Vollie away from the snoops on base and arranged for him to fly to California. While permission for the hard clearing was still under review, a room was arranged for him in a dormitory inside the Presidio of Monterey, where he didn't know anybody and most of his neighbors were squids learning Russian or Chinese at the Defense Language Institute there, college types who ate together at their designated tables chatting unintelligibly. Nobody asked him, If you aren't a student, what are you doing here? because nobody asked him anything. Nobody pretended to give him a job. This went on a couple of days. His orders were to wait. Then it went on a few months. He ate. He ran by the emerald ocean amid deafening winds.

One morning a knock came at his dormitory door. There stood a civilian he had seen in the library and taken for a professor. The man asked for a moment of his time to deliver a message from a friend they had in common and looked inside as though inspecting the condition of the tiny room. A smiling fellow, with an unplaceable accent, wearing a heavy sweater from the pocket of which he took a couple of wrinkled cigarettes.

Vollie offered him the desk chair while he himself stood against the wall. It was the first time anyone else had been in the room with him.

"I find the weather here beastly," the professor said to the window, in which the luminous yellow leaves of a walnut tree shook and a breeze entered smelling of the surf. The smile he wore was of a middle-aged person determined to be grateful for the trials he had endured.

Vollie said, "I think it's the most beautiful place I ever saw."

"But such a monotonous consistency of temperature. I would have liked to be put in Chicago." He spoke as though his life were finished. He scanned the room distractedly. Vollie handed him a foil ashtray. "Yes, thank you. I hope you've found your stipend sufficient to your needs, the accommodations reasonable?"

"I don't need much."

"It was the best I could do within the bounds of discretion. I'm sorry I haven't been able to speak with you before, but our common acquaintance regards his protocols with a certain punctiliousness. I was not to communicate until I received a definitive message. Your mattress is firm?" The professor poked the bed pillow as if testing a steak on a grill. It gave and sprang back. "He wishes you to know that the initial request for a hard clearing has been denied. That was his phrase. Confidentially, I would advise you to pay close attention when that man uses the passive voice to elide the subject of a verb. You might infer, not unreasonably, that he himself is in some degree the subject. Be that as it may, he wishes to know if you will reconsider. That is, if you would agree to proceed on the basis of his original proposition. Again, these are his words."

"Let me make sure I understand."

"You may of course ask whatever you like, but bear in mind that I know nothing more than what I have just related. Irrespective of your answer, you are to remain at the Presidio and wait."

"Do you really teach here?"

"I do," he said with smiling weariness. "I am adjunct associate professor of Romanian. I'm sorry to report that after this conversation we will probably not have another chance to talk. I am an irregular channel of communication, you understand."

"Tell him no."

"He will want to know whether this 'no' comes bearing any conditions."

"Just tell him no."

"Very well. There's excellent seafood in the town. Salmon and . . . now I'm forgetting." He made a yakking puppet gesture.

"Clams."

"Clams, thank you. You shouldn't miss them. The shellfish of no two places are alike, I find."

"Water's different everywhere you go," Vollie said.

"I'm sure that's true."

They shook hands. From the shallow drooping pocket in the breast of the professor's cardigan, a clump of mustard and mayonnaise packets peeked, as well as a pencil, a chewed straw, and several plastic forks still in their cellophane envelopes. The handshake lasted longer than custom required. It suggested a mutual understanding that since they were to speak only once, their parting merited a moment's extended ceremony. It was a handshake with mortality in it. Then the professor left the room.

Vollie ate more. He ran by the ocean, thinking and trying not to think, missing farm chores, wishing he were yanking the waterhemp out of the soybeans, work into which the useless mind disappeared. And he longed for the woods above the meadow on the farm—where the sun might go down, and a night ensue with no moon or stars, and you might walk in the woods without overturning a leaf; no sound; and not just alone but imperceptible; composed of the same material as the earth and the trees, and having no more need of a name than the trees did.

He took a bus to Big Sur on the weekends, when he could count on a crowd. Some folks lived out there, camped in the open, not a few of them ex-marines. He wasn't really an ex-marine himself, he was still missing someplace in Vietnam. The ex-marines, spotting his tattoo, strolled up to him on the sand and asked where he'd been stationed, usually as a prelude to asking for money. They didn't smell so bad since they bathed every day in the frigid water. He usually gave them at least half of what he had in his pocket. They wanted it, he didn't. His spare diminished.

Then two associates from Lorch's shop found him in the Presidio weight room. It was September 1972. They apologized for the delay and took him out for lunch at a seafood shack where Vollie ate the first oysters of his life. After a secondary review the hard clearing had been approved.

OVER SUBSEQUENT MEETINGS, they schooled him on the shop's many tedious and paranoid protocols.

They also briefed him on the initial operation in which he would participate, an intelligence-gathering project that would burn as much as a year of his time to no apparent use at all: only the military could have commissioned it. The associates nevertheless maintained they knew neither the identity nor the motives of their ultimate customer. Such compartmentation was itself a crucial protocol, practiced all the way up the chain of intelligence consumption. Their ignorance of the customer equaled the customer's ignorance of them. No one could be entirely "witting"—aware at once of the intelligence, its use, and its means of cultivation. No single actor bore responsibility for it. This made the chain of consumption resistant to organized interference.

Vollie's own place in the chain must have fallen near the bottom. He was under no circumstances to ask anyone what they knew about the subject on whom the operation centered. The protocols even required that while in the field he never speak the subject's name. His method of operation was to gather not facts but the subset of human intelligence called rumor intelligence or "rumint": subfacts, hearsay. He was to listen for mentions of the subject or signs of him amid the streets of the neighborhood in Queens, New York, where they were renting Vollie an apartment, and where he was to find a job and work for a living like anybody else, and where it was possible, but unlikely, the subject once had lived.

His objective there was not to find the subject but to corroborate that he was lost. If, after twelve months of careful listening, he heard nothing, they would consider his work a success. He was to be a bowl left out overnight to show in the morning that it had not rained.

Further detail would be available after his clearing, which was to be made official at a confab with superiors in Bridgeport, Connecticut, in two months' time.

The subject's name was Egon Hausmann. They were nearly certain he was dead.

THE BRIEFINGS in Monterey took place always over meals. Protocol dictated information be communicated in speech, never on paper, and always in public locations. The associates were both former NCOs, stoop-necked, attentive, quiet. Quiet did not mean self-absorbed or thoughtful. They had the dark unflustering other-directed eyes of horses.

He wanted to believe they weren't liars. But even if the job was as rudimentary as they suggested, what qualified him to do it? He didn't come from the class of people who did work like this. They must have been using him for something else. "Why would I be of any good to you?" he asked. "All I ever did was farm and drive a truck."

One of the men choked on his chowder. The white splatter smirched his mouth.

The other said to the choker, "I told you he'd be like that."

"Sir, you're Staff Sergeant Frade," the choker said through his napkin. This told him nothing.

"You're famous," the choker coughed.

When Vollie recoiled in disgust and confusion, the other assured him this fame extended only to a limited circle within the intelligence community. He said, "You're the one who made it out after the rest of those guys died."

IN THE SPRING, Vollie finally received orders to head east. He bought a bus ticket to Dallas, a second to Pittsburgh, a third to Bridgeport, and put the tickets in his wallet.

The first bus carried him down along the California coast ranges, across the Mojave Desert, through the wastes of southern Arizona, and into New Mexico. There, it made a scheduled half-day stop at Las Cruces, a location stamped forever on his mind because the envelope containing Bobby Heflin's letter bore a postmark from there. While the other passengers were waiting in line for the depot bathrooms, he went outside to inspect the sun and noticed a collection of ramshackle taxis waiting in the slag-covered lot.

He fished Heflin's letter from his wallet and bent before a taxi window and showed the return address to the old cabbie inside and asked if he knew roughly where the place was.

The cabbie drew a map in the air with his chalklike finger and calculated. "Sixty miles that way," he reckoned, pointing over a mesa. "Ninety on the road."

Vollie stood and screwed his torso side to side, twisting the spine and stretching the cramped muscle thereabout, where the slug was lodged. He walked to the paved road and looked at it. Then he went back and asked how much the cabbie would charge to drive him out there, wait an hour while he said hello to some friends, and drive him back here to the depot.

"Fifteen dollars," the cabbie declared.

Vollie said he didn't have that much.

"Meter goes on running while I wait."

"Well," Vollie said.

If the cabbie was considering coming down on the fare, he showed no signs of it. He peeled and ate a whole banana while the noonday sun irradiated every inch of the world where Vollie stood exposed to it as inescapably as to the judgment of conscience.

Only then, the alternative presented itself. He didn't need to do any of this. He could go live with Bobby and his friends instead. The disintegrating three-year-old invitation was right there in his hand.

"Say you dropped me instead and turned around," Vollie said.

"Thirteen fifty."

"I could give you eleven."

The cabbie would go no lower than thirteen, tip included, in light of the uniform Vollie was still wearing. He suggested Vollie borrow the remaining two dollars from the friends at his destination.

Vollie straightened up. The fathomless bright sky around was blue and clean with promise. He tried on, like unfamiliar clothes, the language he would have to use: Will you lend me— Would you float me— Could I ask you for—

He breathed deep.

He put his head back in the window. "I can't do that," he said.

In the night, while he slept across the bench seat of the bus, somebody stole his wallet right out of his hip pocket. Most of his money, Heflin's letter, the bus tickets—all were lost. From Dallas, he was constrained to walk or ask for rides from strangers.

5

Stars.

He came awake shivering in a Missouri meadow where the tall grass had hidden him and the vault of night sky hovered near enough to eat. Too cold now to sleep, he hefted his seabag and went on walking up the road. Not even the birds had yet awoken.

He humped through Grovespring—an Esso station, a P.O.—and was already halfway to Lebanon before a Peterbilt tractor trailer, colossal on little Route 5, passed him at a low, quiet, sluggard coast. The slowing rig exhaled and stopped. Its hazards began to flash. The mud flaps bore in white relief the logo of a citrus distributor in Petaluma, California. He broke into a trot. The yellow-green sky of nearly sunup. Outside a distant hog barn, the fluorescent lights went out. The rig's sulfur exhaust floated over a plowed field where some deer stood, watching: three does, a buck, a twiggy fawn in its vest of spots. The fenders of the rig were tricked out with airbrushed flames. He came to the passenger door and opened it.

The young driver sat spitting tobacco juice from a gob in his lip into a paper coffee container. His thick hair was cropped, parted, and combed. He pointed his chin at Vollie's bag. "I'd recognize that seabag from a mile away," he called over the din of the engine. "You aren't in the navy, are you?"

"Nossir," Vollie shouted. "Marine Corps. Was."

"Me too. Come up where I can hear you."

Vollie mounted the running board and climbed into the light of the cab. His uniform shirt bore a masking scrim of road dust, but the driver made out the chevrons of his rank, counted them aloud, and asked where the staff sergeant was headed. Vollie told him Bridgeport, Connecticut, and the driver said, Lucky day, he was going to Rhode Island, and told Vollie to get on in.

None of the human detritus of long-haul travel littered the cab. Not so much as a pencil stub fallen to the floor. The vinyl bench and dash shone in the glow of the instrument panel as though freshly oiled. But the air smelled of the sweat-funk of small rooms where men have been sleeping alone.

The engine thrummed. Vollie slammed the door. The family of deer outside took to the air, white tails up, and dispersed among the trees. The driver stamped. The rig rattled into gear. The engine roared. They were off.

Sunup. They headed right at the sun like angels in a vision.

The driver asked if the staff sergeant had been in Vietnam, and Vollie said yes. The driver asked where at. Here and there, Vollie said. The driver said he'd spent thirteen months as a PFC in Chu Lai on the coast and had also done some Swift Boat patrols in the rivers and listed the villages where he had camped, naming each of these places as though they were questions. When Vollie didn't respond to any of this, the driver said he'd also manned an M40 recoilless rifle at the battle of Hue, during Tet.

Vollie listened and went on watching the road.

After a few miles, the driver asked how come he wasn't wearing his campaign ribbons on that shirt, and Vollie said he'd lost them.

They didn't break for food until they had crossed half of Illinois. The driver said Vollie had better fill up, they wouldn't stop again until supper; so he bought a coffee and two boiled eggs from the Automat. "Are you that busted?" the driver asked. Vollie said he'd had plenty at breakfast, though he'd had nothing. In truth he was down to four dollars in singles and change, most of it stowed in his bag in a shirt pocket, bound in the money clip that was really a silver-plated barrette he had managed to keep right through the tunnel days when its function was to scrape his teeth, a slim hard thing with a minute pattern of vines and leaves engraved in it that he had bought for a hooker he liked in Da Nang—a hungry-looking, broad-faced girl from the North who smelled of cabbage but paid him courtesies such as taking off all her clothes, every stitch; remembering his name; telling him in her percussive little vocabulary that he was really good at it, she was really liking it now, she could see a glow around him, which, boy that he was, he believed for months afterward—and who disappeared from her corner, just *poof* one afternoon, and nobody in the clubs around there ever copped to knowing her name, as Vollie didn't know it either, looking for her at the same corner at unwonted hours, or the same hours but by different clubs, with his stupid gift in his pants.

When they stopped for the night outside Toledo, he went for a run down a corn road that led away from the truck stop. He ran with his shirt off to save on laundry later. The damp cold air chilled him badly. He ran away from the sun, and by the time he circled back it had set, and having no towel he let the wind dry him while he shivered. The driver already lay sleeping across the seat under a military-issue wool blanket. Vollie shut himself in the trailer and wrapped a tarp around his body for bedding and lay down with his bunched shirt for a pillow on the floor among the cargo crates of grapefruit. The piney smell hung thick in the dark like a blessing given in excess that had become a curse.

For two days on the road the driver didn't volunteer his name. Neither did Vollie, who didn't have one yet. They stopped at a wholesaler

in Akron and unloaded fruit. They swung north to Rochester and unloaded more. Vollie declined a share of the driver's meatloaf supper at a
tavern and drank only coffee that failed to revive him. After sundown,
the night before he was to meet his superiors in Bridgeport, slouching
and limp with hunger and fatigue, he was falling toward a dream when
the driver took three gasps off a Benzedrine inhaler and said, "All right,
Staff Sergeant, I'm sure you want to ask how it went for me over there."

"Not now," Vollie muttered.

"Don't you want to know what all I saw and what I did?" the driver
asked.

"Maybe another time. I need to sleep."

The driver's nerve-jangled eyes speed-read the vacant road. He activated the left signal, checked the mirrors, drew the rig halfway into
the passing lane, rechecked the mirrors, completed the lane change.
There were no signs of cars or lights save the rig's own anywhere. Then
he activated the right signal and performed the whole operation the
other way. The rig accelerated. It slowed. It accelerated again for no
evident reason. The driver started to talk inaudibly, then stopped and
swallowed. The marks on his pallid face were a matrix of uncertainties.
He watched the road as if he feared it. His mouth distorted vividly to
squelch a rising sob. His eyes welled. But he did not fully cry.

They commenced a sudden incline, yet the driver shifted into higher
gear. The engine shuttered and bucked. When he hit the inhaler twice
more, Vollie sat up and said, "Pull over the rig."

"What for?"

"Pull to the wayside. I'll drive."

"You ain't got no hauling paper, have you?"

"I've driven eighteen wheels before."

The driver said, "I'm having a rough time, Staff Sergeant."

"That's all right."

"I thought it would be different stateside."

"You're all right, citizen."

"I thought it would be like a wet sponge on the blackboard. But everything keeps getting louder, and I can't make it stop. I don't got anyone to tell. If I go home I'll fuck everybody up."

"There's a pull-off right there."

In fact it was a crawler lane for trucks on the steep grade of the mountain. The rig merged into it equivocally then swerved again into the through lane.

"Aim back toward that solid white line," Vollie said.

The rig slowed, then darted toward the roadside and came to a shuddering halt straddling the lane and shoulder. They were on an escarpment above a canoe-shaped valley. The driver popped his door.

"Check your mirror now," Vollie said.

The moment the driver poked his foot out the door, another rig, festooned with lights like a refinery at night, shot past them near enough to touch. It shed a tremor in its wake that shook the cab. The driver sucked his breath. Then he checked the mirror and climbed down to the road. He crept in front of the headlights.

Suddenly he was sprinting up the highway.

At first he ran in the crawler lane. Vollie saw him spasmodically check either shoulder as though mirrors were mounted there. He veered to the edge of the road and continued to run. The slope of the escarpment leveled, then quickly tilted up again, but he showed no signs of slowing.

While Vollie slid over the bench and oriented his feet to the pedals, the driver, evanescing in the upward-angling headlights, ran like a tireless dog.

Vollie put the rig in gear and overtook the runner by a half mile before he brought the rig to a stop again on the roadside and got out and lit a flare. He sat behind the trailer on its bumper and smoked while the hazards flashed.

A figure emerged through the intermittent shadows. It seemed to move too slowly to be a person. Creeping closer amid the red- and amber-pulsing dark, it became the revenant driver, hands in pockets, face streaked with tears and snot.

"What fool place did you think you were running to?" Vollie asked.

The driver dragged his sleeve across his nose.

Vollie picked a tobacco shred from his tongue and spat and looked at the tired boy. He was a boy now, his tears unmasked him.

"There's a house back there in the trees," the driver said with timid hope.

Vollie studied him.

"I just saw it a second ago. Maybe they'd let us in."

"Get your crazy ass in the cab."

He stood there cowering.

"I'm not going to hurt you," Vollie said.

"You say that now."

"If I miss this meeting tomorrow I got no number to call, no place to bunk, no way back on the train the other direction. Do you follow? So get back in the cab, and I'll drive us to Connecticut. I'm not going to hurt you."

Once Vollie got the rig going again, the boy, having nothing to drive, sat on his hands and quailed like a child who had been beaten a second time for crying out during his first beating.

The road materialized endlessly at the horizon of the headlights.

In the middle of the night, Vollie said, "You weren't really at Hue, were you."

The boy struggled to reimpose the air of authority he had possessed when Vollie had first climbed into the cab two days before but shortly gave up and admitted he had not been there for the battle at Tet, no. He had gone through—well, he had flown over it later on. It was a stretcher he had got used to telling. Now Vollie would never believe him about anything he said. He felt so fucked up. He really had been in those other places.

"I know it," Vollie said.

"How?"

"I believe you, that's all."

"You don't mind being lied to?"

"Not if I know it."

"The president said we were winning, and the secretary of defense said we were winning, but in private they said we were losing and we'd never win. It was in the papers black and white."

"I heard," Vollie said.

"It doesn't bother you?"

Vollie exhaled slowly through his nose, extending the many aromas in the tobacco smoke.

"I wish I could be that way," the boy said. "I mind a lot. You don't seem to mind anything. You're like the mountain under the trees."

Vollie's father had once told him that if you let someone go on believing you had a talent you didn't really have, you were worse than a braggart, you were a liar too. He said, "I mind being broke."

"Oh yeah?"

"Anymore if you're broke, what good are you?"

"Folks didn't need money before?"

"They didn't always need money for everything," Vollie said. "I hate money."

As they crossed into Connecticut, the sun jumped a low fence of gauzy cloud, and Vollie snapped the window visor down. He hadn't eaten or slept in thirty hours, but his impatient hungry mind was keen amid the rush-hour bedlam of the interstate in Hartford. From there he found his way to an AME church in Bridgeport where somebody was to meet him.

Vollie threw his bag down to the pavement. He offered the driver his hand, and they shook. The driver's face was covered in the still-pink acne scars of a body until lately flush with the hormones of growth. Only now did Vollie really look at him. He asked his name. "Clayton," the driver said. Whether it was the true name, Vollie never knew.

Then the rig was gone, and in its place lay a city street stabbed with phone poles and NO PARKING signs and NO LOITERING ANYTIME.

He sat on his bag on the sidewalk, stretching his back before the iron fence that encircled the untended churchyard, the cracked, toppled headstones lying every which way. One after another pedestrian, catching a glance at him, zagged across the three-lane avenue where the loading docks of a factory loomed in windy rust-flaked sleep.

Midday, the factory awoke. A hundred men streamed out the doors into its acres of parking lot and sat on open tailgates eating wax-papered sandwiches from Styrofoam coolers. They napped in truck beds. Cigarettes jounced in the mouths of four men playing cribbage across the hood of an LTD. From among this assembly two white men emerged, waited as a flight of traffic clamored past, and jogged across the lanes to where Vollie sat at the cemetery fence. One of them said, "Staff Sergeant, that you?"

"Yessir," Vollie said. It took a few more seconds before he recognized Lorch amid the mustache, sideburns, plaid shirt.

"You're a sight," Lorch said. "Are you hungry?"

"Naw." He could have eaten a house.

"You look like Opie the Gimp. He used to stake out Mamma's beauty parlor pleading for alms."

"I was to stay at the churchyard and wait," Vollie said.

"Good man, but you look like, Brother can you spare a dime? I wonder why."

"Sir, I never panhandled in my life."

"It's the shirt—where's your iron? Or it's the whole getup."

"Sir, in my bag," he said, hoisting it.

Lorch didn't introduce the associate, who stood watching Vollie with minute, unswerving, impassive eyes.

"At ease," Lorch said. "You're out now. Nobody cares how you keep your clothes."

"Sir, I never begged, sir."

"At ease, I said. It's lunch hour. Off we go."

Vollie had only ever encountered Lorch at Bien Hoa and at the base hospital in Saigon. To meet him now in America was vertiginous and world scrambling. He briefly suspected he was dreaming this whole encounter: soon he would meet with other such misplaced figures— squirts he had killed in combat would pass on the street; his mother would approach, not recognizing him, asking the way to the train station.

Bridgeport was strafed with sunshine, but clouds impended from the west. The sky was a brain chopped in half. Lorch's associate walked point, Vollie and Lorch following. When a bum on a corner dropped a bottle that shattered a few yards away on the sidewalk, Vollie and Lorch jumped, every bone at once, as though they were marionettes and the invisible puppeteer had sneezed. Lorch's associate reacted not at all and went on walking. He held open the door of a strangely built diner with small stools and banquettes and narrow tables on each of four cramped floors, and narrow iron staircases leading between them, steep as ship ladders. Vollie stowed his bag in the coat closet, and they all climbed to the top floor. The associate sat with his back to the wall facing the landing as the waitress climbed down below decks.

Lorch said, "Home cooking filled you out, some anyhow. I wouldn't have known you from Adam's off ox if it weren't for that bag."

Vollie read the menu.

"I have a sister used to make us all a vinegar pie every time I come home on leave," Lorch said. "It took every ounce of my self-restraint not to eat the whole thing before anybody else got to the table— Hold on. I forgot. You didn't go home, did you?"

"What were you guys doing in that plant?" Vollie said.

Lorch extracted his cutlery from the paper napkin in which it was raveled. He said, "Ask me later."

When Vollie spoke, the associate watched him intently, yet with eyes cast strangely down. Then it became evident he was following Vollie's lips, to read them.

His name was Arthur Van Aken, United States Army, retired. He had lost his hearing from an aerial attack he had called in on a ravine in Laos where he and a group of Hmong guerrillas he was working with had got pinned down. All this came out later. He was fifty-eight, with broad shoulders, but he had lost the upper body strength of youth. His movements were few and smooth, as if unguided by consciousness and untroubled by its interference. His jaw had been broken, so that he frowned—the lined, uneven frown of an old person working a seed from a molar with his tongue. His bloodshot eyes were dim and small. He had never married. He spoke, distinctly but at a whisper, when the waitress came. "Fried chicken, coleslaw, greens, water, lemonade, cobbler."

Lorch pronounced, "For the table," and offered a hand to take Vollie's menu. The waitress went away. The light changed. Their table abutted the louvered windows, but it was queerly dark in their perch under the rafters. The windows gave on the dark street below and dark torquing trees; two hunched people sprinted past with jackets on their heads: it was raining. But nowhere could you see the rain.

"We need you to get comfortable awhile," Lorch said. "Do you think you can do that? Settle down and get recognized. Bore in like a tick does. I'm aware it isn't your training to subcontract personal chores, but we need you to lay up some of your independence. Use the dry cleaner. Firstly on that shirt—what am I saying? The shirt has to go. All them stripes ain't accurate anymore. Pay the girl upstairs to simonize your car."

"I don't have a car."

"Actually, you do, and it's paid for. So's the spinet piano we found for your apartment. Play it with the window open. Let the neighbors hear."

"I forgot to ask you, bread or biscuits," the waitress announced, stopping to address Van Aken from the side.

Van Aken didn't see her.

Lorch said, "Get your teeth cleaned and make a follow-up appointment—biscuits, thank you, honey." He waited as the girl went away. "With the car comes a loan to buy the car, ergo a credit history. When you get yourself a speeding ticket, your name goes on the rolls of the local sinners. That might serve you later. 'For all have sinned and come short.' Romans three, verse twenty-three. I'm saying don't hide. If our subject is anywhere down there, he's probably under a bridge or a park bench. You'll never hear a word about him if you make yourself a homebody."

Van Aken continued with his statuary stare. He had picked up lip-reading in a year. You couldn't tell whether the eyes had their graven stillness from disposition or from training. They were like the eyes of a lieutenant commander from Naval Intelligence to whom Vollie had once made a report, an old-timer trained before the era of subminiature cameras to memorize whole documents at a sitting. An indifferent, acquisitive stare. It didn't say, I see or understand you. It said, You will never escape the consequences of what you are doing right now; I will have the evidence, and I will not forget.

The waitress labored up the ship ladder carrying the chicken, legs and thighs only, the crust thick as barnacles. The men fell to, dabbing with paper napkins at the grease in their whiskers.

Shortly, Vollie had cleaned his plate. He took two more thighs and ate.

"I hope you're happy with your assignment," Lorch said. "We can't afford you to be disappointed, dissatisfied, disabused."

"I'm well-enough appointed," Vollie said.

The rain had stopped. Women and men went bareheaded below the window. From here you saw not their faces but their hats and swinging arms and foreshortened legs.

The cobbler arrived. Lorch asked the waitress to bring them some ice cream. He remembered aloud the greater and lesser ice creams of his youth in the town of Alpharetta, now an Atlanta suburb. "I like that you're not even going to ask what they want with our subject, are you?" Lorch said.

Vollie ate his cobbler.

"You don't think to ask *why*?"

"It doesn't interest me, sir."

Lorch seemed disappointed Vollie would not ask for what he would not have disclosed even if he knew it. "It's only natural to have some curiosity with respect to *why* or *wherefore*."

"Maybe I'm not natural."

"Everybody's natural is the whole notion of natural. And you out there for months or a year following orders without even a question, that's a little—you really don't care?"

"Why should I ask? You'd have to lie."

"Among ourselves," Lorch said, "we tell the truth. Leviticus nineteen, eleven. Colossians three, nine. Revelation twenty-two, fifteen. 'For without are dogs, and sorcerers, and whoremongers, and murderers, and idolaters, and whosoever loveth and maketh a lie.' That's *without*. You're within a family now."

"I don't hold it against you, sir. It's your job to lie."

"A job—what are the *ideals* in a job? Listen, there's an immediate customer for this intelligence. Do I know the immediate customer is the ultimate customer? Of course not. That doesn't mean I'm lying. If I don't tell you something, I'm just not telling it to you. But if I do tell you, it's the truth. You do likewise and we'll make great product. Arthur has some background on our subject to give you now."

Van Aken sipped his coffee. He was older than Lorch. He didn't care whether Vollie believed any of this. He put the cup on the table. He said, "We don't write any of this down."

"I understand," Vollie said.

"We pay attention the first time."

"Yessir."

"I'm not your superior," Van Aken said. "I'm retired."

THE DEAF MAN then reduced the unfortunate life of Egon Hugo Haus-mann to so few basic data points that it could hardly have been worth his trouble to be lying. Born, Budapest 1894. Orphaned at nineteen. Exiled shortly thereafter to Athens. In September 1965, broke and coughing blood, he had entered the Manhattan office of the Immigra-tion and Naturalization Service at 20 West Broadway, requesting resi-dency papers. The request was denied. Deportation proceedings were initiated but then frustrated by the problem that Hausmann had no papers from any other country to which he could be returned. Anyway, by then he had disappeared.

More recently, a woman named Sandy Colt, claiming to share an address with Hausmann in Queens, had filed a Social Security claim on his behalf. This claim had failed because no Social Security number could be produced and no one by the claimant's name appeared on the rolls. Colt's repeated appeals had led a validation investigator to refer the case as a possible attempted fraud to the Office of the Inspector General of the Social Security Administration. By then, however, the Department of Health had already fined her for running a flophouse out of her apartment. And by the time the SSA investigator knocked on her door, she had kicked out whatever tenants she once had had, prob-ably from fear of being deported, since she had no papers herself.

As to how Hausmann looked, they had only the description in the INS report: white male, six feet tall, one hundred thirty pounds. The picture of him in the file had come unglued and was lost.

After Van Aken had finished, Lorch waited for Vollie to betray any signs of having digested the broad strokes of another's life.

Vollie said, "Where's my car, sir? Parked on the street in Queens?"

"You want to act like all you're doing is taking orders," Lorch said. "A fair position. You're getting paid. Money does tend to focus an asset's energies, but I have to tell you, in our experience it can't sustain them over the long term. A deeper sense of purpose is required. Yet because the customer's motivations are classified, I can't provide you directly with a sense of mission-purpose. So we have a challenge.

"Let me give you another example. Some of my friends who work in the strategic planning outfits at DOD have concluded—and this might offend you—that we have . . . not made a success in Vietnam. And their diagnosis—I admit this took me aback—is that it was the vivid *absence* of this sense of mission-purpose among the society writ large that has led to what they call the"—an intake of breath and a summoning of nerve to say the word aloud—"*failure* of our project there. It never occurred to me the defense of our constitutional liberties against murderers and collectivists wasn't a sufficiently vivid threat to focus our will. But that is their conclusion. Political opposition in itself didn't stop us. Political opposition was a *fungus* that grew in the absence of a shining goal that could obliterate all doubt. Do you remember what they used to say the 'U.S.' stood for in your Yankee general U.S. Grant? *Unconditional Surrender.* There was no mistaking his objective. What is your objective?"

"Sir, I am immaterial," Vollie said.

"Good marine. Why should you care? Except I think you might care anyway, because of the money. Because you probably never agreed to take money for a job and didn't do the work. You're vain that way. There's why I like you. And you obviously know how to handle a certain amount of solitude, not one of my talents. Even so, for this job, as you want to call it, you'll have to give a damn to do it proper."

"Sir, this man means nothing to me."

"But the *money* means something to you. You can't help it in your angry bones," Lorch said. "Also you see a person either dead or getting ready to die with none of his own people close at hand. And you see a reflection there."

"You guys think I think life has let me down," Vollie said. "It hasn't. I've had a lot. I've had more than my share."

"Your mother taught you manners." Pause. For all Lorch's motor-mouthing, he had mastered the insidious pause, the moment of letting the hook go in, letting the barb get snagged in the gum, and setting it with a jerk. He said, "You might better have taken some home cooking while you still could have, back at home."

"Sir, fuck you," Vollie said. "What were you doing in that plant?"

"Whatever it is I do," Lorch said. He made his smile of innocent satisfaction. "Sometimes we're in the structure a long time and come out. Sometimes we're out a long time and go in, like you're going in. And sometimes we enter the back door and pass right through to the front and out, and never break stride. And who's to know we weren't in there for a hundred years waiting for just now to come out? And who's to know whether we walked out, or broke out, or somebody unlocked the cell door and said, You're free to go?"

BELOW THEIR PERCH, the postrain midday heat was making the pavement steam, the kind of misty heat that used to mean the corn was about to spurt like mad. Now there was no corn to nag the mind. And wet heat mostly meant defoliated jungle ravines, waiting, nausea from the chloroquine pills the men all took to poison the malaria swimming in their blood.

The check came. Lorch scrawled long division on the placemat, figuring the tip. A silence ensued while the planet of Vollie's mind rotated inexorably. Sun overtook the part of him that hoped. He could no longer resist asking the question that had brought him here: "Am I nobody from nowhere yet?"

That was when Van Aken handed him the envelope, warm from the man's jacket. It was exactly the manila envelope with blue border that Lorch had promised in Saigon, of the kind cinched by a length of ruby-red string figure-eighted around two buttons. Vollie unwound it.

Lorch capped his pen. He said, "You are Sergeant Dwight Elliot Tilly, born 1948 in Davenport, Iowa. Sorry for the demotion."

"Davenport!" Vollie said.

"Best to keep the region of origin. Folks hear it when you talk. What's the matter with Davenport?"

"My folks didn't like it."

"We got your honorable discharge, and no reserve time," Lorch said.

Vollie looked through the IDs, the payment booklet on a loan for a '66 Buick Electra, the insurance policies, the discharge papers, the baptismal certificate. There were documents from an Illinois law firm establishing an as-yet-unfunded trust, and there were dental records and proofs of vaccination against childhood diseases. Words in ink on card stock and carbons, some crisp, some folded and smudged with seeming age. The truth invented. The name and dates. The words the wish had conjured. The woman listed as the mother. The blank unfilled for the father. The letters of the name. The person begotten from a faceless crowd.

THAT AFTERNOON, a train clattered southwest from Bridgeport, stopping in Fairfield, Rowayton, Darien, Cos Cob. A mostly empty, off-peak train that carried a crew of office painters; a suburban opera club; a man at a window seat in a tired Marine Corps shirt, craning to catch the names of the stations. A grown man not one day old. He had the eager eyes of a boy who, never having betrayed anyone, foresaw no harm coming his way, no one seeking atonement or revenge.

The train turned south, following the coast. It stopped in Mamaroneck, Pelham; densely built places, abounding in parked cars, where no people walked the streets. Sculpted trees and blue sky.

He was alive now in his body alone, and in the memory of no one.

The track bed sunk below street level. The retaining walls of a granite trench crowded the racing train. He had hoped to see the great city from a distance, the bridges and office towers, but the walls of the trench came still closer, choking out the sunlight within the car, where blue paper seat checks littered the floor. A final burst of sun as the train crossed a river.

Land again: a new trench, deeper.

Then all turned black as the train went truly underground.

He disembarked at Grand Central Station, secure among the schools of commuters swimming in their lanes, at home as in the throng of the Saigon junk bazaar. He was already a part of the city without ever having seen it.

He would take the Number 7 train east into Queens. He would apply for work at a transmission shop, a Pontiac dealership, finally an ice cream warehouse. The city would seem the whole world, its boundaries the boundaries of space; time likewise would seem to stretch to the horizon of time, as if the people here had never been born and never died, and his place among them—a man of perfect inconsequence—were permanent.

6

POSITION SOUGHT: PRACTICAL NURSE

Ursuline High School student seeks 15hrs/wk. First
position. Will learn all. Prompt, clean. Experience:
bathing/feeding people, mending, fundamentals of
cookery (excl. pastries, sauces, roasts). Touch typing
54 w/m (improving). Own bus pass. Call Trisha: MV
5-3416. Amen.

The girl stood at the chain-link gate of the three-family house
studying a stenographer's notebook. She wore vinyl pumps with
bright grosgrain bows across the vamps; an A-line dress, yellow with
pink piping; linen gloves that buttoned at the wrist. A tied goat regarded her from behind the fence, then went back to chewing the cat-
brier that grew all over the ragged yard. A few milk crates of stripped
paperbacks had overturned in the weeds; the pages were bloated and
gnawed. The girl studied her notebook. She breathed. The bent head

and tense neck did not move. She continued to study in a state of no skeletal motion for as long as a minute while the wind made her ponytail wigwag like a captured snake. She filed the notebook in her handbag. She climbed the stoop and knocked.

It was the woman Sandy Colt who showed her in.

The apartment, ground floor, was like a chicken coop, squalid and fertile smelling. Discs of pressed foundation powders shriveled on the sills. In the sink, an old cake. Along the hall floors, levees of cellophane, pencil boxes, hosiery, record sleeves. Jars of sand evidently collected from deserts on four continents and labeled as such with embossing tape. Six rooms, each of them somehow the living room, with an appliance that didn't belong, in the corner. The tub did not share quarters with the commode. Sleep seemed once to have transpired in every room. Quilts and bed pillows were stacked or splayed about all the radiators; a cot by the stove.

The girl followed Miss Colt as she cleared a footpath through the potted cacti, flip-flops, worn pocketbooks, carpet samples, reticulate canvas folded lawn furniture. The place was arranged less as a home of discrete rooms than a warren of contiguous lairs. Hinges remained in some of the interior doorjambs, but the doors themselves had been removed. You might believe you were picking your way to the rear of the apartment only to find you had circled back to the front. They made their way to a curtained closet. Pushing through its many naphthalene-smelling dresses, you found an opening had been cut through the back wall leading to a short passage. And you wouldn't have taken this cramped space for more than a dead end used to store newspapers and yarn unless you noticed a recess in the wainscoting, darkened by the grease of prying fingertips. With a tug here, a portion of the wall became a miniature door. To fit under the low lintel of this final doorway, Miss Colt stooped into black space. The girl followed.

When the light came on, he was lying there. Just lying there alone.

An old man on a stained mattress, evidently almost naked beneath a

SALVATORE SCIBONA

tangle of afghans. His white whiskers were yellow at the corners of the
mouth. The peeling chest had sunk. The exposed stomach rose feebly
with his breath. A toxic fungoid smell. There were no windows. There
was a low-watt floor lamp. There was no furniture save the bed and this
lamp. The man looked like—who was it who smacked Jesus on the way
to the cross and was damned to walk the earth without salvation or
sleep until the Second Coming? He sat up and spoke foreignly. The
eyes roamed in evident nonseeing. He pleaded in whatever the language. Miss Colt, when questioned as to what he wanted, said, "How
should I know?"

The Wandering Jew. Which a creeping plant had been named for
him also. He said the thing, whatever it was, insistently, again, the eyes
imprecisely following Miss Colt's movements in his all-but-blindness
and decrepitude, in the light of the lamp lacking a shade. The eyes
swerving to the cramped doorway as though noticing the second person
there and making his appeal in that direction.

Nobody understanding him. People in the room looking and talking, two people, not one; but neither understanding him. The tall person, the usual one; and a stripling girl holding a notebook.

MISS COLT SAID she disliked the name Trisha and preferred Trisha's
middle name, Agnieszka, though it was Polish. Having been born in
Poland and got away from there with her life, Miss Colt had long since
forsworn all things Polish, from friends to church to language, and insisted on translating the name to Agnes. When Trisha felt compelled to
correct her pronunciation of the velar-to-alveolar consonants in the
middle of that name, Miss Colt changed the name she used again, to
Alice, with which she was most satisfied.

That summer, Trisha and the old woman, who had hired her to help
look after Mr. Hausmann—her tenant or patient or prisoner or whatever he was—were again watching a CYO Big Brothers basketball game

128

from the makeshift benches the parish had set up on the defunct el, where the view of the game was unsurpassed and even some of the fathers came after work to watch, if they were still attached in some manner to the boys. A rule prohibited the fathers from playing.

Low sun. The Dopplering howl of a passenger jet, screaming as it departed the city. The muggy wind off the bay smelled of molasses.

"Alice, that boy's fingers are too long, Alice. Be wary of them. I do not like them." Miss Colt did not need to indicate which boy. For Trisha there existed only the one boy forever, and not even him, because of her calling. He was not only the only boy she would ever love, he was the only boy she would ever need to prohibit herself from loving. This magnified the normal monomaniacal focus of a fourteen-year-old's crush to a harrowing degree.

She said with a vigorous wave, "I don't have to worry about his hands, we're only friends. And I'm giving my life to the Lord, so none of that matters. You don't know anything about him, pardon my saying."

"Him the boy, Marlon, or him the Lord?"

Trisha said softly, "Marlon."

"And you do know somethings about him?" Miss Colt said, licking her custard. "That are?"

"Nobody knows him for real. All they know is *gossip*."

"Alice, you are not really going into any convent really, Alice. You have been deterred regarding one boy and him with fingers wrapping halfway around the ball. See? Unnatural. The mischief of the hand, imagine it, while with the other you can't even imagine—sinister— what it can do. You are in all cases of a different level than this Marlon. With respect to mother and father both in the home. I admired you making up your mind to go to the promenade. He was just a *way* to go to the promenade in really truth, however." She said with command, "Next time you go, but with someone else."

"One just says 'prom.'"

"Do you know why his mother is in prison? That Marlon's?"

"She is *not*. She's in a rehabilitation hospital." Trisha looked away at the other girls watching Marlon from the el and despised them.

"How old are you?"

Miss Colt returned as often as she did to this question out of sadism probably, to make Trisha repeat the lie she had committed during their first interview. It was not in the woman's nature to forget a number.

"Sixteen," Trisha averred.

"Do you know what they do to sixteen-year-old girls in the cloister? Whole books have been written for centuries about the depravity. And paintings painted. Depraved paintings in very important European art books at the library."

Trisha breathed, looking down at the blacktop. Marlon accepted the ball, which directly sprung away from him toward a teammate on the Shirts who laid up to the basket and was fouled by a sinewy older character on Skins, a white man new to the game in recent months, a veteran, which people had assumed from the tight way of the haircut and the polish on the work boots when he delivered ice cream for the Breyers warehouse. A tattoo of some military or patriotic kind was evident now in his half-clothed state. Marlon and the other Shirts, each in succession slapping the shooter's hand, gathered around the key, bent, and panted.

The thoughtless urgency Marlon radiated standing at midcourt, just dribbling and looking, gave Trisha the impression of a dense object bending space-time around it. The ball came to him from the outer reaches of the solar system, and he put it in orbit around him and made the other boys and men revolve in epicycles merely by calling the play with a hand sign. The ball didn't descend from his hand and bounce as he dribbled, it leapt to his fingers, and he threw it away, and it flew back as if it loved him.

The physical proximity of this boy drove Trisha mad.

"Alice, listen, Alice. I am not well enough acquainted with your"—Miss Colt looked below at the speeding Falcons, Corvairs, Biscaynes, Bonnevilles, and Skylarks for the word she wanted—"with your spirit to pronounce on your vocation."

"Thank you."

"However, it is *inevitable* that you will have sexual intercourses. Vocation or no, promenade or no, Marlon or no, yes or no, *no* or no. In all cases it impends." She raised a fist overhead and brought it down, slugging the palm at her belly. "It is a force that descends on us all."

"Please don't be disgusting," Trisha said, as wanton fantasies carried on in her sex-mad mind, while other parts of her consciousness convulsed with chastity and reproach.

"The mother was a fence on which radios were hanging," Miss Colt remarked.

"*What?*"

"That Marlon's mother. Where they sell a stolen item by fencing, or is it on top of a fence? She was a fencer. She fenced."

Trisha turned her wrist inward and looked at her watch. "We should go home. I always give Mr. Hausmann his oats by eight."

"How would he know the time!"

"It isn't right his supper should wait because I wanted to watch a dumb boy play a game."

"But the sun is *divine.*"

"So stay," Trisha said.

"No, I will go with you."

"Stay. You like to watch more than I do."

"Because you insist, I will go with you," Miss Colt said.

Trisha was a member of the parish, but Miss Colt was not anymore. She had joined the Jehovah's Witnesses and always looked about warily on the el as if a priest might run her off. But it was a porous parish where people joined and left all the time as the borders of the surrounding neighborhoods shifted year to year. At present, white blocks extended to the east, black to the south and west, some Dominican and Mexican and some more mixed-up blocks to the north, with the parish and its basketball court in the middle like the paneled column of a merry-go-round.

A young woman got out of an Impala that had stopped at the curb. One of Marlon's gaggle of sisters, pointless to discern which one—Trisha's jealousy extended even to them. They shared everything: clothes, apartment, the old Impala that Marlon washed and waxed weekly, and Marlon himself, who had been their common doll but now had found his God-given feet and wished to walk on his own, where and when he chose. Trisha understood; the sisters did not.

A break in play.

Miss Colt and Trisha climbed off the girders and went home.

The Shirts passed among themselves a saltcellar, a knife, a brown paper lunch bag from which peaches were extracted. Somebody had connected several lengths of garden hose and found a working spigot in the settlement of brown brick apartment complexes that surrounded the court, the cinderblock walls of transmission shops, television repair, plumbing supply, rug cleaning, alleys no wider than a swinging door. The hose water came on. Each took his turn at the spout, swallowing heavily and aiming the current over his skull.

After the game, the Impala and Marlon's sister, wearing a sleeveless housedress, its pattern washed out, were still waiting at the curb as he departed the chain-link cage of the court. He approached her, shaking the sweat from the long hands, his long neck hanging down while she harangued him, smoking. They got in the car. The engine turned over and burbled and spat. It drove off through the twilight—

Through the dense world. The auto exhaust and rust blowing off the el girders plastered with faded advertisements for milk on sale, enameled aluminum Bundt pans, ratchet sets. Puddles with mosquito larvae seahorsing in teeming hordes in the runoff from garbage piles. The euphoric dismay of car horns. A pretty woman in old clothes catching a breeze on the stoop, smoking and teasing out the knots from the hair of a five-year-old not exactly the same color as she was, both of them crinkle-eyed and sated from supper and bandy-legged on the steps, watching the street; one of the mothers who was still going to be sexy a few more years, one of the daughters with hair incomprehensible to the mother who'd borne her. Everywhere people coming out on the stoop while the breeze passed, the houses ovenlike inside. A girl wheeling a crippled and gasping old woman onto the stoop, then going in and coming out again with a wire-backed chair for herself and a bowl of ice chips and slipping them into the ancient invalid's face, and the uncomprehending eyes alive for a second of pleasure, sucking ice, the cold itself a kind of sustenance. A boy who worked third shift, maintenance, maybe he was nineteen—a couple of years before, his ass would have been sunk in a rice paddy, born too late, lucky him—on the stoop now, the breeze all around, sitting with a pile of scrambled eggs and half-cooked onions in his lap, and coffee. His breakfast hour.

People are standing on the stoops now. The boy stands up and keeps eating: even the steps are hot. The heat off the buildings just blazing. Better to stand up than sit on the sandstone so less of you is touching it. A lot of people outside standing up. You'd think there was a parade coming. You'd think something was about to happen. To be from here and not to have left when you had the chance, before you got entangled in human reproduction or some kind of decent work if you could find it is to say, I don't need anything to happen. My brother, my mother, my car, my gang from school, their girlfriends, their boyfriends, their kids—what's the matter with all that?

Twilight.

This time of year the light is a long time lingering. One particular affiliation of street rats, age twelve to fifteen, is dickering with somebody's car on the street. Talk about hot—that's your back on the Queens asphalt, August, under an engine that was running a few minutes ago.

Their business is curbside oil change while you wait. They'll even do the filter if you have a few minutes for one of them to sprint to the auto-parts store on Marion Boulevard. They have several boosted cases of Pennzoil 10W-40, and for draining, a discarded aluminum turkey roasting pan, and because people live here and watch, they will not dump your former oil down the storm drain, they will dump it a few blocks away in any unobserved patch of exposed earth—in the public cemetery (the one already full to capacity where the dead don't mind) or in the needle park—or sometimes will dribble it in a barrel with gathered trash under the highway and set it on fire, watching the fire, and watching it, and watching in bottomless transfixion, with the ancient mind we carry around that knows the myths about fire to be true, a body could go into the fire and burn down and rise up again in a new shape, a truer shape; watching the flames, the flickering faces around the burning drum, the hundred thousand cars crawling the highway, until on the service road the signature orthogonal Crown Vic gaze of cop-car headlights approaches and they book the fuck out of there. This is cheaper fun than driving around, what with gas more expensive than champagne or cognac or some shit.

It is possible to attract swirling bats by throwing a neon-bright tennis ball high into the air. And this is taking place up on the corner. A smart-dressed old colored lady hobbles by, and those wooing the bats pause while she passes and touch their baseball hats in deference to smart clothes on a weeknight, which may mean she's headed to a wake, although in fact she's only going to the Kingdom Hall for fellowship, and Kool-Aid, and pralines. And when she gets there, in the funky meeting room where the windows don't open, and they sit around the table, heads bent to scripture, a brother reads through the whir of the dehumidifier that the Evil One controls the whole earth. But a sister testifies the son of God came to destroy the Devil's work. And God has chosen Jesus Christ to rule the world. And they pass around the meeting table a crackling cellophane container, lined in dainty corrugated wax paper, of Lorna Doones and study how Satan's rulership will end. The chains of their reading glasses droop, or they hold a magnifying glass to the page, pencils hovering, at a Formica-topped table where the Entenmann's strudel box sits on a dish out of anyone's convenient reach in the middle of the table like a baby about to be sacrificed to propitiate the false god Diabetes.

What will the world be like after its evil ruler is removed?

Whatever force that knows to light the streetlights has not yet turned them on. If you are watching the twilight and waiting for the street-lights because you are the mother, and the time of the coming on of the lights is the drop-dead latest time for your child to report back to the house, then it is possible something has gone perilously wrong with the administration of the city of New York insofar as surely the ap-pointed hour has come, and still you are waiting in the darkening, while the careless receptacle of your life's effort is hidden someplace among the alleys treating his life as though it has no value for anybody but him. A man is busting up an armchair in the alley, and with every blow of the hammer, cigarette ashes, cat hair, decades of human skin cells come flying about him in the light leaking from the window of the house adjacent. And newspapers somersault all down the street on ac-count of a trash can dumped by nobody saw who. The houses having got still hotter and the people coming out in the dark, the stoops seem-ing darker when the cars sometimes pass with their headlights on, so why has the city not taken notice, the administration, the responsible parties? The whole street thick with life. How can you stand to stay inside? Here and there a transistor radio, not too loud, sort of a smooth pulsing, very discreet and continuous. People like to listen to music while the wind comes in. Merengue. Claude Debussy. Eartha Kitt. Or TV, keeping TV on in another room for the feeling of a window that looks through the wall on more deliberate lives, the way the people on TV pay more attention to what they're doing than you have to pay at-tention to them and it makes you godlike in your lofty privilege, to listen to them frantically solve their crimes or to shut them off, and the way the familiar theme music lets you know where all this is happening and whether it's sad or funny or innocent or retrospectful and heartsick about the old days when wood burned under the teapot and John-Boy hunted pheasant with the dog. Now the first of the mothers comes out to say to a football game in the street that when you can't see the ball anymore, it's time to come in. Then comes the countersuit: if they're allowed to play a little longer, the boys and girls in the street, the streetlights will come on, and they'll see the ball that way. This sort of temporizing will fail because it isn't really to the dark itself that the mothers are referring. It is to the fact of the lights coming on. The way, in older places, church bells toll important hours. My children do not play in the street after the lights have come on; I was raised right. Somebody's aerial has a motor attached at the base and can be seen to rotate like a Martian weapon of low-budget film slowly toward the TV signal of another city. A Phillies fan maybe, judging by the southwesterly inclination of the antenna. Not too much extra noise just now. The settling in of night like ecumenical holy time, like Thanksgiving dinner. Not a lot of background hustle. A woman carries a skillet of smoking grease onto the fire escape and leaves it on the grating. An armada of gulls high overhead going back toward the East River after a long day's landside scavenge. These are commuter gulls that spend the nights on the water off Throggs Neck or farther out in the Sound.

In the spillover light from a kitchen window, the veteran from Davenport in the Midwest, Tilly, bends and combs his keys. He plucks one and shakes out the jangling ring and inserts it in the door under the stoop, under the sandstone facade on which graffiti announce the affiliations of local youth.

In the lock, he turns the key.

There are girls up the street, Spanish girls who watch him from their stoops, watch him and others come and go, learn and trade the jobs and names and relations. A man who lives that way, alone that way, at least he ought to have a dog. None of them knows the first name. He has the initials D.E.T. stitched in red cursive on the tan shirts of the ice-cream warehouse where he works, and because of this job and his unyielding looks, some of the kids call him the Iceman. Most folks call him by the last name, the family name, a distinction reserved for those without family.

He has opened the lock and gone in and closed the door behind him. He is on the inside for now.

All the streetlights come on at once.

7

She called herself Sandy Colt, but the DPs all had changed their names. She wore squarish glasses with a bar across the bridge. Blocky shoes. She didn't care about shoes. Trisha admired this indifference to fashion and would have liked to share it but could not yet; her soul was still coming into flower; she hoped soon to love only the best things: mercy, justice.

From the middle of Miss Colt's forearm to the adductor muscle that closed her large thumb over the palm there extended a scar (Trisha coveted it)—the result not of a failed suicide but of a successful escape nearly thwarted by concertina wire. Such escapes had made the woman both sympathetic to persons in flight, living out of doors, and able to see the profit that could be extracted from them. She seemed to forget nothing. The dates of battles and earthquakes; an appointment made six months earlier, in passing, on a bus. If you found a book of yours among the rest on her shelves, or amid the cliffs of printed matter that amounted to shelves along the flanks of her apartment, she made no pretense of having misunderstood you had wanted the book back. She was taking it. It was hers now. She had lived everywhere. She had survived.

The country was still young enough to swallow whole lives, criminal or merely collapsed lives, and leave the changeful human animal, whatever money he might have, and his clothes. Such people as the men who used to pay fifty cents a night to sleep on her floor could live a long time undetected amid the polyglot streets here, in plain sight while underground, aging faster than their years. If the conditions in her would-be rooming house were known to have been squalid, her lodgers had fared no better once the Department of Health discovered her operation and made her evict them. Most now lived again on the street or under it.

On one of these luckless souls, however, she had taken a grudging pity: Hausmann, who by the time the rest had decamped could no longer get to his feet, as she had once confided to Trisha. If the city inspectors should return—as they warned they might at any hour—and find a single other soul sleeping there, Miss Colt would be turned over to higher authorities. That Hausmann no longer had a cent to pay her mattered for nothing with these people. On the other hand, the fact that she could be persecuted for her righteousness in sheltering him made her the more likely, in her reading of scripture, to inherit the kingdom of heaven.

Trisha sort of agreed—she felt a solidarity with anybody who risked herself for the sake of what was right—but nothing the old woman might have said could excuse her bewildering lack of domestic hygiene.

"I disagree it smells *bad*," Trisha said to Lizzy, her friend. "Old people can't help the way their houses smell."

"Irrelevant whether she can help it," Lizzy said. "I call a spade a spade."

"It smells like when we went to visit your cousin at New Paltz. Like the bathroom in the dorm. It doesn't smell bad, it smells loud."

"I call a stink a stink."

"But she won't let me clean *anything*. It isn't fair to Mr. Hausmann, even if he's a fugitive or whatever you think."

The two girls approached the caged blacktop where the boys were already shouting, moving around the court in the slithery way they did before the game began. The girls climbed the stairs of the el to see if Miss Colt was occupying the seat where she often took the afternoon sun, but the old woman was not there. She could only be off studying some doomsday brochure at the Kingdom Hall with the other heretics. And Marlon was not playing, so they continued to walk.

Lizzy, adjusting the big flower she had been wearing ever since her father had taken her to Samoa on a business trip, said, "Once, Daddy and I were in a plane flying over the Rocky Mountains?"

"Here we go," Trisha said.

"And it was night? Like totally black under the plane."

"Again with the mountains."

Lizzy blushed but continued. "And you could see the cities where the light was?"

"How did you know you were over the mountains if it was so black?"

"The pilot told us so on the intercom. And by the bathroom I saw the escape hatch? The big red handle it has? And I go to myself, Who's to stop you from getting a parachute and dropping into the Rockies and starting all over on nuts and berries, and I don't know, trapping and like that?"

Trisha had wearied of this particular pipe dream. She raked her eyes jitteringly up the street. Marlon was nowhere to be seen. "So you think Mr. Hausmann jumped out of a plane?" Trisha asked.

"After his own fashion, don't you think?"

"Why would he do that?"

Lizzy said, "Because either he didn't have anybody to stop him or he wasn't afraid."

Lizzy had hardly any bust, and what she did have was not in balance yet, the one side with the other. Once, Trisha had admitted in confession that she enjoyed walking with Lizzy as much because she loved Lizzy as because Lizzy's cockeyed bosom made her own look more attractive by comparison. Plus, boys must find Lizzy's flower dumb. The priest had congratulated her and told her that to confess her sin against Lizzy this way was in fact to love Lizzy. The key was never to forget you were likely to let people down: one of the ways we loved people was by studying our wickedness toward them.

On Miss Colt's porch, Trisha retrieved a key from under the concrete gargoyle planter that overflowed with crabgrass and pizza parlor coupons and spent matches and a single bright dandelion that presided above on its stalk like the good deed in the naughty world. Lizzy plucked the weed-flower and ejected it into the yard. They went inside. For all Lizzy's fun-making of Trisha's stupid job, Lizzy seemed magnetized by Mr. Hausmann's disgusting old body and on more than one afternoon had stood in the doorway of his secret compartment, dumbstruck while Trisha washed his hair or pared his nails. Mr. Hausmann only occasionally looked toward the doorway as if he recognized another person was there. Because Lizzy never spoke in his presence, she considered herself successfully hidden. She had cleverly refashioned the shyness that had overtaken her during the first months of high school into an alluring and sort of intimidating sexy stare, mute and unreadable, which she practiced around Mr. Hausmann and other men and boys, and which incensed Trisha because it made her have to do all the idiotic talking for the both of them, while Lizzy could stand there bewitching whoever he was with no work at all, as if her breasts matched.

While Trisha was preparing the old man's oatmeal in the room called the kitchen because the stove was in it, she spied, half buried in a bucket of clothespins, a box of Domino brown sugar, petrified for unknowable years. She scoured some on his oats. The two girls hovered over the old man to see if he would notice this adjustment in his regimen. His jaw slowly churned like a steer's with his cud. The tongue clapped against the roof of the mouth. The eyes still closed, the orbs meandering beneath the lids. Lizzy adjusted the strap of her handbag on her shoulder, peering from behind Trisha's head. The room smelled of Hausmann's effluvia, of the oats, of dust, of Lizzy's heady flower. Hausmann's Adam's apple rose. The oats could be heard squishily entering his gullet. The nostrils pulsated. Tears emerged from one closed eye. They streamed around the meager fat of the nostril.

In a distant room, a record began to play. It was a song called "Innsbruck, I Must Leave Thee." Lizzy went away to investigate it. She found Miss Colt in the kitchen dribbling whiskey into a glass of iced tea. Without turning around to see who had really come in, Miss Colt said, "Hello, Alice darling," and sipped the drink. A gush of sigh blew out of her. Her head and shoulders drooped as though deflated. She unrolled her stockings. She said, "My dogs are not hunting anymore."

"How's that?" Lizzy asked.

"Elizabeth!" Miss Colt said, turning around. "I thought you were our Alice. Come talk to me while God curses my feet. Make yourself sandwich."

"No, thank you."

"Come sit and tell me about your flower today."

"Where did he come from, Mr. Hausmann in there?"

"Germany, I believe."

"Was he like a Nazi and killed a lot of Jews?"

"Yes, I believe he did."

Lizzy said, "B.S."

"Ask serious question, get serious answer."

"You're only trying to teach me a lesson about don't be flip."

"Have it in your way then."

"What do you mean you *believe*?"

"I regard as true."

"So you're guessing."

"There were millions of Nazis. Where do you think they all went?"

As though Miss Colt had beaten her, Lizzy said, "Today's flower is a peony."

"Argentina could not be expected to hold every one of them, could she? I met Nazis in Argentina. Obvious Nazis. And in Uruguay and in

Baja Peninsula of California which is in Mexico. Obvious Nazis with accent and foreheads dented from obviously bullets. Nazis now are onions in stew, disintegrated, everywhere."

"Omar gave the flower to me."

"Congratulations! It's enormous. You must be so proud! Do you plan them ahead to match your ensemble?"

"You know Omar, from the newsstand by Firestone Tires? He gives it to me early in the morning, and I go back home and pick the right dress for whatever the flower."

Trisha appeared, soaked the oatmeal bowl in an adjacent room, and stood in the doorway until Miss Colt said, "Go back in there and talk to him."

"He's asleep," Trisha said.

"You don't know that."

Lizzy, using the brave blunt tone that Trisha had long coveted, but that Lizzy had lately forgotten how to use in the company of men and boys, said, "Miss Colt, why are you hiding him?"

"Who says he is hidden?"

"If you aren't hiding him, why do you keep him in his secret box?"

"You have reached the age of showing off ankles and shoulders and whatever other pretty parts. Later you will reach the age of privacy. To lie alone in the dark will be sweet."

"Then why shouldn't we talk about him to other people?" Here was the old Lizzy, daring to ask what Trisha shrank from asking. Trisha knew it was only Miss Colt's dispute with the Department of Health, which she had not allowed to overrule her compassion for the old man, that necessitated this secrecy but had never told Lizzy. A confidence was a confidence.

"Privacy," Miss Colt said. "Privacy, that is all."

"Miss Colt says Mr. Hausmann was a Waffen SS," Lizzy told Trisha.

"Already the child is embellishing on me," Miss Colt said with bemused indignation.

"No, he wasn't," Trisha said.

"Miss Colt believes he was."

"Embellishing with the big beautiful penny in her hair."

"He was not," Trisha insisted.

"How would you know?" Miss Colt asked. "Enter back in there and talk to him."

"He told me is how."

"What did he tell you?" Miss Colt asked derisively.

"Where he came from and like that."

"Oh yes? Where did he come from?" Miss Colt asked.

Trisha tried to speak plain and strong as Lizzy would. "From Greece."

"You never told me that," Lizzy said.

Miss Colt intently turned the ice in her tea, watching Trisha.

"But he was born someplace else," Trisha said.

Miss Colt said, "He *talked* with you?"

"Yes, a couple of times. Why, is he not supposed to?"

"How did he talk with you?"

"What do you mean, how? With his mouth is how."

Miss Colt refreshed her tea straight from the whiskey bottle. She said, "He talked to you with English."

"No, in Greek. I only understand here and there. He isn't very good at it, but neither am I. I tried it out and he answered me. What are we supposed to do all afternoon? I finish my homework, and you won't let me organize or sweep. Is he a prisoner that I can't talk to him?"

"Why are you with Greek? And I thought you were Poles in your house and you spoke only English."

"That's my father's father, the Polish one. His mother came from Athens. Mommy is from the Dominican. I don't, like, study Greek. I'm better at French where we take it in school, but I tried French on him and he just lay there dying."

"Why are you with French?" Miss Colt said, annoyed. "What happened to Latin for schoolgirls?"

"They make us learn a useful language now," Lizzy said.

"*Useful.* I thought it was religious school, but in fact it is vocational where you attend," she sneered. "Then where did he go?"

Lizzy took the pin out of the flower and adjusted it and put the pin back in, all without moving any part of herself except her arms and hands. She was practicing her fornication stare.

"After Greece," Miss Colt said.

"He said, 'Down below.'"

"Below what?"

"Please don't say I did something wrong. I didn't mean to. He's such a silly coot. We only ever talked a couple of times. I'd rather listen to his crazy mumble than just sit there. He said, 'I was down below. But I have come up now in the light.'"

FIVE O'CLOCK in the afternoon.

Gurgling and slow, the Impala rolls up the avenue and stops at the court. Sleek and rounded quarter panels, the hood pointed and beak-like, the whole body bright with wax, the chrome aglow. Its ill-tuned engine, however, is like a consumptive trying futilely to stifle his coughs. The rear door swings open. The boy Marlon emerges, loping to the cage of the court. The Impala rolls away, hacking.

Somewhere in the surrounding apartment buildings, a radio is singing angelically about Raisinets.

The boy approaches the cage gate where the bronze statue of a lady saint presides. An offering has been left in the dish at her feet. Two dollars in paper money. The bills staring up at him like a dare with a rock on it. He assesses his surroundings. Nobody observes from the seats on the el or the apartments. Then he sees the Iceman watching him from the court. The boy waves at the gnats swarming him.

The cage gate slams behind him. Suddenly, the gnats are gone. Before he can strip his windbreaker, the ball comes to him from parts he can't have seen. He catches it and springs it to Fernando, who sends it to Maitland, then to Pickett the barber, Iceman, Julito, Josip, Jerome, back to Marlon, who by then is doing a squat with a jump at the height of the extension, distending his ligaments, getting tall. He catches the ball midjump and shoots it from midcourt.

The ball spins through the breeze tinged with smoke. It comes down on the neck of the rim. It bounces high, climbs, climbs, and dives like a swimmer through the chain-link net.

Shouts and curses. Young and old. Little Maitland asks to touch his shirt. Even the gnats know that in here Marlon is king.

Play continues into the evening. The streetlights come on.

One of the lights stands near enough the court they can go on playing, Marlon untiring, never distracted, a growl when he lays up, using the others as a surface against which to bounce his shoulder. He plays less with the others than among them. The eyes suggest another opponent, a phantom within. He has modest height, a patient shot, a microsecond of pause for thought that serves him at the free throw line but makes him pickable in the key. He's heavier than the other boys, but the muscles, for all their coordination, are slack. Any of the others could crush him in a fight.

All the cars have their headlights on now. Only men and Marlon remain on the court. Pickett tells Marlon he's late to go home, though it's known only Marlon's older sisters remain in the apartment to impose a curfew on him, and while he doesn't quite ignore the curfew, he can be spotted at any corner of the neighborhood these days at any hour loitering with the grown people, listening, hanging back among them, half noticed; until some sensible woman happens by, some old person telling him his sisters are burning up the phone wires trying to find him, get on home, does he know what time it is? his sisters worried sick, what's the matter with him? his sisters with their brains tangled up in worry, doesn't he understand a boy can get abducted, dismembered, dissolved in vats? get home to your bed, you need to sleep to grow.

The game breaks up. The men sit stuffing their legs into sweatpants, zipping jackets. The money is gone from the dish at the feet of the saint. Marlon closes the latch on the cage gate and follows the men up the street. All his grace evaporates once he leaves the court. He shambles and lurches, aping the men's gestures, the walk that shows nobody what they think or feel. Information blackout, the way the men can do. The posture that says they know the price of things and give nothing away for free.

Fernando says, "You do nice work on your sister's chrome, Marlon."

Julito, the pale Cuban, a machinist for the MTA, says, "*Coño,* that ride is fine."

"Tell her to replace her compressor," the Iceman tells the boy. "Her points and her plugs are shot too. You can't hear it?"

"Time to go home, Marlon," Pickett says. "Your sisters need you."

The boy pretends to ignore him, selectively deaf like the men, snug within lightproof envelopes of self. He knows from these men that he must be indifferent to the demands of all women while living only and ever in the hope of sex with the prettiest ones, but he hasn't figured out how to do both at once.

"We drink now," Julito says. "The superstar goes home."

They walk on pavement where, in the hot tar, dead balloons are stuck, stove-in hamburger boxes, the remnants of a rat flattened by many tires. Ants marshal over smashed fruit.

The bartender is outside his door drawing back the canvas awning with a crank. "Marlon, your sister called," he says. "Go home."

The men go inside; the boy stays without.

"Now ASK HIM where is the money," Miss Colt said.

"What money?" Trisha asked, sitting on her stool by Mr. Hausmann's bed.

Lizzy stood uselessly in the miniature doorway.

"Ask him where he put his money."

"To pay for room and board?"

"Ask him if he knows Social Security number and ask him if he has children or interested parties, whether in Greece or other country, who would like to say farewell to him, and ask him if any of them have his money."

"He told me he doesn't have any children or any relatives. Poor coot. The other day he said."

"Is there annuity or pension fund."

"Miss Colt, I don't know those kinds of words in Greek."

"Are there perhaps stocks, bonds, certificates of deposit under other names in other countries. And ask him what are the names and what are the countries and what are the names of the banks."

"I can conjugate, 'Where are the good plates I gave your mother for Christmas?' and like that."

"Is there term life insurance, and what is the term."

"I wouldn't even know how to describe what that is with the words I know."

"Go on. Insurance policies. Or perhaps IOUs. Debts owed to him by interested parties, and who are the parties."

"Mr. Hausmann?" Trisha said. "It's no use. He's sleeping."

"No, he isn't."

"When he can talk—it's hard to explain—one side of his face scrunches and the other shivers, and that means it's a day when he can talk. And he isn't doing that now, so I think it's the wrong time. He's just, what, sleeping and innocent."

"Go ahead and feel bad for him. Then feel bad for me also. And ask him if there are funds in secret somewhere," the woman said and leaned over his body and nudged Trisha out of the way, as if politely. And she turned the yellow-pinkish globe of his head, the inscrutable world of his head, and the long lusterless wisps trailing off it onto the pillow, and the face scrivened with wrinkles. And she swung behind her then briskly forward and smacked his skull, high over the ear where no hair grew, and exclaimed at him in Polish, and carried the arm straight through like they tell you to swing through the ball when batting; her arm, coming across her and reaching its extension, now swung back and cuffed the other side of the head with the knuckle-studded back of her hand.

Mr. Hausmann's eyes came open like two yellow chicks cracking out of their eggs.

Trisha should have said, Why are you doing this to him? Or, Stop it, Miss Colt, he's an invalid. But something prevented her. What was that thing? Call it by its name. The name was cowardice. And it took the form of a backward step toward where Lizzy stood in the dark entrance full of old woolly dresses that guarded the way into his living crypt.

Mr. Hausmann said something. Trisha could not hear it through Miss Colt's incomprehensible Polish imprecating.

Miss Colt asked, "What he said?"

"Say again Greek please, more loud?" Trisha said.

He turned toward approximately where she stood in the mothball haze of old clothes and the fullness of a hundred other smells wafting from within the crowded home. In Greek he said, "You're the girl."

"Yes. Right."

The gray and white untamed bristly eyebrows lifted, opening the old eyes wide in childlike curiosity. "Why are you doing this to me?"

"It's Miss—it's the woman doing it to you." This was cowardly also: she had stood by and was letting it happen.

"Is she trying to help me die?"

"No, she wants to know where your money is."

"I'm so tired," he said.

"Ask him where," Miss Colt said.

"I'm sorry I didn't stop her," Trisha said.

"I beg your pardon?" he said.

"I'm sorry I didn't stop her from"—Trisha could remember only the word her father sometimes used—"spanking you."

He raised a soft hand in pardon or feeble defense, and the woman swung harder and struck it, and the hand flew away from the rest of him and fell over the edge of the bed.

"Why is the woman striking me?"

Trisha made a note of the word. "He asks why are you striking him?" She took another backward cowardly step crouching through the low doorway reaching behind her and flapping her hand so that Lizzy would take it and hold it. But it only slapped the raw wood jamb. Lizzy had forsaken her there.

8

Vollie knew how to lie now. It came to him as the knack of tying a hog had come: first in a flurry of ill-timed swipes and snatches aimed at getting all the limbs of the crazed thing under his control; then with a mastery so sudden and natural he forgot whatever had confounded him about it before; finally with pity for the angry hogs, the facts he had hobbled.

He did not tell stretchers or evade or hedge the truth, he told downright lies in plain speech. He marked them with details distinct from their functions the better to remember them. He told not many lies but the same ones faithfully. The bookkeeper at the ice cream warehouse asked if he had brothers or sisters. Thinking it wise to distinguish new life from old, he borrowed Heflin's first name and gave himself a brother Bobby. In the next breath, he killed this Bobby in childhood lest news or visits be expected of him in the future. Every lie was a new fact forever to which subsequent lies must conform. He avoided new lies only for the nuisance of keeping them in agreement. So long as he spoke of present matters the need for a lie seldom arose. When he had to speak of past times he delivered the lies so squarely as to make them true—except the one that came with trouble every time, the name, to which he would never learn to answer without a moment's calculation, the name, the source lie and the one that mattered and the one that didn't work: he was still there.

The mechanism of erasing who he was had a bug in it that had less to do with becoming the new man than with leaving the old man behind. Nobody in the warehouse or on his route or in the neighborhood doubted he was Tilly, so nothing they said or did refuted the existence of anyone called Vollie Frade. It insulted his independence that he should want a witness, but unless someone from before could corroborate what he was trying to accomplish, he'd never believe in it himself. Yet if someone from before knew what he was doing, the old life would continue; the new one would never overtake it and become true.

Nevertheless, he required a witness. Lorch and the others in the outfit didn't qualify as people from before. The witness had to come not only from before the clearing but from before the tunnel. He neither comprehended this nor doubted it.

There was a boy in him, plain for all to see in boot camp, in Okinawa, receding deeper inside with every day of that first tour. After the tunnel it was obvious no one else could see the boy. They saw a man, a vagrant, and crossed the street, or they saw a marine or a truck driver or Tilly or they didn't notice anybody at all. But down below, the residual boy continued to abide and fester. He must be killed and the remains burned up and scattered. And a witness was needed at the execution or else the whole thing might never have happened. In isolation you could never know for sure what you had lived for real and what you had lived only in the cavern of your mind.

If there was anybody from before whom he trusted to tell about the tunnel and about the new man, it could only be Bobby Heflin, safely off in New Mexico, out of whom he had made a ghost brother. So Vollie wrote him a letter:

Hey there citizen,

Well I got out of the service. That second enlistment seemed to take longer. I kept yours of 4/20/70 on me a long time planning to write. Some of that time I had no opportunity. Some I did I guess. A bus lately brought me a couple hours' drive distant of your parcel out there. Boy it was goodlooking country like you described. I should have stopped to say hey but I didn't. And well there's an awful lot to report but I gotta go.

Your friend,
Vollie Frade
p.s. I'll write again soon.

First, he would wait for a response. For the return address, he rented a post office box. No one else but Bobby would know the box existed. The office was in Manhattan on the fourth floor of a former dress factory on the Lower East Side, far enough from his delivery route and distant enough from the subway as not to tempt him to check it more than once a month, first Saturdays, early in the morning while the service counters remained shuttered. On the sallow walls, people had written their names. They had written telephone exchanges and numbers, slurs, riddles, services offered, obscenities, anatomical sketches, intentions—names high up and near the floor, faces in dark pencil, faint faces etched in the plaster with sometimes a name beneath the face identifying it. The other floors were home to squatters or were vacant. The windows of the sorting room behind the bank of mailboxes looked over the East River. And through the aperture in the door of his own mailbox he could see clear out of the sorting-room windows—he could see planes in the distance over Brooklyn—because only sunlight ever filled the box when he checked it. He didn't even have to work the lock to satisfy himself the box was empty.

After a while the true hope of the box revealed itself, not to hold a letter addressed to Vollie Frade but to stay empty and attest that no such person remained in the world to receive his correspondence there.

THE ICEMAN brings the men and boys on the court damaged product from the warehouse, half-gallon cartons of Neapolitan and butter pecan that have been nicked with the edge of the forklift and made unsalable. They eat it right away before it melts, and they go on playing afterward, stomach-sick but cooler and full of sugar to burn. Because he seldom laughs, the men sometimes call him the Good Humor Man—as speedy Josip is called Leadfoot, and the boy Jerome is called Blanco because he's black as a wet tire.

Omar, the vendor of newspapers and flowers, has his fingers taloned in the chain link of the cage and shouts: Marlon's sisters are looking for him. He better get home on the double.

The boy finishes the game first and begs a ride toward home with the Iceman in his Electra, which is looking deadly cool these days. Marlon's secondary talent is for buffing chrome and waxing, and the men from the court pay him to detail their rides. He treats these vehicles not quite as his own property, more as younger siblings he has to protect from corrupting elements in the neighborhood.

The Electra is coming down the avenue now, a black, sharp, sentient creature that turns the heads of the boys on the street. An older model but clean, modern. Nothing personal. Nothing that's trying to impress. The hardtop version not the convertible, with long, straight brightwork nose to tail and skirts that cover the rear wheels. Steel and glass. Basic and hard. You don't need to own it, you just want to be the one who gets to service it. Get up close and study its ways. A car so cool it could drive itself.

While the Iceman and Marlon are stopped at an intersection, two boys nearly Marlon's age, on bikes, fly to the car like swallows. The white boy mimes a tapping of the glass. The black one backward-cranks the air. The white one holds up a finger. Marlon looks at the Iceman with a child's inquiring eyes stuck in the nearly man-size body, and the Iceman indicates by microscopic raising of the chin to go ahead and open the window.

The white boy on the bike says, "Marlation, a second of your time?"

The black one says, "Yeah, just a second."

The white one says, "Real nice ride."

The black one says, "Yeah, can I touch it?"

"Yo, have some respect," the white one says.

The engine purrs, and Marlon says, "What."

The white one says, "Can we come over later? Lizzy—"

"I don't care if you do or you don't," Marlon says.

"—Lizzy gave me a note for you."

The black one says, "Just I want to touch it the one time."

The white one says, "Show some respect."

The black one cranes below his handlebars, peering through the late-day glare on the flawless glass. He shouts, "Hey, Iceman?"

"Hello, Maitland," the man says.

"Can I touch the hardtop here?"

The white one says, "Will you stop?"

Marlon says, "Go way now."

The light changes.

The Iceman says, "He can touch it, Pinker."

The white one says, "Don't let him, he's a scumbag."

"Can I for real?" the black one says, Maitland, his hand hovering. But the Electra pulls away before he dares.

TRISHA SAW HIM STANDING at the fence in front of Miss Colt's house, eyeing the goat in the yard, the swollen books: Marlon.

He wore boots that didn't fit him anymore, the laces open. A plaid polyester shirt with snaps down the middle and at the wrists. So many faded magazines crowded the window that there was no risk he would catch her watching. God had made every part of him long and perfect. His big hand lay on the gray gate. What business with Miss Colt had brought him here she could only guess. She aimed all her powers through the glass in telepathic effort, willing him to step inside the gate. Willing him to knock and find her inside, though she was alone in here, except for Mr. Hausmann, and it would never do, never, to be alone, alone with Marlon, in a house full of every kind of infuriating garbage. Though Mr. Hausmann *was* there, yes, and while he did not exactly qualify as a chaperone, she might still hold up her head in public and say she had not really been alone with Marlon if Mr. Hausmann was in the room the whole time.

The snap on the cuff of Marlon's hand that lay on the gate had come undone.

He turned and shambled away up the street.

The spot where Marlon had stood outside the gate was without form and void. The goat lay down in the grass. She did not move a single joint or breathe. Someone had set fire to her brains.

Then, as though reconsidering, he shambled back. He took a step inside the gate at the edge of the shallow yard, where a concrete trough was filled to the brim with dirt and abounded with yellowing weeds. He stood immobilized again reading the sign that said, *Please not sit on flowers.*

The moment called for something he didn't seem to have but maybe she did. Maybe she could find it in herself and give it to him. What was the name of that thing? The name was nerve. She went to the door and opened it.

"Hey, baby," he called.

"The lady of the house is not at home," Trisha said.

"I figured."

"She's away reading her Bible."

"I know it. Wednesdays."

"Her mistranslated fraud Bible. You'll have to come back later, or you could wait outside. But it might be a long time before she comes back. You can't come in, she wouldn't have it."

He approached the steps and sat uncertainly. Trisha stood over him, looking at the blue-brown clouds like heavenly battleships getting ready to blow each other to bits, then down at his collar, the discoloring at the collar's fold, and considered the best way a person might address the stain, whether with soaking, a brush, lemon juice, vinegar; the possibilities for removing his oils from the garment were endless.

A fat older boy with a tricorn hat made of folded newspapers slalomed down the street on a bicycle, hailing Marlon as he went, to which Marlon raised his chin in close-lipped, uncalculated, frank, coolly authoritative acknowledgment, a new gesture he had picked up somewhere.

He turned to her his gray eyes, which were underwritten by freckles and blemishes that she could have easily fixed with Noxzema and cold compresses, and said, "I didn't come to talk to her. I came to talk to you, if that's cool."

Trisha had to think fast. "I could show you inside but only for a minute. It's important work I do because no one else will do it is why. Don't you dare take anything. I won't hesitate to inform the authorities."

Shortly they were picking their way through the path of plastic and collectibles, and Marlon was standing over Mr. Hausmann's body as it lay losing its human qualities.

"Mostly I wake him and dry him and shave him and like that. He won't eat much anymore. The other thing I do is I get a straw into his mouth. You start off in life from the moment of birth with the ability to suck even if you're a total idiot," Trisha pronounced. "What is it you were hoping to discuss with me?"

Marlon watched, impressed and appalled at the shriveled tendinous rag that her patient was.

"Please don't think I'd ever live like this," Trisha said. "She doesn't want me to do anything with her treasures, so called. I'm just here for him while she's out with her social calls and like that, or studying. And yes, he has a bedpan; and yes, I change it."

"Do youse talk?"

"A little. In Greek. My grandma speaks Greek."

"You wonder how far down in there he is," Marlon said. "Like right behind the eyes, or bottom of the ocean, or other side of the universe? And what's he thinking about down there?"

She had not taken Marlon for a philosopher. "Sin," she said.

"That look like a sinner to you?"

"And wishing he made better choices in life so he wouldn't be alone at the end in a coma bed with strangers looking after him."

"Is this what a coma is for real?" Marlon asked.

"Not yet, technically."

"Sometimes I think people don't have any choices at all," Marlon said. "Not for real. They're just naturally a certain way and they're always going to land up the same place whatever they do."

"That's called Calvinism and it's a heresy," Trisha said. "There is a price for everything."

"You never heard of bad luck?"

"Luck is for people who don't believe God cares what they do. Egon obviously started all over someplace, and either he didn't come with the people who loved him or he ditched them. You have to go on loving people even if they're total jerks."

Marlon's lip came out, and he chewed it, and she felt him on the verge of an admission, but because she wanted so badly to hear it and because it was her own nature to sabotage her hopes the moment their accomplishment came into view, she kept on stupidly yammering. "Miss Colt's family is dead," she said. "But she's out at her reading group now, and later they're going to have cheese sandwiches at Fregel's."

"I don't get your point."

"My point being she made a decision to go on loving people. New people if necessary."

"This is love?" Marlon asked, indicating the room with his chin.

"What's worse, to treat people not as well as you could have, or to pretend they're dead?"

"Put the straw in, I want to see how he does if he has coma."

Trisha unwrapped the paper sleeve of the straw and brushed its bent end on the old man's lips. He did not seem anymore to sleep or to be awake, but to live in a middle ground between. The wizened mouth fluttered, and the jaws unclenched. He sucked air through the straw. She sunk the straw's other end in a jar of ginger ale, flat. Ginger ale was all he would take without fussing now, and apple sauce thinned with milk.

Trisha asked Marlon, "Do you want some—I don't know what she has, Tab?"

"Caffeine stunts your growth," Marlon said. "I don't drink caffeine."

"How tall do you want to be?"

Marlon had an answer. "Six five," he said.

Trisha swallowed in awe.

"I can do it too," he said. "If I eat right and I'm lucky."

"Who told you that?"

"Mr. Tilly."

"The Iceman? And you believed him?"

"Sure."

"He just said it, and you said, Sure, I believe it?"

"I guess I asked him."

"Asked him what?"

"Asked him, did he think I could make six five. And he said—I guess for real what he said was, 'That what you want?' And I said, 'Yeah, how do I do it?' And he said, 'Eat.' And then he thought a bit and he said, 'But you know you can't do it from trying, right?' And I said, 'Yeah.' And he said, 'I hope you make it.' And I said, 'Thanks.'"

Trisha was annoyed at this turn in their discourse toward a neighborhood nobody who had probably, judging by his tattoos, gone to Vietnam to kill and maim for sport. "Marlon?" she asked.

"What."

"Can we both not talk a minute? Like not say anything at all? For a whole minute, timed?"

"Why?"

"Stop it with your why. Don't be that way."

"What way?"

"Facetious."

"What way is that?"

"Fake-face, when I'm trying to be sincere."

"All right," he said.

She turned her hand, looking at the watch—the watch was the size of an apricot pit, banded to the underside of her wrist—and she said, "Go."

She pulled the straw from Mr. Hausmann's lips. Ginger ale backwashed into the jar. The old man, with nothing to suck on and his breathing even slower, seemed to partake in the experiment with them, the breath his only act, willful but resigned and almost at peace as it often was after a feeding. The eyes hidden beneath the sheer tissue of the lids could be seen in their faint bulge to rotate smoothly toward the wall as though observing another ceremony there.

In the alley, a dog bayed. Marlon leaned against the wall, arms crossed, watching the ceiling, dwelling in time, the separate time that he alone inhabited. His ears and skull. His cabled neck. The long hands she dared not touch lest she die.

Mr. Hausmann's guts yowled. He stirred. He wheezed and settled further away inside his person, behind the layers of skin and flesh in which time had invested the essential self, the innocent being that made no choices, that harbored no illusions of choice making—a tree within its bark within a quiet snowstorm, within its final season, creaking here and there where the accumulation weighed it down but otherwise making no sound, and not yet breaking from the weight of the snow, the cold roots even now fixing the choiceless being inside the frozen earth, alive without needing to betray any signs of life. The life within remote and waiting for the end.

"Marlon?" Trisha whispered.

"Was that a minute already?"

"You wanted to ask me?"

He sat on the floor of the cramped room. A jumble of unwieldy limbs. "I'm embarrassed, but I thought you'd know what to do," he began.

She knew Mr. Hausmann to be awake and listening. No one else but she could detect the signs.

"I got this note from Lizzy," Marlon said.

"Yes?"

"And you two are friends."

A premonitory horror gripped her. "Yes," she said.

"And you and me are sort of friends, right?"

"You and I, you mean, yes. I thought so," Trisha said. His innocence was beautiful, holy, obscene, like a naked human body. Everybody knew he would turn into a thief like his mother. But each word he spoke had the disgusting ring of truth.

"And Lizzy wants to go out just her and me sometime."

"She and I," Trisha corrected helplessly. She grabbed Mr. Hausmann's hand and squeezed it. Her hand was as white as his. All her blood had gone to her burning face.

"I don't really know her," Marlon said. "But do you think we'd be good together? Her and me?"

THE VAGRANT on the post office lobby floor slept within a cloud of reek that held the patrons all in awe. They stood at steel counters licking stamps under handkerchiefs and scarves, breathing shallowly. Their sinuses rang. They scribbled a zip code, glancing at one another. Strangers, but they were in tacit agreement, right? This was no mean funk. A smell to shock and shake you out of yourself. The glances said, Corroborate, please. We're thunderstruck in the nose, aren't we? We're together in this. The figure on the floor a pile of clothes, sexless, ageless: every inch of skin and strand of hair covered, the feet covered, all identifying characteristics covered, the face pushed toward the corner of the tile floor as into a pillow under the inscribed walls, the heavy soiled clothes and blankets rising slowly and falling slowly with labored inaudible respiration. Inside them, a person.

Vollie, nose in shirt, bent to the translucent aperture of the brass mailbox door. The interior of the box brimmed with sunlight and nothing else, and he quickly turned to leave. The service counter was shuttered. A single blueish fluorescent tube in the ceiling lighted the lobby. The smell for the fifteen seconds it took to walk through the lobby and peer into his box was of feces, piss, rot, and it added up to some extraordinary other sweet reek, a new life form or weaponized gas.

Yet this figure on the floor had taught himself or herself to keep living inside the reek. And when Vollie put his hand to the lobby door, his disgust gave way to something else and he turned back around. He approached the figure and stopped a few feet away and did not move. The others in the lobby had hustled out. For a moment no one new came in. He did not speak or take his nose out of his shirt, but he did not look away either. The breath of the figure seeming to falter, stop, and start again in a silent burst. The tile tattooed with skids. His disgust did not subside but opened and disclosed within itself something that had nothing to do with disgust. It was not pity either.

It was pride on behalf of the person within the pile of clothes.

A young woman in a sequin-spangled denim suit opened the door, took a step inside, let out a whimper word, all vowels and lamentation, and ran away.

Pride overcame him like a sudden wind: he was somehow proud of the figure's endurance, as if he participated in the figure's accomplishment merely because both of them were people. The burden of life a person could carry around. The history a person could hoist on his back without putting it down. The history not only of troubles but of the beautiful things that had happened, the dream of flight, the plunge; in his own case the blast of sun on his head after the tunnel, the taste of home water; and the trouble too, all of it, the sorrows of childhood, a slug in the back, measureless time, hunger like a knife in the stomach, his recognition at some moment within the dark after Wakefield had died that the lieutenant was dying too, but that he himself would have to continue being alive, the disremembered acts of greed and thirst that kept him living. All this life, too much, far too much of it, accumulated around a person. And it was only his own weakness to want to drop it, to cut it off, to wash it away, to be naked under the sun, to leave others behind and face the sun alone. He felt pride for this person on the floor who could do what he himself could not do, who had chosen not to strip it all away but to carry the life around on the body and in the clothes. To be a universe, even of bacteria, molds, still a living ecosystem respiring its reek among the coats and undergarments.

A person was a world that walked through the world.

THE TALENTS of Vollie's youth no longer came to him with thoughtless ease—truth telling, fraternity in small groups, spitting on the dirt road while the combines crept north toward Minnesota, and the ease also of solitude, the boy's light step in the woods, hours spent scribbling the fingering onto a piece of music—all these talents he had never considered talents were buried now and lost. New life had overgrown them. Probably he had new talents he didn't see. But he had not yet grown the talent for knowing when he was being played and when he was not being played.

He had asked one of the associates in Monterey—themselves surely liars, though he didn't want to believe it—whether there was anything he could be sure Lorch would tell him the truth about; and in a laugh of what he wanted to believe was candor, the associate said, "Lorch is going to lie about everything from the start to the what's-it-called, the thing before the last thing. But the last thing he doesn't lie about. That's the money."

After six months in Queens, Vollie believed to a near certainty that Hausmann either was not here or had never existed. Neither possibility excited or bothered him. But he couldn't abide any longer the way Lorch had forbidden him to do anything here but listen. Perhaps the play was to drive Vollie mad with boredom.

He met Lorch in midtown at a luncheonette on Forty-second Street, their standard rendezvous and only place of communication. Van Aken didn't join them. Lorch had shaved his hippie whiskers. He wore a blue tweed suit, keenly tailored. He evidently kept an office in the city. When Vollie asked where, Lorch said between Houston Street and the Yukon, west of the Euphrates and east of the Hoover Dam.

Then Vollie said that from neighborhood scuttlebutt, he had identified the woman named Sandy Colt, and he wanted permission to do the obvious thing and approach her to ask if she knew whatever had come of her tenant Hausmann.

Lorch said, "Hold on."

"Why? If we deliver, we're paid. Sir, did I misunderstand?"

"I ask myself, Why this haste? Why this tone of mistrust? He's trying to elicit and prod. Is it because he doesn't believe we'll carry out our commitments? Have we ever let him down as to an agreement?"

"My understanding was the sooner the delivery, the sooner the contract is complete," Vollie said.

"You're looking pallid. I don't like warehouse work on you. It isn't enough to take a constitutional after supper. Get outside at lunchtime. You want the sun direct, not aslant. Arise, and let us go up at noon. For the day goeth away, for the shadows of the evening are stretched out."

"Tell me straight why not."

"This woman isn't the kind of entity who you can knock on her door and she'll tell you things. This is the kind who, if you knock, you are the secret police or the headless horseman. SSA and the Health Department already spooked her good. Don't you undermine my operational security, Sergeant."

Vollie said, "I do the job, and afterward I'm paid."

"It puts me off my waffles you'd already be speaking in terms of some hypothetical 'afterward,' Sergeant Tilly. Put some cream in your coffee. You eat like the slender ladies in the Metrecal commercials. Let me at least get you a biscuit." He waved at the passing waiter. "It's enough for now that you should watch and report. There are protocols vis-à-vis you, me, the customer. Both the proximate and the ultimate customer. What you propose is not just the cultivation of actionable intelligence but something close to acting on it. At that level there are other protocols."

"You give me the job. You tell me I'm working independently. But to complete it I have to rely on superiors who don't seem as eager for me to finish as you say they are."

Lorch, in a low and silky television voice-over, said, "Here they come—the slim ones, the trim ones. Who are they? They're the Metrecal for Lunch Bunch."

"I want to work, sir."

"God doth not need either man's work or his own gifts," Lorch said. The biscuit came. He seemed to forget whom he had ordered it for and buttered it quickly and stuffed it in one side of his mouth. With the other, he spluttered what sounded like, "You haven't even touched your plate."

"Yes, I have," Vollie insisted with annoyance, showing the clumped remains of his omelet.

Lorch swallowed heavily and repeated, "They also serve who only stand and wait."

· · ·

FRIDAY NIGHT. The unfamiliar block lay closed in a husk. Winter on the air and gravel dust.

In search of parking after a double shift, Vollie drove in ever wider rectangles before he found a spot between a trash heap and a Bel Air with a crushed roof and four flat tires. No street lamps or people, except a girl he half recognized, sitting without a coat under the unlit marquee of a dance club that was also evidently a bowling alley called the Bowl-nanza. A halter top, a half-there skirt; barefoot, makeup disarranged. A lurid unseasonable flower perched in the back of her hair. She was crying with great self-possession and shivered. She had done nothing to interrupt her tears and projected an air of resilience in the face of suffering, character earned through long years, although the twiggy girl was barely fifteen. Her cheeks were still the roundest part of her.

Vollie might have let her cry in peace, but she said, "Oh, hello, Iceman."

"What happened to you, there?"

"Nothing happened to me. I did it myself." She wasn't the girl who watched the basketball with Sandy Colt; she was the girl who sometimes tagged along with those two, inspecting the other people on the old el or reading a magazine, the one who hid among sidewalk klatches, turning as the men passed. "I don't regret a thing," she said. "What do I have to regret?" She studied her polished toenails through her nylons.

The leagues had all emptied and left the lanes to the late-night crowd. Teenage screams escaped the building, though the heavy doors were closed. Traffic on the avenue periodically convulsed in drag races. The old did not drive at night for fear of the young.

"Where are your shoes?" he asked.

"What if I never put them on? Did you consider that?"

"Were you wearing them when you went inside?"

She looked at him askance, the wry mouth coming up at a corner.

"I need to go home," Vollie said. "Are your friends coming to get you?"

"What friends? I did it all, I don't deny it. Just because she liked him first doesn't mean she owns him. I'm a girl outside with no coat. And nighttime. And people might get the wrong idea. What do I care what they think?"

"You've been drinking," he concluded.

"Actually, I've taken a barbiturate, or something, to relax, and yes, I've had a little drink, and it all feels *wonderful*." She picked pith balls off her meager skirt. The knees awkwardly crossed and recrossed. With unsteady pride, she looked across the avenue at nothing. It was clear she was about to be sick.

The door to the bowling alley opened. A steel door painted black and freshly graffitied.

Marlon came out. "There you are," he said.

"Get. The fuck away from me. Go have a good time with your *fan*."

Marlon looked at Vollie. Then he looked at the girl. Then he looked at Vollie. He said, "I don't understand what you're doing here, Mr. Tilly."

"Your date is trying to get kidnapped for ransom. I'll leave you both to it. Good night."

"Hold on right there," Marlon said. "How did this all start about some *date*? Lizzy, you never said we were on a date officially."

The girl pushed on the sidewalk as on the gunnels of a tottering rowboat. "The fuck away. I'm waiting for my bus."

"Bus doesn't come out here at this particular time," Marlon said.

"Ask her what happened to her shoes," Vollie said. "See what she tells you."

"There was an altercation," Marlon explained.

"You need two for an altercation," Lizzy said. "Trisha *attacked* me."

"I'm marking a spare on the scorecard," Marlon said, pleading his case to the nearest adult. "Trisha comes in, swoops—I don't know from where, she's flying from the eaves like a bat." To the girl he said, "She didn't actually hit you."

"I look like an *asshole*," Lizzy said miserably.

"Mr. Tilly, can you give her a ride home?" Marlon asked.

The girl's tears started again. "I can't go home stoned!" she said. "Daddy will strangle me."

The door slammed open, and Trisha marched out of the bowling alley toward Lizzy and stood over her. "Get up, tramp," she said. "I'll take off your head. The whole head. Do you understand?"

Lizzy made a listing effort to sit upright.

Trisha said, "Do you want your shoes back? Go take a dive in the grease Dumpster behind the building. Maybe you'll find them. If I come one step closer, hussy, you'll really be sorry. Hey, Marlon?"

"Don't. Please," Lizzy said weakly.

"Marlon, do you know why Lizzy keeps that flower in her hair?"

"Stop it," Lizzy said. "Don't."

"Because," in singsong nasal taunt, "her *daddy* gave her a *flower* once on *vacation*."

"Get a coat on that girl," Vollie told Marlon, trying to walk away.

"Don't leave me here with her!" Lizzy cried.

"Do you know what else she does when he takes her on a trip, Marlon?" Trisha said. "She writes me letters."

"I'm sorry!" Lizzy cried. "Don't!"

"You aren't sorry, you only decided to like him because I liked him— want to hear what the letters are *about*, Marlon?"

"Don't!"

Trisha's breath was white. She wore a plaid sweater with long lapels folded over the collar. " 'Dear Patricia, The beach is awful. I cannot find the words to relate how *friendless* I feel being away from you. Daddy dumped me for the whole day. I love you.' "

"Don't!"

"'I love you, Patricia. You are my *only* true friend,'" Trisha shouted. "'You are the friend of my heart. We should go away together and start *over* in the *mountains*.'"

Lizzy let out a sob and snatched the flower from her hair and smashed her eyes in it.

Trisha took a step toward Lizzy and raised her thin arm high behind her, winding to swing. The hand hovered. Lizzy crouched. "One of you guys has to do something," Lizzy said.

"Mr. Tilly," Marlon said, "you better stop her."

An AMC two-seater roared past them the length of the block. A dirt bike chased it, popping a wheelie at equal speed.

Trisha turned to the Iceman, daring him to intervene. Her nose leaked, but it did not embarrass her. She did not doubt her rightness one bit.

And yet in the Iceman's eyes, spooky and black, she saw reflected what seemed her own plea that he might show her a way out of all this.

MR. TILLY SAID OKAY, he would take Lizzy home to her parents; but Lizzy, who seemed about to pass out on the pavement, refused to go. They were at an impasse. Someone was going to have to get the harlot out of the weather.

No one was going to figure this out but Trisha herself. That Lizzy had betrayed her only lent vigor to her cause. They couldn't go to Trisha's own house because her mother would rat Lizzy out to Lizzy's mother on the phone. So Trisha told Mr. Tilly they would have to go instead to the house of her employer, Miss Colt, who, whatever else might be said of her, could keep a secret.

Mr. Tilly seemed to think a minute. Then he said all right, and Marlon said okay, fine, he was going to go back inside and finish bowling, and thereby revealed himself to be just another boy doing what boys do, turning their backs—one more illusion shot down. Trisha's lust for him evaporated in an instant. She felt cured.

They drove past numberless pizza parlors, pierogi joints, Royal Swedish Warm Bath, Trisha in front, directing. The three of them picked their way through the crates in the lawn, the household appliances. Mr. Tilly held Lizzy by the arm, steadying her. A light came on. With pink foam curlers pinned in her dark hair, Miss Colt opened the door.

"Come back here, poor idiots," she said, clearing a spot on a sofa amid the prodigious trash arranged and stacked as though it were more than trash.

Mr. Tilly lit a cigarette and tried to explain what had happened, but it was all too much for Trisha, who started threatening Lizzy anew and graphically cursing her.

"Alice! Stop it at once," Miss Colt said. "You do not have the first idea what those words mean."

Trisha asked if Lizzy could borrow a spare coat.

"Absolutely not," Miss Colt said.

"Doesn't Mr. Hausmann have one?" Trisha asked.

Miss Colt said, "Elizabeth, go wash your face."

"Yes, Miss Colt," Lizzy said.

"You look terrible."

"I know I do."

"Alice, you go get our guests some tea, Alice."

Trisha asked, "Don't you have a blanket she could use?"

"Will it be ever returned to me?" Miss Colt responded acidly.

"I promise," Trisha said.

"You promise. But does she promise who leaves her house on a winter night dressed like a men's entertainer and loses her shoes in a bowling alley?"

Mr. Tilly's cigarette had grown a long and listing ash.

Trisha went away and brought tea in jars on a tray.

"Alice, bring blanket with teepee on it from second room, Alice."

"Do you want me to check on Mr. Hausmann while I'm back there?"

"Why?" the woman snapped.

Trisha looked at her bright shoes. "I just think I should." Then Lizzy came in the other entrance looking refreshed, and Trisha's anguish choked her all over again.

"You found cold cream in there?" Miss Colt asked Lizzy.

"Yes," Lizzy said.

"And you feel better with your face cleaned?"

Lizzy nodded and took a glass of tea from the coffee table and drank, shaking.

Trisha went away and checked on Mr. Hausmann. When she came back with the blanket that Miss Colt prized for its Navaho theme, Lizzy was sitting comfortably next to Miss Colt on the sofa with her bare feet folded under herself, and Trisha felt her neck go red, her face go red. Miss Colt and Lizzy did not look at her but at each other. They did not speak with her but with each other. For a moment she couldn't comprehend what they were saying though they spoke in her own mother tongue. She was on the other side of the void. The other people were together. And she was alone.

But then Mr. Tilly came through the veil, gaunt and black about the eyes like the one who ferries you over the river into the world of shades. "Don't cry," he said. "What did he have to say?"

"Sorry?" Trisha said.

"You were going to check on your Mr. Hausmann," Tilly said in careful tones.

She stood empty-handed, breathing shame. "He said it sounds like there's a party. He wishes he could come out and be with the rest of us. But he doesn't come out. I wish I could take him to a doctor, but Miss Colt says it's no use. He's a terminal."

Maybe the man who rowed the ferry had compassion for the dead after all. Mr. Tilly in a polite and hesitating way asked, "Why don't we go talk to him and keep him company?"

Miss Colt was absorbed with Lizzy, and Trisha showed him down the hall through the strange doorway in the back of the closet. He didn't show the least embarrassment on behalf of herself or Miss Colt or Mr. Hausmann at the shabbiness of the room. He was so gentle that he went right up to the stool where Trisha often read to the old man in the afternoons and sat looking into Mr. Hausmann's plucked-chicken face with no disgust at all, quietly as if not to disturb him.

"Can he see?" Mr. Tilly whispered.

"No."

Mr. Hausmann's orbs moved beneath the lids in that way she understood to mean he had come to the near side of the void.

"Can he hear us?"

"Right now, I think so."

"Does he understand us?"

"He doesn't understand anyone but me."

"Ask him where he is."

"Mr. Hausmann, do you know where you are?"

"What is that, Russian?" Tilly whispered.

"Greek," she said.

Mr. Hausmann seemed to rouse. The skull rolled amid the ticking of the pillow.

She asked the question again.

"Of course, my darling," he said in Greek. "We are in the world to come."

9

For once, Lorch had nothing to say. He looked across the luncheonette table, up to the ceiling, out the windows that gave on the monumental facade of Grand Central, the arched windows and stone columns and sooty gods lounging in their robes, one of them naked and striding, ready to leap from atop the golden clock into the atmosphere. Then he said, "But Hausmann doesn't speak Russian."

"I said I asked was it Russian, and the girl said it was Greek," Vollie said. He had not yet divulged where the encounter had taken place. He was holding that in reserve.

The check came. Lorch didn't look at it. He had changed his mind about eating. He was off eating for the both of them now. He needed to know everything Vollie had seen, every word they'd exchanged, and he needed to know where Hausmann was living. He distinctly wanted not to be sitting still to hear all this. They would walk; Vollie would disclose; Lorch would attend, mark, and inwardly digest. He wanted to know the color of the clothes, did the posture suggest easeful sleep or was he cramped, in need of a neck stretching? Lorch had all day. Rather, he would call the office and have his schedule cleared. Sergeant Tilly could not possibly appreciate what this meant. To Arthur, to the shop, to Lorch himself. "You'll be a legend among all the people who never speak of such things," he said.

Lorch folded two dollars and put his coffee cup on them and reached for Vollie's hand, and Vollie felt with a foolish pang the hope that Lorch would guide him now through the jungle of his own misgivings. Instead Lorch grabbed the wrist and led him out the door and to the curb where men in plaid jackets boarded a bus and the car horns made an aural cloud through which it was impossible to hear what Lorch was carrying on about.

A bread truck accelerated, and the winch of a wrecker growled as it pulled a cable through a breach in the pavement.

"I can't hear you," Vollie said.

"Give me all of it. Most important, tell me where he is."

"Okay, but what did he do?" Vollie asked.

"I wouldn't know, would I?"

"Hold on," Vollie said. "What did he do?"

"It's enough that the customer knows."

The wind stung Vollie's teeth. "What did he do? I want to know."

"We burn that question. It's easy. We refer to our previous training as to questions."

He had let himself hope for guidance from a man whose work in life was to mislead. His temper caught flame. He hated asking questions. He did not need to know the answer to this one. He had asked it almost by accident. But Lorch refused to answer, so now Vollie *had* to know. "Tell me what he did," Vollie said.

"He screwed your mother with his horns. Does it matter?"

"I'm tired of this. I get to know what he did or I walk from your whole thing."

"*Our* whole thing, you mean. But you can't walk away. You're with us now. The body is not one member, but many. You're in the bowels of your country, Sergeant. You're part of something bigger than yourself. All you have to be is your one part. If the whole body were an eye, where were the hearing? If the whole were hearing, where were the smelling? But now hath God set the members every one of them in the body, as it hath pleased him. And if they were all one member, where were the body? But now are they many members, yet but one body. So tell me where he is."

"No."

"We're in this together, Sergeant. The eye cannot say unto the hand, I have no need of thee: nor again the head to the feet, I have no need of you. Nay, much more those members of the body, which seem to be more feeble, are necessary: and those members of the body, which we think to be less honorable, upon these we bestow more abundant honor; and our uncomely parts have more abundant comeliness. For our comely parts have no need: but God hath tempered the body together, having given more abundant honor to that part which lacked: that there should be no schism in the body; but that the members should have the same care one for another. And whether one member suffer, all the members suffer with it; or one member be honored, all the members rejoice with it."

A bearded figure wrapped up like a desert cleric pushed a cart up the slope calling, "Cigars, clocks, bananas, cashews, batteries."

"Tell me what he did," Vollie demanded. "And tell me what you want with him."

They were standing on a street corner in 1973. The sun fell everywhere like a terrible shower, and they cast no shadows. The light came drenching equally and indifferently the people, the glass and granite cliffs, the luxury vehicles and taxis, and a busted malt liquor bottle's abundant dark shards. All was visible and plain. The winch tore a pipe out of the earth with slow effort. Oil gleamed from the winch's cable. Lorch leaned close enough to kiss him but turned the head aside to address his ear.

"God hath set some in the church, first apostles, secondarily prophets, thirdly teachers, after that miracles, then gifts of healings, helps, governments, diversities of tongues. Are all apostles? are all prophets? are all teachers? are all workers of miracles? Have all the gifts of healing? do all speak with tongues? do all interpret? But covet earnestly the best gifts: and yet shew I unto you a more excellent way."

"You don't trust me to know the first goddamn thing about what you're doing."

"We're *protecting* you, Sergeant. We're bound to each other now. Don't you see that? There are ways, and there are ways—of looking out for a person you're bound to, of taking care of him."

"Shut up."

"Why is it so repulsive to you and incredible that people look out for each other? You know what the more excellent way is, don't you, Sergeant?"

Vollie was walking away again, back down Madison Avenue. But Lorch dogged him. "The more excellent way is love, Sergeant."

"Get away from me."

"Though I speak with the tongues of men and of angels, though I have the gift of prophesy, and understand all mysteries, and all knowledge; and though I have all faith, so that I could remove mountains, and have not love, I am nothing. Though I give my body to be burned, and have not love, it profiteth me nothing."

"You're a liar. Get away from me."

"You think you can make it on your own, Sergeant. You can't."

THE FIRST SATURDAY of January.

Vollie awoke and took an EE train into the city, then the Lexington Avenue line downtown.

The world of etchings and graffiti on the lobby walls of the post office, the rhymes and faces and numbers, had been painted white. The wire mesh cans for trash were empty. The place was dim and clean as a mausoleum. The sun in its winter course did not enter from behind the bank of mailboxes, and the aperture of his own box was further obscured from within by an angled shade.

He unlocked the box and took out the two envelopes inside, but the prospect of seeing his old name written there filled him with foreboding, as if a murdered man had come back to life in search of revenge. He closed the box; the foreboding turned to dread; without looking at what was written on the envelopes, he stuffed them in his coat pocket.

At home, he stuck the envelopes inside the score of the *Kinderszenen*— a new score he'd found in a street stall in the Bronx—at the page for the eleventh of the *Kinderszenen*, called "Fürchtenmachen," or "Hobgoblin," the one he never practiced and the one his father loved the least: the only one that used the tempo marking *Schneller.* But even with the envelopes hidden from sight, the dread did not leave him. It seemed to suffuse the apartment. The letters possessed a terrible power, and he had to get away from them.

He climbed outside to the street. He headed south on foot through the abstruse games of children gathered in every block, children locking arms in circled groups with two of them running around the circle or trying to cut across it like a shot bullet, children ranged in opposition, lacking any sort of ball or stick or sideline but taut and organized and avid to win, sprinting hard then stopping at an invisible mark and turning, running and stopping again, bent and panting, conferring before the next play, huddled in packs, twisted into their common objective like fibers in yarn; and he continued south as best he could determine with the sun hidden by a lid of cloud, through less mixed neighborhoods, Korean or Spanish signage, past figures alone and asleep under trees, alone under a mound of leaves and cardboard scraps, human figures alone and living, and continued midafternoon over what must have been the Long Island Expressway—his feet and hips leading him urgently he knew not where—and skirted a hilly cemetery that teemed with rows of uneven headstones like moon glints on rolling surf, and reaching a wide boulevard he turned west toward the antenna of the North Tower of World Trade, stark on its other island, the faint antenna over the lid of cloud that hid the bulk of the towers and disembodied the upper decks and left them hovering, twin heliports in mid sky for destinations in the ionosphere, the antenna a slim gesture of pointing up and out, and he headed west toward the tower tops, periodically losing them in cloud or amid collections of lower buildings on the boulevard, getting turned around and heading to higher places, climbing a fire escape to find them again, tending toward them as to a lodestone until he got to the Brooklyn-Queens Expressway and following it south along access roads, construction paths, keeping the expressway in sight above him, and more than once probing the interior into strangers' home streets, foreign lands and people, and returning to the expressway contours until not a landmark but a person, a jogging woman with a headband, matching wristbands, seemed to lead him inland through a denser settlement, a row-house canyon of sandblasted brick in ornate courses, each house with its own bold color of trim, until he was watching the windows under the crimson pediments of a house where a stooped and silverhead man had just entered, watching from across the street while the day waned.

As if by merely knocking he could make the man his father's ghost, he climbed the stoop and knocked and waited. A moment later he knocked again and waited. An ancient voice behind the door said, "St. Michael protects this house, the archangel, patron of the police. He slew the dragon of Revelation. He bears a mighty sword. Go away."

He went away. Then on the next block, he was coming out of a pharmacy and unwrapping the cellophane from a new pack of cigarettes when his mother walked right past him on the street. Not a ghost but in the flesh, and she turned a corner, and he followed her and watched her, this woman in a pleated wool skirt and boots with low heels. His mother's unwonted outfit dissuaded him not at all. She crossed the street sorting her keys and ascended a stoop. She went inside the red door. Lights came on in the windows.

So many grackles were trying to roost in the same curbside cherry tree it might have collapsed, or they might have hoisted it away in flight, a cherry that had lost the waxy ringed bark of its youth and adopted the scabrous dark bark of old cherries like a disguise put on for later years. He did not approach the door. He stood apart from the nude branches listening to the yo-yo croaks and whistles of the grackles, as if they might be speaking to him some vehement admonition, and to the soft ticking of the dried-up shoots and branches. He watched the bright windows, pleading for a sign. All these specters meant something, knowledge coming to him from the other side, the way the spirit that spoke only through music had long been trying to instruct him in some urgent business, but knowledge of what? "Come outside and tell me what to do," he said.

At length the window lights went out. He did not approach the house. He found a bus headed toward Jackson Heights and from there found his way home on foot, not having breakfasted, lunched, suppered, snacked, and not hungry anymore, long past hungry, and fell into bed bone-sore and cross-eyed from weakness and dreamt of Wakefield.

Private First Class Herschel "Let'm Sleep" Wakefield. A dream consisting at first merely of an intuition of the presence of PFC Wakefield amid the hungering dark, then of his sick shallow breathing, then the smell that might have been indistinguishable from the smell of the three of them—Wakefield, the lieutenant, and he himself—but that some rot had come into it, then the understanding that he was going to keep being alive and they were not because he wanted to go on living more than they did.

Suddenly, in the dream, the three of them were about to tuck in for supper—Wakefield, the lieutenant, and not he himself but his silverhead father—at the farm with biscuits on the table, pie, a magazine preparation called health salad that was mostly carrots, and a hog they turned on a spit over an immense fire in the middle of the collapsed kitchen floor with the smoke rising right through a hole in the foundered roof, a column of smoke like a tower. He knew himself to be witnessing this impending feast but to be taking no part in it and waited for the others to note his absence, but they only turned the spit, drinking Falstaff beer from cans that did not sweat, near to the fire as they were, so he knew the beers to be warm. "Pop, you don't drink," he protested, but none of them heard him. "Tell me what to do," he said. And the cellar stairs creaked with footfalls. The cellar door opened. Out walked his mother, oak and corn and cherry leaves growing from her head in place of hair. Liquid water composed the rest of her. She shimmered with it through the smoke. She handed her husband a jar of pickled beets to open where he sat by the fire as she turned to a mist in the heat of the flames. "Mamma, don't go away yet," he said. Then the dream left him, and he knew himself to be asleep but not dreaming, in the dark.

FOR WEEKS he saw nothing of Lorch, Van Aken, any of the others from the shop. They could not just have let him quit his duties, but he tried to comport himself as if they had. At the same time, he expected any moment the slowing car, the knock at the door that would mark the fulfillment of the dread that did not abate with time but deepened.

By and by the logic of the dread began to grow on him. Its omnipresence and shapelessness. If Lorch had threatened him with anything particular, he would have known what to fear. Instead he began to fear everyone and everything, and saw no way out but to tell Lorch where Hausmann was.

Yet the more he feared, the more adamant he became to tell Lorch nothing. There seemed no length to which Vollie would not go to defy him. The rightness or wrongness of Lorch's cause—or his client's cause—whatever it was, had never mattered much, and now mattered not at all. This was what it meant to discover your enemy: the only thing that mattered was to defy him.

After winter layoffs at the warehouse, Vollie went looking for new work and through a word dropped by the Cuban Julito with a union representative, managed to get at least a half-time temporary job collecting tolls on the Bronx-Whitestone Bridge, the span to the mainland at Unionport suspended under slim, arched towers. Sheer blue towers lacking any adornment, the ash blue of overcast horizons at rush hour, as if to hide the giant towers in sky. A transistor played faint music in the corner of the booth, but change making left him no time to listen to it. The lurid glare of the lights of every car waiting in his line might be Lorch coming—to do what?

Then on a night of feeble traffic after a snowstorm, the super cut a shift Vollie could ill afford to lose, and he had to go home early. He went inside his dark and quiet rooms. The furnishings were covered with brocade and were very old and dusty. The kitchen having been a wine cellar had no wiring, and he simmered a can of beef stew beneath a kerosene lamp that hung over the stove. He ate from the pot, standing at the range in wet boots. He went to the other room, where he had tacked carpet padding as a muffle to the ceiling, and played the first ten of the *Kinderszenen*. Then a dam of resistance within him buckled, and he flipped the page to the eleventh, the one called "Hobgoblin," and his hands played at a frantic scream where *Schneller* called only for increased speed, and he played the last chord and lifted the pedal and grabbed the first envelope, which had fallen out of the score, and impulsively stuck his thumb under the seal and ripped it open.

The letter was written in pale ink hard to make out against the brown paper of a grocery bag, but the handwriting was tidy and methodical. The sides of the paper had been torn along a straight edge. The letter bore no date or salutation, as if it continued a thought from a previous page and neither time nor estrangement had intervened in the lapse of the correspondence:

> Just when a sumbitch tells his friends we hadn't better wait up on old Vollie because he ain't coming and we'll have to wait for glory till I can introduce you all godwilling, wouldn't you know one of us (her name is Sally) come back from selling our honey up at Alamogordo and a stop at the p.o. and says, Bobby, who do you know in New York City? Not a one dead or living, I say. Somebody knows you, she says, look. And wouldn't it be your own self coming right off the page like I don't know who else. Like nobody else I reckon. Which is the idea I reckon when you got an old friend. He can be a long time gone away and times change but he come back around the fence and you know him right off, like my roan mare Rita did after I got home from the service. She huffed my hand and gave me a look with her big goober eyes said, Where you been, Bobby Heflin?
>
> This business of you're near as Las Cruces but we don't get to see you up here has me sore. I prayed on it a long time, about why was I sore? I couldn't figure it. Finally I reckon the Lord's saying, Boy, you don't have to figure it to forgive it. Matter of fact, Vollie Frade's an unscrutable sumbitch anyhow and if you wait till you figure it, you'll be sore till doomsday. You probably think it's funny me thinking I need to forgive you about not saying hello our way and staying with us some time and meeting the others here, my friends. We all get sore about our own things. I understand if you're sore at me about being sore at you (though like I say I am not sore anymore). I hope you'll forgive me about I was sore at you before, though you didn't know it.
>
> We are living alright here in our way. Getting by just about. And I hope you'll write again soon about all the lot you have to report which we are eager to know. And better than that come

show your face and tell us. And better than that come stay. We got all these rooms.

We are doing our best to love each other. Hard work on the hungry days when we might have gone out prospecting for uranium or hunting the coyotes that eat our cats. It is hard not to kill. Funny thing is my friends know all about you from what I told them about us in jungle school and Oki and them emu-meat days on Coogee Beach and Queenscliff. One of them said, You two been to the bottom of the world and come back on top. They love you like I do. How can they love somebody they never saw but in a photo? When you give yourself over to loving, the need to do it grips you and won't let go. I wonder if that was Nixon's secret plan for peace, spread love over the world like allconsuming fire.

But it only happens one by one. When I don't think about loving anybody particular I can't do it. Sometimes all I have to do is concentrate about a person. Like about Sally's mother. Her mother don't want her out here with us, but sometimes I concentrate about Sally's mother and then I love this old bat in Carson City who works part time in the steno pool for the state legislature and hates our guts. Any one person is a grounds for love if you pick him. You have to pick him is the thing. Paper's run out. I'll find more by next time and write you back right away. Noroomtosign.Yrs.,BH.

He put the letter back in the envelope, and the envelope back in the score, and he had already stuck his thumb in the seal of the second envelope and begun to tear it open before he saw it came not from Bobby but from an outfit called Pierson-Blatt Holdings of Springfield, Illinois, and was addressed not to Vollie Frade but to Dwight E. Tilly. It contained not a letter but a cashier's check made out in his new name for $136,809.27.

That was how he found out that they'd known all along about the P.O. box, that he had been watched as he was watching, that he had underestimated their reach, that Lorch was capable of playing a bureaucratic joke like having the check sent to the address Vollie had tried to hide from him. And that was how he found out, from the check and the memo attached to it, that there had been a liquidation of an estate, and that was how he found out that his mother had died.

BY THE TIME Trisha let the two men into the house—Mr. Tilly and the doctor he had brought to examine Hausmann—only a half hour remained before she expected Miss Colt home. Both men were covered in the heavy snow that had delayed them, but they had come as Mr. Tilly had promised, and she felt within herself the old reluctant stirring that meant she ought to have more faith in people: here they were to help someone in need.

One way or another Trisha was going to get fired for this, but she knew it was right to let them in. She showed the doctor, a deaf man she had to address face-to-face so he could read her lips, toward the mothballed dresses in the closet. He said she'd better stay outside, a full examination would have to be performed. And though Trisha protested the patient spoke no English, the doctor said that was all right; and though Trisha insisted she gave him a sponge bath semiweekly and was not a prude, the doctor said sternly to stay outside. And Trisha went back to the sitting room where Mr. Tilly was standing patiently as a stone, and she said, "You're so kind. You're both so kind to help him."

WHAT WOULD COME NEXT? Vollie had no idea.

He told the girl to get into the kitchen and stay there. She said she was perfectly strong enough to assist in moving Mr. Hausmann if they should need to evacuate him for treatment, and besides he weighed hardly anything.

"Get into the kitchen," Vollie interrupted. "Don't come out." And even then she returned such a repellent expression of trust that the hair on his arms inside his coat sleeves stood up and he snapped as if to a yard dog trying to come inside, "Git away!" And no sooner had she squeezed around the immense roll of sailcloth that nearly blocked the entrance to the kitchen than a barely muffled explosive crack came from the farther reaches of the hall. Then a second, just as loud.

His manners responded before any of the rest of him. The internal voice of a parent admonishing. He knew it to be admonishment before he understood the offense. Some things we did inside, and others we did out of doors, and to fire a round from a gun even with a suppressor screwed on the muzzle was like cursing inside the house, was rude.

And rudeness was what, for a fraction of a second, he told himself the girl was responding to as she darted out of the kitchen. His hands and feet began to twitch as he stood there not stopping her. The girl raced by him, high-stepping like a heron through marsh weeds, heading down the hall as Van Aken came back the other way. "What did you do?" she demanded.

Van Aken's smoothly moving and untroubled arm rose to push her out of the way.

The girl, suddenly in an acquisition of absurd and useless resolve, planted her feet on either side of the cramped hall, radiant with certainty. "You stay right there," she said.

In the dim hall, Vollie saw the pistol in Van Aken's hand, saw him point it, threatening, saw the girl absurdly refuse to move.

And Vollie stood by unspeaking. The girl needed to be grabbed and thrown. Yet in the microsecond in which he could have grabbed and thrown her, he instead stood there telling himself he didn't know what was happening.

And he dwelt within the jammed-up mind that was like the Hog Butcher in need of oil, unable to fire. And he could have done something and didn't. And was supposed to, and could have, and didn't. "Mr. Tilly," the girl had already shouted, "you have to stop him!"

And a light had already flashed, an orange light. A flash and a crack. And the girl had already spun around and bent double, blood in her sweater, her skirt pleats, everything so fast it might have happened at once except there was a sequence to it, and Vollie saw the breath-sucked hurt in the girl's face, and the fear, as she fell on the hall floor amid the stacked newspapers in her blood-wet shining shoes.

She was an adolescent in high checkered stockings, a wool sweater with a stripe across the chest and up the shoulders, and blood soaked the fabric, and the knees splayed behind the inert form. And the sequence of the three cracks had already begun to replay in Vollie's mind. Two eighth notes. A long pause. And a half note. Or did the last only seem a half note because otherwise the measure would go unfinished? That something was not finished. That the rhythmic structure was off. Or the time signature. That somewhere there had been a misreading of notations. That perhaps he had misread. Each shot a crack of demon speed, a not unfamiliar sound but a wrong sound because indoors. Somebody upstairs stamped the floor to shush the racket. And the girl's eyes had already gone blank, the lifeless form unstrung, and the blood was falling out of her into the floorboards. A forever silence intervened, except it could only have lasted a few seconds, before Van Aken came back toward him stepping over the dead girl's pooling blood, which was wicking into the newspapers. Van Aken had already dropped the pistol. And Vollie had already gone back to the door and locked it and stood before it blocking Van Aken's way. And Van Aken said, "Why have you locked the door?" And Vollie didn't move or speak. And Van Aken had already retrieved the pistol, all his motions smooth, unstudied, certain, automatic, had returned to where Vollie stood barring his way out of the house, and had already fired a shot at the floor—all of it already accomplished before Vollie's laggard mind unjammed and he finally asked, "What the hell is going on?"

The reverberant sound. Then a curse and a moan. The acrid smoke smell. But no flash he could see, Van Aken had aimed the pistol so low. Vollie lost his balance. Van Aken pushed him aside and opened the door and left and shut the door behind him.

The curse and moan might have come from Vollie's own throat, and a weird intuition regarding his foot overtook him; it probably had nothing to do with the present and came instead from a moment of remembered fear, but he had to test the intuition anyway.

Vollie sent his foot a message with his mind but then spoke it aloud, "I'll stomp my foot, and if I hear it then it's still there."

He couldn't hear the stomp. Perhaps the pistol crack had deafened him. However, he had heard the message spoken aloud. He was still more or less standing. The person upstairs banged on the radiator and he heard the pipes ring. That was when he fell down.

10

He got up.

He opened the door. His foot smoldered. Smoke rose from what remained of the exploded leather toe cap. He gripped the door-jamb. He stabbed his smoking shoe in the snow. He felt nothing. The girl within was dead. Blood everywhere on the floor. He felt nothing. He steadied his hips and sunk both feet in the snow. He turned and grasped the door. He pulled it shut.

After that night, he never saw any of those people from New York again and he never went back there.

He tottered to the Electra on the next block, dragging the hot foot behind him. He torqued his ankle to engage the clutch with the heel and started the engine.

He drove home and combed his keys in the window light and put the house key in the lock and went into the dark rooms. He filled a laundry bag with underwear, socks, rolled-up T-shirts, his toothbrush and razor, the *Kinderszenen,* a jar of pickled eggs, canned tuna, and a pair of shoes that didn't fit in the bag so he dumped them on the floor and tied it. By the time he had driven himself to a Veterans Administration hospital in Connecticut, the leg with the lamed foot at the end of it was electrified from within by hot wires that ran as far up as his hip. He got the leg out the door, but when he put his weight on it everything went white.

He came to in the snowy parking lot. All about him spun. He had vomited but had managed not to foul his clothes.

When he got to the intake desk, the orderly was eating a sandwich of baloney and mayonnaise from a lunch box that had a sticker on it reading EAT THE APPLE, FUCK THE CORPS; and another reading, PROPERTY OF THE 2/9 MARINES. "What happened to you?" the orderly said.

"Two-nine were at Khe Sanh, weren't they?"

"Before my time, thank Jesus."

"You never knew a grunt in the two-nine named Espinoza? Little guy."

"Can't say I did," the orderly said. "What was his job?"

"I don't know. He was a grunt. He filled a lot of sandbags. Little fellow. Sort of an attitude, like, I know better."

The orderly touched his head and tilted it as though listening for a distant sound. "No. Nothing in the file."

"Well," Vollie said.

The orderly leaned over the tile counter that shone in the fluorescent light and he looked closer at Vollie's foot.

"Two-nine," Vollie said. "Hell in a Helmet."

"That's us. You want me to get somebody to look at that foot for you?"

"All right."

"What happened to it?"

"Somebody shot it."

AT FIRST THEY TOOK the two smallest toes. Then some of the vascular system around the wound became compromised, and before long they took a little more of the forefoot to stave the infection. Then he got a case of osteomyelitis, and they had to take another toe.

"Morphine" came from Morpheus, the god of dreams, and his morphine dreams were so long and sweet and true-seeming despite their taking place nowhere on recognizable earth that he made the hospital people take out the drip. Then followed nights when he couldn't sleep for the pain, or worse nights when he did sleep and dreamt torture dreams: he was the torturer. And in the first moments of waking, gratitude flooded him for the pain that lodged in the body and seemed the body's means of killing what had gone wrong to save the rest. The pain was the wage finally of his errors; of his cruelty; of the deaths he had caused; the deaths he had ignored; the deaths he had not forestalled; the deaths he had watched, frozen and mute, allowing them. Not the whole wage, only the beginning. And once he knew he could live in the pain, he knew he should.

He had to learn to walk again, in a new way, watchful of the pavement as never before. His landlady in the East Haven boardinghouse where they set him up after inpatient treatment showed him how to do it. She was a firm Scot from Ottawa with no medical training, but the VA had been sending her lower-extremity cases since the Second World War. She didn't believe in physical rehabilitation. She believed in putting the heel on the floor, then putting whatever remained of the rest of the foot on the floor, then commencing likewise with the other heel. She permitted no analgesics beyond coffee. So much as a glassy look at breakfast and she would boot you. He learned a more or less steady gait, but it was also more atomized, each step a distinct act of bringing his body back squarely to the ground. She tailored his socks. She did not believe in reminding the foot of its former appendages by allowing for slack in its clothing.

Any day the law or Lorch would find him up here, but they didn't.

Torture dreams. He did all the worst things he ever saw done and more.

In the summer, they told him the risk of reinfection had finally passed, and he loaded his belongings into the Electra and drove down from East Haven into New Jersey, then into the Delaware River basin and Pennsylvania, down across the central part of the state where he had never traveled. The highway snaked among dozens of towns each owing whatever prosperity it enjoyed to the manufacture of a consumer good—a cough drop, the bushing on the crank that opened louvered windows—of which item the welcome signs declared the town the world capital. A much longer state than he had imagined, like a western state but forested. Then he hit Ohio and country more like what he knew. Bright, open, even country a glacier had mostly smoothed. Not hilly country but tottering and well drained. Orchards, pastures, small factories and warehouses, rail yards. Out toward Dayton and then into Indiana, the flatter land knew its work more certainly: to grow corn and beans, but the crop looked stunted and unhomelike. At Indianapolis he made an effortful downward turn away from the due-west course that would have brought him into Iowa and he drove instead south toward the city of Effingham in Illinois, where a truck stop advertised bunks and twenty-five-cent showers. The glass coolers inside offered no beer for sale, and he asked the young bunk clerk if this was a dry county, and the clerk didn't know what that meant, so Vollie dropped his bag on the bunk and went into the town center where he found a tavern: a museum of deer staring nobly and without bodies from the dark cheap wood paneling, the animal eyes quiet and blank as the eyes of Roman statues over the dim mirrored bar.

Then, on the snowy television, Dentu-Creme gave you back your smile. And Arrid had something in it that not every spray had, aluminum chlorohydrate. And Wish-Bone Italian was for people who really liked salads.

His second beer was purchased for him by a certain Clifford from Olney, thus he introduced himself like an Arab or Viking. Vollie said he was Tilly from Davenport. Shortly it became urgent to everybody at the bar that the stranger, Vollie, submit to being taken up in Clifford's crop duster. Tonight, by God.

Vollie said, "Maybe another time."

"Did you ever go up in a two-seater before?" said the bartender, who had taken the lead in imposing air travel on him.

Because Vollie had not, he said he had.

"Where was that, in the service?"

Because it could now have been anywhere, he said, "In Greece."

"I'll be. Over the islands or the mainland?"

"It was over Patmos," Vollie said. He only remembered that the Book of Revelation had come down to St. John while he was on Patmos. While there, an angel with a rainbow on his head gave the saint another little book and he ate it, and it was bitter in his belly later, but sweet as honey while it was in his mouth. Wakefield had loved that story. One time he said, "I'm hungry enough to eat the whole Bible."

"Did you fly over the Colossus of Rhodes?" the bartender asked. "I always wanted to see that."

Somebody behind them at the pool table said, "They blew up the Colossus of Rhodes a long time ago. Nazis did it."

The bartender said, "I have seen full-color photographs."

"No, you didn't. Nazis blew it up for bombing practice before color photography."

"I've always wanted to go there and you're telling me it doesn't exist?"

"Little children, keep yourself from idols. Amen," the pool player said. Tremors beset the man's arms, legs, neck, his individual fingers. But when he leaned into his cue all went still for a moment and he fired the ball into the corner while his opponent stood on a chair and spanked the television.

Was it live, or was it Memorex? And when her husband was out of sorts because he needed a laxative, she got the one that wasn't harsh, Flavored Haley's M-O.

The pool player shook again. He leaned again and shot with a body at peace, still and determined, that knew its work and had made its choice. The ball made a crack as it went in the pocket that was choice made audible, will sending the past into oblivion.

But as the ball dropped into the pocket, a woman came in the alley-side entrance of the bar. When she got a little closer amid the blue TV light, she became the girl Trisha, in a sweater sopping with blood, her skin a deathly blue pallor. The man she had come in with gave no sign of knowing she was dead, but Vollie knew.

To the bartender, Vollie managed to say, "I'm off," and left a quarter on the bar and made it to the street out front, his heart in his throat, scanning his surroundings for others who could not have been there.

He never saw any of those people from New York again—except the girl, dead and yet living. Bearing no message, indifferent to his presence, trapping him in unnatural solitude.

By noon the next day he had put St. Louis behind him, and by nightfall he had made it to Kansas, where he traveled through a hundred repetitions of the same Plains town. The silo, bank, gas station, co-op, all clustered about the depot. Nothing like Iowa. Zero topographical variation. But the roads were sleek and proper. Wet under the headlights. Music on the AM station from Topeka stayed with him as far west as Pawnee County and did not crackle. Party music, crowd music like in Okinawa. He traveled alone in moonless dark. Not tunnel dark, which was more essentially an absence of time than of light; but world dark, a swallowing of all beyond the flying keystone figure the headlights made.

Shortly after crossing into Hodgeman County, nearly at the town limits of Kalvesta, something went funny in the wiring between his eyes and jangled brain. All around him, a vague but wild idea was taking physical shape. A troubling thought became a silver infinite waving. Above this, a second more quiescent idea, unmoving, gray, and peaceful. The troubling idea began to roil more brightly about the car. A rippling of earthly waves on all sides.

It was wheat. Winter wheat with dry heavy bent ears swimming in the dark. And the upper solid emanation was sky—gray sky that when the clouds drifted north turned to a black vault speckled with stars like the enameled pot in which his mother used to boil eggs. The earth descended endlessly at the horizon toward an abyss. The stars receded. Color began slowly to impose itself. He drove through the thickening world and made it into Garden City and pulled into the parking lot of a steak house. He climbed into the back of the Electra and pulled his nylon jacket over his eyes and dreamt of his mother and father.

When he awoke, a patrolman was knocking a key ring on the rear side window of the Electra above his head. Vollie sat up in the yellow vinyl womb that smelled of sweat, of coffee, of plastic under sun.

"Get up," the patrolman said. He seemed a dream figure, about to disintegrate, whose directions the canny dreamer might defy just to see what would happen. Vollie closed his eyes and descended through universes of time, wheat, the bean field where his mother and father walked in rubber boots cutting out thistle and buttonweeds with sharpened hoes.

"Get up, I say," the patrolman said again amid the twisted sky, and the Frades were sucked into the dream wind.

A lean man in uniform, with a pale mask across his eyes where the sun had not burned his face, looked into the window. Either the patrolman had come back later to hassle him, or sleep had dropped Vollie through a warp of numberless years and brought him back again only a moment later.

He sat up. He rolled down the window. The exhaust of the patrol car licked him in the face. Phlegm in his sinuses. A taut rope, knotted among the bones in his neck, ran straight down his back to his pelvis.

"Hello, ocifer," he said.

"State your business."

"Coffee and peanut butter toast, please."

"Get the hell out of this area."

"Sir?" He pulled the lock and rolled his shod feet out of the car into the state of Kansas on a July morning in 1974.

"What are you on?"

"Sir, I was asleep, sir." He sat crookedly, stooped in the doorframe and squinting.

"I dare say. And what kind of drugs were you eating?"

"Sir, I been driving awhile."

"Where you coming from?"

"Topeka, I guess."

"Then how come it says state of New York back here?"

"Because I was east before."

"Where you headed this morning?"

"Sir, New Mexico, sir. I'll get a move on if it ain't all right to sleep."

"No, it ain't all right. Show me your drugging paraphernalia. Your pipes and doodads."

"I was asleep, sir."

"Get the hell out of this area. Go sleep in Oklahoma, you want to sleep."

He made it as far south as Liberal before the need to sleep overtook him again. He bought and ate three pickled eggs from the jar on the counter of a service station. He found a shed behind an institution called the Orthotics and Prosthetics Hangar. There he slept undisturbed with the lawn care equipment in the torrid heat of day and dreamt of pain and death. Death entered from his foot and filled his every cell, and he became its slave and instrument amid the eternity a dream can contain, while all the while he struggled to free himself by waking up.

In the afternoon, all that remained was to transect the corners of the Oklahoma and Texas panhandles before he entered New Mexico at Nara Visa around five o'clock Mountain Daylight Time, wide awake.

The electric quiver rising up his sternum now was hope. The people were on the other side, and he knew where that was.

The country bloomed with rusty rocks and cattle on which rain fell in storms he could see for many miles before the car went under the roofs of cloud.

He slept again, in the back of the car with the windows open to the desert cold. In the night, he went out to piss, and the stars were like a kitchen mess across a dark floor. He had never known himself to be so alone, a sense of the loneliness that was the soul's inborn affliction. The car was parked about a half mile from the road, and in the morning light not a single structure interrupted the landscape in any direction, and no vehicles approached, but long mare's tail clouds streaked a sky that seemed the true sky, the false dome lifted from it, the sky of everything going up and out forever. He hiked along a trail in his new way, step by ground-watchful step, about three hours in the midday sun wearing boots and running shorts and felt his body dusty all over and renewed and darkened and right. Grouse and scorpions crossed the path and continued into the desert weeds. Flowers he couldn't name. Clouds impended but didn't break. Lightning struck on the mountains to the west, too distant to hear. Then he changed into sneakers, the left one fitted with a custom piece of rubber to keep its form, and walked about five miles more along a wash until at last the wedge foot complained and he was too hot to continue and reached a pool where he took off his clothes and stepped to the water's edge. Flies buzzed all around. The sun came at him slanted over the mountains, the sun like a brush on his hide. He was a small entity moving in a wide valley; mountains westward, the rocky plain east. The place did not belong to him; he did not belong in it.

All the life surrounding him was a flowering that would end, every organism bound to return shortly to inert material. But nothing, not even the certainty of its death, could make the flowering less than enough while it lived.

Calf-deep in the shallows, he did not fear the water's cold but knew it completely, recognizing it from his vision. Then up to his knees in the cold, he saw his animal self as it were from the outside, at a distance. In this distant view, a creature had walked without objective by a fast-moving wash through the hottest part of the day and then onward into the afternoon. He watched this creature creeping into the water. The mind's false story of itself went quiet. How much did you fail to see because you had to be there looking? How much more did you see when you were with others? The self projected a sphere around itself and believed that sphere to be the limit of the only world, of which it was sole proprietor. Other people seemed only punctures in the sphere where the light came through, rather than universes themselves. But periodically, as now, he had felt the magnitude of the world pressing against him, the blunt cold of the water, even when he couldn't see the force pressing him; or he couldn't hear it, as when he had tried to listen to the Beach Boys on the headphones in the Saigon record store and couldn't get himself out of the way and let the music inside. To really hear it he needed friends with him, or else imagination, which credited not only data from the filter of self but from elsewhere. The imagination lived not in the center of a world of its own fancy but at the edge of a world that was really there. A world of which it was a witnessing, insignificant element. It required the imagination's eye to see what he really was. A man in a crowd of mountain, dust, road, water; naked and shivering while sweat poured down his back. In the tunnel, on a slab of packed dirt, he had played piano, with only his mind's ear, the dreaming ear, to make the sound.

Sweating, red, and hungry, up to his ribs now in water, the mere body as it obviously was for the present: another living animal amid the teeming life aswirl microscopically in the water and the air. And amid the unliving elements. The desert wind on his face.

The human animal breathed deep. The water moved about its privates. Horseflies dive-bombed a cowpat on the other side of the wash. Dragonflies droned. Clouds collapsed on the mountain while sun burned the southern half of it. Other clouds headed this way. Their heavy contents spilled soundlessly on the plain as they went. The sun still bright here. Cottonwoods lined the wash. The dark eyes of the human animal recessed in the skull, the skull a rock that persisted unliving within the living flesh, the dead rock that contained the living mind. The human being only a pile of rocks dressed for a while in warm flesh. The hair. And the skin irrigated with blood that moved a distillation of inert air among its cells.

The animal up to its lonesome chest now in water brought together its arms and dove, rupturing the surface, and disappeared. The surface formed again shining and seamless as a sheet of mercury.

The wash that fed the pool went on flowing amid its rubble and sandy bed. The chamisa and goathead and Indian paintbrush ate up sun. All around, and sloping up westward, the rocks lay in their present formations while the wind scoured them, shaped them, the slow patient invisible work that changed them forever every moment.

It started to rain.

THE PADDOCK FENCE at the roadside lacked nearly all it rails and some of its posts. The place bore no sign of barbed wire anywhere. The washboard path that led from the road shook everything inside the car that wasn't bolted in place. He maneuvered up the smoother berm and drove the car cockeyed like a banking plane toward the interior of the property. Sage and creosote scratched the fenders. Even the living junipers and mesquite looked dead, or dying from their blighted tops downward. Birds roosted in the thorny tangles. A few old mining tires were scattered around the place as watering tanks for cattle, but the tanks were dry. There were no cattle or horses.

The stone footers were all that remained of the old outbuildings, the debris of which lay nowhere, as though someone had burned it all for fuel. Behind a low wall in the distance the house appeared, piebald, shedding its cement stucco in patches where it showed the chicken wire nailed to mud bricks beneath. The fallen stucco itself had been raked away. The structure had sunken in the pink sandy earth, and rainwater must have collected at the base of the walls, which had coved so deeply all around that the house seemed to hover on its own shadow. Wind and rain had pitted the exposed bricks; settling had fissured them. About half the windowpanes still had their glass. The others had been sealed smartly with tarp. The house was low and long with many doors opening onto a veranda under an attached roof. A skinny cat darted from nowhere with a lizard in its mouth. There were no other cars on the place and no tracks of cars. When he got out of the Electra, a woman came to one of the doorways.

She wore a man's V-neck T-shirt, distended, shapeless, clean; a peach-colored skirt that swept the floor but showed her feet in their sandals and the little rings around some of the toes. Various gewgaws hung around her neck. Also useful things—an extension cord, a John Wayne can opener. She wore her long hair in a knot with a pencil through it. He could just make out the shape of her breasts within the shirt. She looked hungry and very pretty and lonely and disillusioned. She was smoking in the doorway and glanced at the floor behind her and said something.

He approached the house, lacking a hat so he had nothing to remove in her company, and he shaded his eyes from the sun with his hand. He did not come so close as the flags of the swept walk that led to the veranda.

"You need the phone?" she said. "We don't have a phone in here."

"Are you Sally?"

"No."

"Maybe I have the wrong house."

She turned and swatted away the grasping hands of a small boy who was dressed in a kind of singlet sewn together from a pillowcase and was trying to climb the back of her skirt. "Are you a buyer? Who is it you wanted to see?"

"A friend of mine. I thought he lived here with some people. Name of Robert A. Heflin. The house number's welded on a piece of rebar off the highway. It must be around here somewhere."

"Bobby Heflin," she said.

"That's right."

She desisted from shooing the hands of the boy, who directly scaled her like a tree, using her lowered arm as a branch, and perched on her hip, pridefully, as if he were held there only by his own power.

"Bobby run off," she said. "Might as well tell you. The bank owns this whole spread now. Only they're Christians at the bank and they're letting us two crash here so long as I tidy up till it sells."

"Will Bobby be back today?"

"I wouldn't expect him back in a hundred years. Bobby run off last winter."

Once, in the tunnel, only once, he had heard the lieutenant crying. Vollie and Wakefield were in a chamber otherwise filled with junked American transport equipment, and the lieutenant was in another chamber adjacent. In the total dark, Wakefield had a motorcycle carburetor he was teaching himself to take apart and put together without any tools besides his fingernails, and the throttle valve was always clacking. Then the clacking stopped: Wakefield must have heard the crying too. Suspended in the black space between Wakefield and himself at that moment was the question whether Wakefield should go back to noisily tinkering with the device so that all three could maintain the fiction that the lieutenant did not cry, was not crying. Wakefield had often cried. Vollie had never cried.

"You all right there?" the woman asked.

"Yes, ma'am."

"You sure?"

"Yes, I was a friend of his."

"Did you drive that Buick from New York State?"

"Yes, ma'am."

"By yourself?" She made it seem a waste with the boy in her arms.

"Yes, I did."

"None of the others come back yet, why should he?"

"Where'd they head off?"

The woman squinted at him under the high sun. "You don't *look* like a collection agent," she said. "But all the same maybe I hadn't better answer that question. How do you know Bobby?"

"From the service."

"Oh, hey! I know you, cat. Aren't you the Volunteer?"

"Yes, ma'am."

"Golly, you don't look like the pictures one bit."

"Well."

"I'm Louisa."

"Yes, ma'am. Pleasure."

"This is Elroy P. Heflin."

"Can I shake his hand?"

"If he lets you."

"Is he yours?"

"Not in the world's way. You know what I mean? We shared him. But where'd they all go? I guess I'm the sucker."

Vollie held out his hand. The boy held out his likewise and they shook. In a dream, he had run such a child under the wheels of his truck. The boy smiled and shied and turned his face into the woman's round breast.

"What's the *P* stand for, citizen?"

"Why don't you tell Bobby's friend what your middle name is," Louisa said. "He talks plenty when he ain't shy. Elroy *what* Heflin. Say it. P— P—"

"Peas," the boy said.

"What's that?"

"Say it again," she said patiently, a great soft patience. And they waited.

"Piece," the boy said.

"Like a piece of pie?" Vollie asked him. "Like a rifle?"

The boy stuck out his hand again to be shaken.

"He's just being funny, isn't he, Elroy?"

But Vollie still didn't get it. He thought a moment, then shook the boy's hand again and said, "Is it like a distance down the road?"

The perfect boy laughed. And the laggard mind at last caught up.

Louisa said, "No, tell him it's the peace that means we're free from war."

PARADISE

2011

Janis dreamt he led a flock of sheep across a bridge to Riga. The sheep came along without fear while their bells tolled. Up ahead, the city teemed with riflemen, packs of starving wolves. His creatures followed him everywhere. One by one they were shot and devoured, and their souls shot up like blue rockets in the night sky.

Souls are blue.

When he awoke, stillness beset his room. The whorls in the paneling were only wood grain, not tortured ghosts trying to talk to him. A bird attacked the tent of caterpillars in the eave outside his window. A passing train howled. Why should all his dreams take place in Riga? Ever since he'd come to Heaven, this was so.

He felt he had at least to consider the loopy explanation that he had never really left Riga: perhaps what he took for Riga dreams were in fact waking life, and what he took for reality here was just a dream. Because some tubes had got crossed. Like the bathroom after his mother's Russian had finished fixing it: there was cold water in the shower and hot in the toilet bowl. This circus had persisted for weeks before Papa had come on a visit and made it right again.

Janis threw off his covers, went down the hall to breakfast with the other children who lived there in the home and the interns who took care of them, and for a few days gave the theory his closest look; but its flaws were hard to surmount. For one thing, he flew in the dreams and breathed water and ate whole cows in one swallow, which seemed too incredible. The parks, attics, and various other locations where people spoke in Latvian changed too quickly for him to understand how he had got from place to place: a telltale sign of a dream. Whereas the room where he awoke from the Riga dreams stayed the same from one morning to the next. A large room, with a cabinet and drawers of his own where he could keep interesting objects he had found outside. A small bed stood atop an identical other bed, and a window looked out on a sandlot and a bridge where trains of awesome length ran day and night, uncountable boxcars, moving mountains of coal to fuel what?

The sun maybe.

He concluded the Riga dreams were only dreams, and this here was the real place, the sandlot made of real sand. He might have concluded also that the months he'd spent here were real months, but it made no sense to speak of months amid eternity. As soon as one month elapsed another arose to take its place. And so on forever. Time here was just a manner of speaking.

He was led every morning to church. At eleven, there was freedom to nap on a carpet alongside the others or, if a growing pain kept him awake, to lie perfectly still listening to their sleep snorts, smelling their breath and clothes, freely and surreptitiously entering their dreams with his thoughts. It puzzled him that even in Heaven he should suffer growing pains before he got to sleep. He could not in fact be growing. If children continued to grow here, then adults must continue to approach old age and die, which would defeat the purpose of Heaven.

In his previous life, or rather in his *life*, he had often questioned how it could be that some of us would be saved and go to Paradise forever, while others, who were wicked or who did not believe, would be condemned to Hell—because surely some saved children had parents who were condemned, and how could you take part in Paradise if you knew your parents were suffering torment for all time? The only conclusion he had been able to reach was that God cracked people apart like ice cubes in a tray and selected one by one which to save and put them in a bowl where he left them to melt together. What became of the resulting water made of the saved? Probably he drank it. In any case there would no longer be a *you,* strictly speaking, to remember your parents. This seemed a dishonest trick on God's part, even though it seemed at first unlike God to lie or trick.

He would soon learn God did little more than trick us. First of all God had dressed that man at the airport as a pilot and arranged for him to speak to Janis in Latvian—even though they were in Germany! Why?

Also, in the school here, he learned about God showing Eve the fruit and telling her not to eat it. A trick, but *why?*

Also, the teacher read to them about God telling Abraham to take his only son onto a mountaintop and cut his throat. Janis and the other students followed along with the story in their identical books while seated in a semicircle on individual rugs. Beside him, the girl Doina wrapped her long dark hair around her eyes. Their classmates were dumbstruck with fear, looking at the page illustrated with the happy boy being tricked into carrying the wood for the fire on which his body was to be burned.

Janis did not fear.

He put his hand softly on Doina's leg by way of saying, Don't cry, Doina, it's a trick. Above them on a wooden chair, the crinkle-faced teacher with massive old breasts turned the page. The children did likewise, gasping and squirming. Janis did not squirm. The picture now showed the little boy in diaperlike underpants and tied in ropes while his ancient bearded father held a knife over him, ready to stab, smiling with confidence at the clouds. Yet further down the slope of the mountain, a ram had got its horns stuck in a thicket, and in a corner of the sky the angel of the Lord was darting this way with enormous feathered wings. The teacher read. The boy was spared. The ram was killed instead. The teacher explained what the story meant, to no one's satisfaction but her own. Janis closed his book and turned it upside down, considering the trick.

Then he leaned to one side and slipped the book under his bottom and sat on it. The book needed to be punished. It had been unfair to the ram.

Also, the teacher read a rule from the Bible where it said you shouldn't keep on mindlessly repeating the same things when you pray, and yet that very afternoon she instructed all of them in his class to repeat the same three prayers on beads to prepare for their First Communions. He gave the teacher a sideways look that meant, I am just a mouse, but *that* is a mousetrap. She spoke German—he considered it German—but he understood her a little better all the time, and the other children as well. To understand German was nothing to be proud of. He had not worked at it; it merely happened. Although he did feel less alone this way. That he was coming miraculously to understand German without formal instruction was simply one of God's obscure tricks.

He wearied of the tricks. The teacher read to them, "When you pray, pray in your private room and close the door, and pray in secret," and anyway she then led them in prayer right there in the classroom! Heaven was like an obstacle course.

He wondered if all the children had entered Heaven through an airport, as in his case, or whether he had come that way because the plane in which he was flying had exploded. He did not believe the plane had exploded because he had broken his father's crayon. What kind of sense would that make? However, it may have exploded *when* he broke the crayon.

Janis had expected to meet surprises in Heaven. However, when he got there, he was no less surprised for having expected surprises: in fact he *did* remember his parents, although he forgot more and more about his father. There was a plane ride, the crayon he had ruined, a toilet. But the events connecting them escaped him day by day.

He missed his mother badly. He awoke from dreams—his leg bones afire with pain—in which the two of them walked together through the aisles of a gleaming grocery store at the end of their street. But his memories of her were breaking apart. Before he had arrived here, the memories were a single sequence. Now they were episodes. He began to see God did not plan to take all thoughts of her from his mind in one swipe, but to erase them piece by piece. It was probably kinder this way. All the same, if God was all-powerful, surely he could find a way to make Paradise less excruciating. Unless God was not all-powerful. But then he would not be God.

For a week or so during the winter holiday from school, Janis and the other children climbed a hill in the woods and sledded down, and when the sled really found its speed, so they couldn't control its motion side to side but clutched the handles while it shot toward the frozen gully below, Janis wondered, what if he hit that boulder, right there, and was killed, in Heaven? Would he go to Heaven's Heaven? And would he remember nothing?

"Boy," the priest said.

"Yes, Father," the boy said.

They were passing a plastic soccer ball in the sandlot behind the fence at the St. Thérèse Home. The priest was wearing his hiking clothes because he did not play sports anymore. He was too old for games, but here he was.

The daylight waned.

"Give it your laces, now," the priest said, demonstrating with cocked ankle, and passed. "Look," he said, "all this has got to end."

The boy cocked his own ankle sharply, as though his foot were clubbed, swung, caught the ball without a hint of toe, and brought it spinning as high as the eyes of the priest; whose limbic system did not inform the conscious parts of him before it responded—a complex of buried muscle memory, the unforgotten talent of a slowing body that still remembered all the brain had lost: the ball was watched in, was trapped with his chest, was dropped to the nimbly flicking thigh that sent the ball up, up. His gleaming skull waited like a globe in space. The ball fell through the purple sky. The spinning hexagons came close. His neck went back and stiffened. The ball came to his forehead like revelation ricocheting against his brains, and he headed it back to the boy.

"Your *name*," the priest demanded. But that wasn't the right question, was it?

And with great solemn gray-green eyes, the boy watched the ball at his feet: as if to say, *I* don't matter, *this* matters; and cocked his ankle, and aimed, and swung back again, all eyes, eyes not to the ground or himself or the priest, but to the ball: as if to say, *You* don't matter, *this* matters; and aimed again, and shot it.

DOWNHILL FROM THE CHILDREN'S HOME, in the leafy commercial district, on the promenade flanking the channel that directed the Este River through the village, and next door to a boutique trafficking in sexually suggestive clothes for young people, there stood under steep gables a four-story townhouse in the half-timbered medievalist style that had bewitched the citizens of the nineteenth century and promised them the long-lost quietude of life inside a nursery rhyme. But the timbers crisscrossing its facade supported nothing at all: they were only laths. The place was kept erect by hidden beams or hidden walls or some other subterfuge. The upper three floors of this gentile sham had gone unoccupied for a decade; but on the ground floor there still lived a lone, tall, bald, vigorous, worldly, aging, orthodox, volatile, over-scheduled, and very angry priest.

He slammed the house's flimsy door behind him and hustled up the street. A fat briefcase on wheels gurgled down the pavement at his side like a lagging robot. He pressed a button in his hip pocket. The car at the curb flashed, awoke, hummed. He folded his bones inside it. He drove through the vale of sophistry and self-delusion that is our current world.

His smartphone pushed a playlist of smooth jazz through the four-teen-speaker audio system as the car rocketed up the superhighway. He checked the color-coded calendar on the phone to remind him at which parish he was to nearly drown in which bottomless pond of administrative chores today.

And there was no color for the Kinderheim St. Thérèse, you see? He was far too busy to do much more than wash the dishes with the children after he ate supper with them on Tuesdays and let them remind him how to burn mix CDs on the computer in the dining room. His body, mind, and heart seldom convened, and spuriously even then, as now on the road, or over whiskey during a wedding reception, when his slackening body led him to meditations on the grave, at which (while the revelers danced, who made new life out of their very tissues) he aimed his mind with—with wrath. He was not ready to die yet.

Have mercy upon us all, oh Lord. And forgive—

For Christ's sake, forget about the orphans! If he wasn't managing their finances then they were somebody else's job.

However, the boy some scoundrel had ditched at the airport eight months ago would still speak only—for Lord knew what reason—with the priest. And the schoolteachers had called on him often enough that he and the boy had fallen into a shabby rapport as among prison bunk-mates, each resigned that the other was his only meaningful company but bristling at the injustice of it.

The boy had had no name, then suddenly he had one. The priest had given it to him by accident. When the boy had started to talk with him, it was in a screwy sort of English that confounded everybody's notion he could only be a Slav of some stripe. The vowels were wrong. He sounded, faintly, like Bill Clinton—no, less class and more cowboy—rather like a country-western singer from Texas named Willie Nelson, or so the priest had observed aloud, only once, to an intern. This notion got around among the staff, and so began another joke the boy had accepted and that enraged the priest. Once the boy began answering to "Willy," the priest began to lose hope they would ever find out who he was.

"BOY," THE PRIEST SAID.

"Yes, Father," Willy said, walking alongside, scanning the pavement for bugs.

"Look at these dunderheads behind their sunglasses. The current fashion—do they think they're hornets?"

"Sir?" the boy said.

"Does that look *cool* to you, those sunglasses?"

"Yessir."

"They take up half that woman's face. The having of large eyes makes us alluring, supposedly."

"What's *alluring*?"

"Tending to draw others to oneself," he said in German.

The boy made a comprehending nod.

"Look at her—what are you hiding from?" he hissed, quiet enough that the woman passing them wouldn't hear as she crossed the street. "Boy?"

"Yes, Father?"

"Your name," he said.

The boy stomped, lightly, just enough to stun a millipede on the pavement. He stuffed the last of his potato chips in his mouth and slipped the insect into the foil chip bag and folded it. "It's allowed to kill bugs here? Or should I wait to find them dead already?"

"Go ahead and kill them," the priest said. "No one cares."

All around them in the park, the vegetable life of suburban Hamburg was motionless and yet alive, surging under greed-stoked growth; light and water turning into leaf matter and husks. An economy of life continuing so slowly no one had ever quite witnessed it, yet all believed. Life proceeding invisibly everywhere.

"Tie your shoes, boy," the priest said.

"It hurts my feet when I tie the strings."

"We are speaking of a cramp around the toes?"

"Yeah, and the middle too. And the heel."

"Well, that's you growing up."

The boy looked down. He looked up with shock, then fear.

Possibly the priest's English had failed him. "I only mean you're getting bigger," he said.

But the boy was not consoled. He stuck up his neck, stiff and bold, like an angry priest, a habit he was adopting that his companion understood to mean he felt some dread returning and was determined to smack it down.

"What size are those shoes, thirty?" the priest said. "I'll have them get you new ones."

"I HATE A LITTLE BOY," he told his analyst, who made no sound. "Will you condemn me, please, and get it over with?" the priest demanded.

"Why should—"

"'Why should I condemn you, what have you done wrong?' you're about to say. Doesn't it embarrass you how predictable the whole theater of your profession is?"

The analyst, invisible behind the priest's head, audibly sipped some sort of neopagan tea that smelled like used underwear and probably stimulated the gall bladder or otherwise bamboozled the naturists and sentimental scientists who, having gone to medical school, choose to specialize in the psyche, wherever in the body that may be.

"Spit it out, why don't you?" said the priest.

"Spit what out, Werner?"

"Say it, why should I hate a little boy, five years old?"

"I was going to ask why should Willy—"

"Don't call him that. That's just the stupid name they use. And don't say I call him that sometimes. I do it ironically. Get him away from me! This is my hour, not his."

"Why should the boy—"

"Thank you."

"—merit your time if you dislike him?" the analyst asked. "Your time is expensive."

"No," he said, drawn out and vicious. "My time is *free*. Water from the ever-flowing stream. And everybody comes and takes as much as they like. My time is worthless. *Your* time is expensive."

"Your time is worthless?"

"I'm not a priest anymore. I'm a business manager. He's inventory. Get him away from me. Sell him."

"To that Dutch woman you mentioned."

"Yes—no! Not to her," he sighed. "Even if she took him awhile, she'd only bring him back. She knows nothing about him. Nobody does. He doesn't himself. He may have forgotten whatever his mother tongue was by now anyway. I wish I could cut him out of my throat like a tonsil."

"Ah," the analyst pronounced expansively. "He's got down that far, has he?"

The priest groped a moment through the thicket of inferences that sprung before him. Then he sat up and turned so he could respond to the last question by laughing forcibly at the analyst's face. "Sex, sex, sex,

sex, sex. Seek and you will find," he said. "Now you'll say, 'I wasn't im-
plying anything about sex.' But you were. You have an unconscious as
well as I have. I'm sure you don't believe in anything so airy as a calling.
But I had one. I thought I knew what it meant to be a weirdo when
they sent me up here. I mean a Catholic in Hamburg, to say nothing of
a clergyman. That was nothing. People here respected me once upon a
time. We took the children to a street carnival the other day; and do
you know I didn't even wear my collar? When I think of what the saints
endured, and I can't take the snide unspoken innuendo of strangers.
People used to assume I was at least living in service to others. Now
they assume—they assume—" he shouted, a sort of bark, and fell back
on the couch.

After a long silence, the doctor said, "I'm certain you still have a calling, Werner. You're a priest. It's obvious to me."

The priest put his hands over his ears. He did not know why. He was
remembering a woman just now: the clerk at a greengrocer in a French
mountain town where he had stayed one summer as an aimless university student before he had received his calling. Every other day, he did
his shopping there. In his second week, he had tried to buy a melon
from her. At the counter, she said this one wasn't ready. It was for the
Americans, who didn't know any better. Come outside and she would
pick one for him. She found another from the same pile. Its shriveled
stem showed the vine had given all it could and died. To be picked by
her, or to have the doctor tell him he was certain he still had a calling—
simply to be recognized—was the one earthly reassurance for which he
still longed. He had wanted it forever. The hope of ever getting it continually from one inimitable human being to whom you were always a
you, never a somebody or a type—this hope was what he had given
away to God when he had agreed to his calling and pledged never to
marry another person.

The two men had beaten sex nearly to death already. The priest fell
asleep for a few seconds and awoke again. He said, "I think he compre-

hends German quite well already but he hasn't spoken a word of it. It's when they need something extracted from him that they call me. He won't speak to anyone else. Always English. Always alone. I bet you wish you could get your filthy symbol-grubbing hands on him. But you wouldn't squeeze out a syllable."

"You're angry with me?" said the analyst.

"Not really," Werner said, "it's only transference. I do wish you would despise me and condescend a little for my being a religious person."

The ancient analyst, however, had steadfastly neglected to treat the priest's religion as a plague. This had surprised the priest, then disturbed him. He had counted on a jousting match over religion with an atheist adversary, the sort of dispute he could engage by rote. By refusing to fight, the analyst had forced him to examine and admit his true motivation in coming here:

Something had gone wrong in his relationship with other people. The boy had made it plain. The priest had not wanted advice or—he recoiled at the word—therapy. He had wanted old-fashioned analysis. He had sat face-to-face for the first meeting with the analyst, had folded his arms crookedly, had spoken without interruption for three listless quarters of an hour summarizing a childhood that he really did believe, as he was describing it, included no special shocks or reversals. "As you see, nothing of interest to a man of your profession," he concluded with sincere relief. "I have no justification in coming here." Whereupon the analyst suggested that having had a mother crushed to death by a cellar ceiling during a Soviet air raid in Breslau when he was seven, and having spent two days and nights under the rubble with her before he was dug out, and finding in this now "nothing of interest" was itself interesting, and worthy of study.

"Hate is endless," the doctor now said but interrupted himself. "I wonder, does he mistake you for God?"

"He mistakes me for a priest, unfortunately."

"You're very angry?"

"Of course I am."

"With the boy?"

"The woman wants to take him to Holland. What court won't laugh her back into her broom closet? Stop it with the boy, I asked you."

"You're angry with him."

"It's too ridiculous."

"Or with me?"

"Only as a stand in for—" He put a pillow on his eyes like the toddler who hides his head under a blanket and believes his whole self invisible. "I'm angry with the Lord," he said.

"You mistake me for God."

"My emotions pretend, that's all."

"You pretend to hate the boy," the analyst hypothesized.

"Yes, I do. I pretend, like a game."

"A kindergarten game. The kind you play before it becomes necessary to a game that someone should win and someone should lose."

"I feel trapped, under a weight in the dark, thirsty, as though—as though I were breathing dust—all from hating him."

"Hate is endless—" the analyst began again.

"So you said."

"—but love is referring to a number of days."

"You had no business lying to him about that woman's intentions," the priest said to Miss Fuchs, the director of the kinderheim, while he paced her office. "You twisted him up like a phone cord. I had to unplug him from the wall and let him dangle and spin until all his knots were out."

Miss Fuchs, happy and implacable, sat behind her desk and said, "It isn't a lie that the woman's intentions in entering his room will be to clean it. He needn't know right away that she hopes for anything further. They say he keeps a collection of *bees* in that room. We should simply accept this, I suppose? *Dead bees,* Father?"

"He talks English to those bees when he thinks no one can hear. 'This is your wing,' he says. 'This is your butt, where you make poison. But if you use the poison, you will die.'"

"She will come in and explain why he must not keep bees in the room. And they will begin a relationship of direction and trust."

"He sees right through you, if darkly. He tore his paper today erasing some mistake in the mathematics lesson, right after you talked to him. The teacher taped it back together, but he was so ashamed that for the rest of the morning he hid his face in his shirt. He had made a little progress, but now—don't you titter at me! You don't understand how timid and zealous and insatiable he is. Once he thinks he's understood something he won't let it go. He's like an ancient astronomer. He's looking at the same data as the rest of us, but he comes up with entirely different systems to account for how they work. All internally consistent. Elegant sometimes. He told the bees they were in Heaven, so he'd saved some honey from his lunch for them. Because in Heaven many things go backward. The bees did not make honey for people; therefore, he must bring honey to them."

"Oh, please," Miss Fuchs said with annoying patience. "He'll be shy of her. And then like any child he'll get used to her and forget to be shy. Perhaps you misunderstand childhood."

The priest made a grisly smile, showing his dark teeth. The wrinkles from the corners of his eyes spread through his temples and around his scalp like feathers from a carnival mask.

"People have played games on him all year," he said. "Did you hear about the collection those little sadists took up? They put a pastry bag full of ten-cent pieces in his cubby with a contract. It said, 'We wish to offer you'—whatever the sum was—for which they wanted him to go back home. Of course he didn't know exactly what they were saying, but he got the gist."

Miss Fuchs took from the bowl on her coffee table a cashew and threw it at her mouth, keeping the hand there as though to prevent herself from making a flip remark.

"The teacher was beside herself," the priest continued manically. "I told her it was only the natural sadism of little children. Well, Willy, game as he is, bought a cigarette lighter with the money. And showed it off. One of the older children must have sold it to him. Of course he wouldn't tell which. Yet again, the teacher called me. I had to sit up with him all afternoon watching him try to make the lighter go. How could I have taken it away? Absolutely every kid in the class had signed the document. And the ringleader was that girl from Ulm who we used to think was on his side against the barbarians."

Miss Fuchs chewed and swallowed her nut. She said, "You should have told him that there is a lid for every pot."

In one breath the priest spat out: "Can't they send one of the interns into the shower with him to shampoo his hair? That's what the other kids make fun of, his hair smells like a French dog." The priest's eyelids drooped. He had eaten too many of her stale cookies on an empty stomach, and insulin deluged his brain. He lay down on her sofa.

Miss Fuchs emitted a sound like a cuckoo bird and got up. She stood over him as though, having succeeded in knocking him down, she might tie him to the sofa and gag him.

The priest waved her away and cursed the cookies. "But I should have told him about the lid and the pot," he said torpidly. "Meaning?"

"Meaning," she said, "that someday Willy would meet a person to whom he would recount that interlude, and this person would shake with rage on Willy's behalf because she would love him."

The priest lay still a moment, watching the beech fire in Miss Fuchs's hearth.

"I hear he answers to 'Wilhelm' now too," she said. "That's progress."

"You know, I have a younger brother who our mother never . . . nursed." The priest closed his eyes and slipped off his shoes. He breathed with deliberation. "By the time he came along it was just a bottle. Sometimes raw egg in the bottle. He has nothing to do with us anymore. Reupholsters furniture in Cologne. Somewhat autistic. Has a manner of standing askance when you talk to him as if he's staring at you with his ear. I mean, I think Willy—anything might still happen to him. You don't appreciate how dangerous a woman's love is to a boy when she offers it uncertainly."

"Poor Willy. Why not smother him yourself, you pity him so?"

"I don't pity him. . . ." He seemed to sleep a minute, and she went to the fire and dropped on it the rest of the cellophane bag of cookies. The smoke smelled briefly of industrial pollution and anise.

"I don't pity him," the priest said, waking up. "I resent how much of my time he absorbs. He gave that Doina, the Romanian, a little cat he'd caught with a half-empty tin of liver paste and a fruit box. I had to pay to have the animal disposed of. He'd already given the cat a name."

"Oh yes, now I understand," she said. "Someone kept calling her on the hall phone in the girl's dormitory. She was telling about how 'Jack' was doing."

"Never once before had the two of them discussed animals or pets. It was a love gift. Poor Doina," he said.

"Oh, Doina didn't care. The cat gave her hives. She wanted it rendered into food for some other creature. She didn't want to *mother* it, for heaven's sake."

"Which brings me back—" the priest said, reviving.

"Now, look," Miss Fuchs said.

"No, *you* look. He will drive that woman mad in half an hour. Does she even know how he got here?"

"Yes," she said.

"He is a delicate flower, our Willy."

"We are speaking of a *professional* housecleaner. She charges thirty-five euros an hour, not that it's your business to know. I tried her out myself. Spick-and-span," she used the English phrase. "He'll never suspect."

"She's trying him on like a shoe."

"You needn't put it that way, Father. I simply went in there and asked him, 'What's this mess? I'll get a lady to clean it.'"

"It's not just that he can't clean his room. You don't understand how ashamed he is that he doesn't know how to clean his room. Of all the ruses—"

"You must promise to ignore her hairdo, which is eccentric, or anyway, please be fair. Style is only style. But clean is clean. Did I mention she's Dutch? She's living here for now, but she won't keep him here."

"I know all about her kind."

"He could have a new life. Wherever he belongs, it surely isn't Hamburg."

"You sang her his wretched lifesong and manipulated her."

"No, Father. I didn't need to. She saw him at the airport."

"I beg your pardon," the priest said pointedly.

"When he got here."

"What, in the terminal?"

"She'd never considered an adoption before, and—"

"In the *terminal?*"

"—and she tracked us down. I tried her out. Mildew had been growing in the grating of my kitchen exhaust. I said nothing about it; I just assigned her the kitchen and waited to see how she would do. When I returned, the room was spick-and-span. She had disassembled the grating and soaked it in degreasing solution."

"Do you have any idea what you're doing?" he shouted.

"Before you ask, there is a husband, or there was and they're remarrying—I can't remember. My memory anymore . . ." she said, insouciant, tapping her head.

The priest looked at her.

"Be not afraid, Father. We agree on the husband."

"I am afraid," he enunciated, "of impulsive, fickle people. Willy isn't a diet magazine at the cash register. Look! A crying child! Maybe if I take him home it will cure my tinnitus and restore my will to live."

"I said, 'Be *not* afraid,'" Miss Fuchs said.

"And Willy will be afraid too, the whole time she's in the room. He'll be terrified she's getting ready to give up in disgust. Or he'll know she's shopping."

This gave Miss Fuchs, who knew her scripture, having been born a Protestant, occasion to quote from a small Bible she had in her purse, as she was just then coming from Mass at another parish. To bring a Bible to Catholic Mass is to bring one's own groceries to a dinner party, but in her long life she had found it more efficient to be rude and superior if need be than to allow the frigidity of less competent people to foil one's excellent plans. She read, "*Be not afraid of them, nor be afraid of their words, though briers and thorns are with you and you sit on scorpions.*"

JANIS STILL LAY in bed on Saturday before breakfast when his door opened and the trespasser came into his room. She set to work without acknowledging him, spritzing the large window with the distinctively sharp-smelling chemical used evidently everywhere in creation to clean glass. Each pane merited a separate sheet of newspaper, which, folded back on itself two times, left a dry surface for the final polishing. She paid special attention to the corners, where, as he knew from his own studies, less exacting housekeepers had left a dusty film in which the limbs and wings of the smallest of insects had accumulated. In the hierarchy of smells, the smell of glass cleaner belonged to the most elevated rank, along with the smell of a mother's hair dryer on its hottest setting, and of pancake batter (however, not after it made contact with the pan: a nice smell in its own way but by no means the same). He breathed the aroma of the cleaner slowly and deeply, imitating the involuntary breath of sleep; but really he was scrutinizing the trespasser's every motion through the lashes of his eyes, which he made to seem closed but in fact were not. She confused him to look at: on the one side her head was shaven; on the top and on the other side she had the white hair of an old person. Except whiter than that. And both eyes were the fancy-painted eyes of a young adult or teenager, and she had bright ruddy skin like Doina's when she ran in the cold. Perhaps the trespasser was only half dead and half still living.

The reasons it did not immediately occur to him to object to her trespassing were several. Fear of her was not one of them. First, she had already got to work before he had quite decided he was awake. Second, she was good at cleaning, and whenever a person was good at something a sort of jar grew around that person, which let you and others see them do their task but which forbid interruption. By the same principle, dogs, always excellent at eating, must never be petted while they ate. Third, the trespasser believed Janis was asleep. Or rather, she acted as if she believed him asleep. Or rather, she acted as if he were too small to notice. Or no—she acted as if she knew for a *fact* he wasn't there, because he had died and his body had been taken away, and she was preparing the room for its next occupant. The prospect that he had become a ghost even to the creatures in Heaven became so terrible that he sat up and coughed. She only went on scrubbing the upper edge of the window molding, a surface his investigations had shown him was furry with dust, like the pelt of a dormouse.

Ghosts make all sorts of indistinct house noises, so to clarify the sort of being he was, he stretched and did his most exact impression of a human boy yawning as he woke up in the morning.

She wrung her rag in her bucket. He yawned again, angrily.

Then, thank goodness, she spoke to him, and he knew that like the priest she was one of God's chief agents because she did not address him in the language of Heaven but in American. "There, he's up at last," she said, her eyes stuck to her work. "How did Willy sleep?"

Of course he didn't answer. He counted five fingers on one hand and five on the other, as though ghosts could be distinguished from people this way.

She then did what the priest would never have dared. In general the children volunteered their dirty clothes on Wednesday mornings for the laundry interns, although Janis had maybe forgotten of late, and maybe felt too embarrassed the next week to put the clothes, by then all the dirtier, in the hall for everybody to see, and maybe by the week after *that* his clothes were even dirtier and maybe he therefore neglected once more to put them out. In any case, the trespasser now went to his chest of drawers and opened them. She made a little phony sound of surprise to find his shirts in there. Yes, the shirts were wrinkled. And yes, there were sand and dirt and urine dribble and bits of snot in them. But when she said she was going to take them away to wash them rather than framing this as a proposition they might discuss (not that he would have discussed it), he knew she was the new tester. Always, there was a new one. Always in some new disguise with some new challenge to his understanding of the laws. *No one gets to take anything away from you that you have.* Yet into a basket she dropped the clothes, the clothes that were plainly his, that he had. He was very angry but did not show it except by counting his toes and then his fingers again with an exclusive focus to give her an idea how it felt to be treated as though you were a ghost. He shouldn't have been so angry with her. She was only carrying out the mission she had been assigned.

Later, after the playing of soccer, he knelt on the rug in the hallway where the coats and overshoes of visiting adults were hung from brass hooks. He was observing through the low window there as the crows outside took turns with their chores. One crow perched high atop the lamp pole watching for danger, while the others pecked at probably bugs or crumbs within the gravel over which the tracks ran. The watching crow then cawed, swooped down, and foraged. Another crow was flying up to take its turn atop the lamppost, when behind Janis in the hall the white-haired agent passed, carrying his clothes folded and ironed and probably even washed. Her arms, crucially, were full. "Oh my," she asked him, "could you help me open the door?"

This was a trick if ever there was one. And a test.

The Devil is an angel, as everybody knows. You don't think of the Devil as an angel when he stretches you over a dilemma like a guitar string to see if you will snap, but an angel he is (the priest had confirmed it). And like all angels the Devil does what God wants. Whether this woman was herself the Devil or was merely doing some deviltry in the service of God's will was not a question for boys and girls but for priests. It didn't matter who this woman was or pretended to be. It mattered that she had *taken away from him something that he had*. This meant either that she was wicked or at least had done something wicked. And now she stood at the door with her arms full, not looking at him but asking him to open the door. In other words, to help her in breaking one of the laws. Had he not learned that the one who helps a thief to steal makes himself a thief?

He had to choose either to assist her and open the door, or to stay where he was and go back to watching the blessed cooperating crows of Heaven. A test. He feared he would disobey without meaning to and incur the consequences. One of the laws of the Bible even said that disobedient children could be stoned until they died. All his classmates had an opinion about this law. Your parents weren't supposed to do the stoning themselves. They were supposed to take you to the gate of the house where you lived, and the men of the town did the stoning.

Then a slow engine, a yellow and black engine of terrible beauty, lacking any follow-on cars, crept up the tracks, and the crows scattered.

All at once he felt as though electricity had shocked him in the form of an idea.

He had misunderstood. There existed another explanation for everything he had undergone. It explained everything at once with no contradictions. If he was being tested, then he might still do wrong. And if he might still do wrong he could not be in Heaven after all. In Heaven we do only as God wants. And God wants only good forever. Everything Janis had done here, even sleeping, had required work. The tests required work. And the place where you work to learn not to be wicked anymore after you have died is not Heaven, but Purgatory.

You would have expected Purgatory involved broken legs, and fingernails pulled out with pliers. But the punishment must fit the crime. For him the punishments were, No supper, Where has Papa gone?, All alone in a foreign country. And tests such as this Devil woman in the hall asking him to open the door so she could put his clothes back in his room. His punishments here were mental. Therefore most of his sins in life had been sins of his mind. Evidently he had done the right things before, in spilling the milk on the egg sandwich in the airport, for example; because now God was presenting him with a harder spiritual examination.

"Willy?" she said in her Devil sweetness. "My arms are getting tired. Won't you help me?" Still she did not look at him when she said the name.

If somebody takes what isn't theirs but then tries to give it back, does the sin go away? God forgives us when we repent. But first we have to admit we did wrong. And the Devil woman had admitted no such thing. She had merely come back with the clothes. Here was the test: if a person wants to take back a mistake but does not say she's sorry, should you still let her take it back?

Yes, he decided.

He got up and opened the door.

SOMEWHERE IN THE WOODS where the priest and the boy were walking, there lived a nesting pair of goshawks, intensely territorial until their hatchlings fledged. Signs at the trailhead advised that from spring until the middle of summer hikers should be wary and prepared to protect themselves. This was the last day of July.

The priest said, "This beech tree, what does it do?"

The boy disappointed the priest by answering in German. "It glorifies God."

"Which means?"

"It—I don't know."

"Why say the word if you don't know what it means?"

The boy blushed and stuffed his hands further in his pockets. The small clean pockets sagged with new items for his collection. For once, nothing was stuck in his hair but hair.

"Good job knotting those shoes," the priest said.

"Nora showed me."

"The Dutchwoman."

"Yessir."

"Now, likewise, if you know there's a word for something but you don't know the word, why call it by some other word? That's why I don't want them calling you Willy. You're somebody else. God knows your name. Can you say it?"

"Father, I need to make tee-tee or I'll mess my pants."

"Go behind that tree."

The boy made one of his grave looks. "No one is supposed to do it outside," he said.

"Very well, but we won't return to St. Thérèse until the afternoon. And we haven't met anyone else on the trail for at least a kilometer. So no one will see, and it will be all right."

The boy's look now became so lost within itself that the priest almost reached out his hand to touch the boy's head and comfort him. Instead he snapped, "Oh, what is it now? Are you afraid the hawk will see you?"

"It don't matter if anybody sees."

"You've misunderstood. There's nothing shameful about passing your water. It's only that we do these things in private because other people don't want to have to look at us with our pants down. It would be rude."

"*God* sees."

"God sees everything."

The boy bounced from the knees and gave him a more peevish look the priest knew to mean both that the boy must go right away and that he had already deduced, from the general principle of God seeing everything, that God saw him now. He did not want to be told what he already knew, he wanted to urinate.

With the low enunciation he usually reserved for the confessional, the priest said, "If you are in the woods, and you go far enough from the trail not to be seen, then the trunks of the trees become your walls, and the canopy overhead becomes your ceiling. You are inside a room that God has made."

The boy pursed his lips and nodded. "You'll holler when you can't see me?" he asked.

The priest said he would.

The boy ran into the beech forest through the understory of ferns. The priest shouted, "Wherever you are, I can't see you now." He had time to recite the Gloria three times aloud and raised his mind to God with humble trust to earn a partial indulgence for someone suffering the temporal punishment for a sin freely confessed. But he was not humble and did not trust. He believed that everybody else but he himself had misled the boy and imperiled him.

A hawk cawed in the distance, a long peal repeated in increments of six, high at the beginning and descending in tone at the end, a sound that were a human being to have made it would have meant, *Please* help me. But that from the throat of a goshawk meant, *Come* no closer.

All very well to feed the children pretty notions such as that the growth of trees glorified God, but it annoyed him the teachers should

catechize the children so shabbily as to leave them incapable of distin-
guishing "Gloria" from "How's it going?" The boy had had no idea
what he was saying when he had used the word "glorify."

"Finish up now," the priest called. Three more times, he recited the
prayer.

The hawk's caw answered him. Then it called again from nearer at
hand. Another hawk joined it from farther up the trail making the
same plaintive sound, really a curse. He had cut himself shaving his
skull that morning, and the wound smarted as the blood moved
through the taut scalp in the heat of the sun. The boy's returning steps
could be heard soughing through the needles and leaves in the duff
among the ferns. One of the hawks circled above the trail, but so high
up now it must have got caught in an updraft.

A small brown-and-white object flashed from where the sound of
the boy's steps was growing more distinct amid the leaves. The light
swung like the arm of a metronome. Then a fawn's face materialized
before it. He had not heard the boy's steps but the fawn's. The fawn
stepped to him—trusting. Humbly trusting as he had tried to be in
prayer and had failed. The fawn's white flashing tail flicked behind it.

The hawk circled lower, as though following a drain.

Would a hawk really feel threatened by a yearling deer?

The fawn approached him, the head spasming to shoo a fly at its
shoulder. A hind hoof scratched its ribs. All about was green but the
fawn's white tail; its bright spots; its tawny fur; its black hooves, nose,
and unknowing eyes. For a fraction of a second the priest imagined he
saw another pair of eyes right behind the deer. Knowing and human
eyes within the woods. What was it they knew?

He grabbed a rock.

From the periphery of his vision, up the trail, the spreading striped
wings of the hawk's mate darted to where he and the fawn stood in the
clearing.

Four things he did at once. He threw the rock over the fawn's head. He shouted to it, "Watch!" He grabbed his scalp. And he fell down.

The hawk struck him with such speed that when its talons made impact, the priest felt both shoved in the head and stung there.

AFTER JANIS PASSED his water among the trees, he shook the dribble from his thing, zipped up, and got a little lost. He was walking near enough to hear the priest praying, so he was not too concerned. Everywhere the beautiful smells of rotting leaves and of hot pine sap promised he would not be tried forever.

God had made such smells to comfort you while you were being tried. He even made trees that grew out of the moss on top of boulders here, with roots that went through cracks inside the boulders and, over many years of growing, split the boulders in half. What such wonders foretold it was impossible to guess.

And because God's appetite for making wonders was inexhaustible, he made also a spotted creature about Janis's size but with all four limbs on the forest floor and with a wagging and rotating white face that strangely lacked any features—or so Janis gathered at first. But in Purgatory we must remain vigilant not to love our understandings so much that we forget they are only our best guesses for the time being. Every day, every moment, we draw closer to correct understanding: this was not the creature's face but its backside. It was the white rump of a young deer.

The moment he saw that it was not the face but the rump, he saw also through the trees to the lighted span of the trail, where the priest had evidently been planning the punishment assigned to him if Janis should fail the test about where to pass his water. The priest held a rock, and so great was his faith in the orders he had been given that he was evidently prepared to stone Janis until he died; even though Janis knew, if he knew anything, that the priest liked him and must have possessed extraordinary knowledge of God's intentions if he was willing to do such a thing as to kill a child who had already died once.

Everything worked according to God's plan. He made the sap rise through the trees and turned it into needles that fell on the forest floor so that Janis could smell their smell. He made the priest test Janis about where to pass water. Janis had evidently failed. And the priest was willing to carry out the punishment God had assigned to Janis right up to the point of throwing the rock!

Janis saw through the foliage to the priest's eyes—and the knowledge in them.

But at the very moment the hand was swinging with the rock in it, the angel of God took the form of an enormous bird with red eyes and dark stripes under its wings, which opened wide behind the priest's head and knocked him down. The rock landed somewhere in the ferns.

This was how Janis learned to trust in the providence of the Lord. It seemed even unfair that others should have to learn about it and hope for it and trust in it but never to experience a proof of it as he had.

So many innocent people had suffered so much. What had he really suffered? His father, for example, Janis had lately come to conclude, had not died with him in the explosion of an airplane. As best Janis could now understand, his father had closed him in the bathroom stall and left him on purpose, because he knew Janis was to die there, in the bathroom. Whether God had commanded his father to do this or he had taken it on himself hardly mattered. It must have felt as mean either way. His father was somewhere suffering and praying to be forgiven.

The deer did not just run away but vanished. Where it had stood, Janis found the rock and put it in his pocket. He vowed to keep the rock always and to speak of it never with anyone. It was more than the acme of his collection of objects from out of doors. It was a gift and a marvel and a sign. When he lost hope, he held the rock firmly in his hand, and hope came back to him.

. . .

Before the woman called Nora Wolbert had even taken her seat opposite the priest in Miss Fuchs's office, she informed him artlessly that whatever a Christian home might be, hers was the opposite and would stay that way.

The priest found himself revising his opinion of her immediately. He admired true believers of all kinds and recognized them by this very inability to resist confessing their belief exactly when it risked sabotaging their other intentions. That her belief lay in unbelief was immaterial.

Miss Fuchs brought coffee and scones. Her guests ignored them. The priest began the interview in Dutch, intending to leave Miss Fuchs mostly in the dark and, with any luck, to bore her into going away. Nora wore a ruby-colored stud in her nose, various plastic rings in the shapes of insects on one hand, a normal wedding ring on the other, green plastic boots, and contact lenses matching the boots. The priest looked no less nutty with surgical tape all over his head.

"This is not a Pre-Cana consultation, madam," he said. "You needn't demonstrate you'll raise the boy in the Church for us to let him live with you. But you should know that the Working Group of State Youth Authorities stipulates adoptive parents must guarantee the child's free practice of his religion."

"Yes, children should be *free*," Miss Fuchs interjected, comprehending incompletely.

"More urgently," the priest continued, "I must advise you that the stability of your home life will compel the judge's scrutiny in a way that will likely feel intrusive."

"I'm prepared for that," Nora said.

"So if I pry, I hope you'll accept my questions as preparation for what more consequential interviewers will certainly ask you later."

She regarded coolly the photographs cut from glossy magazines that were stuck in the corkboard behind the director's desk: children in a landfill picking through piles of electronic junk; children potbellied, harelipped; children eating mush from the fingers of nuns. "I didn't want to leave you with any illusions about what my husband and I believe," she said. "Of course, we won't stop Willy if he wants to pray, to your God or anyone else's; it makes no difference. All religions are false."

However she might have intended this last remark, she spoke it with a clarity the priest so envied that he could not resist trying it out in his heart. All religions are false, he said inwardly. It gave him a rush of peace, as if he had surrendered in a battle, or admitted an error, or drunk a fatal poison after a long illness. For a moment he knew the promise that in the end his being would not be concentrated to an essence but would disperse; that he was a child not of God but of no one. He sunk for a moment into the warm pool of the dream that he did not matter. The warmth, the complete peace of not mattering. The peace of no one mattering. And yet he could not deny that Willy mattered.

"You might come across as more respectful of the judge's position," the priest said, "if you used a phrase like 'we *wouldn't* stop him.'"

"All right."

"Your husband," he said, "is this your future husband or your former husband?"

"There's only the one. We never divorced."

Miss Fuchs understood enough at this point to say, "There you are. Don't wait for others to find out your deficiencies."

"I fell in love with another man and left my husband two years ago," Nora said straightforwardly.

"At which time you moved here from Holland?" the priest asked.

"That's right."

"You remained married to Mr. Wolbert while cohabitating in Hamburg with the second man?"

"Yes," she said.

"And now you've changed your mind? Don't worry about my judgment. I can offer the court only my observations. I have no authority here."

"My boyfriend—"

A knock came from the door. Miss Fuchs asked who it was. One of the interns poked her face in and asked for a word in the hall. Miss Fuchs went outside and closed the door.

"You needn't feel I'm judging you," the priest said.

"And yet you are."

"What makes you so sure?"

One side of her lean face hid behind the long hank of white hair in which a few blue and green streaks ran, curving under the chin and framing it. Most of her was wrapped in an elegant sweater, handmade, a flea market purchase, old and coming apart at the shoulders from holes that had been stitched along their edges, not to mend them but to keep them artful holes.

"I see the calculation in Willy's posture," she said. "He's so alert. He's so sure he's done something wrong to be here. Who else would have given him such an obscene idea but you people?"

"There it is," the priest said comfortably, nodding. "Your contempt. Tell me about it."

"Sir, I don't need your assistance to make sense of my feelings."

The priest moved aside an amaryllis planted in a bowl of sphagnum moss from the space between them and looked nakedly on the woman who was asking to be Willy's mother. An understanding seemed to pass between them, a potential unrealized, that having each sincerely sought an enemy in the other, they might as sincerely find the ally they had been looking for. Her stomach growled audibly. A queer, contrary emotion began to trouble him. He tried with a spiritual muscle to resist its temptation. It seemed to be the wish, in spite of his earlier misgivings, in spite of her mistrust of him—or because of it—that she was indeed the parent God intended for the boy, and that the judge would let her take him in.

"I hear you don't believe I was in the airport," she said.

"Then you hear incorrectly. If you say you were in the airport I have no cause to disbelieve you."

"Walther had just left me and I was flying back to Amsterdam to ask my husband if he would have me back. You imagine I was smeared in my own shit."

"If you weren't ashamed, who am I to shame you? You must have been very sad."

"Very sad," she said. "Your years of loving-kindness give you remarkable insight. I was ruined."

"I didn't mean to minimize, only to avoid presuming too much. To love and to be rejected is"—he nodded, resisting a glib impulse—"to shed your skin and then to be thrown in a briar."

"What would you know about it?"

"Grandfather used to say he was married, not dead."

"And you're married to the Church?"

"That's right."

"And your eye wanders?"

"Of course." He laughed. "Less than it used to."

"And you fall in love sometimes?"

"I have, yes."

"But you never surrendered yourself to your boy hustler, did you, and prayed for him to love you back?"

"I'm exerting effort not to respond to your provocations, Mrs. Wolbert, but I hope you won't mistake that for an attempt to be more-genuine-than-thou. I'm often sarcastic myself. I don't want to fight with you. In fact, I'll tell you something personal. Often, but not always, when someone else is judging me, I feel a strange calmness. Psychologically speaking, I'll confess I feel momentarily relieved of the burden of judging myself."

"That's interesting."

"Does it sound familiar?"

"Not in the slightest."

"Maybe we can have a treaty anyway. I'll respect that you have suffered in ways I can't share, and you might respect that I have suffered likewise. And you can go on with what you'll tell the judge."

"What is it she'll want to know?"

"The judge will be a man."

"Do you know him?"

"Unfortunately I know him well."

"Is he one of your—what do you call them—communicants?"

"No, he's—how would he describe himself? He'd probably say he was a secular humanist, but humanism implies an allegiance with one's fellow man that he's never experienced. And a high regard for consciousness, don't you think? But he'll never possess the self-awareness to know how disappointed he is that his career has stalled in the guardianship court. I've played racquetball with him. He will die of a coronary playing racquetball someday. The competition going on inside him manifests itself as savagery in any venue where he can find a prospect of winning. In his professional position, he has no obvious adversaries. Therefore he will cast you in that role and he will flay you. He'll believe he's questioning you in the service of the Civil Code but he's really serving the torturer inside him."

"You mean the sufferer?"

"They are the same entity."

"All right."

"The first of the two considerations that the Civil Code requires him to hold paramount is the child's best interest. The second is that it must be expected a parent-child relationship will develop between the adopter and the child. That is the language. In your case, he will most likely go after what *appears*, forgive me, to be the capricious nature of your interest in the boy. I could try to argue that if not you and your husband, no other qualified couple would likely step forward, especially in light of the boy's age and what the court psychiatrist will likely conclude is a severe emotional injury incurred at the airport, if not before, resulting in the boy's refusal to speak and unknowable future problems for the adoptive family. He's a damaged person, and we're lucky to find anyone willing to brave him.

"Perhaps that's all true, but the judge won't care. He will want to rationalize his first impression, that you are using the child as a bandage on your humiliation. Once you feel better about this Walther, you might resent the boy and even drop him. You must know that happens sometimes. The child refuses to bond, or the adopters come to regard the child as an alien presence in the home. Even if you escape that, most children despise their parents for at least part of adolescence. A biological mother, or at least a mother who's cared for the child from infancy, retains a helpless love that usually gets her through the child's contempt at that age. You may believe you love him, but under extreme pressures, the bond breaks at its weakest place. And that weakness, in the eyes of the judge, is the fact of your relationship having its origins in a *choice,* rather than in nature. A married couple begins with a choice too, but their choice is mutual. Therefore it's twice as strong. Even if the young child assents to live in your home, he hasn't reached the age of real choice.

"What I'm trying to say, Mrs. Wolbert, is that the judge views the animal bond as true, and the chosen bond—because it is revocable—as false. I don't share this view. In fact, if you'll allow me an opinion, I think this view ought to be repulsive to anyone calling himself a humanist. I think the choice you're making can be definitive. The judge does not. He assumes you can't love the boy on purpose. And the only true love is the one that strikes you down without your choosing it."

She flicked her hair with the finger adorned with a plastic mantis. "What I saw in the airport," she said uncertainly.

"Go on."

"Yes, I saw him and felt attached to him crying there."

"Who wouldn't?"

"But it wasn't love in an instant. I'm forty-seven years old. I know better."

"Love is referring to a number of days," the priest said.

"You don't mean I can love him just by sticking with him awhile."

"No."

"I saw him, and I want to do this," she said. "Isn't that enough?"

"I'd say it's almost everything," the priest said.

"Okay, but what I saw in the airport . . ." She seemed to concentrate. She put her hair behind her ear—her ears were so prominent it seemed she might have begun wearing her hair over them as an adolescent to disguise them, but at some point during adulthood had shaved the one side of the head in order deliberately to call attention to her ears and conquer her repugnance. "I also saw a man. Late thirties. Shivering, bug-eyed. Maybe he was strung out. I saw him go into the bathroom. People get worked up at airports all the time, right? Visibly stressed. I remember saying to myself, I hope I don't look *that* bad. And I took out my compact and fixed my eye makeup and I felt better. I'm not certain I saw him with Willy. I *think* I saw him go into the bathroom with a little boy, but maybe I made that up. I remember seeing a child in a black parka, a sporty little ski jacket. And that's what Willy was wearing later when I saw him crying. But was there really a boy with that man, and was he the same boy I saw crying later at the ticket gate?"

"You didn't tell anyone."

"I'm almost certain I made it up. There were so many people. And Walther was gone. I thought my life was over."

"When you saw the boy later—"

"Yes. I wondered right away if he was the same child. But I decided, what if he was, what difference would it make? At the time I thought, what difference does anything make?" she said. "Does the judge really need to know about all this?"

"Don't call him a judge."

"You call him a judge."

"He is a judge, but the law also invests him with the care of the parties within the case, so he's a kind of social worker."

"What do you call him?"

"If you call him a judge, even though he is a judge, he'll think you're making fun of him."

"Does he need to hear about the bathroom?"

"You are describing a suspicion. The judge—but he is also not a judge—prefers to do the suspecting himself. It's you who's on trial, not some man you maybe never saw."

"I sat there on my luggage telling myself, Let the airport people worry about it. Let the police find his parents."

"I told myself the same thing," the priest said. "I won't tell you the police investigator was completely indifferent, but when I pester him for updates he lectures me about the agony that he imagines drove Willy's mother to do this to him. It's not as though she left him in the woods, he says. She left him where the state couldn't fail to find him and take care of him." The priest believed he saw a smug and slanted smirk flash across the woman's mouth as he said, "The investigator considers it a crime of mercy." But Nora had not smirked; he had smirked, and he reproached himself.

"Don't you agree?" she said earnestly.

"I think we all have a right to come from somewhere and know it. To come from some people and know who they are. And I think that information is slipping away from Willy. So no, I don't agree. I admit I got angry with the investigator. He asked me, 'Do we really want to spend time and money tracking this woman down—'"

"Or man."

"Or man, I suppose—'and putting her on trial?'"

"What will I be on trial for?"

"How will it look at its worst? I'd say you were an adventuress who had her fun, and now she's lonely and too old to get pregnant without a lot of hassle, but she wants a child because now that she's destroyed her marriage she'd like someone to keep her company. The husband's still loyal enough not to stand in her way. So he'll testify to their continued home life, when in reality they intend to divorce soon or at least to live separately."

"That isn't so bad, I suppose."

"And not too far from the truth?"

"I wouldn't like to say," she said.

"Were there any questions you'd like to ask me?"

"I guess I didn't expect we'd go so soon before a judge."

"Not a judge."

"What do I call him?"

"He is a judge, except something less than a judge. He is a judge manqué. Better not to call him anything."

"I didn't expect we'd have a hearing so soon. I mean before Willy's even lived with me."

"Who told you it was a hearing?" The priest bristled. "A hearing is a contest. It is not a hearing. It is a chat."

"Does my husband have to be there, for just a chat?"

"Wouldn't you want him to be?"

Nora looked at the drab scones.

"The standard interpretation of the guidelines issued by the Working Group results in a de facto requirement that the child be placed into the home of a married couple."

"I know that," she said.

"Or of a same-sex couple living as legally registered partners, whatever one might think of such arrangements."

"I know."

"But not in the hands of a woman living alone, especially a woman born more than forty years prior to the birth date of the child. And your husband realizes that a married couple must adopt jointly? Married couples, at whatever stage of marriage, *may* and *must* adopt jointly."

Nora wiped her eyes and nose with her tissue. "Damn it," she said. "Sorry."

"I'm not judging you."

"If you say you're not, who am I to say you are?"

"That's clever."

She inquired of the ceiling, "How much more am I prepared to ask of this man?"

"What's his name?"

"One more thing I left out."

"All right."

"His name is Kees, my husband. But I left something out and I should just tell you, you're a priest."

"I am a slave in the mines of sin. Whatever you say, I've heard it before."

"You assume it's a sin."

"You're right. Forgive me. To the carpenter everything is a nail."

"Jesus was a carpenter."

"I surrender. What did you leave out?"

"Doubt this all you want. But the moment I saw Willy crying at the gate and wondered if he was the same boy I'd seen earlier, I also knew right away that all of this would happen. All of it. I knew that when I got to Holland, Kees would refuse to have me back. I knew I wouldn't be able to get the boy out of my mind. I knew I would come back here. I knew I would get some dismal job just to stay in Hamburg. I knew no one else would claim him. I knew Kees would agree to be the father at least for legal purposes. I've been living for almost a year in a vision I saw unfold for me all in a moment. I even remember seeing that Miss Fuchs would leave the room just now and then I would get angry with you. And then I would trust you somewhat, and be more candid."

"Quite a vision you've had."

"But that's the end of the vision. You make it sound like we can't win."

"Yes, you can. He will try to make it a contest. If you don't compete with him, he'll see there's no one to defeat. We could send Willy home with you in a week."

"I saw it all, right up to now, but I don't know what comes after this."

"A chat comes after."

"Not a hearing." She ruffled her hair and smiled. "I so hope this will work," she said.

With a rush he recognized that so did he. "Was there anything else you wanted to ask?"

"What happened to your head?"

The priest said, "I was attacked by a wild animal."

"Really?" she gasped.

"A hawk."

"I can't believe it."

"It is because my vocation demands that I espouse a love of truth that no one believes I'm telling it. We live in an era of disenchanted irony. We say we *can't* believe, when we have not even *tried* to believe."

Nora picked up a scone and put it back down.

"I saw the hawk flying toward me, but I didn't realize that I myself was the threat it feared until it knocked me over."

"You knew you were innocent of the threat, but how could the animal have known?"

"Perhaps it wasn't wrong," the priest hypothesized.

"What do you mean?"

"Perhaps I had intentions intolerable to my conscious mind and therefore invisible to me. Perhaps the savage animal in myself was rising up to do something of unspeakable wickedness. And being helpless to stop it, I instead unconsciously invented other, acceptable intentions.

Of course I can't know, by definition: as they say, the unconscious is *really* unconscious. But the hawk that came after me saw only another animal and knew only its animal plot and acted to stop me."

"Stop you from what?"

"What were my acceptable intentions? Or what did the hawk think it saw me about to do?"

"Both."

"There was a fawn at the edge of the woods. I thought I needed to protect it from the hawk. So I threw a rock to startle it into running away."

"And what did the hawk think you were going to do?"

"It probably thought I intended to kill its children."

Part Two

The New Country

11

He had driven the Electra up to Bobby Heflin's house in the desert and had got out shading his eyes from the afternoon sun with his hand, and the woman he mistook for Sally came to one of the doors wearing an extension cord and a can opener like jewelry around her neck saying the house had no phone. "Bobby run off," she said. The others had gone too about the same time. The place was for sale. The bank owned it all.

Her name was Louisa. And while the knowledge penetrated him that the future he had come here for had already ended, she was introducing him to the boy, and they shook hands. She asked if he was hungry, and he admitted that yes, he was a little hungry. He didn't admit that he hadn't eaten a thing since breakfast yesterday in Liberal, Kansas. She insisted he come inside. He followed her and the boy through the door. Piñon wood burned in the cookstove. A new smell to him at the time. The smell was never to lose its mythy power of turning whatever the moment into an eternity. And a pot of meat simmered on the cookstove in a foreign green sauce, not unpleasant smelling. She put some of the meat on corn tortillas, on an earthenware dish, and spooned a little of the cooking sauce over it and showed him how to fold the things up. He'd never eaten a taco before. He opened his teeth. And the combination of the flavors in his mouth was like music. Then he swallowed, and the moment was gone.

The spirit of meat was death, okay, but when the people from the church had given Louisa an old rooster the other day she knew what to do with it. And the boy Elroy must grow in spite of the corruption that surrounded us everywhere. Elroy had her cooking spoon and was licking it while he formed a shaky structure out of the kindling on the floor, realizing a vision he alone could see. She liked the way the boy climbed her skirts. She wanted him to be strong. He hadn't chosen to be born into a dying world. It wasn't for her to make decisions that shrank his bones or made him weak. Some of the others had claimed a mineral supplement could provide all the nonplant nutrition a growing child needed, so they shouldn't even have to resort to milk. This was when they were debating whether one of the guys should go work in the world for cash or whether they should sell the last of the cows. There had been talk of gleaning the material for the supplement from the rocks thereabout on the ranch.

Elroy was in his body a constituent of this place; he was made of the plants grown on it and belonged here; and she believed in the love they'd all built together; but look, she wasn't insane. Let the boy play with the rocks, he shouldn't have to eat them. Anyway, the church lady had already butchered this rooster by the time she drove out with the other groceries that would keep. Corn meal, powdered milk. What with they had no electric anymore, Louisa would have to can the meat, and did she know how to do that?

Of course she did. Who didn't know how to can? At first she ate only a morsel of the meat, to remind herself that not one of us was pure, we all had a beast inside. Then a small jar of it every few days because she didn't want to get weak. The boy's portion she chewed to a mash, then kissed the boy and spat some of it between his lips. He'd never eaten meat before. But she had come to terms with her decision. She needed to show him it was not a corruption to eat another creature's flesh if your hunger was pure. The boy had laughed. Everything was a game. Climb the skirt and get a kiss of rooster and climb down and swallow and climb back up.

She knew that there had been somebody called the Volunteer back when Bobby was a killer. And they'd eaten strange birds in Australia and probably murdered babies in Vietnam, and in a hundred other ways had not kept their bodies pure. Also that the Volunteer was a scary-looking fellow. Now, here he sat in the flesh and didn't look one bit like the half-naked soldier in the beach pictures. She meant, clearly he was the same person, but boy, was he changed. To be honest he looked much scarier now than in the pictures. His eyes, she meant. He looked at her and she looked at him. He said the corn and meat things were real good, thanks. Tacos, she repeated.

Was it true what she'd heard, that his eyes came open in his sleep? And that none of the boys told him, and to see if they could insert stuff in his dreams they'd hung in front of his open, sleeping eyes a magazine cartoon of a devil roasting people in the fires of hell? And then in the morning the boys asked him how he slept, and he said real good, and they asked if he had dreams, and he said no, nothing?

He said no, that was a trick they'd played on Bobby. Though come to think, maybe his own eyes came open too in his sleep and they'd played the same trick on him. He couldn't know, could he?

Also, she remembered the Volunteer was an Iowa farm boy.

But no, not a farm, he said fatefully and without calculation. He came from the city of Davenport, down on the floodplain. His name was Tilly, Dwight. And at that moment he killed and burned at last the residual boy he had come here prepared to revive, the person Bobby knew, and scattered the remains. She said she was pleased to meet him, Tilly, Dwight. Her bare neck and clavicles were red with sun. And thereafter, so long as she was liking him, she called him Dwight. Most others he would come to know used the last name instead. When she was remote from him or uncertain she called him the sergeant, and when he said he was out of the service now, he was free of his past, so why did she have to call him that?, she said because she never wanted to forget that he was a killer.

He had never entered an adobe house before that first day. It was dim and hard in all its surfaces like a cave and very old. The rough-hewn timbers in the ceiling were strong and dry. The place made for sound habitation, and he couldn't fathom what had possessed Bobby to let the exterior dilapidate so. The bank required she keep the packed earth floors clean of mess or toys in case a buyer should come. The world's law said the bank now owned the whole Heflin spread from the leaves of the mesquite to the rocks ten miles underground, so the bank was entitled to sell it, which they were trying to do for the outrageous sum of seventy-seven thousand dollars. Some fool would finance it at 9 percent over thirty years and end up paying three times that much—but look. It was obviously an ego poison for anybody to imagine himself the owner of a piece of land. If the bank owned it now, let *them* take the poison. People belonged to places, not the other way around. If you needed in the world's way to speak of a name that rightfully belonged on the deed, that name could only be Elroy P. Heflin. Because he was born right in this room and had never slept a night off the place in his life.

Tilly slept that first night on a cot in one of the spare rooms. From the second night onward, he slept in Louisa's bed with her.

The world had required that the boy have a name. The law required a name. They called him Heflin, not after Bobby but after the place to which three generations of Heflins before Bobby had lent their name and which they had left him according to the world's law. And it was beautiful, to a lot of them, most of the time anyway, that nobody, really nobody, could have said for sure which of the guys was Elroy's father. They were all the same pinkish color more or less. And the puppy piles of screwing, everybody screwing everybody else, God, it was paradise. They were *making* something. They had chosen love. Right here in this short life, not waiting for the next one, which was how they'd all come to agree that what they were doing wasn't really about Jesus, as at first it had seemed. Even the guys could screw among themselves. That took a long time for the guys to get used to. Was it clean? Was it only a confusion of the beast? Maybe. But the way to treat our beast is with mercy.

They were all practical. They weren't about drugs. If a drug helped loosen something overnight, that was okay. But you couldn't carry water from the acequia for the garden all morning if you were on acid. What would happen was you would spill the water. She told Tilly all this some weeks on, while they were ferrying water from the old rain barrels for the bath they shared. The hand pump on the kitchen sink was too cumbersome for so much water as a bath. The boy followed them dragging a mesquite branch for a pile he was building behind the house. The sun fell all over their bodies and everything else while they hauled the water, and she asked how Tilly kept his balance missing the toes. Practice, he guessed. And she asked if it was his only injury from the war. And before he could tell her that his foot had been injured after he'd returned to the States, but the divot in his back, where she sometimes put the pad of her middle finger as she held him while they screwed, had come from an NVA slug still holed up in his flesh somewhere, he decided to let Louisa make a new past for him. Yes, he said, that was the only one.

Some of the guys had left some of their clothes, and she gave them to Tilly to wear.

They had all seven, women and guys, been in their prime. And they could screw and screw even in the middle of the day outside if the wind was low. Then one of the others would come by and say, "May I come in?" That was the language they agreed on. And the most proprietary thing anybody ever said, if the moment wasn't right, was "Hold on a minute, baby." Mostly they said, "Yes." Or they said, "And how." Or they said, "Oh please, yes." They were lean and strong. And you know, she'd learned something, that vanity only corrupted you when you hoarded it. Because when you were vain of your family, like she had been vain of Lucy's white feet and their painted nails, and Conrad's strong hamstrings, it felt like unstingy love spreading itself out from you to the others and the others to you. If it was wrong to find herself pretty, then it was wrong to find Lucy pretty, or Katerina.

Four women, herself and those two and Sally, who they kept having to hide in the arroyo from the pigs. Now, the sheriff in this county didn't count as a pig. Bobby had it good with the local law from so many years of Heflins out here. But more than once Nevada state troopers had come snooping around, which had to be a hundred kinds of illegal, trying to capture Sally and drag her back to her mother in Carson City. They all came to a strong understanding about that mother. She was a deep teaching to them in the killing power of love when you point it like a gun at somebody and say, You're mine. Their own love was a fire in the dark in the desert that drew them all freely around a central heat, a light that sustained them.

They were all seven of them practical and they tried to be forgiving of the beast we all are in addition to the soul. Everybody knew without saying so that you had to have more women than guys. They had an attitude of, Why pretend? We see how the bulls behave. We have it so good, and we know this is precious and precarious. And we know it'll end. So let's keep it and respect it and love each other and forgive the men for sparks of jealousy, or when he rolls over and decides to screw Lucy instead of me. I have a beast too. I have a gun I want to point, to keep something for myself by killing it. I say to myself, This hurts my pride, okay. And also, Lucy has beautiful breasts. Just beautiful, for now. Her glossy flawless skin like a paint in which she'd just come from swimming. And Conrad's naked ribs, the fresh dense animal hair on his arms and legs. Their limbs working, the ends of the bones showing through the flesh, the muscles doing what they were made for, twisting, gripping. And I get to lie here and watch them. Isn't that some kind of grace?

The togetherness they had. You couldn't have reckoned it unless you were in it. They were practical. They knew we each die severally and alone. But there was love in the meantime. Love to *make,* you know? Not to wait for. But to build up.

Louisa was twenty-five now, and her prime lay already behind her. She still liked how she looked. She rubbed herself in coconut oil every day, down to the toes. But for about three years there, they had made heaven on earth with love every day. Nothing that had happened in the unraveling disproved any of this. Times were always going to change. Not to discriminate between the sexes, but men aren't naturally as open to loving. For example a man could only screw one person at a time, but a woman could take it three ways at once. That wasn't proof. But why deny the body's shape, you know? Men have to learn love, and they can do it, but they have to *decide* to do it.

They all knew they would break. Let's do this *until* we break. She didn't regret anything. But they were over now. And she often felt powerfully alone. Whether worse than the others she didn't like to guess. Anyhow it was probably a grace that at the time they broke she was the only one of them who could still nurse Elroy a little, so they all decided she should keep him. With birth control pills and practice pumping, all four women had tried to make milk. A beast of man in him right from the beginning, he'd change his preference among them week to week. They didn't talk about who was the mother. The mother was Katerina, but they didn't talk about it. He called them each severally "Ma." All the men he called "Sir."

"Sex is glorious, Dwight Tilly," Louisa said one night, touching his nakedness, letting him touch hers. He had been crashing at the Heflin house for two months, excoriated by love and a hope for the three of them together—Louisa, Elroy, and himself—that was so far beyond any previous imagining he wanted to ditch his name yet again and let her give him a new one and start over. Instead that was when he became Dwight Tilly for real. She called him by that name, and he believed her. A door closed once and for all behind him. If Bobby came back around and said, I thought your name was Frade . . . But it didn't matter. He never saw Bobby again.

Except in torture visions. Of Bobby or one of the other two, called Conrad and Luther. Jealous visions of these other men she loved collectively more than him, so that he often left their bed and walked in the desert at night and tried to make himself disappear. The jealousy relentless in assault as a pack of dogs chasing him from the house. Disappear. Leave her the ninety-eight dollars he still had saved. Leave the car.

Then the desert cold bit him and he went back to the house. In the cookstove, piñon fire. Elroy asleep on the cot. Louisa lay beneath a quilt in the next room. He pulled the quilt aside but hesitated to lie down. He wondered if in her sleep, when he touched her, she mistook him for one of the others. She would turn with her small and prematurely wrinkled hand open and pat his beard and scratch it and smile and be nevertheless asleep.

He said, "Louisa." The name itself was a torture. The others must have used it too. Used her. Bent her. Picked her up and put her down. Been scratched by her. Called by their names. The perfect round breasts were not his. As the piñon smoke was not his, or the boy or the house. Someone else had licked this rib; had known it was not his but *felt* it was his; had maybe made a joke, like Baby, I gave God that rib to make you with, and had laughed but *felt* at night it was true, the rib was part of him. The way as a small boy Vollie had *felt* it was true that people, like corn, were made of earth and water.

He wanted to undress and lie in the bed with her naked and spoonwise as was their custom. The door closed on Elroy, the stove, creation. He and Louisa alone in the dark. But if he touched her now he would stick to her. Every part of him that touched her would cleave there. He knew it. And she had made it plain through the private, implicit language of two people together that he was welcome to cleave where he liked, but that when she walked off no part of her would come away. There would just be parts of him stuck to her, and she would bathe and shed them like mud that had dried. While he lay flayed in splotches dying of love.

One night that autumn Louisa fixed a supper of corn cakes and boiled beans. They gave thanks and ate. Tilly asked the boy what he was building with the tangle of mesquite that abutted the rear of the house and that comprehended an opening at ground level big enough for the boy to enter if he flattened himself and crawled into it on elbows and knees. The boy said, "It's a cave."

"What do you need with a cave?" Tilly asked.

"To live in after they run us off," Elroy said.

Tilly snorted.

Louisa stiffened.

Elroy scraped from a jar the last of the peach compote they were using to flavor their corn cakes and showed the empty jar to Louisa, his eyes wide with appeal.

She got up and picked through the cupboards while Tilly enquired of the boy about the architecture of caves, whether an underground or rock-enclosed element was required, whether a true cave must be discovered or could be built, what sorts of lizards one met in caves, where the flour was kept if the cave lacked a pantry; to all which questions the boy gave ready answer. Louisa came back to the table and said there was no more compote and gave the boy a bit of crushed honeycomb. The boy chewed it and then held forth in detail about how things would end here soon, how his ma should probably think of her own cave and so should Sir.

Tilly stole a glance at Louisa, who spooned some more beans onto the boy's plate and put the spoon down and touched her eyes with the back of her wrist and put her hands in her lap.

Elroy turned to Tilly with a constricted brow seeming to ask for manly counsel. It was only then Tilly registered that Louisa was trying not to cry, and that the boy had recognized it right away and had intended all his answers to make her feel better. Tilly returned to the boy a look that said he had no advice yet to give.

The boy told Louisa he was sorry.

She said, "You ain't got anything to be sorry for, have you?"

He was sorry because his own cave was only big enough for himself, Elroy said, or she could have stayed with him. He had only the brush to build a boy-size cave and no more.

That night Tilly closed the bedroom door on Elroy and the stove and lay down next to Louisa on the bed. "I haven't been straight with you," he said, "about money."

Louisa was sitting up, brushing her hair. "You ain't stole any from me, that's for sure," she said. "What do you have, a loan on the Electra? Forget it. They won't find you here."

Tilly slid to the end of the bed and turned to face her and sat cross-legged like a mendicant, and she gave him her foot and whimpered in the way that meant she wished him to rub it forcefully underneath with his thumb, and he took the foot and held on to it with both hands but didn't press it and said, "I mean there's some money I think I can have if I want it."

She dragged the brush through her hair, inspecting the ends. The hair interested her, the money did not.

He said, "You aren't listening."

She withdrew her foot and sat at attention wearing an ironic indulgent smile and said, "Ready cash money?"

"Yes, but that doesn't make it right for me to use it."

"Did you cross the law?"

"No."

"But you done something underhanded."

"It's more what I didn't do."

"What happens if you don't use this money? Who gets it?"

"I don't know."

"You said it mightn't be right for you to use it."

"I didn't think so, but now I wonder."

She made a low birdlike friendly noise which meant something in her personal idiom that he couldn't yet distinguish.

"I let some people down," he said. "There was a lot I could have done for them, and I didn't do any of it."

"So why'd they pay you?"

He did not set right her use of "pay" and only answered, "There was no one else the money belonged to. That doesn't mean I deserve it." She had tucked the withdrawn foot with its shapely be-ringed toes under her, and he wanted the foot back but didn't ask for it. "An envelope came in the mail. There was a cashier's check in it."

"That's bigger than a regular check or what?"

"Yes, but I didn't cash it. It was yellow, the check." His naked wedge foot lay before him on the bedsheets like a creature from another land. "I kept the check a long time in the breast pocket of my winter coat, like maybe I'd forget it there. Then there was a day in East Haven, in Connecticut, where I was learning to walk again. I didn't have any cigarettes left, and my money clip was back in the room where I was living. Only about an eighth of a mile away but I could have told you exactly how many steps at the time. Then it came to me I had the coat on, so I had the check. And I always kept my ID in the front pocket of my pants. And I was standing in front of a corner store, and I could see the cigarettes through the window behind the cashier, and there was a savings bank across the street. So I went into the bank and showed my ID and filled out the card for an account. Then I gave the teller the check and asked for twenty dollars of it, and she said she could never advance money on a check that size. I said how about five dollars, and she said it would take two weeks to clear it, and I took the check back and went into the lobby. Then I felt a shot or a stab under my ribs in the back, but there was nothing there. I got out the check and folded it a few times and pressed the little trapdoor button on the ashtray in the lobby and I stuffed the check in there with the butts and I walked out."

"And you don't reckon it would be right to call these people and ask them to cut you another check? Is that what you're saying? After you let them down and then you done that way with the check they sent?"

"The people I let down are dead."

"Oh."

"It's just a company holding the money. I'm sure I could get another check. But I don't want it," he said. "Unless. Well, that's what I want to ask you."

"You're talking to the wrong girl about money. The last check I saw was in Robert Lee, Texas, three years ago."

Tilly said, "What if I got another check and cashed it and bought this place?"

"That's crazy. Why?"

"What do you mean why? So we could stay on it is why."

She said with a dismissing wave, "You'd have to show regular income to get the mortgage."

He said, "There wouldn't be any need of a mortgage."

"You'd have to keep cattle. It's the only way to get enough revenue out of a spread this size to make it. We tried everything else."

"I could keep cattle. Like—we could."

"And you'd have to learn about keeping cattle. It ain't nothing like the truck driving you done before."

"I might know some already about cattle keeping."

They sat listening awhile to the wind snapping the tarp that covered the window.

She said, "The Lord is asking you a question."

"You too."

"No, he isn't," she said. "It's your money."

"Not if I don't use it."

She sat up rigid against the carved and darkly lacquered headboard of the bed in which Bobby Heflin had been born and said, "This is *your* mistake, or it isn't. Don't make me share it with you."

Tilly said, "You said it was evil to own property. I guess it wasn't evil when your friend owned property and he let you stay here. And you fucked him for his trouble."

Louisa got up and put on her underclothes and pulled up her long knee socks and got into her dress and one of the men's heavy sweaters she wore about the house and stood in the corner with arms crossed low over her stomach and regarded him.

Tilly said, "You'll share Bobby's mistake but not mine. Why's that?"

She stood right next to the door but stayed in the room as if to prove she refused to be wounded.

"You want to walk out and sleep in one of the other rooms," he said. "Go ahead. Why don't you do it?"

"I deserve some of this," she said. "Not all of it. I reckon I'll stand and listen till you're finished."

"All right. Do you want to live here?"

"Not so much I'd be willing to have you look at me every day like you're doing now. You'll say later, I didn't want to cash that filthy check but I done it for her sake."

"Does that mean no?"

"It means what I said. And I'm not going to ask you to apologize for the mean thing you let slip a minute ago. Even Elroy can say he's sorry, but you can't, so I won't ask. I reckon that was your beast talking and not the rest of you. But Sergeant, you ought to know by now it isn't true what you said about me and Bobby. And I don't want you to suggest it again."

Tilly said, "I still have to make a decision whether to get that money and buy the spread."

She got out of her clothes again and sat in the bed and went back to brushing her hair.

He said, "I'm coming up to your side of the bed now, all right?"

"That's fine, but please don't touch me while I'm angry."

He crawled to the head of the bed and punched the pillow and slid his naked shameful body under the sheet which smelled of her, and she sat inches from him but outside the sheet as if she had already receded into the world of visions where people lost to us can be seen and even smelled but never touched.

"I hate money," he said.

"Me too," she said.

"I won't do it," he said. "That's my decision. We'll have to go someplace else."

She tied up her hair and got under the sheet and said, "All right, you can touch me now if you want to."

A few days before the sale of the land closed, the night the church man from the bank came with a pot roast and broke the news they'd finally have to leave, Tilly and Louisa lay in bed again in the dark, sweating from their exertions. She was holding his hand. He wanted to cut the hand off and give it to her.

The boy in the dark outside the worn door of the bedroom could be heard stirring. Then the boy said, "Sir? Water?"

Tilly put on his skivvies and got up and put the dipper in the bucket and brought the dipper to the boy, and the boy took it in his little paws while Tilly hovered over the handle and the boy drank about half the dipper and fell dead away asleep. Perhaps he had never really woken up. Tilly put the dipper to his own mouth and drank the rest. It was the boy's home water. A tang like pennies. The boy might forget this taste, but if it ever touched his mouth again time would swallow him whole.

Later that week they drove into Las Cruces, and Elroy was never on his home place again.

12

They slept on the vinyl bench seats of the Electra, parked in the lot of a Lutheran church in Las Cruces.

The boy sat up in the night behind the wheel and said, "Where'm I at?"

Tilly and Louisa lay in the back under their coats tightly spoonwise along the deep seat. She had not woken up. He waited unmoving to hear the quilt rustle and the vinyl squeak of the boy lying back down. The wind kicked up, and stopped. Tilly lay his head on her neck again and descended through disjoint wakeful dreams—of barns, a shed, a sty, of the grinder worked by hand and screwed to a vertical timber within the barn that cracked corn for the hens. A clapboard house decayed and slanting, its chimney collapsed. Then of Coke box houses on low stilts with thatched straw for roofs, crushed or napalmed, black smoke pouring up like a waterfall inverted.

In the front seat, the boy said clearly, to no one, "This ain't real."

Tilly sat up careful not to wake Louisa and pulled the lock in the rear door and got out stocking footed in the mercury-vapor light of the empty lot. He tugged from his jeans pocket the ring with its two remaining keys, to the Electra's ignition and its door locks. The frigid wind kicked up again. He unlocked the driver's-side door and opened it. The boy sat saucer-eyed and querulous, daring him to pass off this evident dream world as the true world after an apocalypse that had left people without cots or even cookstoves to sleep by, and the only light in the outdoors a high green lamp that made men into ghouls.

Tilly said, "Come here."

Elroy suffered himself to be picked up within the wrappings of quilt. A bleary hum of distant highway traffic. The child's milky night breath, and the stink of the man's night sweat in his several days' clothes. The cold desert night capped in low cloud.

Tilly crouched through the rear door and pressed the quilt with the boy into the cavity between Louisa's knotted arms and lap. Elroy fussed and situated himself, sprawling. There was no room on the seat for a third. Tilly took his slicker coat, which had belonged to one of the other men, and climbed in the front and pushed up the armrest and wrapped himself with the slicker. He stuffed his toes into the warm fold of the seat where the boy had been lying, and gradually the chill left them. He lay facing the exposed underbelly of the heater core under the passenger dash. Shards of snow tinked against the steel roof. He listened to Louisa's and Elroy's snuffly but easeful breathing, the boy's breath out of time with the woman's but their sounds mixed, the elemental animal sounds, the air from one mingling with the air sucked into the other—listened to the two of them but did not see them, saw only the inert surfaces of the interior of the car and the glowing green-misted windows and his own approximate shape in its slicker shroud. Three people in the dark together, one apart from the other two. Like the lieutenant in the adjacent tunnel chamber in the dark when he and Wakefield had heard the lieutenant crying.

In the morning, they drove to a truck stop on the edge of town. They unpacked fresh flannel shirts and underwear and went inside and paid for a five-minute shower. They were all three lean and they fit snugly in one stall, but the shower head was a cannon. The boy cowered from it. Tilly baffled the current with his hands so the water would come down on the boy with less violence while Louisa quickly worked the knots from the boy's hair. They shared the foxed old towel that came with the stall and they dressed. At the luncheonette counter of the truck stop they ate rye toast with raspberry jam and eggs and Cream of Wheat. Tilly and Louisa drank their coffee looking at the television. Elroy had never seen television and looked at it with an air of hostile impatience as though it were a salesman come to the door at mealtime. The show concerned two deliverymen in jumpsuits launched into outer space by mistake.

Tilly paid the bill, and Louisa wished him luck, and he left on his own and drove downtown to the Motor Vehicle Department and showed his New York State driver's license and filled out the forms to transfer it to the New Mexico State chauffeur's license required for all forms of commercial driving. He took the written test and passed it. Then he took the driving test and passed it too. After he read aloud the line of letters on the eye chart, the clerk said, "Okay, pard. You win."

The license would be valid for one year and expired on the last day of his birth month and cost $3.25. The clerk asked his date of birth. Tilly looked at the old license and showed it and said his date of birth was November 14, 1948. The clerk asked where he lived. Tilly said he'd lately moved. The clerk said that was all right, where was he living now? And Tilly told him to put down "no fixed address."

"I can't do that."

"All right. Put down One Hundred Louisa Street, Alamogordo, New Mexico."

"Is that where you live?"

"Yessir."

"Why didn't you say so?"

"We might move again."

"Long drive from Alamo. Why didn't you just go to the MVD up there?"

"They don't do the chauffeur's test up there."

"They don't?"

"Not on Saturday."

"I didn't know that. Now, this entitles you to operate a motor vehicle for the purpose of transporting persons or property for compensation. You can drive anything you want except a school bus."

"All right."

"You can drive a Sherman tank. But you want to operate a bus or motor vehicle transporting children for compensation, you got to wait a year and you got to get three responsible persons who know you well to sign a certificate attesting to your good character and habits."

"Fine."

"All that, you got to file in Albuquerque. You ain't going to drive schoolchildren in a bus?"

"Nossir."

"Set awhile and we'll laminate this thing. Then you'll be a truck-driving son of a gun, like Red Sovine," he said. "Hold on. You wrote brown for your eyes."

"Yessir."

"Your eyes are green."

"Nossir, they're brown."

"I'm going to put green. You go to the head and look. We'll have you back in Alamo by suppertime."

A while later the clerk called his name, and he went to the counter. The clerk said, "Did you look at a mirror?"

"Nossir, I guess I'll have to take your word for it."

He found Louisa and Elroy in the windowless truck stop laundry room where Elroy sat on the floor, his mouth agape, watching the churning clothes in the porthole glass of the washing machine. Louisa was marking up the front pages of a *Las Cruces Sun-News* she'd taken from the trash. She always read with a pencil and underlined and wrote *yes* or *maybe* in the margin, or wrote *lies, shame on you, are we stupid?* right on the printed text as if talking over it.

"Says, 'Ford offers conditional pardon to draft dodgers and deserters,'" she enunciated. "You got to reaffirm your allegiance to the U.S.A. But then you do two years of a public service job, and they clean your record."

He waited for the horsey snort of indignation to follow—he enjoyed all her rhetorical noises, a hiss recognized a stroke of crazy luck; *hmm* meant she agreed, go on; a *hoo*ing like a mourning dove equaled commiseration. But she only let this news hang in the air unremarked upon and looked elsewhere down the page.

"That article gives you a notion," he said.

"As a backup," she said. "Down the line. If you can't find anything else."

"Let me get this straight."

"Absolute and total backup," she said casually but wouldn't look at him.

"I tell them, 'I'm a pansy. I swear it. I deserted.' So I can get to sweep the streets for two dollars an hour?"

She blushed and turned the page.

"I'm sorry," Tilly said. "Sarcasm."

"Forget it."

"You were trying to help."

"I think I was trying to do something different. I think I was trying to make believe you was someone else. I think I was trying to make believe you went AWOL on your own."

"Is that what the others did?"

"Or you was 1-A, and we was hiding you. But you ain't hiding. You're right there with your killer's mark on your arm. And I'm here with you. Sometimes I don't know what to make of myself."

"I'll get something real soon."

"What was your draft classification? I don't even know that. Tell me it was 1-A. Tell me you didn't have practically no choice at all."

"I wasn't drafted."

"I don't understand what you mean."

"If you go in and sign up, why would they need to draft you?"

She stuffed the newspaper in the trash among the clumps of lint and she twisted up her hair and stuck the pencil through the knot. Then she folded her arms and looked at him and looked away and said, "Wow."

"What?"

"That's how Bobby come to call you the Volunteer? Because you signed up on your own free will?"

Tilly thought a minute. He said, "Yes, that's why. What did you think it was?"

"I guess I knew but I didn't want to know."

"I'm not sorry."

"I know you ain't. You never get sorry."

"Doesn't mean I'd do it all again the same way."

"I need to think about this."

Tilly said, "Well, tell me what you're thinking about."

"I'm thinking if the girls in my high school saw me now."

"You look nice. You always look nice."

She laughed. Her eyes were remote with misgiving. She said, "Love don't know any principles at all, does it?"

Tilly felt a catch in his throat and he coughed to scratch it, but it wouldn't soften. He turned to the boy on the floor and rasped, "How'd you like that outer space show on the TV?"

Louisa refolded her arms, watching the boy, addressing the man. "He told me, 'I don't believe *any* of it.' Them were his words."

"They send people into space, Elroy. On top of rockets."

"Go on," Louisa said, "prepare him for the world's truth."

"I like *this* show," Elroy said, pointing at the sudsy window.

"Did you pass?" Louisa asked Tilly.

"I did."

"Let me see it."

He showed her the license, and she smiled at the picture, and he said, "Turn that thing over a minute and look at me. What color are my eyes?"

"Green."

"They're brown."

"Go look. They're green. What does it say here?" She turned the license back over. "Says they're green. That's right."

"They're brown. Eyes don't change color once you're grown, do they?"

"Go look."

"I don't want to."

"Why not?"

"I don't want to, that's all. We have to be careful now. That thing cost us a fortune."

"No more champagne and oysters."

"We'll be all right."

"I know it," she said.

"You do? How come?"

She put her hand in his beard and scratched it. "Ain't we all right now?"

"Yes."

"Then let's keep on going."

"All right. Elroy, time to make tracks."

"Wait," Elroy said.

"Come on. Those aren't even our clothes."

"But wait."

"What's this silly street address you put!" she said, reading the card.

"I had to think fast."

"You sweet beast." She was smiling and crying in the modest perplexing way she did sometimes after sex that didn't betray her feelings but made them more confounding to him. "Have you ever even been to Alamogordo?"

"I figured he'd know all the street names down here."

"Elroy Heflin, come on," she said, touching her eyes on her coat sleeve.

"But wait," the boy said.

Louisa asked him, "What is it makes the sun shine?"

"Love, I know," Elroy said. "But wait. I like the machine."

"Up with you," Tilly said.

"And what do you like about it?" Louisa asked.

"Up you come."

Elroy said, "I like how it keeps on going."

Tilly bought a roll of dimes from the luncheonette cashier, and the three of them went back downtown where he'd seen a public library and they sifted other newspapers there, and he and Louisa took turns at the lobby pay phone chasing leads in the want ads.

At night they built a fire in the desert and made a grill from rocks and two tire irons and cooked hominy on it with stewed tomatoes mixed in. Elroy asked for green chile but they didn't have any. All three lowered their heads. Louisa gave thanks for the fire. Tilly gave thanks for Louisa and for Elroy by name. Elroy gave thanks for chile.

Tilly said, "We don't have chile. Say thanks for what's here. Not what isn't."

Louisa said, "For—?"

"Let him think."

"For?" Louisa said.

The fire spat. No hint of breeze. The smoke drifted about them like a net underwater.

Louisa said, "I could look at a fire forever."

Tilly said, "Me too."

Elroy said firmly, "For my eyes, amen."

"Good," Tilly said.

"Very good," Louisa said.

Later, so the boy could have something to spike up his hominy, Tilly pocketed a bottle of Tabasco from the luncheonette of the truck stop where they took their showers. Elroy demanded the shower every day in determined tones he didn't otherwise use. They went along with it despite the expense. They closed and locked the shower room door and undressed, and Elroy went into the shower making yips of shock and bravery, then stood right under the stream with his eyes closed raising his arms and clenching his teeth while Tilly and Louisa briskly soaped themselves.

Nudity was nothing to Elroy. Tilly was not so bold. Even the language put him out. Before Louisa, he'd never known a woman to say aloud the words for a lady's parts. Nor a man, excepting the dirty versions.

"Vagina," she said, toweling off and pointing.

"Hush. Men don't like that word."

"Uterus."

"Stop. I know what it means. I never heard a person say it out loud is all."

She didn't believe him, though when she pointed at herself his normally frank eyes went cagey. She asked, "What do you call the equipment on a cow at calving time?"

"Once a Hereford cow started crying on the meadow at night. You could hear her from the house," Tilly said. He shivered, waiting for her to finish with the towel. Elroy had already got back into his socks and underpants. "When I was a little boy. An old man had to go call the vet. On the phone he said, 'Come quick, her back end fell out.'"

"No!"

"It's right enough, isn't it?"

She laughed and said, "What old man called the vet? I thought you grew up in a city."

He stood with his penis and testicles hanging out, in front of a woman and a child. He was embarrassed, yet he discovered he wasn't ashamed.

"Who called?" she said.

"I don't remember. Some old man." His father had called. Tilly nearly said so. The old silver head had glowed in the dark of the hall by the phone.

"Who called?" Elroy mimicked.

"The vet came and pushed it right back up inside and stitched her," Tilly said. "He didn't have to call it anything."

At last Tilly found work driving for a wildcatter. They trained him to spin chains on the drill pipe too. His timing with the chains was excellent right away, and the other men on the derrick liked him.

They came from all over, no two from the same state. One of them said Tilly wasn't going to be a bona fide chain hand until he lost some of a finger. Tilly unlaced his boot with his grease-black hands and took off the boot and sock and showed the chain hands his wedge foot and said, "That do?" The men applauded. Two of them got on their knees to appreciate the foot and nodded at it. They showed their own stub fingers, waggling them like a lady with a new ring. At quitting time, the men drank at one or another bar. The one from Wyoming passed around a box of miniature plum cakes made for them by his daughter, Sophie, an ample seducer, in steel-toe boots, whom more than one of the men had known in secret. After an hour, all the men went home. Only an hour. The work was heavy and they prized their sleep. Not since the Calamus Comets high school basketball team had Tilly so well lost himself in a gang.

Louisa cleaned houses in Las Cruces. She liked to work while the wife was home and to hear what the doctor had had to say about little Peggy's croup. These were mining executive families. Copper and lead.

Rocket propulsion families. It interested her to learn how people culti-vated the peace of their homes. The philodendrons and lime trees should be placed in the windows by the piano—not there, just to the right. Yes, *there*. Meantime think of the anguish these people had to carry. The earth-murder, the orgies of human killing that made possible the peace where they slept. She envied the strength it took to ignore such things.

An Air Force wife lay on the divan dying of thyroid cancer. But she had dragged herself to the bathroom and put on her face. Taupe hose. A chiffon blouse that matched her earrings. Her name was Marlene. She was writing a collection of poems titled *My Choice to Continue*. The subject and Marlene herself held Louisa in thrall, and she was desperate to learn what the poems contained.

"You won't let me read them," Louisa said.

"No."

"Please, I want to."

"They aren't finished. And they aren't good. And I won't show them until they're good." Marlene wore a look of endurance, though her on-cologist had promised her case was terminal. A hard look not of accept-ing but of outlasting. She said, "Get rid of that boot on the mantel. Who put that there?" The boot was an amber vase in the form of a lady's button-up shoe.

"I did. It was in the closet," Louisa said.

"Pitch it. Why should I have to look at it anymore? You were trying to make things pretty. I understand. . . . Don't touch the thermostat. It isn't cold in here. It's me that's cold. I won't be one of these people too proud to wear a blanket."

She did not however have a blanket close by. Louisa said, "Let me," and went away to hide the glass boot and find a quilt.

"Don't," Marlene said. "I'll get up in a minute. Come back here. You mustn't let lazy people make you play gofer."

Louisa went back to the living room empty-handed.

Marlene lay there, shivering. "The boot was a going-away present when we had to leave the base at Vandenberg. Henry practically *invented* the A-10, and then command transferred us here before we could even see anybody fly it. I'll get up in a minute."

Louisa polished the large mirror that overhung the mantel. She asked what the A-10 was.

"A jet aircraft. We call it the Thunderbolt. Close-air support, mostly for killing tanks," Marlene said, breathing shallowly. "If the Soviets send their mechanized divisions through the Fulda Gap—heaven forbid—the Thunderbolts will smash them—and statues of Henry will be—erected in every war college in Europe."

Louisa knew perhaps more about the Fulda Gap than Marlene reckoned. "I don't understand. What would the Russians send tanks into Germany for?"

"They did last time," Marlene said.

"But Europe is planted all over with thermonuclear weapons."

"Yes, darling. But we won't use them. Except to respond to a nuclear attack. If they want to come at us, they'll use something milder."

Louisa was like one of those Christians who prefer not to talk about Jesus with anyone outside of her congregation because she was liable to blurt the terrible truth so few people knew. She had no inclination to persuade. She didn't want to frighten anybody. But sometimes the truth came out of her like a sneeze. She said, "Right at the start there's going to be a nuclear exchange, Marlene. Nothing's going to stop it. It won't take a day to finish, maybe a couple of hours. A few folks will survive. Then they'll die from the radiation."

Marlene looked at her. She said, "No one's going to die from radiation except me."

Louisa snatched a cashmere throw from the armchair.

Marlene said, "*Don't.*" But Louisa had already covered her up and tucked the throw around her shaking feet.

"This isn't warm enough anyway." Marlene lay beautiful and stark in her weathered skin, her silver rings, conjuring poems full of deadly knowledge under her blue-painted eyelids.

"WHAT ARMY EVER CAME IN with swords when they had machine guns?" Louisa asked Tilly later. "These antitank planes, whatever Marlene was talking about, these are toys. Why are we building them? Is it really a public works program? There's got to be another reason. What are you laughing at?"

"A little grim."

"What?"

"All you told her about the end of days."

She started to laugh—then saw he'd mistaken what she'd said about a nuclear exchange for mere pessimism. "What did you reckon we were doing at the Heflin place," she said, "praying for peace?"

"Something like that, yes."

"Come on, baby, there ain't any use. I mean, nobody knows when the end is coming, but it's coming. We weren't stupid. We didn't think we could stop it. If you only had a minute left, what would you fill it with? That was our thinking."

Tilly said, "You sound like Bobby."

"Fuck you," she said. "We all sounded like each other. We don't know just when, obviously. But this here war we're in is the last war. It's only having a lull right now."

"You believe this."

"Who cares if I believe it? It's true." She had the desolate look of an eyewitness whose testimony was doubted.

"If you believed it, how come you guys decided to make a baby?"

"Well, we didn't," she insisted.

"Well, you did though."

"We decided not to."

They had known they were taking risks. They had all seven held a meeting, cross-legged on the floor by the cookstove. They could respond to their dilemma in only one way if they were to be decent and loving, but not all of them were ready for it, so they slept and came together again the next day and went on deliberating. They kept talking for three more days until they agreed to go together to Mexico, where operations could be had cheap and they would all get sterilized.

"Oh," Tilly said. "I guess I knew that." In fact, what with the two of them hadn't been using precautions, he'd assumed—but then he couldn't even think now the outrageous, foolish thing he'd assumed. The hope he'd let flower in the garden of his ignorance.

"You thought I was on the pill?" she said. But she knew better. She was letting him save face.

"Yes," he lied.

All seven of them had got into Luther's van and driven to Ciudad Juarez. Everybody was to have it done the same weekend.

"Two of them lied?" he asked.

"Yes."

"What did they do, go into a clinic and fake a limp coming out?"

"More or less."

"You had a pact. And two of them broke it. They lied to your faces."

She said, "At least two, yes." He saw her force herself not to flinch from his questions. But he kept asking, unable to stop now that his ignorance was ruined.

"That Katerina and one of the men?"

"At least one, yes."

"You didn't care to know which."

"Somebody lied, okay. Should we have made everybody defend themselves? Should we have had a trial?"

"Why not? If you wanted to get to the bottom of it."

"I thought you'd understand," she said and didn't hide her disappointment in him.

They were living in a single-wide trailer within view of the depot where Vollie Frade had first stepped out of a bus under the New Mexico sky bright with formless hope. They had lately been laying by a fixed portion of their monthly wages, and he pretended with her that this money represented only a hedge against future hardships. He never said aloud they might use it someday to put a down payment on a house. He seemed to recognize the anguish it would cause her to admit she might be capable of hoping for such a wickedness, a capitulation, as owning property—in fact a particular little cinder-block ranch house in Rincon that came with an ancient peach tree in the yard and half an acre-foot of water rights for the garden. Louisa had found the place in the foreclosure notices. Who did she think she was? Lusting after property. She had damned the bus traffic that harassed her sleep here and had conspired with this man to better their lot by saving for the mirage of a future, even while she *knew* only the present existed.

"We were more important," she said, "the thing we made was more important than nailing somebody with his mistake. Maybe that was the first crack, and we didn't admit it. But you know what, I'm glad we didn't."

"How could you ignore a lie like that?"

"We didn't ignore it."

"You had to decide to do something about it, didn't you?"

"We did. We decided to love each other."

Louisa was never his. She didn't need to say it. She radiated it all the time like a tinted light. On the street in Las Cruces a drifter kid asked them for money, his hair matted and stinking, a deathward look in his yellow eyes. He had the square teeth, plumb as piano keys, of someone whose parents had been vain of him once. Louisa said she had no money on her but she would give him a hug. The drifter kid nodded with his whole spine and said, Golly, that would be great. Then he glanced at Tilly standing behind her, and at Elroy climbing Tilly's flannel jacket, and back up at Tilly, who watched the drifter vividly until he shrank away untouched.

Louisa didn't blame Tilly for *feeling* what he *knew* wasn't true, that she was his. Did she blame his severed nerves for telling him he still had toes that stung him although they didn't exist? He didn't have her because no one had anyone. We didn't belong even to ourselves. The beast in us ordered us to do a hundred cockamamie things that weren't possible. Own land. Possess a person. To tame the beast would be to take it away from itself. When the drifter kid shrank from her embrace, she turned and looked at Tilly and later told him she could see him trying to leash the beast inside. Yes, she was grateful not to be the excuse for violence or the object of violence. But a spurt of physical violence couldn't compare with the way our several beasts savaged us from the inside all day and night when we tried to make them into something other than beasts. He probably thought he'd hidden his beast, but she saw how it fed on his resistance, multiplied his resistance, and threw it back at him.

"What woman doesn't want her man to hold his idiot temper?" he asked.

Whip his temper, more like, she said. Fire guns at it. To do violence to a creature of violence only increased the violence afoot in the world.

Tilly asked what choice did a person have. He might have known what she would say.

"All we can do with the beast is to love it," she said. He had been a killer. He had lusted after the power of America, the tools America had to multiply his killing power. In reality he had been the tool, the mul-

tiplier America had used because it was a killer. A much more dangerous killer because America had no balancing power of love as a person
has. "You only *think* you're holding your temper," she said.

"I never raised a hand to you, did I?"

"Hmm. Course not," she said, scratching his beard. "But you think
I can't see it?"

"See what?"

"The thing you're like to do every moment. And you think it's only
your power what keeps you from doing it."

"Are you saying you think I want to beat you up?"

"I'm saying—do you really want me to say this? I don't want to
change your mind or anything, or scare you."

"Say it."

"I'm saying you look around like the whole world is complete and it
works, and there's only one thing the matter with it. And that's you.
And you could make the world perfect if you only took yourself out of
it. Like disappeared."

Tilly didn't say anything, and Louisa said, "What."

"I'm trying to decide whether I understand what you're talking
about."

She made her low slide-whistle noise that meant she would wait.

THE OIL WELLS didn't pay out, and all the men were sacked. After they
had hauled the last of the drilling equipment back to the rail yard in
Deming, they went to a bar for green chile stew and posole. The chile
was like battery acid and came with a glass of milk to cool the mouth.
They toasted each other's hometowns one by one. Indian Springs,
Georgia; Waldo, Arkansas; Bishop, California; Windom, Texas; Chilli-
cothe, Ohio; Wartrace, Tennessee; Davenport, Iowa; Egbert, Wyoming;
Comayagua, Honduras; Buffalo, Missouri; Mobridge, South Dakota;

and Glendevey, Colorado. At length Missouri toasted the plum cakes of Wyoming's daughter, Sophie. They all roared and laughed but South Dakota, who shot across the broad table a tortilla plate Frisbee-wise that cracked Missouri on the mouth. Tennessee nearly fell from his chair hooting and then Wyoming, the until-now unsuspecting father, palmed a shot glass and whacked it into the skull of Tennessee. There was blood and wrestling. In the melee, bystanders were knocked to the floor. Even while they were still fighting it seemed better that the men should fall out with each other than go away from Deming still possessed by the spirit of friendship. Later, they all got in their several pickups. They signed on to other outfits in Saudi, Venezuela, Louisiana, Canada, Indonesia, Alaska, Bahrain. Only Tilly stayed in New Mexico, with Louisa and the boy.

While he looked for work they had to dip into the money that they had never said aloud was intended for the Rincon house.

Louisa tried to enroll Elroy in school. He was five by then and wondered what it was all about. The secretary at the school wouldn't let Louisa enroll him unless she was his legal parent or custodian. And the clerk at the district court wouldn't let her take out papers to become his custodian unless she was married. So Louisa and Tilly came back the next day, and a magistrate married them, and they filed the initial papers to become Elroy's guardians, and after three months of zero official inquiry whatsoever, not even an interview with a human being at all, they got a letter saying the application was approved and they should come back to the court and they did and signed the documents in front of a notary, and the boy was theirs, and they left. They bought root beers at a gas station to celebrate. Tilly dropped Louisa and Elroy at home and then drove as far north as Elephant Butte hoping to rent himself out as a mechanic on one of the big cotton and alfalfa spreads in the Rio Grande valley. He could also weld, he said. He would have tied hay bales by hand if it had come to that, but nobody was hiring. By then rent and groceries had eaten all the money for the house.

At night in the trailer in Las Cruces he asked her, "You think we'll be all right?"

"I know it," she said.

Lean years. Love years. He knew the three of them would break. No telling when, or who would do the breaking. He hoped it would not be him, but then it would have to be her. *Let's do this until we break.*

13

The people on the Heflin place had told Elroy he came from everyone. No one held more claim to him than anyone else. No one had to feed or watch him, they all did. Just like the mesquite trees, he belonged on this place here, where he was made.

It was only after he had lived in the world a couple of years, among certain people or others, in this or that place, that he figured out how completely those first people had lied. It took exactly two people to make one person; the two people who had made him had left him behind; and no one belonged anywhere.

Only Tilly seemed to tell the truth. Tilly had chosen them, Elroy and his ma, forsaking others, and didn't hide it. Between himself and Tilly, Elroy knew there was a unique solidarity that seemed to become firmer with time.

Nevertheless, Elroy never fully lost his first understanding: that he had come from everyone and that there was a place—somehow smelling of the ranch—where everyone living and dead had their home. Everyone rightly abiding together now and across the centuries past and future. To dwell in it was to be in heaven, to be kept out was to be in hell.

AFTER NONE OF TILLY'S EFFORTS to find work around Las Cruces availed, he finally got hired as a technician with the Bureau of Land Management maintaining barbed wire in remote country and testing the soil and groundwater for radioactive isotopes. Pay was chickenfeed but the job came with an RV, in which they all three lived, along with a weekly tank of gas.

In the mornings, Louisa drove the boy in the Electra—still sound in engine but falling apart in its rattletrap body—across the sun-cracked beds of lost seas and dropped him at school and went off to iron other people's napkins and sheets. Kind, foolish people drunk with hope, planting pecan trees in their yards for a future that wasn't coming. And yet—and yet sometimes the temptation to pretend the future *was* coming bit her like the will to do harm.

They put the boy to bed in the jackknife sofa of the RV. Outside, Tilly unlatched the aluminum card table under the RV's rear window and planted the two legs in the dirt, and they played the version of bridge called Back Alley that Tilly had learned in survival school. You were allowed to off-suit even if you had a card of the suit that had been led, so long as no one caught you. If you got caught reneging like this you automatically went set: you lost your whole bid and your opponent gained his. Catching the cheater out went by many names. A lot of marines called it "putting you in the hole." When eagle-eyed Louisa caught him, she called it "shafting."

"I shaft you," she said, slapping Tilly's pile of tricks and turning it over. "I led the king of spades before, and you off-suited. *There.* See? You go set."

"Aw, fuck," Tilly said.

"Hush, he'll hear you." She took the pencil from her hair and tallied the new score on a scrap of shopping bag under the Coleman lamp within the queerly windless desert night. "You go back three, six, nine, *twelve*. I go up nine."

He looked at her; she looked at him, differently.

They couldn't afford beer or cigarettes. The piñon smoke from the campfire was intoxicant enough. She riffled the cards in her long fingers then pressed down on the overlap and bent the far edges to make the bridge, and the cards interleaved in her hands, and she riffled again and finished with the bridge and offered him the cut. He tapped the top card, and she dealt and turned the last card faceup, which showed the trump suit was diamonds. He had the big joker and three diamonds besides in a hand of seven and he told her his bid was six.

"Ain't you got brass. I bid one," she said and wrote it down.

"We'll see. I got a hole to dig out of now." He led the spade queen, and she followed suit with a four, and he took the trick.

She said, "You never asked how we come a cropper on the Heflin place."

"You want to tell me?"

"Just—you never asked. Why did you never ask?"

He played another spade, and she off-suited, and he stacked the second trick crosswise on the first.

"Did you think we all got mad at each other after our money run out? That wasn't it."

He led with the jack of clubs, and she sat up vexed and off-suited again.

He looked at his cards. He said, "Sweetheart, now I'm going to make you pay for putting me in the hole."

"Does it make you mad to think about you might've come before, and you could've been a part of us?"

She was more than competitive at cards. She would push any advantage to the hilt. She seemed to have no idea the lengths she would go to, to win.

He led with the big joker which compelled her to surrender her highest trump, and she said, "*Damn it,*" and showed the king of diamonds and flung it across the table and looked up at the stars and looked at him squarely and said, "Even if you'd come earlier, it wouldn't have mattered."

Tilly gathered the trick. His trustful mind didn't detect the knife coming. She said, "You couldn't ever have been one of us. You ain't our kind, Sergeant."

He cast about in the surrounding dark of the desert flats where the RV was camped for some impending tidal wave or person he knew to be dead, any telltale impossibility to tip him off that he was having a nightmare.

"The way it happened was one night we all took off our clothes."

"Why are you doing this? Are you trying to make me mad enough I'll hit you so you can be right about my temper?"

"Luther and Katerina were going to Oregon together in his van next day by themselves. And Sally and Lucy were going back to Nevada where they come from. And Bobby and Conrad were going to see about getting to Thailand. And we were all naked and we were all crying. And we were outside like this around the fire. And Elroy was inside asleep like now."

Tilly put his cards down.

"Bobby come up behind me and kissed my neck. Skinny boy. The others had beards, but he couldn't grow one. And I could feel his cock stand up against my leg from behind."

Tilly put his hands on the armrests of the folding chair. He got up. He went into the RV and got a quilt. He took it to the Electra. Louisa was still sitting at the card table. He turned the key in the ignition and he sped off across the trackless desert undisturbed by brush or washout, the fenders trembling. After he had driven about five miles he parked and lay down and tried to sleep under the quilt. But he couldn't get himself to lie still. He sat up behind the wheel alone in the dark asking the instrument panel what to do. Asking his silverhead father what to do. He could see the campfire in its solitary distance. He knew better than to drive back with his blood roiling.

His father would have said, Do nothing fast if you mean to do it right. But his father was not here, and his hands and feet as if automatically turned on the car and drove it back to the RV. He was afraid he would get out and hit her, and he was afraid it would feel good and right.

When he got out of the car, Louisa was feeding the fire, wrapped in his flannel jacket that had belonged to the one called Conrad.

Louisa was crying. She said, "You won't never understand how I miss them. You can't help me. You think we just run out of money. So, we run out of money, so what? If we still had love, the money wouldn't have counted. We would've found a way. We must have gave up on loving. That's the only way to explain it. What was the matter with us? It wasn't anyone's fault but ours." She wiped her eyes on a sleeve of the jacket and said, "Let's you and me finish the game now, please."

Tilly sat down. He said through his teeth, "I forget whose lead it is."

"You don't either forget. You were winning."

But he had in fact forgotten, and when he looked at the three trump cards in his hand a rush came over him in spite of everything, and he saw the four tricks he'd already taken from her, and the sequence of the game repaired itself in his mind, and he remembered the score, that he had gone set in the previous round but was winning the present one and charging now with a hand full of trump.

Louisa studied the score and her cards. She had the damnedest way of crying and letting the grief out, and finishing, and coming back to business.

Tilly played the queen of trump.

Louisa said, "Asshole."

He said, "Remember when you said I think the world is right and finished except that I'm in it?"

"Yes."

"And I wanted out and I was like to disappear?"

"Yes. Case in point you run off just now, didn't you?"

He gathered the trick. He said, "I don't want out. I want in."

She made the dove sound of commiseration. It meant, Poor thing, too bad.

"I want in," he repeated.

"You can't. It's over."

"No, I want in with you."

"How much more do you got to own? We're married. Law says so."

"You know what I mean."

"You could chop me up and eat me like a heifer for all the law cares."

"That letter Bobby wrote me said, 'Love all men. Love everything.' All right. Can't I be part of that?"

"No."

"I can't be part of all men?"

"No, you don't understand. So no."

"Why do I have to understand?"

"I said no," she said.

ACCORDING TO THE NEW RULE, Elroy had to come up with at least one new thing for which to give thanks at grace every evening before supper could commence. He sat looking at the steaming T-bone steaks in their puddle of red fatty juice on the dish in the middle of the table. The potatoes and luscious sour cream. His brow was drawn in thought. Outside, snow fell on the empty mountains. Then he remembered a plan he had made and he asked to be excused.

"Just say something before our steaks get cold," Tilly said.

But the boy promised he would only need a second, and Louisa excused him from the table, and he went to his book bag on the jackknife sofa and took out the list he'd made at school when he'd had a pencil and paper and could think and had anticipated the present challenge and had prepared a list of items for which he would give thanks in the days ahead. He looked at the list and stuffed it back in the bag and returned to the table and climbed onto his chair.

Louisa said, "For?"

"Okay," Elroy said. "For the bear."

Tilly said, "Elroy."

"Let him explain. What bear?"

"The bear in my dream."

"Elroy, we're hungry. Cut this out. Pick something real."

"What color was the bear?" Louisa asked.

"It was brown. It was a grizzly bear."

"What did it do? Why are you thankful for it?"

Elroy said, "When the wolves come at me, the bear killed all of them."

THE BLM REORGANIZED Tilly's Resource Area and closed his operation. The field manager offered to get him trained to inspect and enforce oil and gas leases, but Tilly would have to work in East Texas. Louisa had come from there and sworn never to go back, which he respected. So they moved all the way up to McKinley County, by the Navaho country, where Tilly got work running the crusher at a mill that processed uranium ore.

McKinley County was so distant Elroy had never heard of it. They might as well have gone to another state. The country hereabout was red. The Navaho kids at school didn't mix with him. Neither did the Hispanics, of centuries-old families and ties here. Nor the more recent

Mexicans, who were the smallest in their bodies and the most likely to share food at lunchtime and the most likely to fight. The only other Anglos were two girls; and while in his youth in Las Cruces Elroy had mixed with girls, he didn't want to do it in this new country that was a fresh start offered to him at age seven. Instead he rode his bike alone in the vast arroyos or watched TV or studied the secret world that inhered in the cedar-smelling old closets and defunct appliances of the house they were renting. The hidden history inside of things. The hand that had driven the nail from which he hung the jacket in his room. The man attached to this hand. The wagon trail that had brought the man here. The people to the east or south who had made the man. The trails that brought those people to the place where they had made him. The way each of them came from two other people and they each from two more people, and the trails diverged the further back you went. The infinity of people in the unbounded past it took to make just one person who drove a nail and died.

A previous inhabitant of this rented house had left installed in the pantry wall an old black Western Electric telephone of the kind with a hanging earpiece and a separate cone for speaking that was fixed in the box itself so that you spoke facing the wall. The phone didn't work because they didn't have the money to turn it on.

Elroy closed himself inside the absolute dark of the pantry and sat atop the stool he kept in there. He thought of a sequence of numbers and repeated it to commit it to memory and spun the dial accordingly.

He put the cold zinc receiver to his ear and concentrated but didn't hear anything, not in the normal way, not even the ocean as in a shell.

Nonetheless, after a few minutes, he faced the mouthpiece and said, "Right." He waited again, longer this time. Then he said into the mouthpiece, "I know it." He sat perfectly still in the solemn cave of the pantry, the peace of the dark, pressing to his ear the receiver that had touched the ears of the people who had lived here, the people invisible but present. Those who watched and listened from the other side. After several minutes he said, "Flush that joker out of the jungle, like you said."

The pantry door opened in a burst of light and Tilly leaned inside and took a bag of beans from the shelf. He said, "Sorry, I thought this phone booth was free."

"It ain't either a phone booth," Elroy said.

"Oh no?"

"It's a pantry."

"Who are you talking to?"

"Command, sometimes. Sometimes my lieutenant."

"You don't tell them much."

"I'm supposed to listen five minutes for every minute I talk, like you said."

"All right, what do they tell you?"

"Reports from the front, you know." He wagged his head wearily.

Tilly looked at him. He said, "How's the battle going?"

"There ain't any battle."

"What's the operation?"

"They're looking for somebody."

"Just one person? They send the whole army, or—what is it?"

"A division."

"Okay, a division—after one man?"

"Yessir, that's the operation."

"What did he do, this man?"

"Do how?"

"Do to get in trouble that they're looking for him."

"He didn't do nothing. He's innocent."

"What do they *say* he did?"

Elroy said gravely, "They say he fired without leave."

"Did he hit anybody?"

"Yessir, then he run off."

"Who did he hit?"

"But that's what I mean. He's innocent because it ain't a person he hit. It's a animal. It was a water buffalo."

"What's this joker's name?"

"They won't tell me."

"You're back in the rear getting reports and you're in charge of a division. That makes you a major general probably, and they won't tell you the fellow's name?"

Elroy seemed to think about this.

"I vaguely recall someone wanted to know what division I was in," Tilly said. "That wouldn't have any bearing on the current operation?"

"Nossir," Elroy said. "And you were in two divisions."

"You probably remember which."

Elroy lowered his head and gripped his temples.

Tilly said as if to himself, "Now I'm trying to remember what I told you."

"Hold on! No hints."

"They were—"

"Stop, I know it. You were in the Second Division, then you were in the First."

Tilly didn't frown, so Elroy knew he'd remembered right, and he smiled. Then Tilly smiled a bit and said, "You got it, citizen. And what do you call the Second Division?"

"The Silent Second."

"And what do you call the First?"

"You call them the Old Breed."

"How come these jokers won't tell the major general who they're after?"

"It was you said I was a major general. I ain't. I'm enlisted. I'm on the needenow."

"The needenow."

"Like, the basis. Like you say."

"I see. Tell me when they find him?"

"Yessir," Elroy said. "Shut the door please, or they won't tell me squat."

Elroy meant this. Understandings came to him of the people present yet unseen only when he was in the dark alone.

A MONTH LATER, Elroy was sitting in the kitchen figuring his addition tables, and his ma was bent over the sink laundering his reeky Denver Broncos stocking hat, and Tilly was crouched in the doorway untying his work boots when something happened that seemed an appeal from the infinite population of those who preceded us to the people of the present household: the phone rang.

"What the hell?" Elroy said.

Tilly said, "Elroy, *language*."

Louisa aimed her chin toward the pantry and the phone. "Is that your idea of a present?"

The phone rang again.

"It sure isn't," Tilly said.

"You're going to spend money we don't have and not tell me, and I'm supposed to be surprised and delighted? Take off your radioactive boots or don't come in."

From TV Elroy knew the protocols of the phone but he'd never answered one. "Our number is top secret," he said. "Can I pick it up?"

"We don't have a number, Elroy. Stay away from there." Tilly said to Louisa with quiet emphasis on each word, "I did not have the line turned on."

"*I* sure didn't," she said, seeming to believe him now.

Again, the phone rang.

"It can't ring," Elroy said. "But it's ringing."

They were paralyzed each with his own uncertainty, and Elroy feared that this first and maybe final chance to speak with the people he had known only in his mind would slip away and he said, "*Please* let me answer."

Tilly gave him leave by nodding. Elroy scurried to the pantry and shut the door behind him.

Louisa said, "Keep the door open, Elroy," as the phone rang once more. Each ring might be the last.

Elroy swung the door open again and took the heavy earpiece from the hook and said into the device, "Heflin residence, Elroy speaking."

The miraculous voice that came into his ear said, "Is this number 18422 Highway Fifty-three, Ramah, New Mexico?"

"Yessir," Elroy said. He listened a moment. "Yessir," he said again. "He wants to talk to D. E. Tilly. That's you, ain't it? He says to say . . . 'Dishonest money . . . dwindles away, but . . . whoever gathers money . . . little by little . . . makes it grow.'"

"*Drop that phone,*" Tilly snapped.

Elroy let the earpiece fall like a live grenade down the mouth of a cave and scrambled to the sink by his ma, fearing Tilly's sudden tone.

Tilly shot into the pantry and grabbed the earpiece and put it to his head.

The dark kitchen floor was marked by a yellow dusting of uranium ore in the pattern of the lugged bottoms of Tilly's boots.

He shut the pantry door and said, "This is Tilly."

The world of souls.

At supper that night Elroy was still in the grip of the miracle, whatever it meant, and when the time came for him to give his thanks he said, "For the ones that come in before us."

TILLY WOULD WEAR for years that same flannel jacket that had belonged to the one called Conrad. Likewise for years he would peel fruit with a folding knife that had belonged to Bobby's progenitors, left in the back of a drawer on the ranch. Ignorant of how Louisa's other companions had really looked, he would see them many years later in the guise of strangers: convivial hikers coming his way on desert trails in the Jemez Mountains where he would walk alone when he was old, laughing people in insulated Gore-Tex coats marching with collapsible trekking poles. They never asked for their belongings back, they had left them behind with their previous selves and continued down the snowy path. If he ever met any of those faceless people from Louisa's time at the ranch before him, he never knew.

THE MORNING AFTER THE DAY the phone rang, Louisa was working a comb smeared with oil through her hair when she noticed Tilly's razor missing. His trimmed socks were missing from the bureau they shared. And his folding knife, from the kitchen windowsill.

He was gone from their lives utterly. He left not a boot print, not a shirt.

He had dematerialized—just as he had first appeared from nothing on the Heflin place with his killer's eyes, which had looked at her forsaken body as if to touch it could redeem the deaths he had caused, and as if she were not a rag wrung out and dropped but the tree in full flower that he was discovering only at that moment he had come across the country to find; and now on the morning she discovered him gone, Elroy, recognizing immediately the new order of things, looked at her over his breakfast for the first time with that same killer's cast of eyes, which swore with the zealotry of an eight-year-old that he was never going to forgive her for this: she had arranged it using whatever means for whatever purpose, and with the slow silent manly licking of the yolk of the eggs from his knife, forgoing the effeminacy of toast, he pledged silently by the knife in his mouth to hate her to the end of the earth.

A coffee can sat on the counter, full of crumpled money amounting to $423.

. . .

IF SHE HAD LONG KNOWN that someday Tilly would take off, with no notice and no trace except whatever cash he would leave them—so that she had all along sequestered a tithe from her wages under the false bottom of her sewing box, and had already decided before it happened that she wouldn't try to find him—if she had not suspected but *known,* then why was she surprised when it really happened? Later, she understood: it had not been *her* surprise. She had partaken of Elroy's surprise.

She would take the boy with her to McAlester, Oklahoma, to an apartment where a friend from high school lived. Louisa would get a job in the state penitentiary there. Over the years she would work her way up to the position of administrative coordinator to the Office of Behavioral Clinicians. She would meet a junkie from Pennsylvania who was going straight while in the prison and training to become a welder and learning for the first time to regard his future with hope. He would be paroled.

He would ask to marry her. She would say yes. But she and Tilly would never have properly divorced. She would then make a few unsuccessful stabs at finding Tilly through former employers. An attorney in McAlester would advise she accuse him of desertion, though that would take longer than a regular divorce.

It would be Elroy, age twelve, who would make a project of tracking Tilly down. Beginning with Alabama, he would search the phone books in the stacks of the public library. With sharp pencil on four pages of loose-leaf binder paper, he would compose a list of likely candidates. He would come to know his country by the Tillys in it. The maps of area codes, the place names repeated state by state. The Georgetowns and Franklins and Salems and Bristols. He would walk his bike home cool and collected, and he would hand Louisa this list with the most likely candidate inscribed within a heavy pencil box, *Tilly Drilling & Co.,* in the little town of Vado back in New Mexico in Doña Ana County. He would stand looking into the refrigerator pretending not to listen while she dialed the number. The slow ringing in the receiver would be audible throughout the room.

Then the metallic voice. She would start to say who she was. She would stop and listen. She would say it was good to hear his voice too. She would say she was doing real good and so was Elroy.

Louisa and Elroy would meet Tilly halfway between them, in Amarillo, Texas. They would eat eggs and rye toast at a diner as in old times. In the passing of the jelly jar and the half-and-half, they would all agree to an implicit treaty: no explanations asked, none offered. Elroy, now taller than Louisa but less so yet than Tilly, would smile shyly across the table at him, saying nothing. Tilly would have bought a small drilling rig and made himself some prosperity installing residential water wells. Two men would be working for him part time. He would be saving to buy a second rig.

Not all would be forgiven.

Louisa and Tilly would consummate their divorce before a judge in Tulsa. They would leave the courthouse, and Louisa would tail Tilly's westward-headed pickup for more than a hundred and fifty miles, willing him to notice her Chevette behind him and pull to the shoulder of the interstate so she could pull over too and get out and confess she'd made a mistake on the desert night when he'd asked to come in. She had said no, and she should have said yes. And she would want him to ask again right there with the eighteen-wheelers shaking the very earth as they passed, so now she could say yes. This time—please—she would say yes. But a Monte Carlo and then a Buick LeSabre would merge between them, and the Chevette would be nearly out of gas, and at Weatherford she would stop and fill up the tank and go back to McAlester and marry the other man.

Her mother would drive up from Lufkin, Texas, for the ceremony. A diffident old woman in a dark dress, her withered eyes made ripe again by pencil and bifocals. The old woman would be introduced to Elroy. She would grin with her invisible lips and would fish in her handbag and give him a silver dollar. Once she would understand he was not Louisa's own blood, she would ask to have the dollar back.

Years would elapse. Louisa and Tilly would fall out of touch again.

Then Louisa would call him at the office of his drilling business and relate how Elroy, now sixteen, had come into manhood and gone immediately berserk, throwing a chair through the screen of the television when her husband told him to lower the volume while they ate, slugging a teacher in the mouth, dumping Louisa's laundry onto the highway, his hatred of her like a bomb that had finally gone off, slamming the hood of a car on the hand of another boy in engine-repair class and now expelled from the only high school in McAlester. He had not hidden the drugs he used. He had stolen her husband's truck on a dare from one of his cronies on the football team and smashed it into the front of an abandoned wood-frame house to see if he couldn't bring the house down.

Leonard, her husband, would have demanded that she choose. He was in recovery; he couldn't have Elroy's drugs in the house. Choose. Elroy or him. One would have to go. He would have made his demand in the kitchen of their two-bedroom rented ranch house with Elroy standing right there fresh out of the shower, dripping, wearing only a towel, with steroid acne on his inflated chest and shoulders and smoking a cigarette and drinking vitamin D chocolate milk from the carton and saying with a smirk, "Ma, don't listen to this guy. He don't mean nothing." She would say on the phone her heart was cattywampus. She had to have a place to live, didn't she? She could never make the rent here on her own. And she loved Elroy all the time but okay, yes, all right, sometimes she was afraid of him. And didn't Tilly think they needed right now to get Elroy under the roof of a man he trusted? She didn't know. She would cry on the phone while he failed to volunteer.

Then she would ask Tilly in plain speech to take custody of Elroy, for at least a while, if he could possibly manage it. She would say, "I don't want him to turn out a killer."

Tilly would arrive in McAlester and get out of the pickup sheathed in the dust of three states and open the tailgate, and he and the boy would load and secure and cover with a tarp the few plastic bags of the boy's worldly belongings while Louisa would stand outside the rented house pruning the plumbagos and crying soundlessly with outrage at what she had authored, how she had found no better way. And the truck would drive off with the man and the boy, leaving her pale, thin, strong, desolate.

Tilly and Elroy would drive through the yellow desert of the Texas panhandle and into the redder one of New Mexico. Then to the boy's everlasting bewilderment and outrage Tilly would take him not home to Doña Ana County to live with him but up to Albuquerque where he would install Elroy in a residential Catholic boys' school. There Tilly would pay him weekly visits, and from there Elroy would periodically take the bus south for short stays at Tilly's spartan house where no framed photographs of anybody would furnish the top of the mantels, only history books and drilling trade magazines, and where the rangy man of his earliest memories, who had brought him water in a dipper in the cot where he slept and who had spoken always with the tone of immediacy and mutual understanding that marked a permanent friend, would have been replaced in the intervening years by this heavier, dark-browed, concealed, and concealing person who would pay for Elroy's school and board and room and for his clothes and dormitory coffee maker but would not any longer look him in the face frankly and com-posedly with knowingness in his eyes as in the days of their solidarity.

Elroy would do all right at the school and would finish, despite a charge of simple assault and battery and a second for inciting a public affray, both pled down to probation with the help of a lawyer Tilly would hire. Elroy would enroll at a community college and study aeronautical engineering. He would lose his temper in a dispute over a checkers game with one of his roommates and break the roommate's jaw and clavicle. He would be convicted of aggravated battery against a household member with great bodily harm, a third-degree felony, and the judge of the Second Judicial District Court in Albuquerque would sentence him to eleven months at the Central New Mexico Correctional Facility in Los Lunas.

He would leave prison and travel as far as Maine, hoping for the world. He would call Tilly on holidays. When the occasional friend would ask where his mother lived, he would maintain her whereabouts were unknowable, deciding he had been asked about the person named Katerina on his birth certificate and not Louisa, from whom he had received many letters during his bit at Los Lunas, none of which he had answered, all with the same return address in McAlester from which he had no reason to believe that she since had moved.

He would do six years at Maine State Prison in Thomaston for resisting arrest, reckless conduct, and Class B elevated aggravated assault with a dangerous weapon: a shod foot. The state would release him late in his term. The year would be 2003. He would lust for the world. He would be thirty-one years old. He would lust for hope of any kind. He would visit an army recruiter who after weeks of wrangling would get a waiver allowing him to overlook Elroy's past criminal convictions. He would enlist and shortly be deployed to Eastern Europe. At a bar in Riga with the boys, a shy waitress in a zebra-print microskirt would say, "Tell me if there's anything else I can get you, my friend?"

The last two words would have been picked up from an English-dubbed news item about the sales methods of kite vendors on the beaches of Beirut. Elroy wouldn't know that. He would believe the gap between himself and womankind had been bridged finally by these two words from this woman who spoke them to him and not to the other soldiers and thereby revealed her intention to single him out for love.

His conviction regarding her intent to choose him with these words would persuade even her, for a while, who had meant no such endearment.

He would be deployed to Kunduz and take shrapnel in his leg and would lay down a stream of M4 carbine fire killing three hajis and wounding a fourth, who would escape trailing a stream of blood through a dense street of stalls suddenly devoid of local nationals of any age. A skinned ram, still attached to its horns, its flesh aglow within the long veil of its blood, would hang among the stalls. The parrots in cages would squawk, some trying to fly. His carbine fire would explode a yellow kharbouza melon and riddle with bullets the dresses that had glittering beadwork and matching headscarves in scarlet and bright mustard, outfits women in this country would never let a Westerner see them wear. And not one live person would be among the stalls at midday, save the haji running from the live fire of the carbine and trailing his life's blood.

Elroy would be deployed to Kuwait and to Bishkek and down south to Helmand Province in Afghanistan. As he would remove his helmet to scratch under the armored nape pad, a bit of his ear would fly away from his head, and only then would he hear the sniper shot that nearly killed him. He would fire his weapon again at two more men trying to rappel from inside an apartment building, men hanging from green extension cords tied to the wood shutters of a fourth-story room where the blue laundry flapped. The two men would fall to the street. He would never see their faces. A spotter from Army Special Forces would confirm their deaths. He would fire on a woman who was firing on him, and both would miss. He would fly to Riga and back to Kuwait. To Riga and thence to Bagram. To New Mexico and back to Kunduz. He would lust for the world. He would take the boy Janis to Jurmala, to the Latvian beach. The boy's slight bones would work beneath his pink flesh while he swam, and from shore Elroy would scan the perimeter twenty miles distant in all seaward and landward directions for signs of bodily threat to his only kin.

"Janis," he called, "not so far." The boy kept on swimming but no farther out, parallel to shore now as if he had heard his father and was complying.

Tall, sun-dazzled, electric white, in cheap short trunks, weak with fatigue from his travels, Elroy stood knee-deep in the water, his feet numb. He dared go no deeper for the cold. Young as the boy was, he knew cold; it fazed him but didn't deter him. At home he often had to shower in it. He paddled with strength. Elroy's pride in him was a stab to the ribs of perfect pain. A teenager had come by with an instant camera and sold Elroy their picture. He couldn't bear to look at it; he had stashed it in his pants on the beach; he would have to give it away.

The water was broad, clean, brown at bottom, nearly inaudible in its movements though it formed the arm of a great sea. The extent of its shallows could not be known from shore.

The boy's hair stuck to his skull like a cap. He seemed to recede.

Elroy, cupping his mouth, barked, "Too far."

The boy now turned not back toward shore but farther out. The head invisible as the splashes grew higher behind the body. The kicking feet seemed to learn a new power.

All at once Elroy saw the threat, the willful boy himself, and ran, the water impeding him, the shallows shortly giving way to rib-deep shocking cold. A spirit took him over, a surge in the blood. He dove. He swam, poorly and hard. He shouted after the boy, who under his new-found power had become only a disturbance of the water, a tiny bomb.

The boy was escaping him. The boy was leaving him behind.

His wind gave out. He kept on swimming. The boy, having heard or having given up his escape, stopped swimming and treaded water.

Elroy reached him, the small head bobbing, the limbs below motoring with ease. "You'll come when I call," Elroy said, but no sound escaped: he was sucking air. The boy grinned. A shallow appeared a few strokes away. They swam to it. Elroy's feet found the sand below. The water came to his shoulders.

"Come here," he shouted. He wept with rage. The trustful boy swam right to him, gripping Elroy's shoulder as if to climb it.

Elroy, twisting, caught the boy's approaching head like a ball that had been passed to him and thrust it below the surface. He held it there.

The other body seemed to struggle.

The taste on his lips, though of seawater, was strangely sweet.

The small feet brushed his legs like fishtails. If he wrapped a leg around the trunk, the body would stay submerged.

No one who had not already seen would see.

He bit his lip. The water on his tongue was like food.

The sunlight made the water's surface a foil sheet that blinded him. His left hand arose and wiped his eyes.

His right hand did not let go the head—he did not tell it to let go—but the sphere it held out of sight slipped away.

The body beneath the water had freed itself. The surface broke; Janis emerged, gasping.

In a moment the boy found a higher shallow and stood, drawing his breath in deep methodical pulls like a rower, watching Elroy with his direct, habitual, unquiet look that asked and calculated and theorized—and yet already knew.

All this must be in the nature of things, it said. None of us is protected, I understand. A wave will come that knocks us off our feet.

14

The following year, after Evija wrote Elroy that she was moving to Spain and he should come and get the boy, Elroy asked Tilly if he could bring Janis from Riga to stay for a while in the condo in Los Alamos, and Tilly said yes, and Elroy flew to Latvia to get the boy, but it didn't work out, unfortunately. Just, it didn't work out, you know?

He crashed awhile on Tilly's condo sofa and then got orders to redeploy to Kyrgyzstan. Everywhere he went abroad, Riga, Bagram, Bishkek, he slept in structures the Red Army had left behind. It made him proud to be taking territory directly from the adversary instead of fighting some proxy war in a proxy land like Tilly had done. But every deployment took something out of him, a blood price that left him weaker.

The army promoted him to staff sergeant. He outranked the old man at last, even if army rules, contrary to those of the Marine Corps, required a staff sergeant be addressed only as sergeant—as if he had bettered the old man but nobody could say so.

Elroy was slowly coming up in the world, but what did he own? Technically, he did still own a little Nissan 4x4 pickup that he had acquired on credit during a previous deployment to tool around the enormous base at Bagram, but he had not found the time to sell it before that deployment ended, and had left it there in a base parking lot. This and other financial miscalculations he had made left him so flat-ass broke that when, at the end of the latest deployment in Kyrgyzstan, he returned to the condo in Los Alamos where Tilly let him stay short times, he had to shave with Tilly's razor in secret, rinsing just twice so as to hide any wear on the lubricating strip, carefully dabbing the razor dry on his shirt hem and putting it back in the medicine cabinet, which contained no medicine. That was when he figured out Tilly had no health insurance and decided he was going to have to fix this and made some inquiries at the VA.

A YEAR LATER, in November 2012, at age forty, Elroy was back in New Mexico on a week's leave in the middle of yet another deployment, his sixth, casting his eyes around him for a way out of the army, an escape before his brains burned down, before his body failed him or he failed his body, a route that led him not into temptation but delivered him from evil, a way and a place to live and eat, and finding them nowhere.

The current deployment was again near Bagram, where his pickup had unsurprisingly gone missing from the parking lot in which he had left it years before but where the collection agency that now owned the loan on the pickup still harassed him by phone, email, and text. From Bagram, without Tilly's knowledge, he had forged certain signatures, and submitted certain VA benefit applications on the old man's behalf, and arranged online an appointment for Tilly at the Albuquerque VA, and got himself this middeployment leave; then he had come home, and on the morning of the last full day of his leave, had inveigled Tilly into the passenger seat of Tilly's own Lincoln (on the pretext of needing someone to drive him back from a dental procedure in Albuquerque), and only revealed the true nature of their excursion as they were leaving Santa Fe County, seventy miles from the condo, on Interstate 25.

"Pull over right now," Tilly said. "I'm walking home."

Elroy drove the Lincoln down the road.

"I have no quarrel with Agent Orange," Tilly said. "Nobody dropped Agent Orange on me."

"Sir, it don't matter if they dropped it on you," Elroy said. "It matters if they could have dropped it on you. These people believe they owe you a benefit. You just have to let them give it to you."

The old man faced the desert racing by the passenger window. The back of his white head seemed about to catch fire. He writhed in the sun-cracked seat of the old car. His drowsy dog, Mavis, fell off his lap. She was a pound rescue, a runty thing with the long snout of a pointer, and regarded Elroy always with a look of penetrating indifference: what I know, it said, I do not even care to disclose.

The bitch climbed back atop the old man's lap, wedging her chin between his knees.

To the window Tilly said, "You want me to say the Marine Corps didn't drop Agent Orange on me but they could have. What if they couldn't have but they did anyway? Do they get a benefit, and I pay for it? Turn the car around."

Elroy continued driving south under a pink bridge. A gutted mattress spraddled the guardrail. "You know they used it," he said.

"Elroy, they used it all over the place. Not everybody fights in a desert. If we took two steps out of the defoliated zone, we were blind. But they never dropped it on my head. Nothing is the matter with me."

It was true nothing evident ailed him.

"This is just money," Elroy said. "I don't get you."

"Nothing's just money."

"It comes from someplace, we send it someplace else, that's all. You act like every piece of money has a curse on it."

The dog tottered, watching the billboards that pointed to the casinos off the desolate pueblo roads. Tilly reached under her armpit and palmed the white blaze on her chest. She twisted her head and kissed him.

"If one of your stents all comes loose or you need a bypass before your Medicare kicks in, them bills will clean out whatever it is you got," Elroy said, temper rising. "Then where will you live?"

Mavis objected to Elroy's raising his voice and told him so.

"Girl, I don't mean nothing by it," Elroy said. "But what does your old man have to live on after his mortgage? Is it a thousand dollars a month?"

The dog wouldn't say. A click came from the heater core behind the passenger-side dash. Mavis turned to inspect it. The blower motor had not yet kicked in. She pointed her beard at the vent expectantly.

"Is it eight hundred?" Elroy asked. "Mavis, he ain't got any sense of financial planning at all."

"Who is this talking?" Tilly said. "You come here and you have to use my razor. Don't you think I notice? And what do you owe on that truck you left in the Hindu Kush? And how do your collection agencies get my number?"

"Hang up when they call."

"How much of your money goes to that woman?" Tilly asked.

"I don't know."

"Elroy, you have to draw the line with people."

"All right, I did."

"No, you didn't."

"I told her no more."

"You're lying."

"I drew the line, like you said."

"Wait a minute. No more cruises, or no more money at all?"

"She doesn't get a dime out of me anymore."

"What do you mean? How does the boy eat if you don't pay her? Socialism is over."

"I don't got it, she doesn't get it, that's all."

"Is that why she doesn't let you see the boy now?"

Elroy pulled the arm that controlled the windshield wipers. Fluid splattered the glass, obscuring the road while the wipers wagged. "Yeah," he said, "can you believe that?"

The blower came on with a whoosh that smelled of penetrating oil, and the dog snapped at the air.

Then the means Elroy had sought for trapping the old man came to him. "If you don't tell me what kind of coverage or assets you got, and you get sick," he said, "who's going to pay your bills?"

To this Tilly made no answer. Elroy had him in a box. The old man would rather have to live forever than die with a debt to his name.

When they got to the door of the VA, Elroy strapped Mavis into the red nylon vest labeled Service Dog that he had stolen. She threw her head and snapped at the reflective trim as the vest wrapped around her, but he said she didn't want to have to stay outside in the cold, did she? Did she?

Behind the plexiglass, the service officer took a thick file from the receptionist. They all went back to the officer's fluorescent cubicle, where pictures of her children and grandchildren decorated the padded acoustical modular wall padding and an old set of a baby's fleece pajamas hung from the side of the computer monitor on a miniature hanger. The pajamas were embroidered with the red and yellow insignia of the Tenth Marine Regiment.

"How do you do, sir?" she said. "Are we in any pain today?"

"Tenth Regiment," Tilly said. "Arm of Decision."

"Those were my baby boy's that his abuelita made. He goes to navy nuke school now. His sister's in that same regiment my husband was in. Would you believe it? We put the pajamas uniform on the wrong one. The regiment dropped the old motto. They're King of Battle now."

"I feel fine. Why don't you ask the staff sergeant here if he has any pain?"

SALVATORE SCIBONA

Elroy, studying the pajamas from a distance, stood Mavis on his lap and petted the knobby cartilage behind her ears, though the bitch took no perceptible pleasure in it.

"I haven't read in the file anything about your service dog, Mr. Tilly. Do you use him for anxiety issues related to your tour? We might be able to get you some funding for him." She wore a hundred hair-thin silver bangles on each arm, and a turquoise bodkin in her gray hair, and a brooch of black and white crystals that surrounded the logo of the San Antonio Spurs. Her thumb bore a nibbed rubber thimblelike cap that rapidly snatched the corners of the papers in his file, individuating them, while she cursed the sloppy clerk who had assembled the documents in such shuffled fashion.

Elroy showed the dog in profile. "Mavis is a she. You know what, I might have met your daughter in Kuwait. Wasn't the Tenth over there? Or no, I saw them at Manas in Kyrgyzstan."

"Thank you for your service, Sergeant. My daughter doesn't tell me exactly where she is. It's a game where I have to guess by the color of the sand behind her on the Skype screen."

"Will you explain to me please, Mrs. Baca, why I'm here?" Tilly asked.

"Did your son not tell you? You signed the POA for your benefits representative."

"Did I, now?"

"Yes, you did," Elroy insisted.

"And your representative filed the appropriate forms to get you this far. Excuse me." She opened an Acrobat file on her desktop and scanned it and said to the screen. "You and Sergeant Heflin aren't specially related?"

Tilly looked at her. He did not look at Elroy, who scratched the mangled nub of his ear. The part that itched was no longer there.

"Call him what you like," Tilly said. "I was his guardian."

"Bottom rail's on top now," she said.

"Hell it is," Elroy said. "I'll be his subordinate till he dies."

"The time will come for us all," Tilly said. "But not yet."

"He wouldn't let me guardian his dog."

"Mrs. Baca, I'm going to tell you something that's going to make Elroy mad. He'll say I'm telling it only to make him mad, but that is not quite so. Nobody dropped Agent Orange on me ever."

"Sir, that doesn't matter."

"See?" Elroy said.

"How can a thing not matter if it didn't happen?"

"Sir, because we have a law of Congress. The law treats veterans of the conflict in Vietnam not as individuals but as a class. And we have a policy from the secretary of veterans affairs. I ask you two questions. Did you serve in the Republic of Vietnam, regardless of length of that service, between January 9, 1962, and May 7, 1975?"

"But that's everybody," Tilly said. "That's the duration."

"Yes, sir."

"Yes, I did," he said.

"Secondly, has a doctor diagnosed you with any of the conditions on pages four through seven of your pamphlet?"

"But this is everything that could go wrong with a human at all."

"Dioxin is a more dangerous and persistent substance than command realized at the time. If you were there, and you have these illnesses, then you have a presumptive service connection with your illness and we can treat you for it and perhaps compensate you financially depending on your Service Disability percentage."

"Who said anything about a disability? Elroy, what have you told these people? I thought this was about insurance." He regarded the pamphlet before him with disgust. "What is peripheral neuropathy? My pinky tingles and you'll pay me for it?"

"Sir, I can't make you take the government's money, but I can advise you it's in your best interest to look carefully at this list and tell me all the conditions here that in your adult life you have been diagnosed with them."

"*Webbed fingers.* Look at this. *Imperforate anus.*"

"Sir, those are birth defects in affected children."

"All I recognize here is the blockage in one of my arteries, which they told me it's saturated fats, then it's genetics, then it's smoking, and now it's chemicals that never touched me," Tilly said. "Also my sugar runs high."

Her bangles stopped clinking. Her fingers hovered over the keyboard. "Has a medical professional diagnosed you with adult-onset type 2 diabetes mellitus?"

Tilly sighed.

She looked at Elroy. She looked at Tilly. "Sir, your next of kin needs to know about these things."

"Yes, ma'am," Tilly said.

"To properly arrange your care in an emergency."

"Yes, ma'am."

"Yes, you agree, or yes, a doctor has diagnosed you with adult-onset type 2 diabetes mellitus?"

"Yes, yes, fine."

She typed clatteringly. She turned to the papers, rifling them. "Damn this file," she said, slapping it shut, and she turned back to the screen.

"The next page refers to follow-on medical conditions as a result of wounds received in action. Your POA has no wounds listed."

"That's right."

"Hell fire, look at that foot," Elroy said. "Take off your shoe and show it to her."

"My shoe is my affair."

"Show it."

"I see no record of in-country injuries anywhere in your file. Did we miss something, sir?"

"Damn right, you did," Elroy said.

The dog in Elroy's lap shrieked. Tilly reached over his belly and rubbed her snout.

"Show her the goddamn foot," Elroy said.

"I see a record of treatment for a gunshot wound to a lower extremity in February 1974."

"That's the one," Elroy said, "but you got the date wrong."

"The injury lists as stateside after term of service."

Rarely, as now, Elroy witnessed Tilly's dark and self-contained eyes revert to the uncertainty of a sort of youth, even to the want of advice—not from Elroy and not from inside himself. The one whose advice he sought was present but not visible and spoke only to him.

Elroy said, "He has a Purple Heart for that foot."

The officer looked at Elroy. She looked at Tilly.

Tilly said carefully, "First it's the refined flour that gets my sugar up, now it's an herbicide."

"How do you misplace a Purple Heart?" Elroy said. "Even I have a Purple Heart."

"Thank you for your service, Sergeant."

"He has two of them, actually," Tilly said. "Brave man, our Ellie."

"No Purple Heart lists here. That's not—that's not a mistake. This was a postservice injury. It was the only other time your father appeared at a VA facility."

"I thought you had a Purple Heart."

"I didn't get any Purple Heart," Tilly said.

"How can you not have a Purple Heart? I thought you got shot in the service."

"Nope," Tilly said to the officer as if it were she who had asked the question. "I didn't get shot in the service, I got shot in the foot. Isn't that what it says?"

"Left lower extremity," she said.

"What color does it say my eyes were?"

"Brown."

"What did I weigh?" he asked reluctantly.

"A hundred fifty-two pounds at discharge."

Tilly sunk in his chair. "Gosh," he said.

"You were all muscle," she said. "I need an email address."

"I hear they're easy to get."

She turned to Elroy. "How do we make him more cooperative?"

"He isn't on email," Elroy said.

"What do you do when you buy stuff online?" she asked.

"He uses my email. Then I have to call him from a war zone and tell him, Congratulations, his package has shipped. Do you need a credit card? He uses mine, then he pays me back when I'm here."

"You fly in the dark, Mr. Tilly."

"Yes, ma'am."

"Are you a black helicopter person or a Roswell cover-up person?"

"He's a distrustful cuss is what he is," Elroy said.

"Without an email, the system won't let me go to the next screen."

"Just put mine in," Elroy said.

"Anybody needs me, they knock. What's so hard?"

"For the record, ma'am, that ain't the case. His condo complex has a security guard who's all 'None shall pass.'" Elroy spelled out the address while Tilly faced the dog in Elroy's lap and made a gesture that was like a man recounting the length of a trout he'd thrown back. The dog jumped to him and landed with two paws square on either thigh, then circled twice, tottering as the paws slid and the nails zipped along his corduroys, then found her balance, folded her hips, and sat, the forelegs upright. She looked up at her master; at the others; at her master again, preferring him. She probed with her nose in his jacket close under his arms and snuffed the glandular, minty, dry-leaf odor that was him and him alone. He took a cheeseburger bun from his pocket and fed it to her.

"Says you play piano," the officer read.

He turned to Elroy. "This is embarrassing," he hissed.

"If you develop a peripheral neuropathy that interferes with your piano," the officer said, "we can get you a benefit for lost wages."

"He doesn't play it for money," Elroy said. "He doesn't even play it if he thinks anyone in the house is awake to hear."

"Is he very good?" the officer asked.

"Reckon you do anything much as he plays, you get good," Elroy said.

"Is he just able, or does he play like Liberace where he feels the music?"

"He can put the knife in you for real. But the face is absolute zero Celsius. You ever see that Lang Lang?"

"I can't say I know what that is," the officer said.

"Lang Lang is a clown," Tilly said.

"There's a Chinese piano player on YouTube with hair that's all 1982, and Mr. Tilly likes him but he doesn't like the faces he makes," Elroy said. "Mr. Tilly hears the music on the inside."

"Let me point out I haven't left the room," Tilly said.

"Don't you want to know what folks'll say after you're dead, about how you were and what you did?" Elroy asked.

"Nossir," Tilly said.

"No curiosity at all?" the officer asked.

"Why, is there a benefit for that?"

"Didn't you ever want to know?" Elroy said.

"I never did."

"Why not?"

Tilly again looked at the officer as if it were she who had asked the question and said, "Everybody has to be so important."

"Everybody *is* important, Mr. Frade—" Her eyes squeezed shut; she shook her head. "*Tilly*, I mean *Tilly.*"

At first it seemed the blood had merely left the old man's face. Then something more anatomically improbable, that the flow of blood had reversed. He went white, then whiter, so white he was bluish like skim milk. The facial features bedeviled, helpless. Elroy and the officer waited for him to crack wise, but the shirty tone had left him. The flesh about the eyes swelled.

"Now I'm mad at myself," she said.

"It's nothing, ma'am," Elroy said.

"I'm usually good at names," she said. "That's why I'm good at my job. Your father looks as if his heart's stopped working. Sir, everybody *is* important. But the clerk in Kansas City who made this file should get fired. There are two men in here!" She required both hands to lift the faded green folder and slam it on the table with contempt. Her accessories jangled. "There's Mr. Tilly and some Mr. Frade, and the papers are so mixed up I can hardly tell the two of you apart."

"She didn't mean nothing by it, sir," Elroy said.

Mavis, watching, extended her face and licked her master's throat.

Tilly looked at the service officer. "Frade," he said. "Not Vollie Frade?"

"Ay, Dios mío. Did you know him? That's the nickname all over the documents."

"Was he assigned to the Twenty-sixth Marines at Dong Ha?"

"Yes, by goodness, that's the one. Was he a friend of yours?"

Tilly's look of urgent discourse with invisible counselors had never been more vivid. His defenseless voice said, "Can I ask what happened to him?"

"You can ask. I can't say," she replied.

"You *won't* say. The man is requesting a simple favor," Elroy said, but even in the certain grip of his temper he knew he had misunderstood something.

"Ma'am, I don't need to know anything personal," Tilly said. "Just the outlines."

Finally she said, "He died."

The dog watched the old man.

Slowly the blood came into his face. "He died?" Tilly asked.

She rifled the papers and extracted one. The desk lamp behind her betrayed the watermark. "Sir, in 1971. I really can't show you the document. It says *Death Location, Vietnam Conflict Military Zone 1, Quang Nam.* It says *Killed in Action, Explosive Device.*"

"He died," Tilly said to no one present. He seemed to smile.

And to Elroy's ongoing catalog of Tilly's inscrutabilities and of his own discredited first assumptions about him, Elroy added another: that this Vollie Frade whom the officer was describing had not been a friend whose death demanded Elroy's condolence with Tilly, but had been his enduring enemy.

"He's dead," the old man said with relief.

"But Vollie wasn't his real name," the officer said.

"That's right," Tilly said, "it was Eugene."

THEY LEFT THE VA. Elroy got in the passenger side of the Lincoln and put three Ambien under his tongue to start adjusting to Bagram time and passed out before they made it through Algodones.

When he awoke, darkness subsumed his air-conditioned containerized housing unit somewhere in the moonless sandbox of Kunduz. Then he swung his naked feet onto the Berber carpet and plunged into the living room of the old man's Los Alamos condo. A shallow recollection came to him from sometime in sleep of Tilly taking his arm amid the gloaming in dry wind and hoisting him out of the car over his shoulder while his own feet wobbled under him. Then another recollection, maybe a dream, of the old man yanking at his socks.

He stood up, famished. The room spun. For solid food in the kitchen he found only jumbo packs of freeze-dried pork noodles, cholesterol-free wasabi peas in individual-serving-size foil envelopes, nothing that had been alive within the year. He pulled on his socks and boots, and he got in the Lincoln amid a hypnotic delirium intending to see if the

Quickie Mart was still open in White Rock. The radio announcer welcomed the restless; the rovers; the waking dreamers; the all-night crews of central, north-central, and northeast New Mexico and the Sangre de Cristo peaks to easy listening at 2:23 A.M. Mountain Standard Time. Elroy tried to back out of the driveway, but the accelerator was stuck. Then he realized he had been stomping the parking brake. He got out of the Lincoln and went inside and ate some canned tuna instead, in front of the computer, on which ads suggested that, life being short, he have an affair; and trainers hated this man for revealing the only dietary supplement that burns abdominal fat while you sleep; and with one click Christians could mingle for free; and these Russian sluts were starved for cock.

He put in his camo earbuds and watched Lang Lang play a Chopin prelude while twisting and swaying and making sex faces. Then he followed the link to a suggested video and watched Arthur Rubinstein play the same prelude in 1958, with an iron bar for a spine and an angelic white cadaverous face; then Vladimir Horowitz played it in 1977, the eye pouches drooping, the slow running of his nose the only tell that the head controlling the music might also be receiving the music and be changed by it; then Elroy clicked to the search field and typed *Bishkek* and *enchilada,* which led YouTube to suggest a video he himself had uploaded and disguisingly tagged. The view count of 112 confirmed that no one else but he had yet watched his video. And he waited through an ad for the new Chrysler 200, *Imported from Detroit,* and when the ad finished, the video at first showed only his own knees while he lay on the condo sofa between deployments the year before, feigning sleep but in fact positioning the camera of the clandestine cell phone that was making the video. A jumble of sofa pillows. A blur and a glare while the focus adjusted. Then the gas-burning simulated fireplace, in the next room from where he sat at this moment, and the stony figure behind the baby grand piano. The lens zoomed on Tilly's illegible face while the old man finished playing the "Cataract Rag."

Then a pause and cough, a rebalancing of the torso. Then Tilly began that same Chopin prelude, while the muted football game on the adjacent television projected blue flashes on him, and the image taken by the phone bobbed with Elroy's breath, and Tilly played the last chord and pumped the pedal and played the chord again emphasizing one of its constituent notes, then again emphasizing another, and another, probing the chord for some tone or meaning, while nowhere in his face could be seen the merest suggestion of what he hoped to hear.

At the computer Elroy was still wearing his ACU boots, with carbon-composite toes, half laced, when Mavis, having spied the lighted screen, appeared outside the sliding door and sat in the star glow, waiting to be noticed, listening to the desert sounds, wanting in. The smug dog who got to live here without ever having asked permission. She yipped, plaintive. He got up and slid open the door. The happy dog reared back on her haunches preparing to leap. He waited for her to leave the ground, opening her forelegs to embrace him, before he swung his boot and punted her in the ribs. She screamed, sprawled, tumbling midair. With a luscious crack she struck the high stucco wall that surrounded the compound.

He slid the door closed. He lay on the sofa in the dark, in the wilderness between consciousness and sleep, now and again allowing an eye to open and check if the dog had returned to the door, but she did not. It started to snow.

By morning the piñon branches sagged with the heavy snow and dripped in the sun, which had already rounded off the crests of the drifts. The two men drank coffee on empty stomachs, standing under the *portal* and not talking. Then Tilly said to the air, "Where is Mavis?" flatly as if he knew the air would answer she was dead, as if he had foreseen the time and way she would be killed but would not hold the killer to account. And this refusal of Tilly's to accuse Elroy of what Elroy already somehow distantly knew he had brought about, but had not *done* or *lived*, as if not he but his boot had punted the dog, this refusal—either because he would not blame Elroy for what he always knew Elroy would do, or because he wanted to hang Elroy on the hook of his deed by withholding from him even the comfort of being accused—now caused Elroy for the first time to ask his heart, What have I done?

From nowhere Mavis appeared, breaking the snow beneath her paws, one foreleg folded up to the ribs, hobbling. She approached Elroy's boots. She sat and bent and kissed them. She let the weak paw down and sat firm in her bones, upright.

They all three got in the Lincoln and after an hour stopped for breakfast at a place on the south side of Santa Fe that occupied little more than a lean-to attached to a gas station and where the green chile tasted tangy and thin before it blew up like kerosene afire in the mouth. Elroy ordered only coffee, and the waitress thanked him for his service, and Tilly asked with seemingly thoughtless sarcasm if he hadn't learned to eat without staining his uniform. Elroy said he was only trying to reset his hormones by fasting on travel days until he got to the new time zone.

This remark, offered in explanation, not defense, woke the old man from a kind of sleep. "Do you know what?" Tilly said. "I didn't need to have said that."

"Ain't no thing."

Tilly watched his chile as if reading it. "It was unnecessary. I don't like the tone I take with you sometimes. You've come a long way. You deserve my respect." He seemed about to say something more but didn't.

Elroy, already weak with hunger, pinched a slice of bacon from Tilly's plate and dipped it in the chile and ate it. Tilly offered him the whole plate—eggs, beans, meat—pushing it toward him, insisting he wasn't hungry himself, and Elroy's resolve left him and he wolfed it all while Tilly sipped his coffee. Then Elroy noticed a crinkle in his thigh pocket and undid the Velcro and found a fifty in there and dashed to the gas station and returned with ten Cahtatic lottery tickets and gave half of them to Tilly and attacked the silver polymerized ink of his own tickets with his thumbnail—hope, the wildest high there was— and when Tilly, looking appalled and sick at the expense, refused to touch or even look at the tickets Elroy had given him, Elroy took them back and scratched the ink frenziedly, saying, "You can't win if you don't play," promising Tilly the winnings from these last five tickets, and Tilly only looked on with exasperation in his eyes, or else the vapors of the chile had irritated them, and it didn't matter, every one of the tickets was a loser.

Then they drove on to the Albuquerque Sunport, and Elroy redeployed, and Tilly continued driving another hour south to the city of Socorro.

15

The Lincoln left Interstate 25 and rolled through downtown Socorro and turned into the parking lot of the Olde Camino Real
Regency Professional Pueblo, an assemblage of one- and two-story
stucco buildings nestled amid potted indigo bush, drought-tolerant
grasses, red and yellow succulents, and arranged around rock-garden
courtyards. At one of the spaces designated Guests of FLV, LLC, Tilly's
Lincoln slowed to a crawl and its directional came on. But it did not
turn into the parking spot. Before it stopped moving, its directional
shut off. The Lincoln seemed to change its mind and instead continued
out of the parking lot and headed westward away from the town on
U.S. Highway 60.

The parking space the Lincoln had nearly used belonged to one of
the newest client relations offices in the FLV network—more formally,
the FLV Wealth Partners network, a spin-off of the conglomerate formerly known as Frisk Lambert Ventures, which had dissolved itself
nine years earlier into its constituent aerospace, procurement, water
and wastewater infrastructure, defense engineering, and private wealth
divisions. With assets under management of $4 billion, FLV Partners

might have found itself a niche in the venture capital communities and had made efforts in that direction under its former parent during the 1990s. The results, while not as calamitous as those of other late arrivals to the VC business, failed to impress the board or investors. However, despite losses, the increasingly geriatric client base had shown remarkable loyalty to the company even through the collapse of the tech bubble, and thereby made the private wealth division a valuable brand to spin off. At the same board meeting where it became clear that the directors who had long advocated getting rid of private wealth would finally prevail, the logic immediately became clear for the broader vivisection the firm would accomplish in early 2002; after which the separate divisions crawled away in separate directions in search of bolder returns, especially those foreseen by its defense engineering outfit, which was busily positioning itself to serve both American and allied defense establishments' pending, urgent needs—with luck perhaps urgent enough to justify a no-bid-contract basis—in view of imminent, protracted wars.

Meantime, the brand loyalty of its dim clients had made private wealth the division best positioned to profit from keeping the parent's name, albeit in acronymous form. The rump firm, FLV Partners, continued holding the aged hands of modest investors who hoped to limp toward the grave with little more at the end than they needed to tip their hearse drivers.

This client base typically kept its assets in testamentary trusts. It may have been the flip allusion, by the CFO during a board meeting, to the prevalence on the books of so many clients still using testamentary vehicles, which did not even offer the postmortem advantage of avoiding probate, that had tipped the balance of the parent's more conservative directors in favor of spinning off private wealth in the first place. Whether the managers who had tolerated this prevalence saw even more dimly into the future than the clients didn't really matter: the whole division was dead weight.

After dissolution, the board of the new FLV, LLC, wasted no resources trying to market the staid old brand directly to new clients;
they might as well have pushed Oldsmobiles on college students. Instead, they aggressively pursued established freelance wealth managers
and boutique operations that could bring existing client books to the
new entity together with the managers' reputations and relationships.
These new managers functioned as nimbler subbrands under the corporate umbrella still recognizable to those who wanted to squint at the
acronym and see the sober old names Frisk, Lambert. It was easier to
buy innovation than to grow it in tired soil. Tech companies did this
sort of thing all the time. The assets within the existing portfolios of the
recruited managers tended more often to dwell in such savvier instru-
ments as revocable living trusts, with the manager himself serving
sometimes as trustee. The personal and unwary nature of these client-
manager relationships often allowed for much longer-term strategic
planning and more ambitious growth objectives than the traditional
FLV client wanted to pursue. In rare cases, the new managers cultivated
such trusts without even the knowledge of the beneficiary, either because of a confidentiality clause within the trust instrument or because
the beneficiary could not be located or, in at least one instance, because the beneficiary refused communication with the manager-trustee.

This last quasi-orphaned trust had come onto the FLV books along
with its manager-trustee shortly before the mortgage crisis of 2008.
The central FLV database listed little more information about the trust
than the Social Security number of its sole beneficiary, one Dwight Elliot Tilly, born November 14, 1948, in Davenport, Iowa.

FLV had received no communication from said Dwight Elliot Tilly,
although periodic credit checks showed that the Social Security Administration had not added the number on file for him to its Death Index,
until which time company policy did not require efforts to identify
secondary beneficiaries. However, while FLV's corporate database con-

tained no record of communication with said sole beneficiary, some of the recruited managers had been known to dawdle in the uploading to corporate's database of contact information held in the Outlook accounts and spreadsheets of their personal desktop computers and those of their executive assistants and bookkeepers. These formerly freelance managers who had "come in from the cold" generally had long-established client lists but no longer wanted to deal with the hassle of regulatory compliance and shopping for liability insurance to cover the man who cleaned their office windows. The new managers were notoriously delinquent in duplicating their data for corporate, a lapse that some in Compliance suspected amounted to a deliberate means of continuing to manage some of their clients' accounts under the legal aegis of FLV, while leaving open the option of carrying off such "dark" clients in the event another outfit should court the managers or they should choose to go back out on their own. In practice, however, such hypothetical dark assets represented a vanishingly small percentage of the capital under the firm's management. And the associates in Compliance, all housed at the Vancouver office, who were responsible for actually looking at the dossiers, had usually just finished business school and showed no desire to harass senior managers who might someday, somewhere within the worldwide web of asset management professionals, represent the catalyzing relationship they would need to make their careers blow up. Before the old men died, they would need to pass on their accounts to somebody.

One such recruited senior manager, who was technically attached to the Fort Worth office but was as likely to show up at the Hong Kong or Arlington facility, needing to borrow a couple of summer interns and the laminating machine; and who managed any number of large private accounts perfectly open to the scrutiny of Vancouver, as well, one might fairly have assumed, as several such "dark" trusts, which weren't really hidden from Vancouver so much as neglected by it, in deference to the way the old-timers had done business back in the seventies and eighties; and who in fact did manage the said "dark" trust for the benefit of said D. E. Tilly; and who had earlier that month materialized at the boutique Socorro office, established two years before to service the burgeoning retirement colonies of nearby Las Cruces and Truth or Consequences; was a lean man of seventy who did all his business with the door open, brought coffee and bizcochitos to all his temps, and who had won himself the admiration of everybody in that office by calling corporate during his first week and threatening to retire unless Socorro was authorized to break the service agreement with their bungling and malicious copier technicians. His name was Percy Lorch.

Tilly never having endorsed the long-ago check from Pierson-Blatt, the sum of one hundred thirty-some-odd thousand dollars had reverted to the bank account of the trust, of which Lorch had got himself made the successor trustee according to the terms of the trust instrument's Gone Missing Clause. He had appointed himself manager of its corpus, in which capacity he had had no choice but to continue to reinvest the proceeds, as was his fiduciary responsibility, since 1975.

The Lincoln slowed, its directional flashed, but it demurred to turn into the FLV parking slot and did not stop. Its driver did not enter Pueblito D and Lorch's temporary office suite there, and did not acknowledge ownership of the trust—a step that Lorch had insisted, during several unwelcome phone calls over the years, most recently last Tuesday, did not even constitute a legal happening. The corpus belonged to Tilly forever regardless of his acknowledgment, unless he and Lorch sat down somewhere and reassigned it.

"It doesn't disappear because you won't admit it's yours," Lorch had said.

"How did you get this number?" Tilly said into the receiver of his unlisted home telephone.

"I can't touch the asset except to invest it. Don't you see that? Nobody can legally use it. Crescit eundo—it grows as it goes—for the benefit of a paper entity, until you say it should do otherwise."

"What are you doing in New Mexico?"

"The business of America is business," Lorch said.

"What the hell does that mean?"

"I have a special project here. Do you fish in your old age, Sergeant Tilly? Reading the water is reading the edges of current, the frontiers, the flanks of change. That's where the hungry trout swim. Wherever you find a landscape or a nation undergoing disturbance, there you will find the entrepreneur. The secret of management for capital growth isn't having a stomach for risk, it's finding beauty in the destruction of obsolete systems and taking delight in the prospect of creating new ones. To dwell on the past is to stay poor. Look at the Islamics—"

"Don't call here again."

Lorch made a low inarticulate sound of annoyance. "Live how you like, but is there really no one else you might be of use to?"

"Get away from me."

"FLV in Socorro. Look us up online. I'll tell you our number," Lorch said. "You pretend not to write it down." But Tilly hung up.

NEVERTHELESS, AFTER HE HAD DROPPED Elroy at the Sunport, Tilly continued driving to Socorro.

He went all the way to Socorro, yet he did not stop there. He continued out of the parking lot, heading westward on U.S. 60 through stark and featureless terrain. A cold and sun-shocked nothingness. He was driving across the bed of an ancient sea. No snow had fallen here. The distant red mountains promised the true future that might still possess him. Not the promise of golden cities the conquistadors had sought here, but the remoter world, the dream world that took the form at the horizon of mountains but might have been composed of unearthly elements, home to unearthly creatures. In the mountain future, all things promised would be brought to completion, all things hinted said aloud, the sun would shine equally on all sides of everything it touched.

The terrain softened and colored. Big sagebrush and winter fat burst from the seabed. Elk tramped meaninglessly through the grassland. The flats ended. The ground rolled. The road gathered upward. The shadows of clouds raced up the slopes. The Lincoln was already passing through the higher terrain that moments before had composed the unearthly future but now, having been reached, became only the promise of other terrain that would follow.

A hawk circled under a cloud.

When the road gave way to descent again, a salt-white figure appeared in the foreground to one side below. Soon it replicated itself on the other side of the road. Then it doubled again and became an arrangement of monuments, approximately human in size, identical and isolated, spaced at regular intervals and continuing to multiply. The road drew the car toward them inevitably. As the speeding car persisted in not reaching them, the white figures grew from human to superhuman to colossal proportions. They were blocks with bowls atop them. Any moment the daring road would veer away from them; but it didn't. They grew in intricacy. They shared a common pose, a facing up and out, identical as salt-white flowers seeking all the same sun, with identical white pistils pointing.

In an instant the disguise of distance evaporated—or he entered the reality the figures had occupied all along. He was driving toward an immense plain of hemispheric antennae, spaced over many desert miles, pointed in silent concert at the sky and listening. Alone but, given their identical inclination, together. And the road did not veer away but shot through them as if to rattle their family peace. The car, the road, changed nothing about them. They surrounded colossally. They stood indifferent, listening. They showed nothing of what they heard, were not changed by it in any visible way. Each antenna a white bowl with flights of white stairs leading into its concavity for people who were not there, who seemed never to have been there and who would never arrive; each bowl inclined on identical white plinths mounted on railroad tracks through which the blue grama and rabbitbrush grew. Antelope walked among them. The hawk was gone.

Twenty-seven white antennae that, though mere half worlds, lacked for nothing, that listened and made no sound.

Then they were behind him. The terrain empty but for scattered yucca with leaves like a clutch of swords. He continued through Datil and Pie Town, heading not so much westward as sunward.

At Quemado—to circle Socorro rather than flee it, to concentrate his route and thus his mind—he turned to the north-northeast and followed the road through dead ground, keeping the sun on his left. Where the road bent toward Cuba, he veered onto a trail that led up a mesa toward a cluster of clapboard buildings, long abandoned. This arrangement once had made a town. He needed sleep. A windowless shack had a cross on it. A path down a slope led toward a collapsed ridge, a pit, and the massed tailings of an old mine. A rattlesnake lay atop a mud oven—an earthen bowl inverted and cracked. Mavis ran at the snake and hollered and darted back to his feet and hollered, but the snake was dead. He poured some water on his hair, though the wind was cold and the desert dusk was coming on fast, and the dog bit at the water flowing off his head, and he scratched at his scalp, and the sun began to go down. He had not eaten lunch or supper. He sat on a red-brown slab of particleboard nailed across the chapel porch, and the desert rose up finally and touched the sun.

Hunger honed his vision. The whole earth was red. Then it was purple. Even the scant grass. He looked toward the sun and yet away from it, at everything else but the sun, until it was weak enough not to blind him.

The same sun rose now on Bagram.

The car cooled and ticked in the dust.

The sun, as the mountain began to eclipse it, became an aperture in space-time through which every person who had ever looked on it from whatever outpost could speak and be spoken to. And he told the lieutenant he was still alive. And he told the hooker in Da Nang he had thrown away her barrette at last when Elroy had sent him a wallet from Dubai. And he asked his father to tell him what to do, but his father didn't answer. And he told his mother he had made a mistake, but she didn't answer him either, as if she was waiting for him first to admit what the mistake was. And he told Bobby Heflin he had come to Bobby's ranch like he wrote to do in his letters, but Bobby wasn't there. And he told Wakefield he had stolen his food. And he told Louisa, wherever she was, his real name. And he looked at the sun on the ridge and told Elroy—but he couldn't say it, he couldn't even think the thing that needed saying.

Because he did not ask forgiveness, none was offered him, not by any of them. And he asked the girl Trisha what in the world she had been trying to do, planting her feet in the hall, telling a man with a hot gun she wouldn't let him pass.

Of all these specters, only the girl Trisha answered. Over the years, she had crossed his path in visions at least as often as the others had, and always, like the others, looking away from him as if among them he had succeeded in becoming the no one he had meant to be.

This time, however, the girl turned to him in her bloody sweater, and asked what Lorch had once asked, "You know what the more excellent way is, don't you, Mr. Tilly? The more excellent way is love."

THE PURPLE ILLUMINATION of the bones of the dead town and of the ponderosa pine in the gully behind included the man on the porch watching the crust of sun that remained. His head bent low, and he shook it and sent the purple water in his hair flying. He seemed to think. The dog got up and trotted to his feet and sat. He ran his hand over the hair twice and smoothed it. When his face came up again, the sun had set.

All night invisible animals scurried under the floorboards of the airless chapel where he slept and dreamt, and in the morning he had made up his mind.

He ate no breakfast. He drove straight to Cuba and southward through Albuquerque and made Socorro again by midday. He ate no lunch either. He parked, and the dog shot automatically over him to the door as he opened it, and he grabbed her neck and tied her to the steering wheel and went inside.

Mr. Lorch was not in, the girl said, looking at her phone, and at Tilly, and at her phone. Could another manager help him?

"I'll wait," he said.

"They all say that," she told the phone—but no, she was addressing Tilly while texting someone else. "Mr. Lorch is special. Are you an existing client?"

"No, I'm not."

"For existing clients I'm allowed to call him."

"Perhaps I am."

She laughed toward her thumbs tap dancing on the phone's glass face.

Her desktop computer pinged, then pinged again complexly. Two short tones, then a long, a short, and a long one.

"He'll see you now." Without looking up, her head inclined to the side to indicate the desktop. "That's our code. Don't tell him I told you."

"How does he know who I am?"

She indicated a peephole camera on the back of her computer.

"Do I show myself in?"

She smiled warmly. "Mr. Lorch would like to meet you in the Regency Courtyard outside Pueblito C."

In the courtyard, a gently frowning white-haired man wearing a tailored business suit and cowboy boots paced in the snow and talked on a smartphone. Had Tilly passed him on the street he would not have known him. He had grown taller, which was impossible. Perhaps he had only lost weight. His face was averted.

He glanced sidelong in Tilly's direction and pointed at the phone and held up a finger. With a wave he invited Tilly under the *portal* to a bench decorated with a mosaic in the forms of bright cows and snakes, but Tilly did not sit. The natty man wore the sort of glasses that used to be called horn-rimmed, though his frames were made of iridescently marbled acetate.

"I know, darling," he said. "You're stretching a limited resource beyond its capacity—no, you're—thaaat's right, and that's why your dermatitis is flaring up—thaaat's right." He took a pen from his pocket and thumbed the top and wrote on the outside of a folder, *granddaughter, rehab*; and showed the folder to Tilly without looking at him and held up a finger. "You should bring that one to your mother—thank you—no, but we love you and we want you to come through this like—thaaat's right. You're our trooper. We all love you, and I love you." He looked down his bifocals at the phone and tapped it quickly many times with his thumbs and put it back to his ear. "Yes, that's exactly right. And you promise to call in a week? Just call one of us. I know I can trust you. That's right, show it to me in La Jolla." He looked down his bifocals and squeezed the edge of the phone and turned to Tilly, and all at once Tilly saw planted in the skull the eyes of the man he had known.

"I'll be a suck-egg mule," Lorch said. "What did you think I was going to do all this time, poison you?"

"Do you have a piece of candy?" Tilly asked.

The *portal* began to swim about him. The floor tiles and the mosaic tiles of the bench swam with it. A Phantom fighter-bomber approached the perimeter of the town. Its roar ascended in volume and frequency. Lorch did not appear to hear it. It was the roar of a passing Phantom, except the sound didn't abate. It reached a screeching peak and stayed there as though Tilly had been plucked up and carried beside the engines of the aircraft. He knew he was falling the moment before he fell.

WHEN HE CAME TO, Lorch was trying to push the spout of a carton of mango-flavored coconut water between his lips. Tilly coughed.

"Don't breathe it, Hawkeye; swallow it. You aren't allowed to choke to death until I get a secondary beneficiary out of you. Siri, ask Gloria to get Doctor Beavers on the line." The phone dinged twice and said it was calling Gloria Pacheco before Tilly swallowed the sweet liquid and passed out again.

When Tilly came to the second time, Lorch said, "Don't be embarrassed. Glycemic issues are the plague of our times. All empires in decline are alike. Some lay the fault for the end of Rome at the feet of the homosexuals. I blame diet. The islets of Langerhans of a great nation can only tolerate so much domination of trade routes before the homeland is swimming in sugar. I was diabetic myself for a while there. Then I went paleo and licked it. I'm very strict these days. Sit up now and tell me how you been keeping. Lacking the clearance I once had, I really don't know. The internet's better than any recon outfit we ever used anyway. I only had to ask Siri to ask Gloria to do a LexisNexis search, and she brought up some of your condo docs on my phone. Look at that—snow. Don't try to stand up till I get back."

He returned with a plate of crackers and two polyester blankets. Snow was accumulating on the pea gravel of the courtyard. Where it fell on the pathway flagstones it vanished as though it had never been. Tilly sat slack limbed in an iron chair. Lorch threw a blanket over him and tucked it around his sides leaving the arms and hands exposed. He put the plate of crackers in Tilly's lap and wrapped the other blanket about his own shoulders like a serape and watched the snow.

The crackers had green chile baked into them.

"Remember when we could still smoke?" Lorch said. "God, I loved smoking in the snow. Yankees don't get it about snow. My grandkids used to bitch about the shoveling when we all lived up in Stamford. I said, 'It's *snow*. Can you believe it? How can you all look away from it even for a minute?' The attitude wasn't their fault. Snow was normal to them as groceries bought on the Visa card. I'm just grateful some notions of scarcity I developed in childhood have persisted despite the riches of later life. You know what I mean? I always pegged you that way, loyal to your cash-poor youth. I reckoned you were living off whatever you made and didn't want to crack your nut until you absolutely had to. Course, you might have been politer about telling me so."

The flags were cold enough now that the snow grew up on them. Tilly might have lain down under the rumpled snow and slept.

"Will you let me tell you a little about the career of your assets? You understand after a while I began to doubt I'd ever see this day—your distribution horizon was effectively never, which allowed a management structure of very long-term growth and freed you up for some exposures to risk that might otherwise have been a little alarming. You got plumb near cleaned out twice before I accepted the gospel of diversification. Once was with Hill Country oil fields. The second was an airline venture that never—well, it never flew its planes. I don't apologize in this business, but when it looked as if Eastern and Pan Am were going under I saw opportunity among the wreckage. Like everybody else, you recovered in the middle Greenspan period. You made some good trades, you made some bad trades. But all in all, I want to compliment your nerve."

The cracker shattered in Tilly's teeth.

"One regret—I didn't see Big Pharma coming. Why didn't I notice all the fancy new illnesses my children were being diagnosed with?" He took off his glasses and dabbed a finger at the inside corner of his eye and looked at the fingertip. He put his glasses back on. "They were too close to me. I hope you don't mind the principles are commingled. The land sale proceeds and the profit share on your operation that you never let us pay you all went into one pot."

Tilly ate another cracker. His delirium was lifting. He said, "I used to wonder why you didn't keep that money for yourself."

"Don't think I wasn't tempted. But I look at the name of the legal instrument by which I have custody of these assets and I see a word derived from the Old Norse *traust*. This word has traveled across icy seas and barbarous tongues losing only a single letter. It has passed many times from the conqueror to the conquered who in time became the new conqueror, but it has kept its meaning unchanged. I had no place undermining two thousand years of history. Trust is trust."

Gloria brought chamomile tea in steaming earthenware mugs. "Beavers sent a text," she said bashfully. "It said *Take him to the hospital, di—*"

"That's all right."

"*Take him to the hospital, dickweed.* Here, look."

"That's all right. He's been calling me that since junior high school."

"Do I phone for an ambulance, Mr. Lorch?"

"Why don't you run get us each a couple of chicken tacos? How's that, Sergeant?"

"Red or green?" the girl asked.

Lorch said, "Red."

Tilly said, "Green."

After she went away, Lorch said, "I started worrying for you about four years ago. I said to myself, Think of his age. He'll probably break down sometime soon and put a couple of kids through college. So I reined you back. Obama was probably going to win the primary. People would ask me, 'Percy, are you in gold yet with this Obama coming?' You know what I said? I said, 'Hell no, I'm not afraid.' I said, 'Yes we can.' Then I said to myself, But Lorch, are you really going to make ole Tilly the victim of your hopefulness? I just didn't think Obama was good for you. I had a feeling. Too bad I didn't have the same feeling about my own assets. You sold a lot in early 2008. You paid your capital gains. Then he actually won the nomination, and I listened to that speech at the football stadium in Denver and I got a little paranoid for you. You know I don't have a racist hair, you know that, but I know my people and I thought, We are not going to feel comfortable with this man at the till. For myself, I was confident; for you, I feared. So you shorted the market broadly—just in time for the follies of September.

"Don't worry about me, I've recovered since the crisis. Everybody with any patience has already recovered. You, however, had nothing to recover from. You walked to school downhill both ways in sunshine. Since 2009 you've taken a special interest in emerging markets, especially India, but at your age you're sick of paying the fees of actively managed funds; you've taken diversification to its logical extreme and you've put most of your assets into index funds, except for your bond exposure, which is mostly in individual T-bills you plan to hold to maturity. You believe in the credit of your government."

"What kind of paleo is this where you get to have tacos?" Tilly asked.

"Mine will come in a dehydrated crisp flaxseed product. No cheese, no guac."

"What will mine come in?"

"White corn, soft shell. I would not recommend that you immediately sell anything in the portfolio once we transfer the trust to your name. Get to know your assets before you decide which of them to liquidate and in what order. Each has its own charm, you'll find. Except within the index funds, you're totally out of defense and security. We've already hit peak security, in my judgment. It isn't undergoing the disruptions anymore that lead industries into ruin or into convulsions of growth. I believe security is heading into a refractory period until the next era of world-shaking terror, which may be a long way off. For now it still appears to be growing, but that appearance comes mostly from the forward momentum it experienced over the last decade.

"An entrepreneur with a taste for history instead seeks out industries that seem to have been long asleep, in enervated states of technological drift. Think of men's formal wear, bottled ketchup. Nothing important has changed there in a hundred years. The technology has become invisible, unquestionable, as though discovered not invented, closed to change. But at any given time, a few of these sectors are really waiting on the cusp of the historical event or technological breakthrough that will change everything forever for everybody. Hence my new project here. Will you let me tell you about it?"

Clumps of snow fell with uncanny slowness through the windless peace of the courtyard. Snow on the stone benches and the yucca in the rock garden. The bittersweet ionized air of snowfall on the desert.

"Some don't welcome the technological change the entrepreneur seeks. What he calls drift, they call peace. I understand. What was the matter with the old TV remote control? How have all these infernal new buttons improved the state of the man on his throne? This man believes he can recede into a distant continent of self and prosper there. But he has mistaken the status quo for a state of nature. He doesn't recognize that cycles of devastation are necessary to continuing life. Many species of conifer have cones that hold their seeds in resin so dense they can only be released to the wind under conditions of fire. The manzanita shrub and the jack pine are two examples. The entrepreneur is not the forest fire. He is the wind that spreads the seed on the ash-black and newly fertile ground. Would you like to know what I believe will be the next old industry on the cusp of breathtaking change?"

Tilly had eaten two crackers and decided to eat no more of them.

"It's a new old industry, as these matters often are. Telephony was asleep for decades—now look how you carry the computing power of a thousand Reagan-era mainframes in your pocket and you quaintly call this thing your 'phone,' as if it were an unexceptional household object. I'll tell you what I see.

"I see a moment when the requisite technologies will shortly converge for a new final frontier. In a few years all the men who walked on the moon will be dead. The future of space would seem to be a thing of the past. But I believe now is the moment when capital invested in the right way can perform its catalytic magic. And here is the place to do it. I mean New Mexico. The convergence here of the world's best rocket-propulsion minds together with the best nuclear engineering know-how. They already live right here on the Interstate Twenty-five corridor from Los Alamos through Socorro and down to Las Cruces. I am not alone in my belief. State and local authorities are right now nearing completion on a two-hundred-million-dollar facility, a *spaceport,* twenty miles south of Truth or Consequences. It is a breathtaking piece of desert infrastructure. It makes use of thermal labyrinth earth tubes to precondition air for passive cooling and heating. Its roof is clad in ethylene propylene diene terpolymer. From the air it resembles a giant orchid in earth tones. My colleagues in the public sector and my partners in the private sector believe we have arrived at the sweet spot in history, the inflection point. I see from your gleaming eye that you hope I'm not referring to mere low-orbit tourism. You might even be wondering how you might invest your own resources at this crucial time if you're unexcited by the slow projected growth of the fixed income products in your portfolio. It's only natural that entrepreneurs and not governments should take the lead now. Think of the joint-stock investors back in England who formed the Virginia Company and got Jamestown going in 1607. The income potential of this new project is going to seem obvious the moment I tell you about it.

"I am speaking, of course, of the private-sector plan to construct one thousand nuclear-powered, oxygen- and greenhouse gas–producing mineral furnaces to create, in a few short years, a heat-trapping and breathable atmosphere conducive to comfortable and *happy* human life on the planet Mars."

"Whatever happened to Van Aken?" Tilly asked.

"Arthur retired. But listen—"

"He was already retired when we met."

"That was from the army. A while after your operation, he retired also from the shop."

"I always thought deep down you had a code," Tilly said.

"Thank you. Arthur married finally, a mining executive from Hong Kong. I liked her right away. She was in her seventies, but if you asked her what was so special about the carbonatite deposits in Tanzania she turned back into a Chinese schoolgirl infatuated with rock formations. Right before he died, I visited the two of them at the golf course where they lived on Bodega Bay in California. Deer were climbing all over the slopes on shore; no one was allowed to hunt them. Arthur was very calmly obsessed with lobbying the housing association to let him build an electric fence, to keep the deer out of his wife's roses. It seemed clear he was taking a benzodiazepine. That made me sad. He was in all the nontrivial respects a great man. He helped me out when my son was going through his teenage moods and I felt I had no one else to call. You know, the indifference to schoolwork and the thousand-yard stare like his mother and I were the biggest assholes in Virginia. It passed, thank God. Arthur said it would, but I didn't know it. I miss Arthur every day. Let's get back to Mars."

Tilly said, "Do you remember a man named Egon Hausmann?"

Lorch looked at him. "Funny way of asking that question."

"Was that his real name?"

"I know for a fact that was his name at birth."

"Arthur killed him."

"You don't say."

"I walked Arthur into the house where this old man was living. I thought, They're just going to squeeze him for information. I was lying, but only to myself. Then Arthur shot him. He died, right? I didn't go back to look."

"Why are you talking like this? I don't like your dreamy tone."

"There was a girl who took care of him. She used to watch the boys play basketball. Always neat. Sometimes a little notebook in her hand. I talked to her maybe three times. I don't know if you remember, I told her Arthur was a doctor who'd check the old man out. Another little lie I hardly noticed. Did Arthur ever tell you what happened? After he shot the old man, the girl tried to stop Arthur from leaving the house. What did she think she was doing? Arthur shot her in the heart."

"Eat another cracker," Lorch said, shoving the box at him.

"I'd seen people get killed before," Tilly said. "Even up close like that. Sometimes I had a hand in it. I didn't know they'd go on living in my mind. Every year they're more alive."

Lorch's mouth opened. For once no words came out. He was recalculating his position. Tilly's implication that he might be informing Lorch of operational details that Lorch probably already knew seemed to irritate his vanity; however, to challenge Tilly would be to admit knowledge. Lorch glanced behind himself over either shoulder. His phone rang, a jingle of computerized wind chimes in his jacket pocket, which he ignored. "If you have the impression that you were misled in your dealings with Arthur, I'm sorry."

"My dealings with Arthur? That's slithery, even for you. Did Hausmann even do anything wrong?"

Lorch asked, "Are you wearing a recording device?"

"I've had a long time to think about this," Tilly said. "I think you were telling the truth about one thing at least. You don't know who your ultimate customer was or what he had against Hausmann, and you'd never want to find out. Your whole operation depended on you not asking who was moving you around or why. And because none of us is ever going to know, our own hands are sort of clean. I shot people in Vietnam and I don't even know how many. I never saw them close. I didn't know what any of it was for. I didn't ask.

"But some part of me must have known you'd kill that old man. Why take that kind of trouble over a person unless you mean to kill him? I said to myself I didn't know what was happening, but I told the girl to get into the kitchen. Why did I do that if I didn't think she could get hurt? When Arthur was leaving, she came out in the hall. My whole body started to twitch. I had this impulse to get in front of her or throw her out of the way. But I resisted it. I stood there telling myself, I don't know what's happening. That was another lie. I knew enough to stop my hands and feet from doing what they were trying to do."

Lorch's phone had quit ringing. He put his hand to his breast pocket as if to reassure himself the phone was still there. He said, "Investigations of the motives of ultimate customers in their commissioning of intelligence products were not encouraged by protocols. Is there a bug in my phone?"

"This is where your code comes in. I could never figure out why you wouldn't stop hassling me to take that money. I think I understand now. Your code says if we're all getting paid then there's no blood on your hands. The money cleans it all by magic."

Lorch rewrapped himself in the blanket, staring with flushed deliberation at his stitched and inlaid boots. "What I can tell you is that Hausmann, in his career, while engaged in a field of operations not unrelated to ours, would have committed offenses that triggered internal protocols of moral balance. Were our shared field of operations within an overt jurisdiction, Hausmann's offenses would have to have been adjudicated by people who could not possibly have comprehended the sensitivity of the operations in which we were routinely employed."

"You think if you keep talking, you won't have to hear what happens in your mind," Tilly said.

"At these levels, intelligence agencies may cultivate informal understandings as to jurisdiction. They come to see it's best if they themselves depose whatever witnesses and gather whatever evidence, and any recommendations for correction are referred internally."

"Referred internally," Tilly said.

"The decisions that were taken regarding Hausmann were probably compelled by understandings of moral balance that Hausmann himself would have advocated were he—"

"What in the world is that, 'moral balance'? I don't even know what that means. You think you can do something and then *undo* it?"

"Why are we talking about this? Are you trying to rattle me? Are you still mad over your foot?"

"I never heard of that, 'moral balance.' Did you make that up? The girl is dead. What's going to balance that?"

"Are you here to take ownership of the corpus of your trust or not?"

"No," Tilly said. "I wanted to make sure you knew about that girl. I figured you did. I guess I was right."

"Don't be a loser your whole life. You know the money's what you came here for. I paid the commission as agreed. I paid what was owed. Why are you rattling me? You're needling and oppressing."

"You feel that commission is a debt you owe against something you did wrong," Tilly said. "Whatever Hausmann had coming to him, you can't ever justify what happened to that girl, and I can't either. By your code I'm the only one you can pay, because the people you really owe it to are dead. By your code, until I take that money the debt's on you."

"You are bound by a verbal contract to accept payment."

"I figure if I don't take your money then I never worked for you."

"We gave you a car!"

"I figure I stole that car." The cold air made Tilly's body seem all the warmer under the blanket. He smelled piñon smoke from a chimney somewhere—the smell of eternal life happening right here around us and we were a part of it. "I had an idea just now while I was out. I forgot all about the future. The past too, for a minute, except I remembered I hadn't eaten and I was hungry. All I need is a little to eat. Two tacos sounds good. That'll be plenty."

"Take your money," Lorch said. "Go on. You take it right now."

"As the money grows, I imagine the stink only gets harder for you to ignore. It's like an organ inside you going to rot. We're not so different, you and me. I wonder what kind of magic thing money is. You have to have it to live; it makes you sick; and it doesn't exist."

" 'Let no debt remain outstanding except the continuing debt to love one another,' " Lorch said. "That's Romans thirteen, eight. I always tried to do right by you, Sergeant. Why won't you do right by me?"

When Gloria came back with the tacos from the truck around the corner, there were three in the large paper sack marked *D.E.T.,* along with a sheaf of documents in an accordion-style expansion folder embossed with the FLV logo, a convolution of stems and loops at once familiar and illegible, like his silverhead father's mark.

He stuffed the folder back in the sack. He unwrapped one of the tacos and opened his teeth. And the combination of the flavors of the meat and chile and tortillas in his mouth was like music. If he had ever before known relief like this he had forgotten it. It had come to its perfection in the moment, because of the moment, and he had let it go. Every part of him awoke with gratitude.

Then he swallowed, and the moment was gone.

16

The drive home to Los Alamos took three hours, clear thinking time, the mind as clean as the cloudless northward sky. His mind became the sky. His thoughts were blue. They seemed to touch on no fixed object; and yet, in a region of the mind unlit by consciousness, unvisited except in dreams and visions, a wall was collapsing under the force of the past. He knew this only by the intensity of passing sensuous recollections—piñon smoke, chicken simmering in a foreign green sauce, hunger that tore the stomach. A woman standing at the cookstove spooning meat onto tortillas. He had buried her far from thought, but she had never lost her power. He touched again with his mind her electrifying skin, dusty, sticky, cool, and felt her ribs beneath.

Piñon smoke—the smell of hope destroyed and renewed in the same moment. The renewal occasioned by the destruction. Bobby and the world of friends he had promised had not been there. But she had.

The guard raised the yellow boom gate at the entrance to the condo complex, and Tilly parked, and Mavis shot over his lap out the open door. He unwrapped the third taco and threw it on the rock garden, and Mavis scampered over the rocks and swallowed the taco whole and sprinted past him into the dark foyer. He turned on the light of the small tiled kitchen, the cupboards too packed with cans to close, and sorted his mail.

Coupon books. One hundred fifty dollars cash back on Cellular+ Cable+Internet bundle. Twenty percent off crystal healing workshops for new subscribers. A postcard alerting him to Mavis's dental appointment next Thursday.

There was also a business envelope of wrong dimensions, metric dimensions. He flipped it right side up. The front bore a square stamp with the number 165 in a corner and the words *Mitteldeutscher Fachwerkbau, 1644/64 Bad Münstereifel* at the bottom. Above this caption was a painting of a six-story half-timbered building with many windows painted in white trim. Along the stamp's upper border, the word *Deutschland*. The left corner of the envelope itself included more long unpronounceable words representing perhaps the return address of a church: what appeared to be a saint's name was embedded in it.

He opened the envelope and took out the letter it contained and began to read. By the second page, what he was reading stopped him short. He folded the letter and returned it half read to the envelope and put the envelope in the kitchen utility drawer and closed it.

He looked at the drawer.

He poured himself a root beer, then he dumped it out and rinsed the glass and filled it with tap water and opened the drawer and took out the envelope and started the letter again from the beginning:

Dear Mr. Dwight Elliot Tilly,

I write this from underneath an accumulation of professional responsibilities so smothering I hardly have time to sleep. And yet here I am at two in the morning writing in regard to a dilemma that has been foisted upon me by forces beyond my control. Please do not disregard this correspondence assuming it may come from a hysteric or from someone with too much time on his hands.

I repeat. I have no time. But here I sit.

I am a Roman Catholic priest in the archdiocese of Hamburg, Germany. I have the pastorate of three parishes, within the territory of one of which is situated a children's home, over which, I take pains to underscore, I have no legal or pastoral authority. Nonetheless, my attendance in the company of the children has become a regular expectation which I have been unsuccessful at shirking.

Slightly more than two years ago, personnel of the State Youth Authority placed in the care of this children's home a boy of four to six years who had been found in the international airport Hamburg-Fuhlsbüttel.

I attach here our earliest photo of him for your reference.

Shortly after he was discovered, he strived to communicate with airport personnel in a language unknown to any of them but now presumed to have been Estonian. By the end of the first day he had closed up, as it were, and spoke to no one further.

It was only after several weeks in the children's home that he began to speak again a little. I beg you not to infer from the regrettable circumstance of his speaking only with me that I have formed with him a special bond. I have not. Nor that I take pride in his having taken me into trust. The boy speaks to me in English, in which I am conversant. This preference for the use of English seems to be the beginning and the end of his motivation in having, as it were, chosen me as his interlocutor.

Of his past, the boy does not relate a thing and has as yet refused to give out his name. The desultory efforts of the authorities here to locate anyone responsible for his arrival at Hamburg-Fuhlsbüttel have failed. Our most promising chance to place him with an adoptive family has also failed utterly. I will not get into the demoralizing details. In short, the judge said no. He even compelled us to sever the relationship with the would-be mother.

Last month I took the horns of the bull into my hands. With a certain moral suasion, I acquired from an element within the *Kriminalpolizie* an edited version of the PNR (passenger name record) listing the 35,438 ticketed and boarding passengers who had used Hamburg-Fuhlsbüttel on the day at issue. Everything had been redacted but the names.

Here I admit I quailed, not at the length of the task, but at my inability to see how in practical terms I was to achieve it. I prayed before my computer and slept and awoke and prayed again, and on the second night a theory and a method came to me both at once.

I ask you to consider with me the possibility that his custodian, in dumping the boy, might not have acted according to plan, as I had always imagined, but instead might have improvised. That the custodian might have bought tickets for the boy and herself or himself but for some reason changed her or his mind and boarded alone. If you infer my pride in this hypothesis, you are mistaken. I am appalled not to have considered it before.

After two weeks' study, taken from sleep, as I have nowhere else from which to take it, and having stricken from the ticketed list all the names of the actually departed, I find too many instances to mention of people missing their flights. (A strike in France and storms at Copenhagen caused delays and missed connections all day.) But I find just three instances in which a pair of ticketed passengers share a surname and in which only one of the two full names appears on the outgoing lists. One of these paired surnames derives from the Kwa language of the Igbo people from the Niger delta; another is shared by two passengers with female given names. These I have eliminated.

The third is shared by one male name and another sexually ambiguous name. Internet searches for the latter yield nothing. Searches for the former yield a criminal conviction in the American state of Maine for one Elroy P. Heflin, with a birth date in 1971. Cross-referencing the name with this year of birth yields nothing useful except the address (on a lien associated with a loan for a Nissan automobile) in Los Alamos, USA, that you will see printed on the envelope in which this letter will be enclosed. Please forgive any impertinence on my part in having telephoned the office of Los Alamos County Assessor to uncover your name in association with this property. I find online no references to persons seeming to be you and can infer no other connection between you and Mr. Heflin. I had hoped to encounter a relative but am forced instead to appeal to you, with the hope that you may be the landlord or subsequent owner of the domicile in which this Mr. Heflin once resided and that you might thereby be in a position to corroborate or to confirm the final hypothesis I shall describe below.

Please do not conclude from my investment in this endeavor that I wish my government to attempt to return the child to the care of someone who, if my guess is correct, has treated him so savagely. Note that I am not writing him directly at this address: even if he lived there now, it seems to me obvious my inquiry would meet only with more evasion. Please do not conclude either that I wish Mr. Heflin to be apprehended and convicted of a crime. Let the judgment of the Lord obtain.

My wish is more modest. Since the boy's first arrival here, when at first he would not communicate with the others, he has begun to speak quite good German. If I were his relation, I would take pride in his alacrity. But so determined and successful have been his efforts to disclose nothing of the time that preceded his coming here and, as it were, to overwrite whatever he knew before with his new knowledge, that it is now my firm conviction the boy no longer remembers his name.

I turn to the adoption procedures laid out in section 6.3.2 of the Guidelines of the Working Group of State Youth Authorities which, for the sake of the child's pedagogical and psychological development, explicitly contraindicates the changing or loss of the first name of the child.

If the child is incapable of carrying, in the present, the record of his past, it is the responsibility of those undertaking his guardianship to hold this knowledge for him until such time as his maturity allows him to carry it himself.

I wish in short only to verify that the entity—surname: Heflin; given name: Elroy Peace—is as I suspect the parent of the child in the enclosed photograph. And thereby to confirm that the entity in the original ticketing list—surname: Heflin; given name: Janis E.—is indeed that of the child installed here.

I hope for your corroboration and await your reply.

Yours very truly,
Rev. Werner W. Wurs

17

If only Elroy would talk with her, Louisa would be able to get this stuff off her chest. The shit, news, heart-scramble, all of it. Listen, there was a lot. She carried it inside her ribs, between the lungs: it crowded her breath. She took care of her body—she stretched and walked briskly on the highway sides with heavy rocks in her fists, and ate roughage, sardines, almonds, and drank calcium-fortified orange juice—but someday the weight she carried in front would buckle her backbones and leave her stooped, watching her feet as she walked. *Just this once, let me tell you what's been happening with me.* She wouldn't ask him any other favors.

Then after, if she could be of help to him, Elroy might contact her for whatever the passing need. She wasn't asking him to buy the whole suite of family attachment software. They might just check in with each other from time to time. Maybe he needed somewhere to have his stateside mail forwarded while he was deployed. Something like that. Or maybe he had kids now, small kids with scabies, and what did you do to relieve the itching and the sores? She'd tell him over the phone how to make an oatmeal bath. *Let me be a resource of some kind.*

Every week, during the time he had been incarcerated at the prison in Los Lunas, she had written him a two-page letter in her Palmer hand. He responded to none of them. After a while her letters started returning to her, stamped ADDRESSEE UNKNOWN, so she reckoned he had got out of prison and had launched upon a new life. She knew he would make it. She *knew.*

She had chosen Leonard, her husband, over him. However reasonable her decision, however misguided, still she'd made a choice. No one else but she had been its author. Elroy in turn had meted out the consequences as was his right. She did not mean to appeal to his sense of what was fair. She did not mean to beg forgiveness. But if only he would talk to her she did mean to propose that they engage in an adult understanding. They need not overcome their grievances. They might even accept the grievances as facts. Similarly they might accept the fact that for sixteen years they had lived together as mother and son. History was rigid. To ignore it was phony. Why not *use* its rigidness as a support against the anguish of future uncertainties? He was not going to *have had* another mother. She was it.

Poor sweet star-crossed Leonard—*just listen a minute and let me tell you what happened, then go on hating him if you want*—tattooed and dentured Leonard; strung out Leonard whom she'd first seen dragging himself through the narrow lobby of the Office of Behavioral Clinicians with fear and determination in his eyes on his way to group; who got clean at last by God's grace; who walked out of prison ready to be reborn; who wanted to marry her and whom she married; who years after his last fix still soaked their sheets in sweat from shame-dreams of getting high again; who woke up scratching the great saphenous vein on the inside of his thigh where in the dream he had injected the needle, woke up sure he was back in Pennsylvania, tying off in the passenger seat of his big brother's Catalina, woke up in prison, woke up in a ditch.

"You ain't either," she said. "You're in bed with me."

And they went back to sleep together in the shotgun house they rented and woke up together in daylight. And she dropped him off at the McAlester Army Ammunition Plant where he was employed as an assistant welder in the pallet production facility that produced the frames on which munitions were shipped from McAlester to naval and air force facilities all around the world. State of the art artillery projectiles. Warheads for the GPS-guided SLAM and Harpoon missile systems containing two hundred fifteen pounds each of Destex high explosive. And after work at the vast penitentiary called Big Mac, she picked him up in the Pontiac Sunbird they shared, and they went home.

After supper, she sent him back up to the Phillips 66 for bananas and aspirin. A state trooper pulled him over: the light above his rear license plate had gone out. Leonard knew every white trooper and policeman in Pittsburg County, Oklahoma, because he swept the floor and cleaned the toilets at the bar they frequented in Longtown, but this trooper was the same brown as his uniform shirt, hat, belt, holster, and the stripes of his pants, and he told Leonard to step away from the car. And while the trooper was feeling around the backseat of the Sunbird a backup unit pulled in behind them, and this second trooper approached them along the shoulder with his hand on his gun, glancing behind him at the interstate traffic. Coming closer he greeted Leonard by name, asking after Louisa's flower garden, and announced that he hoped the other trooper wouldn't find anything in the car here of a fellow Christian that might endanger his freedom after two felony drug convictions that were way in the past, paid for, repented of.

Leonard didn't say anything.

The first trooper emerged from the Sunbird in the changeful light of the oncoming traffic, holding a crumpled lunch bag and asked the white trooper how he knew this gentleman, and the white trooper allowed that they might be acquainted via the McAlester Victory Baptist Church, but anyway the first trooper had better go about his search.

And the first trooper apologized for the intrusion but once he'd run the plates he really did have to check the car, and both troopers later testified Leonard had acted always with the civility owed to their station as law enforcement officials. The first trooper pulled from the lunch bag the crusts of a baloney sandwich, a crushed and empty yellow box of Mallomars, and a nectarine pit. He handed them to Leonard, and Leonard took them. The first trooper stuffed himself back in Leonard's car, and the white trooper said, Well, he'd better check Leonard's person for formality's sake and patted him down from the neck to the shoulders and at his armpit asked if Leonard might be carrying an unlawfully concealed weapon there up under his arm. And Leonard said, Naw, he wasn't, and they laughed. Then, before the white trooper could pat him all the way down, a dispatcher called via the speaker-microphone looped by a Velcro strap to the epaulet of his uniform shirt and informed him he was needed to address a roofing ladder fallen on the interstate at the Route 64 overpass heading into Muldrow.

Which was how it happened that, having finished searching the car and finding nothing of concern there, the first trooper was the one who completed the pat down and found the bulge inside Leonard's tube sock, at the touch of which Leonard at first maybe twitched or winced. And the trooper said, sorry if he'd hit a bruise there, and rolled up the leg of the jean and tugged down the tube sock and peeled off the bandage that had been affixed to Leonard's ankle, revealing the pale and hairy skin unmarked by any remnant of wound, and the trooper weighed the bandage in his hand, his mouth taut with misgiving, and weighed it some more while Leonard stood there stocking footed on the asphalt and then the trooper pulled apart the cotton wadding of the bandage and found a shrink-wrapped bag the size of a thumbnail containing one eighth of an ounce of brownish chalky methamphetamine, and the trooper poked it and looked embarrassed and said, "I didn't mean this to happen to you." And though the eighth of an ounce the trooper was poking with his thumb constituted an offense that might have been knocked down to misdemeanor possession, the forty-seven identical packages he then found in the fuse box under the driver's-side dash were enough to establish intent to distribute.

And Louisa knew every infraction in Leonard's old prison jacket and she knew the sentencing guidelines for habitual offenders, and the night she received the call that he had been arrested she walked amid her astonishment alone behind the house she would not be able to afford to rent on her own, through lately timbered hardwood forest, the dead misshapen trunks of junked trees, by the muddy reservoir, over cattle guards, into a residential development and onto a paved road. Walking and thinking over the choice that lay before her.

These were the things that had happened and what she had done.

Walking through other people's yards. The whir of air conditioners. No one outside. Knowing somehow that unless she made a choice right now at this swerve in fortune, seized the unspeakable opportunity, she would die like this, exactly like this, walking alone and all the houses sealed up against the heat, outside and unknown to those within, a woman without any people. Looking for an open door anywhere.

In the gravel apron of a driveway, a girl sat revving the engine in a car and calling for somebody to come the hell out of the house, a white girl with dreads and purple braided extensions. Louisa got right inside the car like she owned it and said she needed the girl to take her to the pay phone at the gas station. And the girl gave her the fish-eye, like Bitch, I'll take you out. But then Louisa must have looked a fright, and the girl asked suddenly what had happened. And when Louisa later asked herself why she could not have simply gone home and placed her call there, she discovered that she must have felt it would be too cruel to Leonard to make such a treasonous call from his own home, felt it even before she understood the nature of the call she intended to place.

When they got to the Phillips 66, the pay phone had long since been ripped out of its aluminum enclosure, and the yellow and red tangled wires protruded like the vessels of a shorn limb. And the girl said she had some spare minutes and lent Louisa her cell, and Louisa called first neither a lawyer for Leonard's defense, nor his work, nor church people who had by then for years included in their prayers the hope that Brother Leonard might continue to walk the narrow path, but called instead the number of Tilly's drilling business, memorized but not used once, not once, since the fateful call four years before when she had pleaded with Tilly to take Elroy off her hands. *I never meant it forever. I meant you to get some sense of your power and your trouble from a man you trusted.* The phone rang while she gamed out the words she would say which all amounted to one or another version of treasonous confession that she'd made a mistake on the desert night when he'd asked to come in. She had said no, and she should have said yes. And would he ask her again right now? Please? All while poor Leonard was at his hour of direst need.

She was not asking forgiveness. She was stating facts.

After four rings a recorded voice told her the number she had reached had been disconnected. The girl driving the car said, "Lady, you don't think I should take you up to see your deacon?" And Louisa called information in Albuquerque, Las Cruces, Santa Fe, saying the name and spelling it in various ways, and none yielded a number for Tilly anywhere.

And Leonard was charged with possession with intent to distribute six ounces of a Schedule II substance, his third strike on a felony drug charge, and they put him away for life. For life.

And soon thereafter she divorced him, despite his tears, a grown man's tears in prison, and she saw him at work as he went for group. She did not hide her face. And all along she had been lying in wait to do this thing to him and not knowing it, waiting for him to fail. And this was her life, did Elroy understand?

And she lived with a lady friend, then by herself in two rooms over a muffler shop, always keeping her same job at the prison where staff and inmates alike knew she had a boy locked up elsewhere. They had a

modem now in the reentry coordinator's office and Louisa had asked
the admin assistant to help her do a search of the World Wide Web,
and with one click they scoured newspapers across the earth in whatever the language and found Elroy incarcerated again in the state of
Maine, and she wrote him there also, letters never responded to.

And Leonard died in prison of pulmonary edema in May 2004.

And sometime around there a collection agent called her at work
trying to get her to divulge the address of a Corporal Elroy Heflin, U.S.
Army, and she asked how could she know they were even speaking of
the same individual? And the agent quoted to her the last four digits of
a Social Security number. And it was as if lightning had shot through
the phone into her ear. Her boy had been turned into a number which
she knew unmistakably as a cow knows the scent of her calf. Then it
was she trying to pry out what the agent knew, but the agent would not
say any more. Then why should she say? If the agent wouldn't, why
should she? But at least she knew now Elroy was in the army, which
after all included many jobs not specifically linked to being killed and
killing. She had hope for him always.

What the others at work knew of Elroy they knew only by hearsay.
She did not speak of him there, only at church where she spoke silently,
amid the company of other people, with God, whose ongoing relationship with Elroy could safely be presumed, whether Elroy accepted it or
not, and through whom she imagined she could pass notes to Elroy in
the halls of a celestial high school, God palming the many-folded note
as they passed and slipping it to Elroy later during math class.

While the others sang in church and gave witness, Louisa spoke inwardly with God also on a different matter. Namely that one night in
her youth, in the desert during a card game, a man who had come from
what amounted to another world had asked her for the very thing she
claimed she was most willing to give to all people, but because he was
an individual person, not all but himself alone, asking for it from her
and her alone, she had said no.

She sat on the cushion she had brought to her dark pew within the whitewashed pine walls of the Victory Church in McAlester while she and God together tried to figure out what cheap spirit had possessed her, or failure of will or vision. Or possible flaw, God admitted with reluctance, in her design.

Then her mother fell getting out of the bathtub in her rented house in Texas and shattered her femur and pelvis, and Louisa forsaking her sacred vow never to go back to the town of Lufkin, took unpaid leave from the Department of Corrections and washed the demented woman who had nobody else, nobody, and stirred her Coke to get the fizz out as her mother liked and mashed up her sweet potatoes with margarine and fed them to this woman whom she no longer had the stomach to judge and kept up her mother's thick eyeliner, which seemed less tacky now than singular, and no one came to visit, no one. And then during *Jeopardy!* the category had been Flags of the World, and a bright red field appeared on the screen with a yellow sun in the middle and stylized rays and two sets of three red rows banded across the sun, and the clue said the red of this flag stood for valor and the yellow for both peace and wealth, and the bands across the orb of sun stood for the yurt or family home and also for the universe, and Louisa shouted at the screen, "What is Kyrgyzstan!" knowing as she did the flags of all the belligerent nations where Elroy might be stationed as part of Operation Enduring Freedom, and she had been right, it was Kyrgyzstan, and she slapped the back of her mother's hand in vindication, and the bone-bag hand did not respond but lay there: her mother was dead.

I'm only telling you what I got to put down or it'll break my back someday.

She sold her mother's things. She paid everybody in Lufkin—the hospital and the podiatrist and the gasoline station tab and the church loans. There remained $720 of inheritance for herself. But when she got back to McAlester she discovered that notwithstanding promises of family medical leave, the work of her department had just been bid out to contractors. And after three months living in the Sunbird, and not touching the inheritance, which she kept under the passenger-side floor mat, she got a job out in Sallisaw as simulcast teller associate in the off-track betting parlor of a casino owned by a Cherokee Nation conglomerate with their fingers in health care, environmental and construction, hospitality, real estate, security, and defense.

And what would that younger Louisa—proud vagabond, who owned nothing but her looks, her love of mankind, and her certainty that the race was doomed—have said to this later woman, gray bangs held back from the face with her mother's celluloid comb, and still thin, able, though lacking several malignant moles and lymph nodes, a portion of one breast, and living now in Sallisaw, a place named fittingly for old meat kept edible with salt, on West Houser Industrial Boulevard in a former motel complex of cable-ready, air-conditioned, attached, four-hundred-twenty square foot, single-story, single-occupancy units with ceiling fan, some paid utilities, shared laundry room, no dogs, birds, snakes allowed, thirty-day renewing lease, one crabapple tree in the courtyard?

That girl would have said, "Better here, like this, than presuming to own."

And what would that girl say if she should learn that the older Louisa had resolved now to add to her inheritance some small sum every week—because she was going to effectuate one last betrayal of that perfect girl in the perfect body who knew almost nothing except that love was true and owning land was wicked and on whom she had not yet much improved—what would she say if she should learn that Louisa was saving up money to buy land of her own and build a house on it?

Nobody gets to run me off: that was what she wanted. If that meant owning, she'd own. If owning was wrong, she'd do wrong.

She wasn't going to apologize. She scrimped by dropping her cell phone contract and eating brown rice from a fifty-pound bag kept in a resealable bucket. The rice and other bulk nonperishables she purchased from a survivalist supply store where the cashier knew her by name and said courtingly he was glad to see a woman keep herself strong enough to lift the bucket on her own and ready to consider some of the truly unprecedented things that had happened in this country and were happening now and were going to happen soon, government coming, radical Islam about to establish sharia, but at least one woman was to be ready, looked like.

Such talk was general also at church. Her new church, Shiloh Missionary Baptist in Sallisaw. The present they called Today's World. The future, Harvest Time. The catalyzing event between the two world-times was called an S.H.T.F. situation for when the shit hits the fan, pronounced letter for letter to avoid profanity, or else TEOTWAWKI, a word like a Polynesian cocktail. The end of the world as we know it. We had entered a long middle period, and not one of us could know how long, and the challenges for which to prepare were not limited anymore to nuclear holocaust but, these days, extended to land invasion through the porous southern border, EMP attacks, electromagnetic pulse, which an enemy might use to fry the whole North American integrated electric grid, leaving the internet destroyed, your bank accounts a memory, the cyborg nation exposed, helpless, gasping. The sun might cause a phenomenon such as occurred in the solar superstorm of 1859 called the Carrington Event when a white light flared in the sun's photosphere, and eighteen hours later the earth's magnetic field convulsed, and you could read a newspaper at midnight by the lurid aurora.

In church they spoke of the inevitability of future such CMEs, coronal mass ejections. And of LTS, long-term supply. And they spoke also of old-fashioned rapture, of the four horses in Revelation, the white, the red, the black, the pale, of the winnowing of human wheat from human chaff. And when they said, "In those days shall men seek death, and shall not find it; and shall desire to die, and death shall flee from them," the words were a comfort to her, but why? Because these were the old-fashioned end-times she had expected from a little girl. Men on horseback, opening seals. And because even though she knew this wasn't what the verse meant, she still read into it that death might flee from Tilly and Elroy both, even though they sought it. They might hide in their holes but love would dig them out.

If you were not raptured you would have to wait. Some would eat, some starve. The beepers that sounded from garbage trucks and construction vehicles when put in reverse were omens warning that to go back was perilous and probably unworkable. They've already taken our country away from us.

Beans. Bulk lentils. Church people had first told her about the store, and whenever she went there somebody from church was rummaging the stocks of milk- and soy-based protein powders in multiple flavors. She couldn't bear to confess to them that she shopped here to save as much as she could in order to commit herself to the folly of owning property so she could put a home on it. This vegetable oil was specially formulated from Canadian rapeseed to be usable in a generator if the oil went rancid before the time came for its consumption.

The store stocked ammunition in large crates for every conceivable handheld weapon. The individual elements for the making of the cartridges of basic armaments, manual presses for loading bullets into spent brass casings, single- and two-cavity bullet molds for the forging of new bullets from recovered ones or from the cames of old windows or wherever else you would scavenge your lead. They had tin and zinc and antimony to mix with the lead, harden the alloy, lower its surface tension to better fit the grooves in the mold. There were Aquatabs and liquid tincture of iodine for your drinking water once the taps stopped working and solar-powered Geiger counters with snap latches so you could affix them to the collar of a dog. There was everything you might expect to need if you were determined to survive. Still there was not enough, and Louisa wanted to grab these people in the aisles and shake them and ask who were they neglecting now to save later?

I'm saying I made a mistake, Elroy.

The store had bumper stickers. They had DON'T BE JUST ANOTHER VICTIM. They had THE PRICE OF FREEDOM IS VIGILANCE. And they had GOD RECYCLES: HE MADE YOU OUT OF DUST. And they had NOT PERFECT, JUST FORGIVEN. And they had Lenin's face, Gandhi's face, Jesus' face in various attitudes, loving, angry, weeping. And they had MY SON IS IN THE U.S. ARMY. And they had ARE YOU READY? And they had MY ZOMBIE ATE YOUR HONORS STUDENT. And they had WHEN TYRANNY BECOMES LAW, REBELLION BECOMES DUTY. And they had REPENT.

She bought her rice and took it to her car and drove to the casino, a windowless fortress of reckless hope insulated against manifestations of the local hour, where she dispensed wager tickets under the banks of the simulcast screens with live feed of the sprinting greyhounds and thoroughbreds across the continent at Hazel Park, Los Alamitos Race Course, Palm Beach Kennel Club, Thistledown, Vernon Downs, Assiniboia Downs, Wheeling Island Racetrack, among the solitary men in flattops, faces pitted like sandblasted brick, smoking and taking notes with pencils worn down to half the length of a finger, men who took in hope with every breath, hobbling behind a steel cane, gripping the foam sleeve about the handle, the vinyl case for the eyeglasses bulging out of the breast pocket, men in wheelchairs and scooters trailing oxygen tanks, still seeing the money ahead, still chasing it. And at the end of her shift she went home. Her headlights caught the crabapple tree in the courtyard standing shocked and solitary over the mass of shriveled blossoms it had shed, grateful to have endured where no others of its kind had even tried.

And this was her life.

The other tenants customarily backed up their trucks and hatchbacks to their doors when they parked, as though preparing for sudden escape from the law. She recognized the faces of the vehicles even if not the faces of the owners when she espied them in daylight, coming out of their houses looking down at their phones, and getting into their vehicles looking down at their phones, and speeding away glancing toward their laps and up at the road.

She had been saving for nine years and after subtracting occasional outlays—for medical insurance deductible, people from church in need, people not from church but known to people from church to be in need—she had amassed about sixty-five hundred dollars, enough for a two-acre lot, and at this rate she would have enough for the house around the year 2055 if the price had not risen. She'd be a hundred and seven years old, and the hideous logic of debt had finally begun to work on her—once you gave in to the core idea of people owning places you got embroiled in the whole garbage storm of greed and killing.

And this was her life. Having been strong it was now compromised, trembling and mortal as the filament in a lightbulb, and she was dependent on no one, and no one depended on her, and she knew the faces of all the cars that lived in her parking lot as though the face of a car were a human face. And all the cars faced out tonight toward the road and were known to her, but one.

God protect you, wherever you are—

She slowed the car. The night was hot. No overhead lamps lighted the asphalt perimeter of the building where she lived.

—and don't give up on me yet.

UNCOMMON, THE CAR of an overnight visitor here. The living units did not fit sofas. She backed in several spaces away from the unfamiliar car, in which a figure sat aslant, inert, reclining. As she moved to get out, the figure in the other vehicle stirred and did likewise. And she had already incautiously got out of her car and was standing with both thoughtless feet on the pavement before the tremor overtook her of carjack, rapist, killer. Women got killed like this in the parking lots outside their own rented front doors, old women whose deaths accomplished nothing but to slake the killer's need to kill. She and the figure had closed the doors of their respective vehicles, the darkness everywhere. The killer seemed to mirror in the dark her every smallest motion. If she should reach into her backseat to lug out her rice, he would reach into his and pull out his gun or club.

And because the angel of death calls us each individually, and though we might live together we must each die alone, this killer in the dark said her name—not like a bureaucrat from hell droning from a list of the condemned but like someone to whom saying the name was an expenditure he couldn't afford, and yet he had chosen to pay it anyway. "Is it you, Louisa?" he asked.

In the dark, she said his name.

It was by her saying his name, not by her knowing it and *then* saying it, but by her mouth itself, her body making the word aloud and the mind hearing it, that she knew she was standing in the parking lot with Tilly. But the name she had called him was Dwight.

THEY STOOD IN THE KITCHEN AREA under the hanging wagon wheel festooned with compact fluorescent tubes within frosted lamps that overhung the table. She offered him a sweet tea. He said okay and stood, not drinking it.

The glass perspired in his fist.

She took out her mother's comb and refolded her hair on top of her head and put the comb back in. Her heart beat like mad. "Why don't you sit down?" she asked.

"That's all right."

"Why are you whispering?"

"Isn't Leonard asleep?"

She felt herself go insane: from a high ledge she took a step into the open air, and the foot came down firmly and rested on nothing. Then she stepped backward onto the earth. She said, "We—" but the words crowded her throat and stopped it.

"Tell me if he'll mind. I would have called ahead. The computer didn't have your phone number."

"Which computer?"

"The web. It even knows how old you are and where you lived before this. Everybody's on there."

"You aren't," she said. In this way she intended to expose everything—her heart, all of it. She waited to see if he understood.

A flush emerged in his cheeks. All at once it rose straight to the roots of his hair. He made no effort to disguise it.

The silence between them was a torture.

He wore an iron-colored waterproof jacket that whizzed synthetically when he moved; and black jeans, formless, as if he had borrowed them from a larger person; and a belt that went around him one and a half times with jagged holes in it punched at uneven intervals; and running shoes with green soles and neon orange laces. His eyes were hard and very tired and perplexed, and he smelled of himself, a smell of their former bed. His accent, when he spoke, of Nowhere, America. The hair uncannily silver and shining. The strong hands, red and wrinkled and veined, and spots the color of browned meat that ran up the backs of his fingers.

Sometime in the previous century, somebody had fitted into the window an air conditioner now long empty of its refrigerant but with a fan that still worked, and Louisa went to the living area and switched on the machine and opened the window opposite, and an unnatural breeze moved in the place, and she breathed it.

When she turned around he had taken from his inside jacket pocket a worn business envelope with foreign writing in the corner, and she saw in a flash of delayed recognition that he had come to tell her Elroy was dead.

The ice snapped in his glass. He took a letter from the envelope and flattened it and handed it to her. She unfolded a pair of drugstore reading glasses from the utility drawer and read the letter through rapidly without speaking.

She knew herself to be falling in the dark at slow then zooming speeds, through an infinite void to no hard place but only toward further falling in a universe with no one else in it.

When she had finished reading, her hand went to her forehead and gripped. She said, "Oh my God, I'm going to be sick."

She read the letter again repeating aloud certain phrases mechanically, drilling them into her mind. Stapled to the final page was the picture of a boy in a black ski jacket, the thick hair disarranged. He wore a horrid look of hunger.

"Are you sure this is him?"

"I didn't look too close," Tilly whispered. He slouched. He shrugged and squirmed as if the true person she knew were trying to grapple his way out of the false envelope of this old man's skin. "Anyway, I never saw him. Elroy was supposed to bring him to stay at my place. He flew to Europe to get him. Then he came back empty-handed."

"He never showed you a picture?"

"He never did."

"This letter is from six months ago. You done nothing that whole time?"

"I've been trying to understand first what it means."

"What did Elroy say when he got back from Europe?"

"He said, 'Just, it didn't work out.'" This fateful datum dangled in the air. Tilly had pronounced it precisely, with no intonation that might betray what he believed to be its secret import, leaving her to read it for herself, to imagine the Elroy she knew saying it, to follow the chain of implications.

"What in the hell happened to the mother?"

"She was supposed to let the boy go, for a visit," he said with equal deliberate impartiality. She had forgotten this talent of his never to impose on you his own reading of things, instead to leave you free amid your own conclusions, however they frightened you.

"But where has she been all this time? Don't you have to assume she's been looking for the boy? And with whatever authorities looking for her, is it really possible they couldn't find each other? Someone's lying."

"All right. Who?"

"It must be someone trying to make Elroy look bad."

"But who?" If he had his own guesses, he disliked or distrusted them and didn't show them. They had trapped him, the way his money once had done.

"I don't think it's the priest," she said.

"Is it the mother who's lying?"

"The mother isn't even here," she said to the letter. "Somebody cut the mother out."

"Let's go outside," Tilly said. "I don't want to wake him up."

"Somebody's lying who doesn't want the mother there. What was it exactly Elroy said when he came back from the trip?"

Dwight told her again.

"He was trying to hide the truth and he wanted you to ask him about it," she said. "So you could tell him what to do. I think the mother reneged after he got there. But if that was all there was to it he would have said so. That would have taken him off the hook. For some reason he was evading you. Somebody doesn't want the mother there. Somebody did something with the mother. But what?"

He stood at the front door with his hands stuck in his jacket pockets. "The mother was always trying to shake him down," Tilly said. "Silly things he couldn't afford. She wanted to travel and she wanted him to pay for it. I'll tell you more outside. I don't like to be in another man's house at night when he's asleep."

The fan in the air-conditioning unit shivered, and its false breeze made the pages ripple in her hand.

She said, "I can't bear this picture."

Dwight watched her with strain.

"It's the eyes. They're Elroy's eyes. They're the same."

He came back to the kitchen area and dumped the tea she'd given him and filled the glass from the tap.

"The water's no good here," she said. "There's hexavalent chromium and fracking and fertilizers and I don't know what else."

He drank anyhow, looking away.

"Someone transplanted his eyes, or he could be a clone," she said. "It's so clear, it's disgusting. Look."

"I believe you."

"But look."

"I'd rather not."

"Look."

"No," he coughed.

"Look at him."

"I don't want to."

"Look at the picture."

"This water tastes like the puddle under the drain trap, in the cabinet where you keep the cleaning chemicals."

"*Look* at it."

"I won't."

"Yes, you will. You look at it this minute."

"No."

"Yes. You go on do it now."

"No."

"Here."

She shoved the page at his hand. He submitted to look at the picture.

He gave it back. In his discriminate eyes she saw reflected the conclusion that had just come to her. A distraught communication was happening. A resifting of the data. Both of them contending with the information, struggling to come to some conclusion other than the one he didn't want to say.

She said, "You already figured this out."

"I wouldn't say that."

"But you believe you know the answer. And you came here to lay all this in front of me. And see if I came to the same answer you did."

"I want to know how you figure it," Tilly said. "You always had a better mind."

"You think the mother hasn't turned up because Elroy killed her. You think he went there to get the boy, and the mother changed her mind and wouldn't let the boy go, and Elroy's beast came out, and he killed her."

Incredibly, Tilly stood there waiting for her to say something more.

"Please don't make me be the only one of us who said this out loud when you're the one who believes it," she said. "I don't believe it one bit. I can't. One of us has to be the one who doesn't believe it, or we're being too cruel to him."

Tilly said, "All right. That's half of what I thought."

"It's your guess. You're the one who knows him now. All I know is how he always was. He wouldn't hurt somebody he cared about, would he? What do you mean, 'half'?"

Tilly asked why she thought he had left the boy in the airport—a question spoken as a statement.

She was unsure. She had heard the airports nowadays were crawling with police armored to the teeth, their fingers on the triggers of machine guns to make the people feel safe.

Tilly's neck minutely twisted in the chemical light. The thing within him struggling to get out was not knowledge as he seemed to believe, but slander, and it was festering in him, and she could read it, and he could not, and he was asking her to extract it for him. He believed he knew why Elroy had left the boy in the airport.

She said, "You think he was afraid he'd kill the boy too."

. . .

EVERYTHING HAD GONE BADLY WRONG. And yet its going wrong was not the end.

Dwight cast his eyes about the place taking in its smallness for the first time and asked if she and Leonard were not living together any longer.

They went to the parking lot and got in her car, and she drove to the reservoir, and they got out and tramped along the dirt trail watching for the night-black cottonmouths that lived in the mud below the embankment. The moon came on them. Among the woods, fog. The blue-white LED floodlights of distant farms irradiated it. The twisted trees the loggers had left behind made jagged black stripes in the glowing air.

She told him what had happened between her and Leonard. What she had done. The choices she had made. His last days, at the hospital in Tulsa with a corrections officer outside the door. After Leonard's lungs had begun to fill with fluid, his kidneys and liver had begun to fail. She sat in the hospital room reading him the underlined passages in his prison Bible. No one else came. They had cuffed his ankle to the rail of the bed. Occasionally his eyes would come halfway open. They seemed to see. Then they closed again. In the hallway, nurses hooted. She went out to talk with them, two black women named LaQuanda and Ruth. They were watching a video on a smartphone. They asked her where she was from, and she said East Texas. They were from Little Rock and from Barbados. They asked where Leonard was from, and she told them a little coal town in western Pennsylvania where nobody lived anymore, she had forgotten the name. The one called LaQuanda asked what Leonard had done to get life.

The other looked away at a chart.

Louisa told them, but they were not appalled at the injustice. Ruth said that last month they had had a killer in from Big Mac for brain surgery. The attending had advised them before they started their shifts that the killer belonged to the Aryan Brotherhood and instructed them as to when he was required to be in restraints. As they were prepping him for surgery the killer asked them to save him the dark ponytail that would have to be cut off. They obliged. When they shaved the back of his head, two tattoos were exposed in matching gothic capital letters. One read WAR. The other, ARTIS. When LaQuanda asked what Artis was, he said she was his mother.

"Gosh," Dwight said.

That had been his father's word, Louisa remembered—the father he always claimed never to have met. One time, just once, in Ramah in bed after they had fucked, Dwight had said, "Gosh." And she had laughed. And as he'd fallen asleep he'd slurred, "That was near as my father ever got to cussing. He'd say it over a piece of pie." Dwight had made a slip, but she never pressed it. He had lived in another world, played another self there. Did he really think she couldn't tell, or that she hadn't done the same herself? Who among us has lived only once?

"Who gave you this shirt?" she asked amid the shadow trees. "It fits you like a tent."

It was his own, he said. In the months since he had received the priest's letter, he had lost interest in eating. He had lost a quarter of his weight. He had taken to walking long hours in the Jemez Mountains, trying to figure out what choices lay before him.

In the Jemez, at Bandelier, he had climbed among the cliff dwellings of the Anasazi. The ash of a volcanic eruption had compacted over the millennia into cliffs of welded tuff from which the ancient pueblo dwellers had hollowed out their homes, and he scaled the wood ladders into the dark smooth high caves from the mouths of which families had watched the bright night sky for centuries, snug in their cliffs and safe from raiders, and the smoke of their fires had drawn away through holes carved above in the domes of rock. The Anasazi had disappeared from that place four hundred years ago leaving only caves and petro-glyphs carved in the cliff faces, hardly visible for the sun shower, of birds and crude human beings, open-mouthed and shouting, elegant spirals turning ever inward on themselves, the same spirals replicated in the rock all over the settlement, their meaning unknowable. Even the name these people had called themselves was lost. *Anasazi* was a Na-vaho word meaning "ancestors of our enemies."

All night the two of them walked through woods and in the thickets of tall marsh weeds taking counsel together and asking each other what they would do.

18

Tilly didn't know how to put a knot in a necktie. Louisa did it for him. She had become adept back at the prison, where she had maintained a collection of ties in various lengths so visiting boys could look their best when they went inside to see their fathers.

At her little bathroom mirror, she and Tilly stood in their finery. His stippled neck was red and warm, and her fingers turned the silk with confidence, and their bare feet pointed crookedly allowing them to be together in the tiny space, and when she drew the broad end through the front of the knot she stood up on the balls of her feet to watch that the edge should not curl in on itself, and as she did so he looked from her sternum down to her legs where her contracted soleus and gastrocnemius muscles were separately visible, and the two of them inhaled through their noses the mixed air of their separate breath and the smells of their bodies.

This time a minister married them. After the ceremony they drank coffee and ate donuts in the church basement with some of her friends from the casino who came to congratulate her and say goodbye.

Later that week they packed her things into cardboard boxes and rented a truck, and at the Texas panhandle town of Higgins she put the state of Oklahoma behind her once and for all, and they continued into New Mexico and unloaded her things into a former warehouse for logging equipment on the outskirts of Bandelier where Tilly had been storing his own things since his small condo had sold. The walls were steel sheeting kept together with screws and did little to hold the heat inside or impede drafts, but the stacked boxes of the possessions from their separate homes formed a windbreak inside the dark structure. Here they lived like squatters, cooking on a camping stove that burned gasoline and taking their showers at the Y in Los Alamos while their new house was being built.

They were unused to spending money but they had bought a new car with all-wheel drive and airbags, and Louisa drove it daily to the construction site they had chosen together, fifty miles away, along a westward-facing slope of the Sangre de Cristo Mountains within walking distance of the school in the town of Chimayo. There would be no mortgage: Tilly would pay for everything.

While they were still in Oklahoma, he had gone to an FLV branch office to sign a direct-deposit form for the distribution of the trust, and when he came back out Louisa was waiting for him behind the wheel of her old car, which they were about to scrap. "End of the war?" she asked.

"Yes," he said.

"Did you win?"

"Nobody won, but we get the spoils."

She started the car. Tilly was crying. She asked, "It ain't all spoils, is it?"

"Guess not," Tilly said. "Some of it was a gift."

Days later, his account was credited with a sum so large, by their lights, that it made the work they'd done to accumulate what savings they had—the years of hours, the deferred medical procedures, the private daily austerities that each had represented its own small accomplishment—meaningless.

But they had made their choice.

Weekdays, on her way to the construction site, she checked their box at the P.O. in Los Alamos. Her passport arrived within two months of her application. His, for some reason, was delayed.

She liked to watch the house taking shape. A shelter made on a place that was theirs. It was a true adobe house with bricks made from mud and straw, and a *portal,* and vigas in the principle rooms that extended outside beyond the edges of the roof, and kiva fireplaces in the bedrooms, and long canales to keep the rain from undermining the foundation as had happened to the Heflin place. She wanted this house to last a thousand years.

Having no refrigerator in the warehouse, most nights they boiled soup from a can for supper. Afterward they read or talked outside by a wood fire—or sometimes drove deeper into the Jemez to an unmarked trailhead and got out wearing wool socks and winter coats and followed the trail guided by flashlights that showed their breath in the cold as the trail switchbacked through densely smelling pines and around fallen boulders, and the trail made a final sharp turn downward, and they stepped over a cleft in the rocks and arrived at a hot spring where they took off their clothes and got in the water and watched the galaxies or the clouds while snow fell through the mountains and lost itself in the steam above the pools. Hippie kids came there from Santa Fe, shyly taking off their clothes and talking softly and smoking pot, and one of them took a long breath and put his mouth to a didgeridoo and submerged his head and played dirges from underwater. Other nights the two of them had the place to themselves.

After three more months of wrangling—as well as a final intervening phone call to Washington from Lorch—Tilly's passport arrived, and they drove down to Albuquerque and left the car in the long-term lot and checked their bags and passed through security and boarded the plane.

As it was taking off she said a prayer. She had never flown before. Once they reached cruising altitude, he asked if she was all right. She said she was fine, pressing the button inside the armrest as if to see what it was for, although inwardly she was still speaking to God and listening for any guidance he might be willing to give. By the time the plane was hurtling toward the runway in Newark, God had indeed begun to speak with her—of his darker proclivities, his taste for mayhem, his willingness to lead us into wildernesses and into further wildernesses inside them.

One by one the passengers went down the aisle of the plane into the jetway and through the terminal door where they merged into a human current, thousands of people flowing as one substance through the veins of a creature unknowable by them because they were a part of it.

And God spoke through the burble of roller bags, the birdcall alarm of electric shuttle carts ferrying the elderly to their gates, the many spoken tongues she couldn't identify, the skidding soles on tiles, the rhythmic thumping of the moving sidewalk: all of it feeding into one voice, answering her in a way she strained to hear.

At passport control she stood beside her luggage, waiting, listening hard.

She handed the agent her document. He opened it and laid it flat on the black screen crisscrossed with red lasers, and she understood at last what the voice was saying and why. Her arm was crooked in Tilly's arm, and she pulled him close.

She had to stop here, she said. She mustn't go any farther from home than she'd already come. She was very sorry. He'd have to go the rest of the way without her. She would rent a hotel room outside the airport and wait for him to return.

. . .

"I THOUGHT YOU WOULD BE a physicist or mathematician," the priest said, "from the secret desert city of doom."

He showed Tilly to a miniature chair, a one-piece polypropylene shell affixed by concealed rivets to a frame of steel tubing. A dozen such chairs were arranged in groups of three around similarly miniature work tables, and there was a knee-high drinking fountain and bookcase and little garbage cans for little garbage. No adult-size desk presided as in the one-room Calamus school of Tilly's youth: if he had rightly understood, this facility where the priest had arranged for them to meet was not the children's school but their home, and the present room a place not for instruction but for independent and group study. An adult here felt the wrongness of his size, the extent of his unbelonging, and wished at last to know his right place among things both seen and unseen. Light as Tilly was these days, he feared his wrongful weight would break the chair. Carefully, he sat.

The priest said, "They say the sand was sucked into the fireball and turned to liquid glass that rained down on the desert and it crackles under your foot when you walk. Is that true?"

"Maybe down south at White Sands," Tilly said, "where the shot happened, the test. Los Alamos was where they did the calculations and the metallurgy. They do a lot of other kinds of research now. I play gin at the VFW with a condensed matter scientist. Also a theoretical biophysicist, a couple of nanotechnologists. Professors come from South Africa and Bangkok to use the linear accelerator. I don't know what any of these things mean. I never worked at the labs."

"Then why, may I ask, do you live there?"

Tilly nearly retorted, Why do you live in Germany? but recognized in time his habit of regarding as an enemy anyone who asked to know the contents of his mind. Still, one of his Frade uncles had in fact been killed not far from here, in the Ruhr Pocket near the end of the Second

World War, his father's brother Fred, whose name his father never spoke and whose bed upstairs became Vollie's bed.

Tilly had landed a day before in Paris and boarded a train of lightning speed that shortly arrived in Brussels, where he changed to the InterCity Express, which shot through reaped fields by stout brick homes with skylights fitted in corrugated roofs, and crossed the Belgian frontier, where through the window the signage whipping past along the gravel ballast of the track bed turned to German, which was to him, lacking any other enduring associations with it, the language of mass murder, and German trains the vehicles that had carried unknowing crowds to their deaths. His body passed at three hundred kilometers per hour through the lingering spirits of the disembodied dead. Why had no such intuitions ever haunted him in Los Alamos? The dead didn't care to go where their death had been invented; they haunted the places they had lived. "Why did I live in Los Alamos?" he said. "I wanted a condo with the radiant-heat flooring option and sliders onto the patio. I don't live there anymore."

The cruel music of children babbling in German came from the hall before the children themselves passed the doorway in single file. On the cork floor their sneakers made no sound. Farther down the hall they could be heard snapping and zipping themselves into outdoor clothes.

The two men spoke of Oppenheimer, Harry Truman, Harry Belafonte; then of people utterly obscure, sinners in the confessional. All interested the priest equally. It was the *variousness* of other people that engrossed him. Their deviations and stinks. The inimitable self responsible for what the person had done. And Tilly wanted to ask whether he had misunderstood all along, since the dream from his fever bed that had convinced him his self was the obstacle he was meant to defeat, and why it persisted despite his efforts to erase it.

"One of my former neighbors used to be Edward Teller's maid," Tilly said. "Ever heard of him?"

"Oh yes, Teller. The so-called father of the hydrogen bomb. I suppose we all must be the father of something. His reputation was inflated by his own conniving."

"That's what they say."

"It was not Teller who solved the dilemma of fusion ignition but the Pole Stanisław Ulam. This has been well documented in recent accounts. A slimy figure, Teller. He could never fully admit he had done wrong. An intriguing figure. A tragic figure. We all live in his shadow. He had an artificial foot."

"She never mentioned it."

"He fell under a railcar in Munich when he was a young man, and the foot was smashed. What in the world could fate have meant by that?"

On the wall a life-size portrait hung of a skinless human being with her muscles finely labeled, also a candy-colored periodic table, in the seventh row of which gray squares had been taped for elements with the atomic numbers 113, 115, 117, and 118, which had not been given names because they could not yet be proven to exist.

"Munich," Tilly said. "But I thought he was Hungarian."

"A certain class of learned man has no proper country. What else does she remember of him?"

"Not much. She's senile. Whenever I met her walking her dog in our complex in the daytime she always knew right where she was. But at night—"

"My sister was that way," the priest said. He had seen all his siblings die. He did not say so. The American's drawn face and unswerving eyes disclosed nothing except that he would listen closely to whatever the priest had to say. The priest wanted to tell him what there remained no one else to tell, that over the years he had given each of his siblings the last rites and watched them go—all but the final brother, a soul wrapped clumsily in aluminum foil, like a sandwich he wouldn't share, who had left orders with the administrators of the hospice to let no one visit.

"Teller proposed using thermonuclear weapons underwater to create a harbor in Alaska, also to free the oil in the Canadian tar sands, also to deflect asteroids that might strike the earth. Enrico Fermi said of him he was the only monomaniac he ever knew with several manias."

"You speak English like a native."

"Of where?"

"Of anywhere."

The priest looked at his white fingers. "And therefore of nowhere. Perhaps I missed my calling, if I am using the idiom correctly. I could have been a criminal impostor."

"People in town say Teller was a rat."

"A rat. Now you will instruct me, my friend. I am going to guess. It must mean an eater of cheese, but the deeper significance eludes me."

"Somebody who double-crosses a person he's supposed to be loyal to."

"Oh, yes. When I spoke earlier of the wrong he would not admit, I was speaking not only of the super bomb but of the betrayal and destruction of Oppenheimer. Now tell me, what brought you to New Mexico in the first place? If I recall your dossier, you came from one of the fertile states."

"I went looking for a friend of mine who lived there."

"Did you find him?"

Tilly shifted his bones on the plastic chair.

"You don't mind my asking? I can imagine a young man going to the desert in search of something that would be invisible in other places. It seems an odd destination to go for friendship. Of course my associations with it are almost entirely related to weaponry."

"I never saw him again."

"And what kept you there?"

Tilly made his eyes unreadable, or believed he did.

The priest waited for an interval determined by what seemed a hard-won sense of empathy and decorum. Finally he asked, "What was her name, your reason to stay in the state of New Mexico?"

"Is it that obvious, even to you, a priest?" Tilly asked.

"I would like a business card to hand out. It would read, *Reverend Werner Wurs—Physical Being, Possessor of Flesh and Glands.*"

Tilly snorted.

"It sounds different in German."

"She was the same woman you see there, the woman in the documents."

"You don't want to say her name," the priest observed.

Not since the Romanian professor at the Presidio in Monterey had Tilly felt the present intuition that although he had met this person only an hour before, he must do all his life's business with him now, because they would not meet again. Impertinent questions begged to be asked. Advice he'd long wished he could have got from his silverhead father. Personal news begged to be disclosed, through the priest, to the old man buried in time. Things his father deserved to know. *I lost your name. I sold the farm.*

"The name never loses its power over us," the priest said. "I knew a woman fifty years ago, a greengrocer in the south of France. To this day I see her given name even backward in a newspaper being read opposite me on a tram. Wherever the name appears it seizes my heart with crushing force. I forget to breathe. But you didn't come all this way to talk about women."

A heavy door slammed, and the voices of the last few departing children were extinguished. Shortly Tilly saw them through the window in the playground outside, sprinting in fevered loops, blindfolding each other with the sleeves of jackets, watching the sky with grave expectation.

"Not that I expected you to *come* at all," the priest said. "You might have telephoned first."

"I don't speak German."

"Or emailed."

"I don't have an email. Maybe we didn't want to give up the element of surprise."

"Are we in an adversarial position, you and I?" the priest asked.

"I hope not."

"But if I knew you intended to come, you expected I would try to dissuade you? Perhaps redouble our efforts to place the boy in a suitable home here and keep him out of the hands of people such as yourselves who might return him to his father?"

"We are not going to do that," Tilly said. "The boy's father doesn't know I'm here. I've lost touch with him."

"Cut him off, you mean," the priest said. "None of us is permitted the fiction of losing touch anymore. In the internet age, we either drop our relationships or keep them. If the court requires it, are you willing to guarantee Mr. Heflin will have no contact with the child?"

"I guarantee it right now."

"You won't let him in the house?"

"He won't know where the house is."

"And Mrs. Tilly agrees?"

"She doesn't like it, but she agrees it's necessary."

The Brandenburg Concerto began to play thinly around the priest's person. He convulsed with swatting at his many pockets like a man attacked by flies until he found his smartphone and squeezed its edge within his clothes. The music stopped. "It's taken you rather a long time to get here."

"My passport was held up. A military document had my birthdate wrong. It triggered an extra level of scrutiny."

"And had you done anything in regard to which it concerned you to be scrutinized? You'll forgive my habit of inquiry, people do often come to me hoping to be asked what they regret."

"Are you trying to make me confess something?"

"To *make* another confess—a pointless enterprise. Contrite words that don't come freely from the heart are perhaps an interesting perversity for the study of psychoanalysts, but no one is fooled, and no one is helped. I see no reason for us to be adversaries. If the facts you've laid out in the dossier should pass scrutiny, I would be open to supporting your petition. Let's come to business. Mr. Heflin, your—" His thumb tapped the glass face of his phone. He asked it a question in German and squinted at the instantaneous response, "—your stepson?"

"Not exactly. There wasn't any father before me, and I was never married to the real mother. Come to think, I never met her."

"There was no father Heflin. Therefore Heflin was the mother?"

"No."

"Heflin was the name of the true mother's spouse, who nonetheless was not the true father?"

"No."

"Heflin was a name drawn at random from a shoe? Please elucidate."

"They picked his name."

"No, no. The surname Heflin."

"They picked it. And they picked the first name."

"No, no. We have crossed our wires. By 'given name' I mean the chosen name. The surname is the fact."

Tilly looked away at the chalkboard, freshly washed and waiting for someone to write something on it. "We took legal guardianship of Elroy when he was five. No one else had custody of him after that but us. Practically speaking, I'm his father. None of the rest matters."

"On the contrary, it matters absolutely and forever."

Outside, a screech of ecstasy arose from the courtyard. Tilly started; the priest remained still, erect, leaning slightly forward, like an optician performing an examination of the retina. Through the gray German atmosphere snow had begun to fall on the hats and bundled limbs of the hysterical children.

"Is he out there?"

The priest said carefully, "Can't you tell him from the others?"

"Not with all their winter stuff on."

They went to the window and stood watching—the silverhead man and the bald one.

"He's wearing the green coat with the fur in the trim of the hood," the priest said. "Don't be offended, the fur is acrylic."

The tall boy labored hand-over-hand up the chain of a swing while the others barked at him. His hood fell down. A peculiar face was exposed, small and blunt, a surprising face in that it did not right away mean to Tilly anything. The priest watched Tilly, while Tilly watched the boy ascending through the snow like a salmon fighting the rapids.

"The dossier you left was in sparkling good order," the priest said.

"A lawyer prepared it."

"He seemed to have excellent command over our law on these questions."

"We hired a consulting attorney over here."

"Sounds expensive."

Tilly said, "The consultant doesn't think Elroy will come to grief from the authorities unless he tries to come back here. Do you agree?"

"I suspect Interpol has more important work to do, if that's what you mean. The judge will likely accept you and Mrs. Tilly as next of kin. Given your ages he wouldn't give either of you custody by yourselves, but together as you are I think you have a clear case, at least morally. However, I'm confused about something."

Tilly went on watching the snow and the strange child climbing the chain while another child stood apart looking at a phone and chanting the time.

"You and Mrs. Tilly were divorced."

"That's right."

"And she is Mr. Heflin's stepmother."

"In practice, his mother."

"In the same merely practical way that you are to be considered his father. And you have reconciled and remarried."

"We have."

"But the dossier is mute as to when this second union took place. Was it before you received my letter? The court will want to know when exactly you and Mrs. Tilly remarried."

"It was six months ago."

"Goodness. Congratulations. It must be—no, I can't pretend to imagine the challenges of marrying at our age. But you see the question about which the judge will wish to satisfy himself, regarding the stability of the home? A marriage cobbled together for the placation of the court—forgive me if I presume."

Tilly waited for some veil to lift, to see in the distant boy what Louisa had seen in the picture.

"Why has Mrs. Tilly not come with you? If I am being intolerably intrusive you might simply say that she has a phobia of flying."

"We flew together from Albuquerque. Before we went through passport control at Newark, she changed her mind. She feels a life has a right perimeter that's unique for everybody, a fixed distance from where you started. You get a warning when you're about to cross it. Once you do, you can never go back."

"Yet here you are."

"I crossed my perimeter a long time ago. She's at a hotel in Newark, waiting. She believes if she went back home to wait it would be like saying she doubted you would let us take him with us."

"Saying to whom?" the priest asked.

"You know," Tilly said.

"I do not."

"To God."

"If you'll permit me to advise, when you speak to the judge, you might better say that your wife has a phobia of flying rather than dragging God into it. Also, the judge will want to assure himself of the household's material capacities."

"Did you not see the financials in there?"

"I should think three point two million U.S. dollars is sufficient, but I am speaking of the home itself."

"The house is almost done. We're halfway moved in. I can have her send photos. There's a school down in the village. Will the judge be an obstacle?"

"Where?"

"Near Santa Fe. A town called Chimayo. Will the judge be an obstacle?"

"The judge will never grant your petition if he believes there is only one of you to look after the boy. He will conclude, and I won't disagree, that the boy is better off here under the supervision of the state system than if he were likely to be orphaned in his teenage years."

"Fine."

"You see the boy coming down the chain there? In the green coat. You see his face clearly now?"

"I do," Tilly said.

"I'm sorry to confess a trick, Mr. Tilly, but that boy is Georg. He arrived only last month."

Tilly turned around.

"Don't be angry."

In fact the American looked less angry than betrayed, and the priest feared the nascent bond between them had broken, and he had broken it, and made himself again an outcast, when he might have made himself a friend.

"I don't understand why you'd do that," the American said. "I never said I'd met him. Listen, we won't accept the boy growing up this way."

"Which way?"

"Alone," the American said.

"I wonder whether you and Mrs. Tilly have any true relationship," the priest said in a prosecutorial spasm he immediately regretted. "I wonder whether either of you has any relationship with the boy at all."

"Nobody else does."

"Nobody save one perhaps." The priest did not identify this one. The question who this one was hovered like a spider building a web in the air between them, one man seeing its backside, the other its front. At certain angles the web was invisible, and each saw only the creature moving in space according to a path of its own imagining.

"We have to do this, Louisa and me."

"And what if the judge should say, 'Too bad. Your "have to" is not my "have to" '?"

"I let Elroy down, I know that. He started with his reckless nonsense when he was a teenager. He tore things apart. He kicked and slugged. I don't know if it gave him relief or some kind of euphoria, but it was my job to straighten him out, and I failed."

"What if the judge should say, This boy is not a table for you to atone yourself upon?"

The American infuriatingly refused to be angry. "You have your rules, I understand. But if there's no one else to take him, why stop us?"

"Yet there *is* someone else." The priest recognized they were on the brink of a miscommunication and chose to exploit it in order to impose on the American his own version of who the someone else was. "Her name is Wolbert," he said.

But the American had already pulled his wallet from his trouser pocket and taken out a slip of paper and was saying, "We've prepared for this."

"Her given name is Nora."

"Do you have a computer in your phone?" the American asked.

"I advised her not to give up."

"Can you use the phone to get on the internet?"

"But the judge obstructed her at every turn."

"Do you know how to use email?"

The priest's neck stiffened. "Of course."

The American read a web address. The priest conceded to enter it in the navigation bar on his phone's browser. The American read him a username. Then the password *Freedom ToFire1971*. The priest said he had understood Mr. Tilly not to have email, but the American, as if reciting from a script he had committed to memory, asked if he knew how to access the file of personal contacts inside of an account.

"Why?"

"Search for last name, D-R-U-V-I-E-T-E. First name E-V-I-J-A," he said.

The priest's adroit thumb jabbed the letters. He read back an address.

"You should see a phone number for that name in the contacts file."

"I see it, but if this is not your email account is it instead Mr. Heflin's?"

"That's right."

"We are violating the law. Whose phone number is this?"

"The mother's," the American said.

A thump came at the window. Snow splattered it. The priest did not look to record the party responsible.

"I *deny* it," the priest said.

"You're so sure about Elroy, but your letter makes it sound like you never considered the mother even existed. That's her phone number. Call it."

"I am not sure of anything. That's why I wrote you. What will happen if I call this number?"

"Try it and see. The boy has a mother like anybody."

"Mr. Tilly, if I've fallen to treating you like an adversary, I hope you'll forgive me. But please understand that for forty years I have been confronting this assumption based on my vocation that I regard women as poisonous or doers of dark magic or not-exactly-human creatures or that I don't notice when women are there. I don't deny the boy has a mother someplace. We have used every means to identify her. We have used all the relevant NGOs. We have made inquiries from Argentina to Switzerland, all of them blind stabs admittedly. No one is missing the boy anywhere. With any reciprocal action on her part, any whatsoever, she would surely have found us by now. I refuse to believe she's dead. So then—and it costs me a lot psychologically to admit this, I don't want it to be possible—the only conclusion I can reach is that she wants nothing to do with him."

"Why not call her and find out?"

"You've already done it, I presume."

"She doesn't pick up," Tilly said.

"If I have treated you as an adversary please understand that I have to, but only to a point. Have you called always from America? She would see that and know not to answer."

"Go ahead and try from here. If you can get her to answer the phone, I'll stand up and applaud."

"I am not your adversary," the priest repeated.

"Don't worry, Father, I know that," the American said. "Is the judge my adversary?"

"The judge is not your adversary. The judge is Mephistopheles."

The American laughed. Neither a scornful nor a polite laugh, but a true laugh. Easy in his body. The air went in and came out in a burst. "Good," he said. "Let's lick him."

The priest was alarmed. The American explained the usage. The priest did not understand and asked for a synonym.

Tilly said, "Let's you and me together knock him down."

They shook hands. The priest's skepticism left him at the moment of the handshake, and he recognized it was on this man's side that he had been working from the beginning.

Yet the priest had to dial the number. The fluids of his inner ear seemed to slosh. Up resembled down. He rifled his jacket pocket and found a strawberry-flavored wafer cookie and tore open the foil wrapper and scarfed it while the phone rang, praying no one would answer, or better yet, the line would prove to have been disconnected. He offered his heart to the Lord with trust, thanksgiving, misgiving, fear. He gave back to the Lord the entirety of the life the Lord had given him, and the phone picked up, and a voice spoke in a language he knew for a fact was not Estonian. He had been studying Estonian in the free time he did not have.

WHEN TILLY GOT BACK to Newark he took the hotel shuttle and found Louisa in the lobby bar looking daggers at a newspaper and scrawling all over it.

It was almost suppertime, but neither of them could eat and instead they talked over what had happened: the voyage, the priest, the boy climbing the chain, the pensioner who had answered the phone, the priest trying four languages before with elementary Russian he was able to communicate with the draggle-voiced old woman who suggested that if he should manage to track down Miss Druviete, might he please remind her that a certain pensioner was still owed four months' rent? Four months! One month of which perhaps Miss Druviete might be forgiven as the pensioner had long ago pawned Miss Druviete's cheap furniture, and another let us say one month for the phone Miss Druviete had left in her apartment and which the pensioner had appropriated, although the pensioner still had had to pay for a charger, so let us calculate approximately seventy-five days' rent was still owed. A considerable sum for one who had only the savings of a florist's assistant. But she was not trembling in wait for her compensation. She had not seen Miss Druviete in three years.

Rather than eating, Tilly and Louisa each drank two shots of bourbon—they had never drunk liquor together before. The occasion called for wild departures.

She touched his speckled hand. She said, "I think it'll work."

"Me too. But we have to go together next time. Unless there are two of us, they won't let him go. The earliest the judge will meet us is March."

It was the seventeenth of January 2014, a Friday. Louisa made a door-creaking noise in the back of her throat. It was a new noise, and he didn't yet know what it meant.

UPSTAIRS IN THE HOTEL, with the blinds open to the thronged highway, they lay in the dark, naked and unashamed. Talking over things, then not talking.

He thought about every part of her as he touched it, calling it by its right name and attaching it to the corresponding place in his mind. The deep mind that knows the elementary things before learning. Water and feet, sunlight and food. The mind that knows the time of our going out of being, and bears the record of our coming in. Memorizing her once and for all. There was a rock at the center of him, and he carved her name in it.

19

Potter Frade showed Annie Frade into the dark house.

He stood behind her in the little foyer, and she held back her arms, and he pulled the loden coat from her shoulders. She stomped her overshoes on the rag mat to dislodge the snow on them. She poked her head toward the doorway that gave on the parlor, not stepping away from the mat, as though it were home base in a tag game. She looked aside to the kitchen and upstairs toward the bedrooms.

Frade sang, "Home again, home again," shoulders tight, his back bent as he unbuckled his boots and tied on his kidskin house shoes. He resembled a wood sprite, his ears pointed. "We could change the paper if you like," he said, indicating the crinkled walls. "Mother won't mind."

"Do you show me the room now, or how does it go?" she asked.

But he said, "Larder's over here."

She went with him and his lamp around the corner.

"Mrs. Frade sleeps in there," Potter said, pointing down a narrow hall to the room of his mother, who had gone away for the night of the wedding and was staying with relatives in town.

The powder on Annie's chest gave off a smell of peaches. He lit a lamp and showed her through the larder, stacked with pickled beans and watermelon rind, then to the kitchen and the back door. He opened it and pointed in the dark to the invisible barn and the old salt shed, which he had lately dismantled, fitted with glass walls, and turned into a greenhouse for the kitchen garden.

She asked, "May I have a glass of water, Frade?"

He worked the iron pump handle in creaking heaves. The room was dark and foreign with a wife in it.

The water sopped her mouth: a bitter mineral tang. Before long, the town water would drain out of her, and her body would be composed of this here, her husband's own element. To inhabit a place is to drink the water there.

He rinsed the glass under the pump. Even his best clothes smelled of hay. The open rear door let in the stink of the cow manure in the near pasture. He said, "We could build an awning out there, for a place for you to read."

The wind pricked her face and she shut the door.

She said, "Shall we go to the room now?"

He took her ponderous bag for her, and they went on up the stairs. The freshly painted spindles of the banister shone with white lead in the lamplight. Her big haunches pulled the legs up each step, and the nailheads flashed in the soles of her shoes.

Two bedrooms comprised the second story, one to each side. Her belongings lay stacked on the landing where her brother had left them that afternoon. A vanity lamp stood atop the heap, but the old house had no electric yet.

Frade said, "You choose which room you'd like to have. I sleep in this one here, but you could have it. This other was Louis and Fred's." He showed her the unused room, which had only a bed and bureau.

Her eyes pursued him into the empty closet. Her stout red face tried to conform into a smile but failed. She said, "May we see your room, please?"

In his own room the taller ceilings did not impede his head. Brass pins affixed topographical maps to the deal paneling. Bunk beds; a sawbuck table by the window and a plate of oatmeal cookies. The disassembled parts of a two-strike chainsaw engine sat atop the bureau alongside a diagram ripped from a catalog. A photograph of his two brothers who had died, one of diphtheria, one more lately in the war; a hand mirror next to a basin by the window; in the dustbin a mound of his hair he had cut for the wedding. She opened the top bureau drawer and found three pairs of his striped underpants, ironed, and a stack of tobacco plugs.

He would not stop telling about the pieces of the engine, and she saw the larynx moving inside his shaven throat, exposing the place where his blood fed his brain.

She took her bag from him. Then she approached his throat and seized it between her jaws. He was a lean man, and she had a big mouth, and she pressed her hand behind his neck, her teeth around the larynx, which tasted of wintergreen.

He had been trying to tell her the chainsaw engine needed new gaskets, that was all. Then she bit him. It hurt some. And he stopped talking. Some part of his innards was killing him. A pain he could not exactly place, near the bottom of the pelvis, something inside, as though inflating. His hands took her shoulders and turned her backward. It seemed to him impolite of them to have done this. Though he stood in his own room, he was confounded as to where he was or what he was doing. A row of costume pearls ran like rivets along the bones of her spine, and his fingers began to undo the pearls from their loops.

She breathed—the stiff white wool dress, originally her grandmother's, itching terribly. The door was ajar. The door was ajar, yet she took a step and closed it.

He followed her, all the time fumbling at the stays as though trying to pluck a mis-sown pea from the dirt.

She pressed herself to the back of the door, willing it to let her out, asking it to forgive her for being such a fool, praying it would spare her.

He had spent his life in a cloud of pollen, chaff, and the steaming excrement and offal of livestock; yet his sinuses throbbed as though in torment as they absorbed the perspiration from her scalp and the egg white and cocoa butter she had used to set her hair. Who would have thought a woman's hair could hold so many pins? Her ear was felted like the leaf of an eggplant.

Down to her kidneys a corset snugly contained her, a second set of ribs, transverse on the outside.

In the pasture, a pack of feral dogs found the litter of kittens he had drowned that morning in the horses' watering trough and buried in the snow. The dogs could be heard shattering the ice scrim of the snow and yipping.

She told him, "You have to pull the bows first. Then the hooks underneath." Whichever of her womenfolk had cinched the corset bows had tied them on themselves in double knots the size of a newborn's knuckle. He rifled the bureau and found a pencil, but it was dull, and in four swipes of his pocket knife he shaved a point onto the pencil and introduced the point between the silk ribbon knots and prized them open.

Her face still pressed to the door, she told him to douse the lamp, and when he did, she stepped out of the dress and the corset, leaving them on the floor, and turned, her arm covering her breasts. She went to sit on the bed, ducking so as not to hit her head on the upper bunk. She wore only her stockings and her underpants. She had gone red everywhere. Her belly glowed in the vent of moonlight that radiated from the snow outside, and her midriff bore the impression of the corset stays. She twisted her mouth into an implacable smile, but lost it.

He came toward her in the dark, shuffling off his jacket. He slouched out of his suspenders and unbuttoned his shirt, neglecting his tie until the shirt came off, and packed the shirt and tie in the bureau. He bent artlessly, stepped out of his trousers, steadied himself on the wall, and removed his sodden socks.

He had gone hungry in his childhood, and now he could not distinguish the pang in his gut from the pang he had known as a boy, the need for oats in the morning after he had gone to bed without supper. His father would give him an apple at lunch and the boy would eat even the seeds.

Now his body was wracked from his sore feet to his searing inner organs to his brain swelling against the sides of its case. And he saw her holding herself under her armpits, covering, the long thumbs up around the shoulders.

Somehow she was roasting, although it was manifestly very cold, as the wind from outside rippled the curtains in the draft. She bent double and removed one stocking, then the other, sitting on the lower bunk, the relics of boyhood all around. He had wept once, talking with her decades ago outside a dance, explaining that Harold, his goose, had died.

She held out her stockings, meantime covering her front with the other arm, and asked him to put them away. In the vent of light, his silver hair swirled around the spot where the plates of the skull had fused when they had stopped growing. His long back showed its bones when he bent low and removed his drawers. He stood again and put them away. She watched him approach. The darkness cloaked his face so he seemed to be watching her with the back of his head. He was a predatory monster with its front on backward and its tail pointing the way for its face to follow. He approached, wicked, nude, and shivering. He made to cover his thing with his hands, and he sat next to her on the bed.

She unfastened the buttons in her drawers and lay naked on the bed redolent of him, a smell like the smell of the parlor when her father had finished his bath. A repellent smell like too-rich cake.

The hair on Frade's front side made a "T" across the top of his chest and down the middle, leaving the flanks bare.

He turned and lay on top of her, his small mouth closed. His wet and frigid feet smelled of mildew.

He craned to face the whitewashed wall, stained yellow in splotches from the grease in his hair over many years. Her body where it touched him stuck to his like paste. She had covered herself everywhere with powder. Where he didn't touch her, she radiated heat like a stove.

She said, "*Frade.*"

She wanted to say, "Tell me you're an honest man."

A sound rose in her throat that she tried to form into the question, "Are you an honest man?" but came out only as a little sob like a chair creaking.

Then a shock of pain.

At first she didn't feel it. And then she did. But between not feeling the pain and feeling it, between fearing she would die and knowing her long death had started, she had time to say to herself, Time will tell.

20

During the second week of February 2014, on the day Elroy completed final outprocessing and was free of the army at last, he flew in a C-117 from Bagram to Incirlik Air Base in Turkey, then to Frankfurt where he picked up a commercial flight to Heathrow. During the layover at Heathrow he hid in a toilet stall crying until the final boarding announcement of his flight to Dallas/Fort Worth.

From there he flew to Albuquerque, where he took the Rail Runner train to the depot in Santa Fe, then a bus toward Los Alamos that dropped him at the turnoff to Tilly's condo complex.

He hiked up the washboard road to the entrance. The guard within the glass cabin looked up from his puzzle and inquired as to the nature of Elroy's request. It was midday, but fluorescent light filled every corner of the terrarium where the big man sat consulting his clipboards. He found nothing on the access control spreadsheet that a Mr. Tilly wished his current residence to be disclosed.

"What, he moved?" Elroy asked.

But the guard had not said that. And he found nothing on the sheet that a yes or no should be given out regarding conclusions such as what the gentleman was suggesting.

Elroy walked back down the washboard road. When he reached the highway, he unpacked his phone and sat on his ACU rucksack in the rumble strips of the highway shoulder. His cellular plan had lapsed while he was deployed, but he turned on the phone and stabbed at its screen as if to provoke it into giving him a signal. He put the phone away. No cars passed. No buildings were visible in either direction. Snow was falling on the Jemez peaks. Purple pinweed bloomed among the rocks. The rest of the desert was MultiCam-colored like his rucksack. Already his boots were cloaked in homelike dust.

He stood and headed back toward the complex, this time eschewing the road and circling through the piñon. He heaved the rucksack over a barbed wire cattle fence and climbed a tree near the fence and jumped down to the other side. He climbed a butte. Then he descended through dense leafless aspen woods. When the woods ended he was standing on the slope above the rear of the complex, but the entirety of the perimeter visible from here was protected by a high stuccoed wall he would have needed equipment to scale. Inside it, the passive solar windows of a hundred adjoined, single-story homes faced the canyon to the south, each opening through a sliding door on a concrete patio big enough only for a single chaise lounge. On some of the patios a potted yucca grew from a clay pot but otherwise nothing visible within the perimeter was alive. The perfume of fabric softener sheets in the exhaust of a dryer came from somewhere within the walls. A woman laughed. He thought he heard a measure of piano being played, but no. A TV commercial for Storm Squad 3—the most trusted weather team in New Mexico. He couldn't distinguish which of the identical red steel roofs was or had been Tilly's. He continued around the complex wall but found no gap in it.

Then he unpacked his pocket knife and a Chocolate Supreme Protein Whey Power Bar, and he hid his rucksack amid the khaki land-scaping of the complex perimeter and walked back toward the town. He didn't eat the power bar. He was still fasting. It only protected him from the fear of going hungry. He felt it against his leg and imagined opening and smelling it. The crinkle, the cocoa powder bouquet. He would keep the fast until he got wherever he decided was home and then would eat the full proper meal for the time zone at that time of day. Then the body would know where on earth it was.

A few miles outside White Rock, a gas station had added a burrito canteen with a placard on the door advertising free wi-fi. The interior smelled of power steering fluid and carne adovada. He asked the stoner-eyed and dough-faced young Anglo clerk at the register for the wi-fi password. The clerk pressed to his chest the phone receiver he was us-ing and said he didn't know what Elroy was talking about. Elroy turned to the Mexican girl cleaning out the steam table behind the sneeze guard and asked her in Spanish for the password, and she gave it to him. He asked if there was any carne adovada left, but she said she'd already put everything away. He asked if there were any cold carnitas or chicken, and she sopped a towel in the basin of the steam table and wrung the towel over a bucket and said firmly without looking up that she'd already put everything away.

The Skype app on his phone searched for the network. He stood in the corner by the door, by the rack of truck trader magazines and cata-logs for crystal healing workshops, polarity and chakra balancing, Joy-ous Journey Reiki Retreats.

The app failed to locate the network. He reentered the password and waited. The power bar in his pocket was nearly touching his junk. Then the app successfully connected with the network, and he used his remaining Skype credit to dial Tilly's phone number. A pearl gray Lexus flew by outside in the weak light. The phone gurgled as it rang Tilly's line.

But the number he had reached had been disconnected; no further information was available about the number.

He had not slept since Incirlik. The new moon desert winter night was coming on.

He tried to think.

He looked at the catalogs. Depending on the organs under study, the human body's proper frequency had been found to vary from sixty to seventy-two megahertz. Subadequate frequencies left tissue systems prey to corrupting viruses, bacteria, and fungi. But Sacred Mesa Seminar participants would learn the use of rose oil and selenite crystals, with frequencies in excess of three hundred megahertz, that when applied through energetic smudging or laying on of stones fostered tissue ecosystems inimical to disease. By configuring contemporary breakthroughs in mitochondrial processes with the wisdom of the Aztecs, purified human tissue structures were now achievable. Previous understandings of safe levels of toxins were obsolete. Once purification was achieved it could be maintained through colonic rejuvenation and the right balance of plant-based lipids in the diet. Learning your proper frequencies was the work of a lifetime. That lifetime began again today. You would take the consciousness of a lost ancient people into your mouth. There was a new way based on an old way once forgotten and now recovered by archeologists working in the Yucatan.

He tried to think. But to think he needed blank paper and pencil, and he had neither.

Healing was voltage. Oil of lemongrass was crucial for flexible tendons at any age.

The clerk put his phone to his chest and told Elroy he was blocking the door, and Elroy went back out to the cold highway and headed into White Rock. More snow up on the Jemez. After the bus from Santa Fe, he possessed all of twenty-six dollars. He might have gone back to Santa Fe and spent the night at the St. Elizabeth's Shelter, but by the time he reached the depot in White Rock the last of the buses had left. His credit cards were maxed out. The final deposit of his salary wouldn't come into his checking account for another two days.

Starved for sleep, he walked into a canyon beneath the highway in the dark. He stomped three dried-out junipers clear from their stumps and dragged them over a little wash. He surveyed the desert winter scrub and low grass. Then with his knife he cut some of the chamisa thereabout and crawled up the wash under the junipers and lined the pebbled ground with chamisa and lay down warm from his work. He watched the stars through the reticulate twigs and scales of the juniper tent. He grew cold again.

He opened the power bar and ate it—and his pancreas, his adrenal glands, whatever the elements of his endocrine system erupted at the breaking of the fast. He chewed and swallowed. Then the food was gone and became a love-ghost haunting his cells, protecting him from nothing, and he fell asleep.

In the morning, he pissed amid the standing chamisa and walked up the highway toward Los Alamos to the diner Tio Rudy's and ordered a pitcher of hot water, a cup of coffee, and three sopaipillas, all of which would run $4.25 with the tip. The sopaipillas were simple carbohydrate and fat, a carnival snack rather than a meal, but he could afford them and ate slowly, watching the door that faced the road.

The diner had wi-fi, and as he drank the water he turned on his phone and opened the ESPN mobile site and watched a two-year-old microdocumentary about Peyton Manning's fifteenth year in the NFL, with the Denver Broncos, a season Elroy had missed watching while deployed but had followed in the news and returned to by looking at this video in times when his phone had service and he needed some-body to watch and admire: because everybody had written Manning out, everybody said he was finished before he got to Denver that sea-son. He was coming off a devastating neck injury that had ruined him in Indianapolis and should have ended his career. But the surgeons had put his head on straight, and he had come to Denver a new man—

though he alone had seemed to know it—and then he started putting up the best numbers of his life.

Manning was called the Sheriff. He had an old boxer's crushed nose. On the screen in Elroy's hand, Manning's remote and fleshy eyes moved behind the quarterback's face mask, commanding eyes that were in themselves an organ of decision. You felt them telling you what to do. He had become more dominant in old age than before, more self-possessed. He nodded throughout the huddle, nodded approaching the line of scrimmage and scanning the defense, flapping down his out-stretched arms to quiet the crowd, raising and lowering a foot to audi-ble, nodded scanning the field east to west, north to south, nodded coming under center, like Everything I see I approved. What I did that worked and what I fucked up. I made it all. I accept the outcome. Man-ning was also called the Old Sphinx.

It was half past seven and the last of the sopaipillas had already gone cold when Tilly came through the front door of the diner. Elroy might not have recognized him if the waitress had not called him Dwight when he came in. He resembled a handsome rat, the gray clothes hang-ing from him. He had lost perhaps fifty pounds.

When Elroy took his coffee and the last sopaipilla and the plastic honey bear to Tilly's booth and sat, Tilly glanced about for the waitress, like, Is there no place else this joker can sit?

"Sir. It's me," Elroy said.

After a moment, the eyes betrayed a sudden recognition—and something else Elroy couldn't decipher. "Elroy," the old man said. He cussed and grinned. He looked awful strange grinning with so much weight off him.

"I hoped I would catch you here," Elroy said.

No, it wasn't the lost weight that made Tilly look strange. It was the helpless grin itself that had overpowered a competing force in his drawn and frazzled face. By and by, however, as if against his will, the face re-verted to the familiar watchful one that betrayed nothing of his inner movements. Neither approving nor disapproving but watching, missing nothing. The sphinx of whom Elroy had once aspired to make himself a copy.

The waitress brought Tilly a pot of coffee with no milk in it. Elroy offered him the last sopaipilla, but Tilly didn't eat.

When Elroy asked when Tilly had planned on informing him that he'd moved, Tilly said, "I'm telling you now."

"And the phone?"

"I didn't like it anymore, having a phone."

"What if I needed to get ahold of you?"

"Write a letter to the P.O. box. That's how Bobby Heflin and I would do it."

"I done that. Because I knew you didn't like the phone."

When Elroy asked if it would be all right to crash at his place for a while, Tilly hesitated almost imperceptibly before he said, "Of course."

He was driving a 2013 Subaru Impreza Premium these days, with ivory leather interior that smelled fresh from the dealership and with a continuously variable transmission: an alarming feature in that Tilly would never be able to service such a transmission on his own. It was a concession not to luxury but to impending helplessness. They drove as far as the highway turnoff to the condo complex, and Elroy jumped out and darted through the piñon and fetched his rucksack.

They continued to the outskirts of the Bandelier National Monument, where Tilly was evidently reduced to living in a cavernous corrugated metal structure with a rolling overhead door big enough to fit a wrecker inside. The piano stood in the corner by a glowing space heater and under a fluorescent shop light that hung from a chain in the uninsulated roof. On the concrete floor, the rug that Elroy had sent from Kyrgyzstan surrounded the couch from the condo and its brown easy chair thatched with the dog's white shedding. The rest of the scant utility furnishings Elroy didn't recognize. The wire shelving units were piled high with boxes comprising many more belongings than he would have thought Tilly owned. A full-size mattress lay on the floor with four pil-lows and wool blankets. A low bulkhead of cardboard file boxes separated from the rest of the interior a sawbuck table with a desktop computer and a laser printer. The air smelled of dusty electric-coil heat, and the gas generator outside made a racket that shook the walls. The only window was over the dry kitchen sink. Mavis came in with them and scampered to the tidy kitchen in the corner and turned herself three times inside a crate of shredded copy paper and lay down. A woman's hairbrush, an eyebrow pencil, a spiral bound notebook, a Bible, and two hands of cards lay on the table as though a game that had been interrupted soon would recommence. Tilly stashed all these things in the white steel cup-board that had been a first-aid cabinet. Also on the table a large atlas lay splayed on a page densely printed with rail lines and names and twist-ing borders. An unfamiliar contour of seacoast. Tilly closed the atlas and tried to stand it up in the shallow cupboard but it didn't fit.

Elroy said, "You don't need to make room for my shit. I'll keep it in my bag."

"You're all right. Put your stuff where you want."

There was no refrigerator, only a pantry. And Elroy, looking inside it, said, "Alls you got in here is spring water and soup."

"I feel bad there's no beer for you."

"Forget about that."

"You should have written you were coming."

"I did write," Elroy said.

He saw within the old man's skull the workings of thought. He saw the thoughts themselves, the electric pulses and chemical surges and bondings. He saw them but couldn't read them.

Tilly slid the atlas next to the refrigerator alongside his broom. He did not need to hold the wall to help him stand back up. Lacking the weight, his movements were spry and strong as if whatever ailed him had also made him young again.

"Sir, you look like yourself minus a third. Is the VA sending your check?"

"Probably," Tilly said.

"Well, is it coming or not? I get all these emails, say the checks are coming. Wait a minute. Did you get none of my letters? Go to the P.O. box, or go to your other mailbox at the condo. There's checks you're not cashing."

"I got your letters. I told you I don't need any checks. I got plenty right here."

"Sir, with respect, except for that car you got nothing. Let's go back to town and buy you some groceries."

"You go ahead. I'll wait here."

Elroy picked a piece of weed from his hair.

"Take the car," Tilly said. "What's stopping you? Are you short?"

The weed was a chamisa husk with a rust-colored pebble stuck in it. "I won't be short in a couple of days."

Tilly opened his wallet and fished out the cash there and handed it to Elroy. It was about a hundred dollars. Then the reticent old man for once betrayed more than he had intended. "Go ahead," Tilly said. "I should stay here and make some calls."

Elroy felt the floor beneath him give way or pitch sharply as on a foundering ship.

"Why do you got to make shit up like that?" he asked.

"What did I say?"

"You know what you said."

"What? I forget."

"You don't forget anything. You said it. You meant it."

Tilly watched the floor as if a roach were scurrying over it. He said, "I wasn't even thinking."

"The hell you weren't thinking. You're always thinking. You didn't get rid of your phone. You changed your fucking number, man."

"I meant to say I changed the service, before, that's what I meant to say."

"You're doing it again."

"What am I doing?"

"Like when you up and run off."

"Elroy, I was going to write you and tell you where I was."

"No, you *weren't,* man." Elroy was crying openly. "You were going to do it again. And good luck to me tracking you down in Vado or wherever the place."

"Why don't you sit a minute?" Tilly said, though he himself was getting up again. "I don't want to see you like this. Stop this. You'll pull it together. You're all right."

"I *ain't,*" Elroy said. "Don't you get out of that chair."

"Elroy, I want you to tell me what this is about."

"Stay there."

"You're all right."

"Nobody listens. I *ain't.* I'm *off.*"

"When you go back, you have to tell them. You shouldn't be in a forward position if you're like this. Think of your unit."

"You ain't read any of my letters at all," Elroy said.

"Sure, I have."

"You haven't. I didn't re-up. I told you all about it. I get you. I know what you did. You got my letters and you kept them, but you didn't open them, did you? That's how you would do. Where are they? They're in here someplace."

The dog approached the old man, and Elroy raised his hand and the dog flinched and came no closer and sat watching them.

"I told you all about it," Elroy said. "Why didn't you answer?"

"What did you need, money? Is that why you were writing?"

"Why don't you open them and find out, and why don't you cash your checks and buy some fucking food? Don't you dare get up," Elroy said. He wiped his nose on his sleeve, and the snot came out in a long stretching tether.

"Ellie."

"Don't call me that. Set back down. You aren't hobbling away again. I got you now. I know what you're doing. You're sick and you're giving up. You'll say you just ain't been hungry, but it's a lie. That ain't even a real bed over there."

"All right, you got me."

"Damn right I do."

Tilly had gone to the makeshift office in the opposite corner of the interior and opened a brown paper sack into which he was stuffing some documents and he rolled the top of the bag and fixed it under his arm. "I'm living in Pecos, only I haven't put all my stuff in the new place yet. The car only fits a few boxes at a time. If I'd known you were coming I would have made better arrangements. Stay as long as you need. The place heats up quicker than you'd think. I'm here most mornings emptying stuff out, but I won't bother you."

"I need to get my feet under me," Elroy said, trying to hope.

"Good. There's a propane service that fills the generator. Use all the light you want."

"I think a guy from high school can get me on a highway crew. Then I'll pay you whatever the rent."

"Forget the rent," Tilly said. "What do you mean you're *off*?"

"Don't let's get into it now. Tell me why you got to live in Pecos."

"I'm not at liberty to say."

"This is more of your bullshit."

"Elroy, I'm sorry I said that about the phone."

"Oh yeah?"

"Yes, I'm sorry I was hard to reach."

Elroy had finished crying and started crying again more calmly. "Prove it," he said.

Tilly said, "There's something I owe you."

"You don't got to tell me anything that's your business."

"I don't know if you remember once, when you were little, we had a phone that didn't work."

"When did we ever have a phone that worked?"

"It was in Ramah. One day the phone started ringing and scared the hell out of you."

"I don't remember this."

"It was an acquaintance calling. I'd gone out of my way to break ties with him. Then he got me assigned a phone number and called it, and you answered and passed me the phone."

"You don't owe me any of this information, sir, if that's what all you mean."

"He had some money he felt belonged to me, and I didn't want it. But I've changed my mind. I want you to have some of it. I want you to get on your feet."

"What?" Elroy said, aghast. "You think you owe me *money*?"

"Let me give it to you. You can stay here as long as you like. Just let me get a few of these things out of here, and I'll leave you be."

"Why can't I stay down in Pecos?"

Tilly's eyes seemed young and in conflict, large amid the newly slim face, awake and undefended. He breathed with effort. He said, "I can't take you where I live."

"What did I do?" Elroy asked. "I didn't do anything."

"I'll come out and see you, all right?"

"Do you have a girlfriend I can't meet?" Elroy said, getting up. "I see her hairbrush. Are you embarrassed of me?"

"Stay where you are."

"This is crazy. Are you living in a nursing home? What kind of sick are you that they won't let you have visitors?"

"I'll bring the Lincoln today for you to use."

"All right," Elroy said. "So let's go."

"You stay here," Tilly said.

The sugar from the sopaipillas reached its peak in Elroy's blood and began to go the other way. The crash, the nausea. At the same time he couldn't be sure it wasn't the composition of Tilly's blood he felt rather than his own. Once, while the two of them were working on a truck, a pulley had started turning and crushed Tilly's thumb between the groove of the pulley and the timing belt, and the smart had shot right up Elroy's own arm to his brain as if his own thumb had got trapped in the machine. He said, "But you wouldn't be able to get back home to Pecos if you left the Lincoln here."

"I'll get a buddy from the VFW to help me."

"Let me do it. I'll come with you."

"Elroy, I can't have you at my house."

"But I didn't do anything wrong," Elroy said.

Tilly took his bag and headed to the door.

The dark room seemed to go white. It was insulin or adrenaline or testosterone or glucocorticoids. Or the old man's spirit passing through Elroy's body on its way elsewhere. Elroy's tissues seemed to invert their functions: blood in the nerves, electricity in the arteries and veins; and he got up and pulled his knife from his pocket and before Tilly had reached the door he grabbed Tilly's shoulder and turned him and shoved the butt of his hand under Tilly's nose, pushing the head and stretching the neck backward and exposing it, and stabbed the knife into Tilly's neck.

The blood came immediately everywhere.

Tilly seemed to smile and said, "Elroy, don't." His breath met with the blood in his throat and the words came burbling as though he were underwater and he coughed choking as his in-breath sucked the blood back down the throat into his trachea and lungs.

There was blood. It was beautiful red and it was Tilly's, and Elroy loved him with a focus he had never summoned in loving anyone else. He pulled the knife from the neck. He rotated it in his hand. Elroy felt how Tilly had already become too weak to struggle. He gripped the old man's silver crown, moving the knife to the other side of the neck, and slid the blade across the length of Tilly's throat and the scarlet blood came out like a garment, a veil of Tilly's blood.

Tilly's eyes in their slowness seemed only now to comprehend something and looked at Elroy with recognition, seeing something Elroy himself did not yet comprehend, looking with horror and admiration at Elroy's folly, his strength, his youth, the courage he knew Elroy to have though Elroy did not know it himself. The knowledge Tilly seemed always to have possessed of what Elroy was. The knowledge he'd held for Elroy in trust until the moment so long hoped for when Elroy too might consummate his lust for the world and become real, a man not a child, a full-blown person cognizant of what he was and his place and rank and serial number, and licensed thereby to hold the knowledge of others not yet knowing themselves, to have others entrusted to him.

He saw Tilly falling away from him into the world of souls, where he had sent the dangling hajis, the one gripping the green extension cord, kicking the window shutter that smacked against the tan stone building, under the blue laundry that flapped over him like a spirit, and who Elroy shot at the base of the shoulder blade and saw explode while still gripping the cord. The body dove away from the arm. The lust to go on living that lived in the arm—in the hand that gripped the cord. Even while the body attached to it fell away and lost itself among the low roofs. The disembodied hand.

The parents who had made the hand. Who had had names. Who themselves had been made by two others, who each themselves had once been bodies unknowing what they were, unknowing the past, and the selves held in trust for them by the ones who had come before them, and theirs in turn by the ones before them. The ones who made us, all of them knowing what came after them, none of them knowing what had come before.

JENSEITS

2029

When Willy was twenty-four, the priest died. The medical director of the archdiocesan nursing home called to tell him. In Willy's apartment, while she spoke, nothing moved. "An hour ago, he was outside reading," she said.

He thanked her for the call and left his building and walked along the street until he passed a shop window, where a second-hand Kross touring bicycle was hanging. He stood on the pavement looking at it. Others walked around him.

Then he went inside and bought it and rode it down through the Augustusplatz, stopping at the university library to get a sweater from his study carrel, and continued riding out of Leipzig into a formless beyond.

The time was three o'clock in the afternoon. He had been working as a junior researcher at the Institute for Geophysics and Geology in a unit dedicated to Arctic stratiform clouds and the radiative transfer effects within such clouds of horizontally and vertically distributed ice crystals. Here, there were no clouds. The highway continued through Naumburg. To one side, rapeseed grew in tight formation at an oblique angle with the road; to the other, rye. Night fell on the pastures, the pine woods, the rider alone on the machine that blinked in warning to no one and quickened the pace of its flashes the harder he pedaled.

He rode for two days and three hundred kilometers before at lunch-time he stopped in a Kashmiri restaurant in Würzburg. With the slot-ted spoon at the buffet he drained the gushtaba thoroughly of its sauce and piled the balls of mutton on his plate. He sat at a table that faced the rear exit where stairs came down from a residence above. He ate. The hostess went to the kitchen. No one else occupied the dining room. His mobile pinged, and he switched off the ringer and ate again ravenously. From a separate bowl he ate rice. The stairs began to creak in the pattern of two people descending, one behind the other. They were speaking Hindi or Kashmiri or Urdu in the soft private tones of long marriage. Their feet on the steps showed through a grate: a woman's feet in bright sneakers, and a man's in black orthopedics and argyle socks exposed below the rolled hems of linen trousers. As the couple came into the dining room, he stood and went to the cashier's station and put a twenty-euro note on the counter and left.

In the next town, he bought a compact repair kit, front- and rear-riding rainproof panniers, an ultraviolet water purifying pen, and a hel-met. He continued riding into Switzerland. He texted his roommate and asked him to return his library books to the university and listed the titles. He disassembled his mobile and used a sewing needle to re-move the magnesium power plate and threw it away and stowed the rest of the mobile components in one of the panniers. He followed the Rhone west into France. He slept in national forests and in a vineyard, leaving the bike propped for the night against the steel post of a frost fan that stood like a sentry amid the dense foliage. He made camp after sun-down and cycled out before daybreak. He did not steal. To eat he car-ried cheese and muesli. He followed the Rhone to Lyons and south to the suburban districts of Vaucluse. There, he turned east through the massifs of the Luberon and the Mercantour, keeping away from the crowded coasts, the cities. In three days he shot across the top of Italy into Slovenia. No one knew him in any of the countries where he went. He rode through the Adriatic side of Croatia into the town of Petrovac in Montenegro, where in the morning at the beach he turned all the pockets of the panniers inside out looking for the notebook in which he had been logging his expenditures, kilometers traversed, high and low temperatures experienced, wind conditions, the periodization and duration of an ibex's pattern of drinking from a pond in the Mercantour. He had lost the notebook. He rode on. Farther inland at midday he spread his polyamide camping towel on the rocks at Lake Skadar on the Albanian border and napped beside the water. He awoke beside the green lake, amid green cliffs and waterfalls. The sun, occluded by low nimbus clouds, did not warm him, but he got up and stripped and took a bar of soap into the shallows and washed and threw the soap back to the bank and swam far enough into the lake that he lost sight of his things on shore, of any other animal, the dark water numbingly cold. By the time he swam back to shore, his bike, clothes, food, and equipment had been stolen.

Wearing only his towel, he picked across the stony trail to a campground and borrowed a hiker's mobile and ordered a car to come down from Podgorica and gave the mobile back to the hiker, and the car came and took him to the city. Still wearing the towel, he walked into a sport supply store where the car had dropped him off. The children there looked at him, the mothers looked away. The self-checkout kiosk confirmed his access to his Deutsche Debit account by sampling his body odor. Shortly, he stood outside again in vivid Lycra clothes and stiff-soled mountain bike shoes, stuffing the translucent packaging of his many purchases into the Dumpster of a Montenegrin shopping mall, having drawn down by 70 percent the money remaining in his account. He strapped new panniers onto the new bike he had bought and filled the panniers with his new equipment and rode into a disused park on the city periphery and bought a beer and a loaf of barley-flour bread and ate watching the traffic.

He continued eastward across the Dinaric Alps through Kosovo and Serbia to the edge of Romania, where news reports in a coffee shop said that a ceasefire between Romanian-Moldovan forces resisting the Russian-backed rebels from Transnistria had broken down; non-Romanian EU nationals were strongly discouraged from crossing the Romanian frontier. Instead he pedaled north across the Great Plain of Hungary and up the steep trails of the Carpathian Mountains in Slovakia. He fell twice and got back on the bike and kept going. For an entire day he passed no one on the dirt roads. In the High Tatras at sunset, he was squatting by a current irradiating his drinking water when a fox appeared upstream and began to drink. It saw him too and screwed its head as if listening to something he was saying. When the length of it emerged from the spruce and fireweed, it was not a fox but a wolf. He did not move. They observed each other murderously.

With a rustle of the spruce needles the wolf dematerialized.

He coasted into Poland following highways along the Oder. He pedaled fast amid marshes studded everywhere with windmills and finally into the Polish city of Wrocław, once the German city of Breslau.

He uploaded to the new bike's navigator an applet that superimposed the map of Breslau 1942, intercoded with the parish registries of that time, onto the Wrocław of the present, where the German citizenry had long since been expelled and the streets and place names Polonized. The neighborhood in which the navigator placed the home of the family Wurs had not been renamed but obliterated. He tapped on the trapezoid designating the lot of the Wurs home, sent the directions to the processor, and supplied its locomotive energy while the navigator guided him to lean into one or another turn. Shortly he arrived outside the cold storage facility of a Syrian grocery store. He froze the sprockets of the bike and went around front and inside.

He asked the boy cashier if he could see the manager. She emerged, an old woman frowning. He asked in German, then in French, if there remained nearby any token, a blackened cellar wall or fragment of brick from the homes on this location before the Soviet siege of 1945. The manager asked if he was an inspector from the Department of Foreigners. He said no, he was a scientist of the atmosphere. She asked if he was from the state Geodesy Department or the Agricultural Market Agency. He said, if he were an employee of the Polish state, would he not have addressed her in Polish? She said, "We came here in 2016. The only pictures or records I have of this place are those of my family living in the apartment in the basement and working up here in the store." She offered him a Mylar bag of dried apricots. He chewed them, standing, reeking of the road. She asked if he was German. He said he was. She asked if it was his own family he was looking for, and he hesitated for half a breath and said yes. She asked if he had a girlfriend or boyfriend. He said no, and she asked why not?, a strong young fellow like him. He said perhaps he would hope for such things after he had a fixed home. She said, "I came here with my mother, my sister, my husband, my son, several toothbrushes, and a roll of toilet paper." "Yes?" he said. She said, "Other people are your home."

He unlocked his bike outside and continued northeast along the Baltic coast through what had been the independent states of Lithuania, Latvia, and Estonia before the late conclusion of the Wars of Slavic Reunification and were now mostly Russian republics, with rump coastal areas of ethnic Baltic concentration under a UN mandate. He crossed the whole of Latvia in two days of pedaling that took him four hundred fifty kilometers along the Gulf of Riga while his legs shook and stomach growled and hair dripped with sweat on the road. He did not sleep until the next day when he made it to Tallinn in Estonia, where he boarded the ferry to Helsinki. He rode up the Finnish side of the Gulf of Bothnia and down the Swedish side on paved roads like channels carved through forests of pine trees and birch gone yellow in the shortening days. At Malmö he merged onto the elevated cycleway above the Øresund Bridge, sleek at night as the tongue of a dragon with the lights atop its towers like flaring eyes, and down into a throatlike tunnel in an artificial island. After four more kilometers underground, the road expelled him into the Danish night with the lights of Copenhagen coloring the clumped undersides of altocumulus perlucidus clouds. He rode through Denmark, taking two more ferries. He rode back into Germany near Flensburg, onward through Schleswig, Hamburg, Uelzen, Flechtingen, amid the aluminum and concrete of familiar towns and cities. Magdeburg, Gommern, Zerbst. When he crossed the Elbe, the road went due south toward Saxony and finally into Leipzig again, where with the last of his savings he bought two three-egg omelets adorned with no sauce, no spices, cheese on the side. He rode to the university from which he had departed three months before and left the bike in the rack outside and climbed through the marble lobby, under the glass-paneled roof of the inner courtyard, up the steps not worn but cleanly edged from their renovations. Sunbeams warmed shafts of the white interior, the long marble tunnels segmented with arches on which rosettes were carved amid statues of fawns and dancing girls in frocks. He turned into an alcove that housed the two elevators where along the wall someone had left, on the steel cabinet that housed a fire extinguisher, an empty paper espresso cup, its lip chewed all around by an absent stranger's teeth.

He was looking into the stone corner. Behind him some people milled, inquiring of each other as to the library's closing hour. He waited while the elevator made its ding, and the doors slid open on their tracks, and the people got on, and the elevator swallowed them, and the alcove went silent; before he put his nose into the corner of the cold marble, hiding his face, and cried: the priest was dead, and he was alone.

. . .

"I HAD A SMALL WHEELBARROW, practically a toy, and a Wehrmacht folding shovel," the priest told him once. "And I went outside to build the Fatherland."

Day and night the boy Werner had loaded the wheelbarrow with rubble from houses the army had demolished. He shuttled the rubble where the Volkssturm engineers directed. They were building an airstrip through the center of the city. Soviet fighter-bombers strafed the streets. Flying low and firing and pulling up. One made a tweedle like a sewing machine. He saw the face of a boy in the cockpit firing. They wrapped the dead in bedsheets. They buried them in mass graves. "Chin up, chin up," his mother said, "even when things are bad." He had not seen his younger siblings, away in the country with an aunt, in more than a year. Few had the privilege of sleeping at home. Earlier in the winter his friends had left on foot with their mothers. Westward through the snow by night and thousands died. His mother worked as a doctor's assistant assigned to stay for the siege. The city was closed now, a fortress.

He drove the wheelbarrow home, weaving around mounds of snow-sheeted shrapnel that might puncture the tire. He cleaned the wheelbarrow with a hand broom. He propped it against the tidy house in the ruined street. "Leave your shovel outside, please," his mother said. "It's dirty." Mother and son ate by a carbide lamp. They washed and dried the china. They went below to sleep.

In the night, he lay in the fruit cellar having a dream. He awoke in midair. The ceiling above him exploded. His body was thrown against a wall. He lost consciousness as the house collapsed on him. He awoke again amid choking fumes. Half his face was buried in ash and rubble. The eye, the nose, all but a corner of the mouth. Obscure forces cramped his head, preventing him from moving it. A clamminess clung to the bottom of his foot. He pressed his toes against it. It gave slightly, cold and wet.

It was his mother's flesh trapped against the bottom of his foot. His mother had been crushed and was dead. Under the fallen concrete, the pressure of the hot bricks on his chest and limbs, he could neither fully breathe nor remove his foot from where it touched her.

Absolute dark.

He was only a location of breath, time, and pain. He was not the vessel of these things. He was the phenomenon of their coinciding, a wave on a black sea.

He told Willy all this when the boy was fourteen. He withheld nothing. The dirt he had swallowed. The smell of the excrement in his mother's clothes. Everywhere infinite black. The prayer that he would be permitted to die—

And then, some days later, amid the black, the shade that appeared. It quivered and dimmed. It grew sharper. It had a vivid edge: a light that defined it.

Light. Dust in the light. And human voices.

The excruciating pain of hope being driven like a nail back into his small body right through the socket of his eye.

The priest served the boy a roasted pork knuckle, fried potatoes, radish salad he had made in the rectory kitchen in Bremen. Willy moved the food around on his plate. They each drank a small beer. The priest did not wear his collar but a blue necktie under a wool sweater. It was the first night of true autumn. Willy had worn no jacket, and afterward, outside, the cold went through him. The priest drove him to the curb of his boarding school. Finally, the priest said, "I'm finished deflecting Mrs. Tilly's correspondence for you. If you don't want her flying in for your confirmation you're going to have to tell her yourself. Your indifference to her is a childish mistake. I won't be an accessory to it anymore."

"All right."

"You think everything has to be paid for. Even if it's the innocent who are made to pay. Some things come to us for free."

"All right. I'll text her myself and tell her I don't want her to come."

"For goodness' sake find some other way to say it if you must. Have you no mercy at all?"

But he did not yet know what mercy was.

HIS NAME WAS WILHELM KÖHLER. They had had to call him something. He liked the name. It came from nothing and pointed nowhere and left him free.

But he also owned another name. He told no one. It had no legal force. He never wrote it down. The priest had known it, but the priest had died. It was his true name, and he doubted he would ever confess it, because if the person to whom he could tell it existed at all, she existed beyond the boundary that separated him from everyone. The impassable verge. And yet he suspected we all believe we live outside the verge, while in each other's eyes we appear to be one of the rest living together on the inside. Whoever she was, her face, her voice, certainly her name—all were hidden. All awaited. He had not confessed the name to Doreen in gymnasium, or to Verena during university. It wouldn't come out. Or he had not yet become the person who would confess the name. Even as a teenager he had known how naive it was to believe a unique other person awaited. But knowing the belief was naive did not disprove it. It meant in fact she must be seen, identified, the name confessed, before he gave way to the truth that no such communion with another person was possible. A drawbridge existed over an abyss, leading us, if we crossed it in time, to the bright world that was not there, sun-drenched and crowded.

As he aged, the bridge drew up inexorably before him. He coarsened and knew better. He felt perhaps *her*—but was disillusioned. He accused her, or else *her*—recognizing as he did so his own complicity, his skepticism and deathward-pointing mind. Hoarding his name as if it really had the power he had ascribed to it in his childhood, by not revealing it, to cloak him in invisibility. To become a part of the earth, of the water soaking it, of the ants in the courtyard, the shining bits of quartz in the gravel of the track bed behind the kinderheim. The name was a foreign object snagged in his lungs.

In the summer of his thirty-ninth year, he would board a thermospheric jet and land in Windhoek, Namibia, for the biennial conference of the International Global Atmospheric Chemistry Project. He would take a seat in a stifling sixth-floor auditorium drinking a marula-fruit soda and listen to a discussion of heterogenous aerosol nucleation. Midway through the lecture, the power would fail. After a few seconds of comprehensive dark, the individual mobiles of two hundred sweating scientists would start lighting up, the interfaces in myriad languages telling the news; the correspondence; the flight updates; the cricket scores; the fluctuations in the sovereign bond yields of proprietary city-states inside gaming metaverses where populations of virtual citizens lived and died without ever knowing who owned them or that they were owned, or why their owner took such interest in them, why he played this game, whom he was playing against, what constituted winning.

He would step into the labyrinthine halls and grope along the concrete surfaces for a way onto the balcony. He would find a cargo hatch emblazoned with a warning sign illegible in the dark and fitted with a malfunctioning access control device that had defaulted in the power outage to its fail-safe rather than fail-secure setting: a way that should have been locked was not locked. He would push open the door and step into a moonless night on an unlit landing way, less than three meters deep, for light unmanned airborne deliveries to the sixth floor, an unfenced cargo slip above the street. Starlight would describe the distant ridge of the mountains behind the powerless city. Behind him, the door would open.

A figure would rush out, mobile in hand, ears holding back the long hair from a face absorbed in blue light, a mole in the declivity below the mouth. She would stride unknowing toward the edge of the dock, the abyss. His arm would shoot before him. He would reach for the back of the collar of the shirt of a woman he didn't know. His fingers, luck-bitten and undeserving, would grip the collar fast. With all his force he would lift her back from the dark below, into which she had already begun to stumble, and pull her into their common afterlife.

.

Acknowledgments

The author wishes to thank the Dorothy and Lewis B. Cullman Center for Scholars and Writers at the New York Public Library; the Civitella Ranieri Foundation; the John Simon Guggenheim Memorial Foundation; the Jentel Artist Residency; Aleksis Karlsons and the Baltic Writing Residency; Ellen Levine and the New York Community Trust; the Dora Maar House; the MacDowell Colony; Maddalena Fossombroni, Pietro Torrigiani Malaspina, and the Castello di Fosdinovo; the Whiting Foundation; and the Corporation of Yaddo for generous support during the writing of this book—as well as Elisabeth Calamari, Bill Clegg, Nicola DeRobertis-Theye, Marion Duvert, Will Heyward, Sophie McManus, and Justin Tussing for their wise counsel.